Ch
or
ww
www

50706

DREAM BREAKERS

A Northern lad's struggle to make his dream of football stardom come true...

Jenna Duncan's only ambition is to marry the boy she loves and have a little terraced house away from her dull job and her parents' boring life. Ruari Gallacher wants to be a professional footballer. When Ruari lets her down Jenna becomes involved with the son of the chairman of the local club, and when Ruari asks her to go with him when he leaves, it's too late. Will Ruari become the next football star, or will he come home with his dreams broken? Does it matter if you get to the top when you've sacrificed the person who means most to you?

DREAM
BREAKERS

by

Elizabeth Gill

Magna Large Print Books
Long Preston, North Yorkshire,
BD23 4ND, England.

British Library Cataloguing in Publication Data.

Gill, Elizabeth
    Dream breakers.

    A catalogue record of this book is
    available from the British Library

    ISBN   978-0-7505-3194-8

First published in Great Britain in 2009 by
Severn House Publishers Ltd

Copyright © 2009 by Elizabeth Gill

Cover illustration © Rod Ashford

The moral right of the author has been asserted

Published in Large Print 2010 by arrangement with
Severn House Publishers

Magna Large Print is an imprint of Library Magna Books Ltd.

Printed and bound in Great Britain by
T.J. (International) Ltd., Cornwall, PL28 8RW

For Jill, Jennifer and Simon, who look after my summers

One

It was Saturday and already noon. Jenna Duncan was standing in the queue in McConachie's fish shop, taking in the reek of chip fat and wishing Mr McConachie could hurry things up. Her mam would be cross if she was late but what could she do? She only got an hour for her dinner and was using up precious time standing there.

Finally, her turn came but the fish that had already been fried had been taken by Mrs Emerson in front who had a big family so Jenna had to wait again because the fish that were in the fryer were not ready. They were better just fried her mam always said but she had been a good quarter of an hour now and her mam would complain when she got back even though there was nothing she could do.

The fish were finally ready. Mr McConachie, who was so skinny that Jenna was convinced he never ate any of his fish and chips which she thought you wouldn't when you fried them day in and day out, wrapped up the fish carefully in case they should

9

break, put the chips into bags and laid it all neatly together before expertly dabbing a moistened finger to separate the sheets of ready torn-up newspaper then wrapped it diamond-shaped from the corner, folded in both sides and ended up with a neat parcel. He did the same thing a second time. Nobody who bought fish and chips at McConachie's ever got home with a cold dinner.

Jenna paid and thanked him. They were good fish and chips, which they should have been, the town being by the sea and the cod sold fresh not far away. She put them into her mother's shopping bag and then she ran around the corner and across the street and down the side and into the unmade back lane.

Ruari Gallacher, her boyfriend, was there. He loved fish and chips and would beg chips from her. She always ended up stopping and unwrapping one of the parcels and he knew that she had had salt and vinegar put on them in the shop and he would eat the biggest and fattest of her chips before she complained.

Ruari spent his life in the back lane with a football when he was not at work, kicking a ball off the back gate or dribbling it endlessly up and down, banging the ball off the walls and outside buildings. He worked as an apprentice electrician in one of the Sunderland shipyards and played football for the apprentices' works team but even so he practised every minute he got.

Ruari was good with a football, that was what everybody said. Jenna couldn't see it really. All the lads were good. There wasn't much else to do when they weren't at work. They took it seriously. Football was a serious business here in the north-east where there was nothing for working-class lads to do other than the pits or the ship-yards and a lot of the pits were worked up. The chance of becoming a professional footballer was the big dream, either that or to start a group and become famous like the Beatles or the Rolling Stones and Ruari had no interest in such things.

He dribbled the football all the way down the road but when he turned around he saw her as she had known he would and he aban-doned the football and raced up the back lane so that she unwrapped the chips and gave him a whole bag. Ruari's eyes widened.

'Are these all for me?'

'I thought it would be easier buying ano-ther bag and then you wouldn't eat mine,' she said though her mam would question her about the money.

Ruari grinned in appreciation. He was a nice-looking lad, she thought warmly, feel-ing proud. He had lovely black hair and cool blue eyes like the sea in July and he was taller than she was but it was not that she

11

liked best, she liked that he liked her, that it was unsaid.

He started in on the chips as though he hadn't eaten in a week, licking the salt off greasy fingers until she was too hungry herself to wait any longer. That and the fact that her parcel was fast getting cold propelled her away from him at top speed.

She heard his 'Ta, Jenna,' following her on the cool wind.

She didn't have far to go, they lived next door to one another. She ran up the back yard and in by the door, past the pantry and took a step down into the kitchen. She didn't think how cold it was outside until she got inside and her mam said,

'Wherever have you been? You could've been to Seahouses for those, the time you took.'

Her mam always said something like that, as though Seahouses wasn't way up the coast and took ages to get to. She knew because they went there for a fortnight in the summer and the fish and chips were even better than McConachie's.

'And where's my change?'

Jenna handed the change, watched her mother scrutinize it and then her mother shot her a straight look as she put the parcel into the oven to warm it back up.

'Have you been buying chips for that lad again? I've told you...'

Finally her father said, 'It was a bag of chips, Vera, let it go,' because he had heard it all before as well and no doubt he was tired of it. 'I just want my dinner in peace.'

He had to get back to work in a few minutes so because Jenna had been late with them he would have to shovel them down and dash back. She felt slightly guilty about that.

Her mother sat down and shut up and ate because as she said Jenna's dad was head of the household and he worked at the Store, in the grocery department. When they had finished eating he sat back in his chair and smoked his dinner-time Capstan and then he said,

'I've been promoted. I've been made head of the department.'

Nothing, Jenna thought, could have pleased her mother more.

'You should have told me when you came in,' her mother said.

'I wanted Jenna to hear it too.'

'Oh, Wilf,' she said, 'now we can move.'

'Move?' Jenna said and her parents looked at one another. Obviously this had been discussed when she was not there.

'It's been on the cards for a while,' her dad said, 'and I promised your mother that we would have a better house if it happened.'

'There's a lovely house for rent in Wesley Road,' her mother said and her eyes shone.

13

Jenna couldn't believe it. She didn't like to say that she didn't want to leave Back Church Street, that she couldn't leave Ruari. Wesley Road was in the posh end of town.

'Shall I see if we can go and have a look at it?' her mam offered.

'Aye, why don't you?' her dad said.

Jenna had to rush to get back to the drapery department of the Store where she worked in one of the big main streets, Durham Road. It was just beyond her dad's workplace, both were part of the Co-operative Society and he had got her the job there. She wished very much that she could work in a boutique but her mother wouldn't hear of it. She would have to travel into Newcastle or Sunderland for that, there would be buses to pay for and her dinner and her mother liked her to go home for dinner. Jenna comforted herself by thinking that at least she saw all the new clothes which came into the department and her mother let her buy pretty things. She had just this week bought a short flowery dress and new long white boots to go with it and had her fringe cut and the ends of her long blonde hair. She thought she looked really good.

All I need now, she thought, is somewhere to go, somewhere to wear it and she wished for the umpteenth time that Ruari had some money. She wanted to go out, she wanted to go dancing. She wanted excitement.

14

More than anything she would have liked a trip to London, to Carnaby Street, to the famous boutiques there. She dreamed of buying clothes at Biba and being very fashionable, she knew that she had the figure for it, not as skinny as Twiggy and not as glamorous of course but she was tall and slender and fitted into fashionable clothes.

The town was busy. The big local football team, Dunelm North End, were playing Arsenal that day so the streets were full of fans from both sides and the pubs were open. There was singing in the streets and there were a lot of policemen about just in case there should be any trouble.

By mid-afternoon when the kick-off began the streets would be empty of men and boys, and the women would come out to do their shopping in peace and even in the drapery department of the Co-op you would be able to hear the roar of the crowd, especially when the home team won. The sound of the cheers when one of their strikers scored echoed through the little alleyways and across the long wide beaches and even further over to the dockyards, the sound would travel for miles, Jenna thought.

Jenna wasn't interested in football but like everybody else in the place she was glad when the team scored and wanted them to win, as much out of pride as anything else. Today however, she listened in vain for the roar of the local crowd and she had the feeling men would be drowning their sorrows after the match and there would be fighting and somebody's shop window would get broken and several people would end up spending the night in jail.

Her dad resented that he had to work on Saturday afternoons and usually when the team played at home he would finish at six and be in the pub with everybody else soon afterwards but he would have to come straight home tonight, she knew, because her mother would have arranged for them to view the house and he had promised her they would look at it and her dad did not go back on his promises. He said it was just to keep the peace.

Ruari and his friends would be at the match, they never missed especially since it was almost the end of the season but later on she and Ruari would get together and go for a walk on the beach or maybe to the pictures if they had enough money. Saturday nights were sacred that way.

When she finished at tea time her mam dragged them to Wesley Road. It was several streets away, through the centre of the town, past Church Street where the parish church was, just in front of where they lived and through Chapel Street where the Wesleyan chapel was and then further up where the Bethel Chapel was and past the main streets where both Jenna and her father worked and where the schools were and the library and the station and the car-sale showrooms and the garages and small business premises and warehouses.

Jenna hated it straight away. The house looked so posh, too big for its boots, with a little front garden and at the back there was another garden, a piece of grass surrounded by flower beds and there were trees and hedges and it was quiet as though the whole of the people there had died.

The man who owned it was to show them around. It had a dining room, something they didn't have now and her dad probably wouldn't like, he was keen on having his tea by the kitchen fire with the telly on and his chair turned sideways to it though her mam thought everybody should put their chairs right to the table and make conversation.

The kitchen here was tiny, just somewhere to cook and wash up, and there was a big front room beyond the dining room, a lounge her mother called it, so that was two rooms they would never use. There was also a bathroom upstairs. The bathroom they had at their house was on the end of the kitchen and had been built as an afterthought because the houses in their street had had outside lavatories a few years back. Here was a huge spider in the bath so Jenna ran out again and left her mother admiring the fittings.

It seemed daft to Jenna to pay so much more money so that they could have more space when they didn't use what they had already and she wasn't convinced she would like going upstairs at night on her own when it was so much bigger – there were three bedrooms and though they never had anybody to stay her mother had been so enthusiastic about having another bedroom and had gone in and looked admiringly about it and Jenna knew that she was deciding what colour she would have it and how the furnishings would be and it just all seemed so silly somehow and the house was a long way from the sea.

The bedroom that she would have, looked out over the little back garden and the road behind so she was no better off because that was what her bedroom did now and she spent so little time there, she wasn't like a lot of girls who spent their lives upstairs, having secrets and making plans with their best friends and talking about boys.

Ruari had always been her best friend. She knew the girls at school had thought it odd that she went home to spend her evenings with a boy when they were younger but she didn't really think about it, it had just always been so. Ruari was the most important thing in her life and now she felt, stupidly because it wasn't far away, as though she was leaving him.

18

She was convinced you couldn't lie in bed there on summer nights when it never got dark in June and listen to the tiny waves barely breaking on the warm sand and imagine the flowers in the sand dunes, green, yellow and white. She listened hard when she was left in the bedroom alone but all she could hear was the distant sound of traffic and the shouts of some children playing in the road.

She didn't want to be away from the beach, it seemed ungrateful somehow, as though you had forsaken it, the foghorn which went off when the weather was bad and the lights which flashed from the lighthouse and sometimes you saw seals in the water when you were on the beach, they were so friendly like big dogs. And people walked their whippets and Labradors and spaniels and threw sticks and children built sandcastles with moats. She couldn't leave all that and most important of all she couldn't leave Ruari.

And then she saw her mother's face and it was shiny with pleasure so she couldn't say anything. She tried to make the right noises and all the way as they walked back home her mother talked about how she would redecorate and where each piece of furniture would go and how nice it would be to live in such a place and she thought, this was her mother's dream and it was such a small dream that she couldn't bear to be the one to break it.

Her dad saw how she felt. When they got back to the house he squeezed her hand and he said, 'Do it for your mam, there's a good lass,' and she knew that he didn't want to go either.

'And you needn't think that boy's coming to visit neither,' her mother said as they went into the house. 'Him and his mucky boots.'

'They're football boots, Mam,' Jenna objected, 'and they aren't mucky either.'

She knew that his mam had saved hard to buy Ruari football boots for his birthday and he treasured them. Ruari would have given up anything for them and looked after them really well. They were never mucky, he would have been horrified to hear her mam saying that.

An hour later Ruari came to the yard gate for her. He didn't often come up the yard, he knew that her mam didn't like him. Jenna thought it was one of the reasons her mam wanted to move. She thought Ruari was common and his family of course. He kissed her briefly and they walked away hand in hand from the house.

Ruari couldn't afford fashionable clothes and Jenna thought it was a shame because he had a really nice figure, a good shape. She thought he was beautiful and though she wouldn't have told him for the world she thought he had the perfect bottom which didn't show to advantage because he couldn't afford tight hipsters with T-shirts and boots like other lads wore on Saturday nights in town. Or nice suits, she loved a nice suit.

She wished they could go to town and she could wear her new dress. Ruari liked her clothes, probably, she thought, because most of her dresses were very short and showed off her long slender legs. He liked it when she wore boots. Her legs, Jenna thought, were her best feature but the rest of her wasn't bad either. She thought her nose was a bit big and maybe her thighs were a trifle heavy but other than that she was happy when she looked into her mirror and saw her blonde blue-eyed looks. She was striking, she knew. Lads gazed at her in the street and she enjoyed it.

'Do you want to go to the pictures?' he enquired and she sensed he was about to tell her what was on so she said quickly.

'No, I want to talk to you.'

He pulled a face.

Nobody said anything else until they got to the beach. What she loved best about their beach was that there was hardly anybody on it, even on a fine night like this, just the odd person walking a dog down by the shore. The tide was out, the rocks showed and the sand was warm because it had been a fine day.

The beach was black with coal where earlier that week there had been a big tide, flat strangely shaped pieces of it like broken roof slates glinted in the evening sunlight, like jet against the sand which was almost white in the spring evening. A cool wind came off the sea, lifting the sand in swirls and through a sky which was almost blue, small flakes of blossom from the trees in the gardens of the better houses drifted like pearls.

The spring tides had left other debris, small mountains of glistening brown seaweed in frills like some of the net curtains which hung in the windows of the pit houses which were too close together for any natural privacy. Mother-of-pearl hills of scallop-edged shells and blue-and-white mussel shells opened like butterflies to the pale cream sunshine which fell upon the beach of the pit town.

The wheels of the three pitheads which graced the blue sky like giants along the edge of the seashore dominated the area. Behind them, like poor relations, crouched the pit rows.

Jenna and Ruari took their shoes off and walked at the water's edge where the waves were moving back and forth and were warmed by the sand and Jenna thought there was nothing better than this though she loved a storm in October when you could feel the sea spray on your face from well up the top of the beach. She loved its noise and movement, something you couldn't control.

'We're moving,' she said, 'not far,' she added hastily, in case he should think she meant another town or even another area, 'to Wesley Road. My dad got promoted and we've been to look at the house tonight and my mam is ever so pleased.'

Ruari didn't say anything. He never went into her house but she very often went into his so in a way she would be losing his house as well as hers because it wouldn't be the same. You couldn't drop in casually the way that she did almost every day and see his mam for a few minutes.

'It's not far,' she said.

'No,' Ruari agreed but neither of them meant it, it was in a lot of respects a whole world away. 'It'll be nice,' he said, 'for your mam.'

And Jenna thought, yes, although he didn't say it, her mam had never fitted into Back Church Street the way that she and her dad had, and her mam would be pleased about that, proud of it.

She kissed him, long and slowly on the mouth. He tasted wonderful. How could a boy taste that sweet? And his kisses were perfect. It had been one of the things she had liked best about him from when they were very young. Ruari's kisses were to die for. She lingered and then he began to get the wrong idea and slide his hands up her legs when she still had something to say so she stopped and said,

'I'm not like my mam. I don't want to leave Back Church Street and I don't want to leave you, ever.'

He smiled, she felt his lips curve under hers.

'You're not going anywhere,' he said.

'I shall never go anywhere really you know, not without you.'

'I'm not going no place,' he said.

'Are you sure?'

'Aye, I'm quite certain,' he said and then he kissed her and this time she didn't stop him when he slid his hands up her thighs.

Together down on the dunes in the spiky grass there she had him all to herself and in the late evening when the darkness came down and hid them they could have each other and be close and there was never any problem about it. There was never any risk because he took care of it, like he took care of everything, Jenna thought. She looked up at the stars and was glad that he was hers and that he could make her feel like nobody else ever did or ever would or ever could.

She didn't have to stifle her cries of pleasure here with nobody but the birds to notice. This was their place, the little town and the pitheads and the sea, the sounds of their childhood were just the same as now and somehow their relationship was like that, it was unsmirched, untouched, unspoiled. She loved him.

It frightened her in a way, how much she loved him, and then he would hold her and she would stop being frightened because she knew that he was hers and always would be. She just wished they had more time together.

She had the awful feeling that when she moved away she would see him less, she knew it was so, it would have to be planned, it could not be two or three casual meetings a day, waving to him in the back lane, knowing he was there, that he was sleeping just a few yards away, they would have to make sure that they saw one another and what with her job and his job and his football and her mother not wanting her to see him and Wesley Road being at the other side of the town she panicked.

It wouldn't be the same. It would never be the same any more. She wanted never to let him go, she held him closer and closer until there wasn't closer to be for fear that she should let go of him and they would never see one another again.

She wished that they could get married even though they were so young but Ruari's mother needed his wage at the moment, his stepfather drank.

Jenna could only dream of them having a tiny house together somewhere not far off, it didn't have to be anything much, just so that they could be together all the time, somewhere very close to where they had been born and lived. She wanted never to leave this place and never to leave him.

Two

On a weekday evening several weeks later Sorrel Maddison heard the knocking on the door of his office and recognized the rapping as Harry Philips, the manager of the club. Being chairman of Dunelm North End Football Club was the pinnacle of Sorrel's career. He had done many things in his life but always he had had this goal – he laughed at the pun – this in his mind, this had been what he had intended and now he was here in this great big office and everybody did what he wanted and everybody listened to what he said.

The new stadium had been built not far from the sea and on the site of an old pit and not that far from the old site so that people could not complain about the football being outside the town or inconvenient to get to.

Somehow they wanted to feel as though

26

the place was completely theirs. The move had been his idea and he had wanted it in the very heart of the town because to him the two were indivisible. The new stadium seated fifty thousand people and there was enough room for it to be expanded further and eventually he would get it there, he knew he would.

During the World Cup the year before, two group games and a quarter-final had been played there and he was very proud that his new stadium was chosen for this. There was also very good floodlighting so that matches could be played at night and in bad weather because football being an almost all year round game and this being the north the weather was at best unpredictable.

He had been very fond of the old stadium which had been used by the local people for over ninety years so they had taken a bit of shifting when the idea was proposed but there was no way they could hang on to the old one, things had to move on and he was the man to move them. He thought of the team and the ground and everything about it as being his, completely belonging to him as nothing else in his life.

Harry was a little afraid of him, Sorrel knew. Most people were. It made things easier, it meant he didn't have to explain himself, it meant that what he said went, everywhere.

'Harry. Come in.'

He was genial because Harry hesitated in the doorway. He shuffled in.

'I wanted to talk to you, about Ruari Gallacher,' Harry said.

'Who's that?'

'Stan Robson's lad, his own father died down the pit years ago and Stan drinks. His mam's a nice woman and Ruari works at Dixon's. He's good, Mr Maddison, really good. Other clubs are sending scouts to watch him. Any day now somebody's going to offer for him and he could be what we're looking for.'

'You think he's special?'

'I don't think he's brilliant yet and I doubt he ever will be but I think he'll make a useful player, I think he could score a few goals, make enough decent passes to make other players score goals. It's good to have local lads who play well and don't cost much.'

Harry had played for Sunderland in his young day but had had so many injuries so often that he had had to come out of it but he knew the game, he knew what made a good footballer. He had been with North End for two years now and Sorrel trusted him. He looked for new talent and sent scouts all over the place, so to find it in his own backyard was very sweet.

'Offer him a deal. And offer Stan a bit of something, Harry, to cement it. If you think he's special then he must be.'

'Aye, I will.'

'But don't go mad. There's no need.'

'They've got nothing so I don't think I'll have to do too much to get him and besides, I'm mates with Stan. It could be cheap and quite lucrative in time.'

'Good.'

Harry looked relieved. He went out and Sorrel sat back in the chair behind his desk and thought how much he disliked Harry. How could such a man manage a football team with success? And yet he did.

The players responded, they worked for him. Sorrel had no idea why. He had seen other managers screaming at their players from the stands, chewing gum and scowling. Harry did none of that. He didn't curse or blame them unless things were really bad, nor, as far as Sorrel could judge, did he do much to encourage them, yet somehow it worked.

Sorrel thought it was the training. They trained in the afternoons and had brand-new facilities for doing so, not just the pitch like so many clubs. The rest of the time they could do what they liked and they were punctual and ready, keen because they knew where they were, they knew how to please and they wanted to please Harry.

Ruari Gallacher would be an asset to the team, Sorrel was sure of it.

Sorrel went home to the twelfth-century manor house he had bought when he had begun to make real money from the betting shops he had started up. He had just sat down on the sofa with a whisky and soda and the local newspaper when his eighteen-year-old son, Paul, came in. Paul had just finished school. He didn't know what he wanted to do next and to Sorrel's frustration didn't want to go to university. He was scowling.

'I heard you're going to sign up Gallacher.'

How in the hell had he heard that, Sorrel wondered, but then a number of people would know since Harry Philips had been at the Dixon's shipyard games lately so there were bound to be rumours.

'So?'

'So he's not that good.'

Sorrel looked at him. This was interesting. Paul had never yet cared about football. Sorrel had taken him to innumerable games when he was little and he had been bored. Paul hated sport. Sorrel could not believe he had fathered a son who didn't like the national game.

'Harry says he'll do well. Have you ever known Harry to be wrong?'

Paul hesitated. He didn't usually argue so this must matter to him a great deal.

'What is it?' Sorrel said.

'What do you mean?'

Sorrel took another swig of his drink and put down his *Evening Chronicle*, folding it carefully as he did so.

'There's something else to this, you couldn't tell a decent footballer from a fried egg.'

'I don't want him here. There are other clubs.'

'He's a local lad, which is good for us, and Harry reckons he could make a striker. What the hell's going on with you? Spit it out, for God's sake.'

'He's getting in my way with Jenna Duncan.'

Sorrel stared at him.

'What?'

Paul moved uncomfortably.

'Jenna Duncan,' he said again. 'She's a local girl, I like her.'

'Yes, well, I didn't think she was Miss World,' Sorrel said.

Paul didn't say anything. Sorrel could have kicked himself for the sarcasm, it wasn't often they had a conversation and then only when Paul wanted something, he thought with regret.

'You want me to turn down the prospect of a good footballer because of some lass? Are you a complete idiot?'

'There are half a dozen lads around here just as good if not better than he is, I don't know why everybody goes on about him,'

Paul said.

Sorrel stared so hard even he noticed he was doing it. His son was jealous because some lad from a back street was screwing whatever her name was. How ridiculous.

'Ruari Gallacher is poor, uneducated, works in a shipyard to support his mother because her bloody stupid husband is a drunk and he has nothing going for him other than a good right foot. How in the hell could he compete with you? Take her some-where nice to eat, buy her champagne. How difficult can it be? And if Gallacher is as good as Harry thinks he is we would be daft not to make sure of him.

'Never confuse sentiment and business. Money makes the world go round, at least our world. And business is money. And women for the most part like successful men. Yes?'

He looked hopefully at Paul, who still said nothing.

'Pour me another drink,' Sorrel said and watched his son mix the whisky and soda, not too much soda, he didn't like the whisky drowned, it was expensive malt, he bought it specially, his family knew that and when he had accepted the glass he said, 'Who is she?'

'Her father works in the grocery depart-ment of the Store.'

'So she's poor as well and no doubt has no education and lives in a back street too.'

'I don't see that it matters, you came from a back street or so you're always telling me.'

'You're right, it doesn't matter and therefore you're Santa Claus, yes?'

Paul smiled.

'Why don't you ask her out and then if you like her you can invite her to dinner? That way we'll get a look at her,' Sorrel said.

Paul's young face lit like he was still a child and Sorrel could not help being pleased that he had got this right.

'Thanks, Dad,' he said.

Really Sorrel thought as he sipped at his second whisky and soda, the world was a very simple place.

Three

Paul Maddison had a car, that was the first thing Jenna noticed about him, other than the fact that he was the richest lad in the area. His car was not an old banger like a lot of the lads' cars, it was an MGB, green, and he had the hood down.

When he stopped to speak to her in the street she noticed the other girls noticing her and being envious. She could not help thinking that Ruari did not have a car, not even an old banger. When she went out with him they couldn't go anywhere much, he couldn't afford to take her anywhere. The furthest they ever went was the local cinema. She didn't really mind but it was nice to see how the other girls craned their necks when Paul stopped his car and said, 'Hi, Jenna,' like he was American or something.

'Hi, Paul. Nice car.' He was good-looking too, fair-haired and tanned.

'My dad bought it for me.'

Well, she didn't think he had gone out and got it for himself. He had just left school, by all accounts.

'Actually, I think he bought it for himself but he never has time to use it. I wondered,' he said, that balmy summer evening, 'if you would like to go for a drink with me. I know a lovely little pub in Bamburgh.'

Bamburgh was miles away, one of the most beautiful of the seaside towns, with the best beach in the area and a castle right beside it. She could imagine going on the beach and putting her feet in the water and then sitting outside a nice pub with a lad like this who wore expensive clothes and could afford to buy her a drink. And she could have worn her new dress, she thought with regret.

'I can't,' she said.

'Why not?'

'Because I'm going with Ruari Gallacher.' Jenna felt awful saying it in a way. She loved Ruari but to somebody like Paul Maddison,

Ruari was nobody and she was ashamed at how that made her feel, like she was nobody either. 'We – we're going out tonight, he's taking me somewhere nice.'

It was a lie and she was sorry that she had said it but somehow she felt she had to. He had been distracted with the football of late as never before and she was starting to hate it. They saw one another in passing every day but she did not have him to herself, it was almost as though he was so used to her that he didn't need to take her out or spend time.

Paul smiled at her. 'I didn't know,' he said and drove off.

Jenna went into the back lane. She had just finished work and she wanted to see Ruari but she had the feeling he was playing a football match that night. She was right, he was just coming out of the house with a bag over his arm which no doubt had his kit in it.

'I really, really want to go out,' she said. 'I've hardly seen you in weeks, you've done nothing but play football, you've been out every night practising.'

Sometimes he would give up matches for her if he had enough time to make sure it wasn't putting anybody out but this time he couldn't, she could see. It had been happening more and more often, the football always came first. She was lucky if she came second. She understood how he felt about the game but she was starting to resent how he was treating her.

'I'm going early for practice,' he said.

'Can't you not just this once? I've had an awful day. Somebody nicked something and Miss Hammond got upset and we had the police and it isn't nice, you know.' Miss Hammond was the manageress of the department. It was Jenna's ambition to have Miss Hammond's job but it didn't seem likely to happen since Miss Hammond was about thirty and not very pretty. Nobody would ever want to marry her, she would be manageress of the department forever.

'I'm sorry Jenna. Mr Hutchinson is hoping there'll be scouts.'

Jenna raised her eyes. 'He's been saying that every game for months.'

'It's nearly the end of the season, it won't last much longer,' he said.

Suddenly Jenna could not stand the idea of going home. Her parents would be sitting over the television and the smell of shepherd's pie would be filling the house.

'Oh, please, Ruari, we don't have to do anything, just go for a walk on the beach.'

'I cannot, you know I cannot.'

Jenna tried to be sensible but they had been going on like this for so long.

'It's never going to happen, you know,' she said. 'There are thousands of lads who want to be top footballers.'

Ruari looked down. 'I'm good,' he said.

He wasn't given to saying such things but she thought, yes, he believed in himself, perhaps he always had done.

'I know but you can't build your life hoping for something like that. You've been going on like this for years, ever since you were a little kid. You aren't going to help your mam like this.'

She had hit the nail on the head, she thought as he looked up.

'I won't do it being an electrician at Dixon's either,' he said.

'It's a good steady job,' she said. 'What's wrong with that? Nobody expects you to do any more. What about us?'

He hesitated. 'I will make it up to you.'

'You're always doing that, always making up to people for what they haven't had. You can't help that. I want to have you to myself. I want us to have a little house, just you and me, to get away from my mam and her big ideas. We could manage. I've got a job and you've got a job and... I know we aren't very old but, Ruari, I love you. It isn't going to change. Please, just this once, just this one time. I won't ever ask you for anything else.' She was almost crying. 'I don't want to be by myself tonight.'

'Come to the game,' he said, missing the point completely.

The tears began to slip down her face and she could not bear that he should see them, could not stand the humiliation of him letting her cry and not doing anything. She could see by the way he was standing that he wouldn't compromise.

'I should have known better,' she said and then she ran down the back lane.

He shouted after her but he didn't go after her. She thought he might, for a few moments she waited when she got to the beach but the time slipped past and he didn't come for her.

She stayed down there. It was the perfect spring evening or was it early summer, she could never remember when one started and the other stopped. The weather didn't necessarily make any difference. It could be cold in July and warm in October.

The fields were yellow with cowslips away from the town, she had seen them when she and her mam went into Newcastle shopping. We could have gone for a walk, she thought, the hedges are white with may, the forests are full of bluebells, there's cow parsley in great big swathes beside the river and in the fields rabbits are running around and the lambs playing and you can hear pheasants calling in the fields and here I am all alone on an evening like this when I should be with somebody.

She walked slowly back up the beach. It still wasn't late and she really didn't want to go home. She was beginning to think that her life would go on forever like this, smiling over the counter, being nice to the public, bringing her wage home for her mam and dad when she could have thought of a hundred other things to do with it. Oh, she didn't want to be ungrateful but she wanted a home of her own, a little house with Ruari. Was it so much to ask?

She went slowly up the steps which led to the main road and began to walk home. As she did so a car stopped just in front. It was Paul Maddison.

'Hello again. I thought you were going somewhere,' he said.

'I'm not going anywhere,' she said, trying to ignore him. He stopped the car and got out.

'The sea's so calm,' he said, 'it's more like July, isn't it?'

It was, she thought regretfully, it was so beautiful.

'The trouble is it's never like this in July,' he said.

That was true. You hoped the summers would be lovely but up here in the north half the time and more you spent watching the rain run down the windows. The local joke was summer's different, the rain's warmer.

'Do you go away in July?' she said.

'Sometimes sooner. Dad's finished with the football season then and—'

'Oh, the bloody football season,' she said.

'Don't you care for the game?'

'No, I don't.'

'To be perfectly honest neither do I,' he confessed.

She laughed, she looked at him to see whether he was stringing her a line but he seemed genuine.

'But your dad owns the club,' she said.

'It's his dream, not mine.'

'What's your dream?'

'Oh, it's very modest,' he said. 'I just want a nice house and a decent job so that I can marry and have a couple of children.'

Jenna looked harder at him. Was he just saying it? She didn't think he was, how funny, no lad wanted that, it was what lasses wanted.

'I want to be able to come home at night and have a nice dinner and chat about daft things and kiss my kids goodnight. My dad never did that, you see, he was too busy making money and being important. I suppose he started from so far down that he wanted to succeed so badly. I don't have that need, I suppose I'm lucky, he did all that so I don't have to do it somehow. Does this make any sense?'

'Oh yes,' Jenna said, 'it makes perfect sense to me. Ruari's like your dad, he has everything to prove to himself and his mam.'

'What are you going to do now?' Paul said.

'Go home, I suppose. What are you going to do?'

'The same. I'd rather go for a drink. I suppose you don't fancy it? Just one?'

'I shouldn't,' she said regretfully. 'I don't drink.'

'Oh, come on. You know me and it's just a drink. It would be nice to have somebody to go with.' As though he was lonely which he couldn't be, him being so popular and his family being the most important people in the area.

'I'll bring you back in an hour.'

She gave in. And she was glad. It was lovely to sit in the sports car and have the wind make a mess of her hair and to see the coast road whizzing past, the sand dunes and the little villages, and the sea was so bright, glittering like sapphire and people looked as they went past and the speed and the car and the fact that she was with a lad who could afford such luxuries made her feel as though she was having fun.

They went to Bamburgh which was one of her favourite places and had one of the best castles she had ever seen, right on the sea-shore at the top of the beach, it stood there so proud, she loved it. They left the car on the dunes. A gentle warm breeze was making its way through the spiky grass where people had trekked sand and on the beach boys were playing football and people were walking dogs and little kids were running up and down the shoreline. The shadows were lengthening but the evening would go on and on as it did at this time of the year.

The light was incredible here, bright, not like it was during the day a whole new white light and just for the next two or three weeks it would be like that nearly all night so that even if you woke up at three in the morning it was not properly dark and there was something very comforting about it.

You made up for it in the winter of course, when it barely got light for weeks and weeks, but she liked that too, fires and sitting inside and listening to the wind and the waves and when you went to bed you had a hot-water bottle.

They paddled, the water had been over the sand and was warm and he was so easy to be with, his trouser legs rolled up to his knees like the old men and she carrying her shoes in her hand. He laced his fingers through hers and he looked so good, the evening sun turning his hair almost cream and when she commented on his tan he said it was because he had been to Spain with his family in February and then to Greece later, what a luxury – she thought it sounded so glamorous and she was envious.

He told her how warm it had been in Spain and of the hotel where they had stayed with a big kidney-shaped swimming pool and how he had drunk cold white wine in the evenings. She thought to be in Spain and to drink white wine and perhaps to wear a long dress and sit in the garden in the late evening and talk with his family must be wonderful. She would never have anything like that, she knew it. Her life was dull.

There were bubbles among the foam at the water's edge but it had been a hot day there had been four hot days in a row and here in the north-east that didn't happen very often which was why she felt even worse that Ruari was playing football that evening.

The sun went down in spectacular fashion like a big fiery football and after it had done so they went to the pub and there he ordered a bottle of champagne. Jenna could not believe it. They sat out in the garden which overlooked the beach and the champagne came in a silver ice bucket. It was Veuve Clicquot, he said, the label was orange and it tasted delectable, like nothing she had ever tasted before. It was the most wonderful evening of her life.

When the champagne was finally finished it was very late indeed and there were stars. They left the hood down on the car and they sang songs to the night air. There were few other cars on the road. Finally he stopped and with the sound of the sea all around he took her into his arms and kissed her. He tasted of champagne.

They got out of the car and ran down in the darkness on to the beach. It was a blue sky and the stars were so many that Jenna was amazed at them, thousands and thousands of stars. She ran into the waves and there he caught hold of her and kissed her again, lifted her off her bare feet, ran his fingers over her bare legs, picked her up and carried her so that she squealed, thinking he was going to throw her into the sea but he didn't. He carried her back up the sand and into the grass. The grass was cool now but not cold and his mouth was warm and his body was warmer and she was so very happy, happier than she had ever been in her life.

She didn't stop him. It seemed inevitable that she should give herself to him, she wanted to, was glad and it was not that he was arrogant or difficult or filled with triumph. He was a bit clumsy, a bit apologetic and it was only then that she realized he was not Ruari. Ruari was not clumsy or apologetic but Ruari had no need to be because they knew one another's bodies so well.

She had somehow expected him to be Ruari though it was not so much of a shock when he was not. She was even sorry for him that he was not Ruari, that she did not love him. She liked him enough to give him the night, that was how it felt, that it was such a wonderful time that she would not ruin it by refusing.

He told her that he loved her, she did not doubt it. She was aware all the time that she did not love him but it didn't matter. She cared enough about him to be there with him, to enjoy being close, to like that he wanted to be with her. There was nothing taken for granted. The stars had already provided what they could, so she did not need him to give her that. The champagne had done the rest.

If it was not the best sex she had ever had she thought it was not his fault. He did not know much about it, he did not know what to do and his very innocence was her undoing. She did not want to disappoint or upset him when he had given her such a wonderful evening, such a good time. Any girl would have been pleased to have been with him. He faltered, when it was over, he said, 'Jenna ... was it all right?' and she said it was, she said it was very good, she could not say anything else because he was downcast somehow and not like she had thought rich boys were.

He kissed her. They got dressed, they made their way out of the now cold sand dunes, where the wind had got up and the sea was like black oil and the sand was lifting in little mean drifts against the breeze. The skies had blotted out the stars.

He put the hood up on the car. He put the heater on but Jenna shivered and all the way home she was cold. He covered the distance so fast that she was afraid, the roads snaking

45

and the little car flinging itself across them. She was glad when they finally reached her house, she giving him terse directions. He brought the car to an abrupt halt outside her front door. He said her name but she got out and ran.

Inside she could hear her mother shouting her name because she never came in the front way and had had to hammer on the door so that her mother would unlock it but all she said was, 'Thanks, Mam, I'm going to bed,' and she ran upstairs and when she got into her bed she found that she was shivering.

She could not stop crying. What had she done? Whatever had she been thinking about? She contained her sobs. She could not indulge herself here. The walls were thin, her parents would notice. She could hear their footsteps as they climbed the stairs to bed. They had waited up for her.

Somehow that made things worse and normally she would have been called upon to explain herself. She had no doubt there would be questions in the morning. She tried to breathe quietly and not to cry. It didn't matter. It wouldn't matter. It would be all right. She had done nothing wrong. She and Ruari were not engaged or married or anything like that. She could do what she liked. It was her life. She turned over and slept for a while but she kept waking up because the night was so long, the hours

46

crawled and seemed to go on forever.

It was only when the morning came that she welcomed the light. Another day. She would do better. Everything would be all right. She went off to work early not only because she couldn't sleep but she knew that her mother 'wanted to have words' with her, as she called it. She would have to face the music tonight no doubt.

Four

Stan Robson, Ruari's stepfather, had known the manager, Harry Philips, since they were little lads. Stan grinned at him when Harry turned up at the Black Lion on Church Street that evening.

'A pint?'

'Aye, I wouldn't mind,' Harry said and they sat down in the depths of the corner and nobody came over and disturbed them. They were a bit nervous of Harry nowadays, Sorrel Maddison's right-hand man and nobody got in his road.

Stan came back with the beer. Harry, a small skinny man, he was only five foot two, had been fast, Stan could recall having seen him dribble the ball past three or four men. He had been good but it hadn't lasted. Nothing good, Stan thought, ever bloody lasted.

'I saw your Ruari play the other night.'

'Oh, aye? Like he was still at school. You'd think he'd find summat better to do. He thinks he's Jackie Milburn like.'

Harry nodded.

'Aye, well, I like the look of him so Mr Maddison and me we thought we might sign him up, you know.'

Stan blinked.

'For the team?'

'Why not ... but give him a trial, a couple of years, and then we'll see.'

Stan downed the rest of his pint, he was so surprised.

'Another?' Harry offered.

'Aye. That would be grand,' Stan said, smiling.

Ruari was still up when Stan got home though his mam had gone to bed. Ruari watched him carefully to see how drunk he was, he might need helping up the stairs or he might only get as far as the couch but Stan, though bright-eyed, seemed more sober than usual.

'I saw Harry Philips in the Black Lion.'

'What did he want?'

'You. They want you to sign up.'

'Who, me?'

'Aye, you. Who do you think I'm talking to?'

Ruari hesitated. 'What?' he said.

'Is that all you've got to say when you're being given an opportunity like this? I have to admit I never thought you'd manage it,' Stan said.

'Mr Hutchison said there was a scout from Carlisle and some other bloke from Tee-shaven at the game tonight.'

'And you think they were there because of you?' Stan said.

Stan looked at him and Ruari knew what he was thinking, that Ruari was soft in the head to think he was that good, that any top First Division club other than his own would have him.

'And did any bugger say owt?' Stan demanded, staring at Ruari from cold eyes.

'No,' Ruari admitted, downcast.

'Well, then. Mr Maddison wants to take you on. What do you think to that?'

'I think it depends how much they're offering to pay,' Ruari said.

'How much? Lad, you've got to grab your opportunities with both hands. You're not that far off eighteen. You're going to be too old to play football if you have to wait much longer. I said we'd meet him at Dunhelm Hotel on Friday night.'

Friday night was a long time off, Ruari thought, and he couldn't help but notice that the man from Teeshaven, a man he hadn't seen before at the ground, came over when he was training the following evening. He was short and stocky and kept his hands in his pockets while he talked to Mr Hutchinson who ran the games at the shipyard and Mr Hutchinson introduced Ruari and he said he had come to make Ruari an offer. Ruari didn't know what to think or say.

He looked at Mr Hutchinson for guidance and Mr Hutchinson said would Mr Hodgkin excuse them for a second and he drew Ruari to one side.

'Does he mean it?' Ruari said.

'Yes, I think he does.'

'How come nobody did before?'

'You're just a late developer,' Mr Hutchinson said with a grin. 'Everybody's different. Two years ago you were just another lad playing football. Now...'

'Now what?' Ruari said, eager for praise.

'Now it's different.'

'Mr Maddison wants me, so me stepdad reckons.'

Mr Hutchinson's face darkened.

'Well, you have to make your own mind up and in the end it's down to what you want and the money.'

'How do I make up me mind, though?' Ruari said.

Mr Hutchinson looked at him.

'Well, you know Ruari, they say that there are three things that matter in life.'

'What are they?'

Mr Hutchinson paused and then he said softly. 'Money, money and money.'

They went over and sat down and Mr Hodgkin made Ruari the kind of offer that got him excited. The money sounded good and Mr Hodgkin didn't make any special promises, he put the offer plainly.

'Think about it, Ruari, and let me know if you think it's a good idea. Then I'll come over and talk to your parents. They have to sign the contract as well as you.'

'Me mam.'

'Your mother then and we'll see what she thinks. There's no rush. Take your time. See if it's something you want. We want you but we know it would be a big move for you.'

Ruari stuttered his thanks and left.

Teeshaven was one of the local rivals and it was about thirty miles away, a bigger town than this and industrial with a chemical works and a steel works, on the coast but it had bigger shipyards than here. He was scared but he thought Mr Hutchinson was right. He would be a fool if he didn't go for the team which offered him the most money. He would be able to tell Jenna, once it was sorted out, and he would move and she could go with him and get a job and he would be able to send money home to his mam and everything would be wonderful. He was so excited, his dream was about to come true.

Jenna went to Farne House, Paul's home, for dinner. Her mam had tried to talk to her about coming in like that and Jenna had told her who she had been with and that was enough to make her mother happy and it was nice for her to feel that her mother approved.

She couldn't help being impressed when Paul had stopped her in the street the day after they had been out and said that he had been worried, was she all right and his father would very much like it if she would come to their house in the evening for a meal and somehow she didn't remember how to refuse. She hadn't known what to say

'I know you go with Ruari, I know it was just...' Paul had hesitated. 'But we could be friends, couldn't we? What's wrong with that or are you busy tonight?'

She was never busy, she thought, she never got to do anything exciting and to be asked to their house and to something as posh as dinner was too much temptation.

'I won't get you drunk, I'll come and collect you and fetch you back.'

He had done so, shaking hands with her mam when he came to the door. Her mother thought he was wonderful, she could see. She only wished her dad was at home to see the lovely little sports car as it stood in the street at the front of their house. She was glad then for the first time that they had moved, it would have been too awful for Paul to have to come to their old house, she would have been so ashamed.

Farne House was a wonderful place, the kind that people went to at the end of fairy tales. It was big and stone and reassuring, the sort of house which wrapped you around like it was hugging you to it and she loved it from the moment she saw it.

It was nothing like she had thought their house would be. It was an old manor house, not a brand-new one like a lot of rich people had. The building was long sideways and the roofs came to three points with three storeys of stone mullioned windows. Paul showed her around the gardens. Furthest away there was an enormous swimming pool.

'There used to be a kind of orchard here, a nuttery.'

'A nuttery?'

'A place with lots of nut trees. My father had them cut down and the place cleared so that we would have somewhere to swim.'

He showed her around. It was wonderful, Jenna thought and must have cost a fortune to build. There were changing rooms and there was another building and inside it a sauna and a steam room, a plunge bath and showers, all things she had never seen before. She wondered if she would ever be invited to use them.

But also she kept thinking about what the

nuttery would have looked like, the shade in the summer, the little spreading trees and the long grass moving in the warm breeze. Would it have had that wonderful smell like almonds had and how were nuts harvested? It was such a novel idea that she wished she had seen it.

The rest of it held half a dozen garages and a huge area for turning. Three Mercedes cars were parked on the drive. There was a very big lawn on which reposed large statues and a fountain which had a big green statue of what looked like a semi-clad nymph in the middle of it and water spouted from various places around the statue.

'It used to be different,' Paul said, frowning as he tried to remember. 'I think there was a Jacobean garden with herbs in it and things like lavender. My mother loved it and she was really upset when Dad changed everything.'

Inside the house was very big, the kitchen had narrow stone mullioned windows and deep thick walls and an Aga set in a huge arched fireplace. Jenna thought every woman must want a house with a big cream Aga like that one.

The walls were white, rough plastering in the big sitting room too and it had a huge open fire which made her wish that the weather was bad because she thought it must be wonderful when the rain was pouring down the four big leaded windows. It had a beamed ceiling, black beams and cream in between. There were lots of big leather settees which were bliss to sink into and little tables and a variety of modern paintings which were lines of pink and purple.

The dining room was her favourite room, the walls were covered in oak panelling and it had a flagged floor with rugs all laid out, and the table was oak too and long enough for a dozen people but laid with four places so the dinner was just because of her which made her feel very important, with the candles burning and their light reflected in the crystal chandeliers.

There was a white cloth, the kind which would have taken ages to iron, and starched serviettes and crystal glasses, three or four of them at every place setting, and there were flowers in the middle of the table, plucked from the garden no doubt and dying but they looked pretty.

Jenna felt shabby and rather silly in her cheap flowered dress. Mrs Maddison came downstairs at the last minute, wearing a very expensive frock. Jenna, working with clothes, knew the real thing when she saw it. Faye Maddison was tall, slender and had a tan, which proved she had been abroad recently. She wore gold jewellery, several chains around her neck and gold bangles on her brown arms. Jenna was also impressed because Mrs Maddison did not go into the kitchen, she offered drinks but the food was cooked and served by other people which Jenna had never seen before.

Jenna didn't like her. She barely spoke, nothing but courtesies and Jenna knew nothing about drinking and Mrs Maddison was no help, asking her in a flat voice what she would like and Jenna couldn't ask for champagne, it seemed so rude so she shook her head and stuttered that she was all right, thank you. Mrs Maddison merely turned away to pour champagne for herself which she opened without asking her son to. Usually Jenna thought, men did things like that but Mrs Maddison opened the champagne with such expertise, a quick twist of the bottle and out the cork came with a discreet pop, that Jenna realized she must have done it hundreds of times before.

Mr Maddison came in at the last minute full of apologies like Jenna was somebody special. She was in awe of him, had heard stories about him, how he had started in the gutter and made lots of money with night-clubs and betting shops. It was said that he was a millionaire. Sorrel Maddison was tall and dark and seemed to tower over everybody but he was nice to Jenna that evening and she liked that he was so fond of his son that he would put himself about for her.

'What do you think of the house?' he said to her. 'It cost a fortune. I had to fight the planners at the council to change everything but I got what I wanted in the end because it was dropping to pieces when I found it, they were going to pull it down and build something entirely fresh. I rescued it if you like.'

Jenna smiled and agreed and Mr Maddison insisted on showing her over the house, including the six bathrooms all of which had gold taps and gold and white tiles, like something from Greece, she thought.

The bedrooms had thick carpets and built-in wardrobes and there was an exercise room in the cellar with things like a running machine, Jenna had never seen anything like that before, and down there in another room was a bar. There was another bar in the sitting room, which ran the full length of one wall and behind it was every kind of drink you could imagine. Jenna caught sight of herself in the mirror opposite before she sat down at the table to eat, badly dressed in comparison to everybody else and pale. She was so nervous.

They had wine. Jenna had never had wine before, except for the champagne she had drunk with Paul, she thought guiltily and nobody talked about her being too young to drink it. She didn't know what kind of wine it was, just that it was so golden it was almost green and tasted of summer, gooseberries and butter.

The food was better than anything she had

tasted before, salmon, chicken in some kind of pale cream sauce and a pudding made with raspberries and meringue. They had coffee outside. It was, she thought, a different world than the one she knew and she felt real gratitude towards the whole family. She didn't want to leave, it was as though she had come home somehow.

There were lights strung between the trees. It was like fairyland, Jenna decided.

On the way back she said to Paul, 'I had a lovely time.'

'I'm glad. My dad liked you. You can come again any time,' he said.

Jenna hesitated, wondering why he had said his dad and not his mam though it had been obvious his mother didn't care for her so perhaps it was nothing but the truth.

'I shouldn't really,' she said.

He stopped the car and for a moment Jenna was frightened he wanted to kiss her but he said, 'We can be friends if that's what you want.'

'It wouldn't be fair.'

'I don't mind, really I don't.'

'Thanks, Paul, that's lovely of you,' she said.

Her mother had waited up for her.

'Did you have a nice evening?' she said, ready to be glad.

Jenna couldn't remember her mother having ever been interested before in what she was doing. She told her all about it, her mother was enthusiastic and it was lovely just to sit there and talk about what she had done and for her mother to be so pleased. Just before they went to bed her mother hesitated, a foot on the stairs.

'Oh, by the way,' she said, 'Ruari came to see you.'

Jenna stopped in the hallway

'Did you tell him where I was?'

'It wasn't a secret, was it?' her mother said.

'No, no of course not,' and now her evening was ruined. She couldn't sleep thinking of Ruari, wondering what she was doing.

Five

Stan met Harry Philips before Ruari got there on the Friday evening.

'I wanted to see you first,' Harry said and he took from his pocket a great big roll of five-pound notes and pressed them into Stan's fist. 'Here,' he said, 'this is just as thanks.'

'But...' Stan wasn't usually given to stuttering. 'Nowt's signed yet.'

'No, but you're his dad, aren't you, as near as, and you can sign for him.'

'Aye, I suppose I can,' Stan said.

59

'Well, then, we don't need to wait for Ruari.' Harry Philips gave him a pen and showed him where to sign and Stan, sweating so much that it ran into his eyes and he could hardly see the paper, signed with a flourish and he thrust the big wad of money into his pocket. He needed a pint to stop the sweating and another to chase it.

Ruari was ten minutes more. He was late, Stan thought, and he could hardly sit still as Ruari came into the foyer of the hotel.

'Isn't this grand?' Stan said.

Ruari said nothing.

Harry Philips said, 'Sit down, Ruari. I would offer you a drink but I know you aren't old enough.'

'I don't want owt, thanks,' Ruari said.

Harry waited until Ruari sat down.

'I've talked to Stan here about it and we want you for two years, that's usual at this point and we'll see how you go. We'll give you twelve pounds a week—'

'You'll have to do better than that,' Ruari interrupted.

Harry looked at him. Stan glared at him.

'Don't argue with the man, lad,' he said.

'What do you mean?' Harry said.

'I've been offered twenty pounds a week,' Ruari said, 'and more if I make good.'

Harry Philips stared at him and Ruari was suddenly aware of how much he disliked this man. Harry Philips was almost sneering at him.

'Twenty pounds a week?' he said as though he couldn't believe it. 'That's a fortune for an untried lad like you. Who is it?'

'Teeshaven.'

'You can't go and play for them,' Harry said with a dismissive snort. 'You belong here with your own folk.'

'I belong anywhere they'll pay me,' Ruari said and in a way he wished he hadn't, in a way he wished he didn't have to say it but the truth of the matter was that he thought Mr Hutchinson was right and that it all boiled down to money in the end.

He couldn't afford to stay here just because he liked it and it was home when they wouldn't offer him the same money.

'I don't think I like your attitude, lad,' Harry Philips said and Ruari thought, he wasn't used to people speaking their minds, saying their piece, he expected to have everything his own way. Harry Philips' face had gone dark and his eyes had narrowed and his mouth was nasty and thin.

'If you offer me the same money I'll talk to me mam about it,' he said.

Harry Philips laughed and Ruari didn't like the look in his eyes.

'That's big of you, lad,' he said.

'So, are you offering me?' Ruari said because he couldn't see how they could do any less and his mam would be really pleased.

'No, I'm not. They're lying to you.'

Ruari was sure the look in Harry's eyes was supposed to make him feel small but it didn't, it just made him more determined not to go with North End.

'I won't sign, then, I'll take what Tees-haven is offering.'

'You can't take it. Your father has signed the papers and you're ours for twelve pounds a week now,' Harry Philips said and there was triumph, and it was mean, in his eyes. 'What Mr Maddison wants Mr Maddison gets and he told me to get you and I have so we'll not have any of this lip from you my lad or you might learn to regret it, especially when I have you in training.'

'Is that right?' Ruari said, suddenly hating him.

'Aye, it's right,' Harry Philips said, showing him the paper. 'You're ours now, we can do what we like with you, train you, not train you, play you, not play you, drop you...' He let his voice trail off.

Ruari looked at the paper and then he looked at Stan and then he looked straight at Harry Philips.

'That doesn't mean anything.'

'What doesn't?'

'His signature. He's not me dad, he's not me legal guardian so it doesn't mean owt, and I haven't signed. The only person who can sign with me is me mam and she's not

62

here,' Ruari said and he got up and walked out.

'Yer mam'll sign. She'll have to and so will you,' Stan shouted after him. 'Come back here, you little shit.'

Ruari didn't want to go home, he hadn't told his mother about the meeting with Mr Hodgkin, he had wanted to see what Mr Maddison had in mind but he could see that Harry Philips and Stan had cooked things up between them, he wouldn't have been surprised if Philips had already given Stan a backhander and that was why Stan was so enthusiastic.

He had heard that such things went on in football and it would be naive to imagine people didn't go on like that but it was not just a hard game it was a hard business, he had not realized until this minute.

He hadn't thought either that he would be so angry that he would behave like this, like he was much older. Behaviour had consequences, he knew it did. He made himself go straight home. He didn't want to bad-mouth Stan to his mam either, he mustn't do that, it wasn't right.

She had been out when he left, she worked at the local school, cleaning after the kids had gone home. Ruari had gone back as early as he could after work and changed into his best clothes because he knew how important it was that he should make a good impression even though he didn't like Harry Philips and couldn't bring himself to think about signing for North End, especially when Mr Hodgkin had made him what he thought was a good offer.

It was mid-evening now. His mother was sitting at the kitchen table when he got in. She glanced up and then looked hard at him.

'Where have you been?' she said.

Ruari pulled off his good jacket, put it over the back of a kitchen chair and sat down.

'Stan wanted me to go and see Harry Philips.'

She was really interested now, her eyes were bright.

'Honest?' she said.

'Aye.'

'You think they might take you on?'

'They offered to.'

She put her hand over her mouth in surprise.

Ruari didn't go on. Harry Philips had scared him. He didn't like to admit it even to himself but it was true and worse still somehow Harry Philips had made him think that when he was a bit older he was going to be a very unpleasant man, difficult and bad-tempered. He didn't remember his mam saying that his dad had been like that and she certainly wasn't so who was he like?

At that moment the back door swung

64

open and Stan walked in. His face was red with sweat and fury. He came straight across the room and he walloped Ruari hard round the face and because Ruari hadn't been expecting it he fell over, the chair clattered and he went with it. It was a hard landing on the kitchen floor and he was dazed and couldn't think for a second so he just stayed there until he could.

There was no way to avoid whatever would happen now. Ruari wished he had had time to explain more to his mother. He got up gingerly and then stood for a moment and Betty stood too, eyes blazing, and taken aback at what had happened, Ruari thought, and then Stan said in a deceptively soft voice,

'You'll sign for North End.'

'No I won't,' Ruari said. His face hurt, he could taste blood and feel it running inside his mouth and it angered him.

'What gives you the right to hit my son?' Betty said, her face white.

I am only 'my son' when things are going wrong, Ruari thought and he wished he had handled things better though he couldn't think how.

Stan glared at her so much that Ruari was afraid of what he might do now, he was so angry.

'Your son,' Stan ground out the words, 'made me look a fool in front of Harry Philips. North End have offered him a perfectly good two-year contract and he told them he wouldn't do it and that I had nothing to do with it.'

There was silence. Ruari didn't want to talk about this in front of Stan, he wished he could have had a little more time. This was worse than he had anticipated. His mother looked at him, thinking, maybe hoping, that it was Ruari's fault because she knew as well as he did that most of the grief in their house was because of Stan and she blamed herself.

'Why didn't you tell me about this sooner?' she accused him. 'I'm your mother, am I not entitled to know what is happening?'

'I've been made a better offer,' Ruari said, looking at her. He could see now that she was very annoyed because he hadn't confided in her before, normally she would not have endured Stan touching him.

She was full of suspicion and why should she not be? Nothing good had ever happened to them without hard work and even then nothing like this.

'You,' Stan said, 'you would trust anybody. Have you seen anything on paper yet?'

'Mr Hutchinson voiced for them–'

'What is this, Ruari?' his mother said. 'Explain yourself this minute properly.'

'I've been made an offer by Teeshaven–'

'By a football club that all the locals hate,' Stan said. 'It's a stupid idea and I'd already signed him up for North End and he comes

66

in and humiliates me and says I've got no right to sign for him, like I didn't matter, like I was nobody.'

'You turned them down for an offer of another club?' his mother said as though she couldn't believe it and her eyes searched his face and they were troubled.

'Yes, I did.'

'When there's nothing on paper?' His mam was suspicious. Ruari panicked. She was right, he had turned down a good offer right here where he lived. Had he been wrong?

'I've got the—'

'You're not going,' Stan said.

'You can't stop me.' Ruari could hear himself shouting and he was glaring at Stan, something he had never done before and he was amazed at himself.

'Aye, I can. Your mother won't sign and you won't be able to go. You'll stay here and I'll talk to Harry Philips and you'll go to him and apologize.'

'I won't,' Ruari said.

Stan made as if he was going to hit Ruari again and Ruari's mother put herself in front of him before he could stop her.

'It's up to Ruari, Stan. He has to make his own decisions,' she said.

'Is that right?'

'Aye, it's right,' she said holding his gaze. His mam, Ruari thought gratefully, had always been like that, always willing to take the responsibility for everything, it was hard but she did it.

'I thought I was the head of this household,' Stan said, 'it turns out I'm nowt of the sort. Well, I'll just take meself back to the pub, then,' and he turned around and walked out, slamming the back door after him.

Ruari listened to him clash the yard gate. He didn't know what to say.

'Mam, I'm sorry. I would have told you but it all just happened. I didn't get a chance.' It was not quite the truth, he thought with a flash of guilt, he had wanted to sort this out his own way.

His mother said nothing for a few moments and her face was white with fury.

'You have no excuse for this,' she said, 'you shouldn't have put Stan into that position.'

'But, Mam—'

'You have to do what's best for you, it's nothing to do with Stan or with me,' his mother said more softly. 'If you can get out of here you should but it sounds to me as though you don't know what you're doing. Have they made you a proper offer or is it all hot air?' Her voice was so quiet as though she was sure he was wrong but didn't like to tell him and she didn't look at him. He felt sick.

'I have the papers here for the contract. I need you to sign them.'

She was looking at him now all right and her eyes began to fill with hope. Ruari produced them and a pen, his mother looked through the whole thing and her eyes began to shine.

'Do you think it's all right?' Ruari ventured.

'It looks fine to me,' and his mother signed the paper.

Ruari was ashamed of himself in so many ways he couldn't think and his face burned.

'Mam—'

'We won't talk about it any more now,' she said with a brief smile and she went back to the sink to wash the dishes from tea.

'I need to say something,' he said.

He waited until she stopped as he had known she would.

'North End offered me twelve pounds a week.' He paused there but his mother said nothing. 'Teeshaven offered me twenty. If I'd thought you wanted me to stay here and take the lower offer I would have but I didn't think you would.' She still didn't say anything. 'If I was wrong, Mam, I'll take it all back.'

She dried her hands and came to him and then she hugged him to her as Ruari had known she would.

'You should take the better offer always,' she said. 'I'm proud of you, Ruari, you did the right thing.'

Ruari went round to Jenna's and banged on the back door. Her mam answered it and she seemed to draw herself up when she saw him. She didn't smile. She never smiled at him. She had never liked him. He didn't know why and then he thought, Yes, I do, she thinks I'm not good enough for Jenna, that's what it is. Maybe she'll change her mind now. He smiled broadly.

'Hello, Mrs Duncan. I wondered if Jenna was in?'

'Jenna has gone to a dinner party,' her mam said. Ruari thought he hadn't heard her properly.

'Is she out?'

'She's gone to Farne House to have dinner with the Maddisons,' Jenna's mam said proudly and she closed the door.

It was suddenly as cold as if it was autumn and Ruari was not dressed for the weather. There was nothing for him to do but go home.

Six

'That girl is common,' Faye Maddison said to her husband as she watched him pulling off his tie when they went upstairs to bed.

'Isn't she?'

'You looked as though you liked her.'

'I am hoping he finds somebody better

70

than that but what is the point in trying to direct him, he won't take any notice.'

'You think she's a passing phase, then?'

'I'm hoping she's a passing something,' he said smiling grimly and he looked at her. She was sitting on the bed pulling a file across her nails and not looking at him. 'I'm sure that's what your parents hoped I was.'

She said nothing to that and he didn't expect her to. They had reached a truce of sorts. She didn't care who he slept with because she wouldn't sleep with him. He made the money and she spent it. They tried to do the best they could together for their son, their only child, and neither of them wanted a girl like Jenna Duncan, a badly dressed kid from a back street who couldn't even talk properly, to be his choice of woman.

It brought back uncomfortable memories. Sorrel was tired and didn't want to think about how things might have been or might be. He had sent Paul to an expensive public school, had hoped he would do well, go to university, be a doctor or a lawyer or anything really which didn't involve nightclubs, betting shops or the lower echelons of society where he dwelt most of the time. He was used to it but it was not something he wanted for his son. He should have known by now. Dreams were only there to be shattered. His were. Faye's were. They went to bed in a single bed each in the same room.

They could have had separate rooms but somehow it would have destroyed the point, they slept together and yet alone, they had kept up the pretence of their marriage for so many years that it had in some ways ceased to be a pretence.

It had been for Paul, they had wanted respectability so badly, but tonight Paul had unwittingly made a mockery of their attempts and Sorrel was so tired now that he was glad to get into bed in the darkness and not think about anything. It was too late for all the things he had wanted except for his football club. It was the only thing that mattered any more, the only thing he had to look forward to.

Ruari waited for Jenna when she came out of work on the Monday. She didn't seem to have been around all weekend, he hadn't liked to go to her house again but had hung around in the streets and not seen her and he didn't like to go to the drapery department when she was working.

Then he had waited for her to come to him, surely her mother would say he had called but she didn't and he felt guilty about neglecting her and also he was desperate to tell her about his progress. He waited outside the Store until she finished. It was a cold dark day, like November, and there was a bitter wind screaming across Durham Road.

She didn't see him, he could see when she left with a scarf over her hair that she had her head down against the wind and the rain. He shouted her name behind her. She stopped.

'Jenna?'

She looked guilty, she looked unhappy. He wanted to take her in his arms. There were lots of people about so that he couldn't even speak to her really and also he didn't want to put any pressure on her.

'Can I talk to you?'

'I have to get home.' She stared down at the pavement and then she turned around so that she had her back to him.

'Have you given me up?' he said.

The frankness of this stopped her. She didn't turn around but she didn't move either and he gazed at her thin back which seemed to shrink from the words.

'You could just tell me,' he said.

She said nothing and then her shoulders hunched and he thought she was crying.

'It cannot be that bad,' he said.

She didn't move. He went to her, around to her so that he could see her face, her eyes. Both were wet, her lashes were black, and all he could think of was that he loved her so much and it hurt. People hurried past, nobody noticed that she was crying.

'It is,' she said and her voice was harsh.

Ruari was frightened now.

'Why?' he said.

'I went with Paul Maddison,' she said.

The pavement was suddenly the only place for his gaze. He couldn't have lifted it if they had told him he was going to play for England in the next World Cup. He watched people's feet, they hurried and their trousers and stockings were wet with the rain, dark and the day was getting darker or was it just his imagination?

He didn't know how long they stood there, it must have been quite a long time because the legs going past lessened as though everybody had gone home while they stood. He always thought people were going home to more than he was, to more than his overworked mother, Stan's beery breath, a house that wasn't big enough, a back lane full of holes and a future which he had dared to think he could better.

He wanted to run. Jenna didn't love him any more, she couldn't have done or she would never have gone with Paul Maddison, and the side of him which said she was his was so angry that he felt he might hit her and though things were bad they could be worse. He could turn into the kind of man who thought hitting women helped. He had to remind himself that he was much bigger than Jenna and that she did not belong to him, not now, not any more.

'You could say something.' Her voice was even harder now, like the kind of sandpaper you would use on rough wood. 'You could tell me I'm a slut, you could be angry, you could shout, you could even ask me why and then you could judge me. You could say that I did it on purpose because you went to your stupid football game!'

'And did you?'

'Yes,' she said, 'yes, I did,' and then she ran away.

He went after her, not immediately, somehow he had to try and remember how to move so that by the time he reached her she had left the main street and when he tried to get hold of her she turned and pushed both fists into his chest and that was when he got hold of her so she couldn't get away and dragged her down a side alley and slammed her up against the wall. They were both breathing heavily by then and the rain was running down his neck.

'I don't love you no more,' she said, shouting against the rain. 'He does it better than you do and I liked it. I went to his house and we had salmon and they had this great big dining room and they had white serviettes and a white cloth on the table and a crystal chandelier.'

Ruari said nothing. They weren't touching any more but still she stood back against the wall like it was more of a friend to her than he was. And then she started to cry and it was different than it had been before, she started to cry like she'd never ever done it, hard and bitter. Her whole body shook and because there was nobody to comfort her she turned from him.

'Why don't you just go away?' she said.

'I'm sorry,' he said and then he turned her from the wall to him and he unbuttoned his coat and pulled her in against the warmth of his shirt and he put a hand on to her dripping wet hair. She cried until he couldn't distinguish between the rain and her tears. He was soaked.

'I'm sorry Jenna,' he said again and she pulled away and she said,

'You stupid bugger.'

'Aye, I am.'

She drew back properly and she lifted her wet face, it was shiny. 'I'm going home now,' she said.

'But–'

'No. I'm going. Don't you come after me, it won't do you no good. Don't,' she shouted when he put out a hand. 'Don't.'

She turned up the collar of her coat as if it would make any difference and then she walked away into the rain.

Jenna had never thought that she would be pleased they had moved for more than the odd few moments when Paul had picked her up in the MGB but by this time she was quite ready to be somewhere else than Back

76

Church Street, something she had not considered. She wanted, more than anything in the world, not to see Ruari daily, not to have memories of what they had had thrust into her face all the time and because they had moved she didn't have to. She was so grateful to her mother that she almost liked her.

She and Ruari never met after that. She escaped to work. She had taken to going out of the front door straight down the stairs from her bedroom in the morning without seeing anybody or having anything to eat. Her mam had been surprised at first but rather pleased that things had changed and when her mam questioned her as to whether she was seeing Ruari she shook her head and Jenna did not miss the look of satisfaction that they were no longer together.

She had never seen her mother so happy. She greeted Jenna's dad with wonderful meals and a kiss when he came home so he seemed happy enough. Presumably Ruari was still kicking a bloody football up and down the lane of Back Church Street day in and day out, Jenna didn't know and told herself she didn't care. She didn't even miss him.

She cried a lot in the toilet at work and had to repair her mascara and her mother gave her money for new clothes so she was always in the latest styles now. Her mother was determined that she should have a chance to marry Paul Maddison, Jenna thought bitterly.

It was soon full summer, the hedgerows were covered in willowherb, the breeze making the long purple stems sway. The gardens were pink with roses and the children were on holiday so on fine days the beach was littered with sandcastles and buckets and spades and little kids in bathing suits and parents with red and orange windbreaks at the top of the beach.

The tinkling bell of the ice-cream van reminded Jenna of all the summers when she and Ruari had played swing ball or cricket on the beach with the other kids. They were not kids any more, she wished the time back but wishing would not make it so.

Seven

Ruari lay in bed in the late evening for a short while, listening to Stan's voice as it came up clearly from the floor below into the bedroom. It was cold and dark up there like it was the middle of winter instead of summer, it had rained for days, even now he could hear it, pattering off the roof. Usually he liked the sound. Now he didn't, it reminded him of his meeting with Jenna after she had gone with Paul Maddison and of the hours he had spent devising all manner of deaths for Maddison.

He didn't move until his mother's voice began to join in and it sounded feeble by comparison, wavering as though she was about to cry. His mother had never been feeble. Stan's behaviour had worn her down. Ruari tried to tell himself that he hadn't made it worse with his signing for a club thirty miles away but it was right. He had altered the delicate balance of power somehow in the house.

They began to argue. Usually it died down, Stan wasn't much good for argument when he had been at the pub so late, his voice was slurred and he had difficulty in getting his words out, but his voice was getting louder and louder.

Ruari slid out of bed and pulled on his jeans, he wasn't wearing any clothes, he hadn't had any pyjamas for years and had got used to sleeping in nothing but his pants even when it was cold, things like jeans and sweaters were much more important, and football boots – but he didn't want to go down there feeling vulnerable.

He didn't try to disguise the sound of his footsteps as he went down the stairs but his feet were bare so the carpet muffled the noise. Maybe they would be too caught up in what they were saying to notice but when he was low enough to see into the room Stan was glaring at him.

Stan, Ruari thought, but he had already known, was drunk. His face was shiny, beefy with beer. Had he stopped loving the woman who was standing with her back to Ruari and her head down? Ruari shook his head to alter these thoughts but they wouldn't go away. He wished he didn't know so much, understand how people felt. He didn't want to understand how Stan felt, only his mother.

She heard or at least sensed his presence. She turned around and in that moment, her face wet with tears and her eyes full of foreboding, Ruari couldn't understand how anybody could not love her. She had given everything of herself to them.

She had been beautiful once, he could remember when he had been very little, now her face was lined, she was too skinny, her bones showed everywhere, there were great bags under her eyes which nothing could lessen; she was ill-dressed and her hair was going grey. How could life do this to his lovely Mam?

'Go back to bed, Ruari,' she said.

Always she put everybody before herself. Women did that. How could men not love them for it?

'Aye, gan on, lad,' Stan said with a touch of nasty humour, 'listen to yer ma.'

'Who could sleep with all that noise?'

Ruari said.

'We'll keep quiet,' his mother said.

'This is all your fault,' Stan said, 'if you'd made your mind up to sign for North End this could all have been avoided.'

'They didn't offer enough money,' Ruari said for perhaps the fifteenth time.

'What on earth were you thinking about? Did you think I would get a job in bloody Teeshaven?'

Ruari wanted to say that Stan never kept a job for more than a few weeks so it wouldn't matter anyroad.

'No, I thought I'd go on me own,' he said. 'They've said they'll find digs for me.'

'Mr High and Mighty,' Stan sneered. 'Not thinking about your family. Maddison offered me good money if you signed. Did you not think about that?'

'It would all have gone down your throat, you and the Black Lion are like that,' Ruari said, crossing his fingers to indicate closeness.

'Ruari,' his mam said, shocked even though it was the truth, Ruari thought. It mustn't be said, the truth could never be uttered, it hung between them all and he thought that made it worse somehow.

'You never let me be a dad to you,' Stan said.

'Oh, give over,' Ruari said, losing patience. Sober, Stan would not have said such a thing.

'You didn't. You never liked me. You went on and on even when you were a little lad about your dad. You didn't even know yer dad, how could you have remembered him? You were nobbut a bairn when he died. It was her.' He jerked his head at Ruari's mother. 'She filled yer head full of him. She didn't tell yer that three months after yer dad died down that bloody pit she had it off with me.'

His mother didn't even defend herself. Ruari thought of her, alone, grief-stricken, wanting to cling to the first person who offered, thinking she could bring back his dad with another man.

'Please don't talk about it,' was all his mother said.

'What for?' Stan said. 'I never stood a chance. Things would have been different around here if anybody had really cared about me. She never even gave me a bairn of my own. Do you know what that feels like?'

The trouble was, Ruari thought, like most other things, that there was some truth to it, just enough to make him feel guilty and wrong about everything. He wanted to say to Stan that he had made a mistake, that he should have gone with North End, that it would have stopped all this but it was too late now. This was all his fault and there was nothing he could do. He couldn't sign for North End, he couldn't make himself do it, there was something about it which was not and never would be right.

'I'm going,' Stan said and he even had sufficient grace to look ashamed and that was worse than if he had cursed and blinded and been hateful.

Going where? was Ruari's second thought. Where could he possibly be going at this time of night?

'It's dark,' Ruari said stupidly.

'Aye,' Stan said, 'I know,' and even more stupidly Ruari wished he wouldn't go, wished as no doubt Stan also wished that he was a better man because he had to live with the person that he wasn't.

Ruari had liked Stan, had even wanted him to replace his dad. Ruari knew that in his mind he had glorified the man his dad was, that no man could replace the golden image in his head which his dad had never been, that no man had ever been.

Poor Stan, he had been on a hiding to no-where right from the start, Ruari thought sadly. Stan had been the cavalry coming over the hill for his mam after his dad had died and his mam had been so broken up. Stan had rescued Ruari and his mother from loneliness and from one another and it had been so brave of him, Ruari thought. Now it was over. It didn't matter what anybody said or did.

'I've got somebody else,' Stan said, a bitter

kind of pride in his voice.

Ruari was shocked to think that now he had found a reason to despise Stan and it was a release from love.

'Oh aye?' Ruari said.

His mother put a hand over her mouth so that she would not cry out, so that she would not offend the neighbours. Ruari wanted to hit Stan.

'You came between your mother and me,' Stan said.

'I never did.' Ruari's voice was unsteady because he felt guilt slay him.

'You did,' Stan said, 'right from the start, you never gave me a chance, it was always your mam and you against me. I never felt welcome here, never felt at home. I was never good enough for you. You always made me feel pushed out and second best.'

'How in the hell could it have been my fault?'

Stan didn't reply.

'And you've got another woman?' Ruari's mam said as though she couldn't believe it.

'Aye, I have.'

She stared but only for a second or two.

'Well, then, you'd better go.'

Stan began to move towards the door.

'No,' she said but it was a reflex action and she put both hands up to her face and then she turned away. Her back was so narrow, stooped, defeated, Ruari thought.

Stan seemed to pause but it was only for a second and it was as if he had willed Ruari downstairs, deliberately provoked a scene so that he would be able to leave. Ruari's mam didn't even look up, didn't say anything, didn't attempt to stop him or follow him or even cry.

She had been left before and even though the circumstances were different the result, Ruari could not help thinking, and it made him feel sick, was the same. She had seen this before, must be getting used to the brutality of such things by now if you ever got used to it which he doubted and maybe he was too because all he did was stand there while Stan walked out.

Stan didn't take anything but Ruari knew he wouldn't be back. There was something so final and yet so vulnerable about his leaving. His hands shook when he opened the door but he didn't turn around.

There would be no funeral, no gravestone this time. Stan was disappointed not only that Ruari would not be playing for the local team but also because in a way Ruari had made him feel small over the business of signing or rather not signing. It had not just been the money. Stan had thought of him- self as Ruari's father, had been happy to make the decision for him, maybe was even ready to be proud of him. Ruari had humili- ated him in front of Harry and also in front

85

of his mother and things had not been the same since and never would be again.

When Stan had gone Ruari had to remember that he was seventeen and could not cry. He was not entitled to but nothing could lift from him the terrible weight of what he had done.

'You mustn't think this is because of you,' his mother said.

'But it is. If I'd signed for North End none of this would have happened.'

'Oh, I think it might,' she said, smiling in spite of herself. 'I think all he needed was a good excuse. Sooner or later one of us would have given it to him. Don't blame yourself, Ruari, it was really nothing to do with you.'

Ruari tried to remember, when he went back to bed, what his mother had said but there was a nasty worm in his conscience which would not absolve him of guilt.

Ruari tried to talk his mother into going with him to Teeshaven but she refused.

'I don't need you to look after me, I never said I would come with you and you certainly don't need looking after, what you need is to get away.'

If she wouldn't come with him he couldn't go, his conscience wouldn't let him.

He started to think he would never get out of there, that he would end up going and begging that bastard Harry Philips to take him on after all that had happened because he wouldn't be able to go to Teeshaven or anywhere else and he would have to try and break his contract with them. He didn't know how people went about things like that.

'Me friends are here, Ruari, and it might not look much but I like this house. I don't want to move anywhere.' When he didn't say anything she said, 'If you stay here you'll never get a chance like this again and you've wanted it all your life, worked for it always. You must go, I want you to. It would waste everything if you backed out now.'

'I'll send you money, then.'

'I'll manage,' she said.

Eight

It was not the nausea or even when she threw up or again when she fainted that made Jenna think she was pregnant. Somehow she knew. She felt as though her whole body was standing on some kind of cliff edge, that something was happening and everything had changed.

She tried to ignore it at first. And she knew why. Because if she was pregnant the baby was not Ruari's, it was Paul Maddison's, and she could not consider the possibility.

87

She and Ruari always used something, they never took risks and she hadn't seen him at the right time. She and Paul had just done it, nobody had thought, nobody had done anything about it. She was pregnant and it had to be Paul's.

The shock stayed with her for days. She got to the point where she could not think about anything else, it took up all her time, all the space in her brain. She could not believe it. She could not believe she had done anything quite so stupid but in a way she knew why she had done it.

Glamour. The worst word in the language but that was why. She had never had anything like that in her life, never felt expensive fabrics against her skin or champagne on her tongue. She had never driven in a sports car and known how the wind rushes past. Was it wrong to want such things? She was sure it was and now she was paying the price for what she had done but why did it have to be so expensive?

She had betrayed Ruari and she had felt awful but now ... now she did not know what to do. She had nobody she could tell.

Jenna had not expected Ruari to be waiting when she got back from work that late August evening. He looked wrong outside her new house, as though he had no place there and he was standing awkwardly as though the very stones upset him.

Jenna's face felt stiff. She attempted a smile.

'Ruari, how are you?' she said.

'I'm leaving.'

'Leaving?' Jenna stared at him. They stood there for a long time while the words sunk into the very pavement, she thought.

'Aye. I've been offered a job like.'

'A job? What sort of a job?'

Ruari looked as awkward as any ordinary lad at that second, she thought. In fact it was worse than that, he was embarrassed.

'Working, in Teeshaven.'

'What kind of job could you get there? Is it another shipyard? Can you move like that?'

'I've signed a contract for two years with the football club.'

Jenna stared at him.

'Are you serious?'

'They've taken me on. It might not come to anything of course but I'll work and maybe it will.'

Jenna was stunned. He was leaving not just his job and his house but the town. How on earth had this happened? How had things gone so badly wrong?

'What about your mam?'

'She won't come.'

Suddenly Ruari looked older. He stood up straight. He was six foot tall by now.

'They must think you're going to do well,'

Jenna said.

'It's the only chance I've got.'

'Didn't Mr Maddison offer? Then you wouldn't have to go anywhere.'

'Aye, he offered,' Ruari was all awkwardness again, 'but it wasn't enough. The others offered more. Will you come with me, Jenna?'

'Me?'

'We'll manage. You can get a job and eventually we could get a house and ... get married and ... you know.'

His face was almost but not quite shining, he was so excited, so pleased, to have within his grasp something he had worked so hard for so long to achieve. He could offer her a life which any girl around here would have fallen on gladly, an escape. Who got that?

She didn't know what to say. The whole world was falling apart and she knew that for him to offer to take her when she had gone with Paul Maddison was a long way beyond what any lad around there would have done, it was not just big of him, it was monumental.

'But...'

'I don't care what happened, if it doesn't matter to you then it doesn't matter to me either. I can't believe you care for him like you cared for me. We can get past it.'

Jenna didn't know what to say. She wanted to cry, she ached to, she wished more than she had ever wished anything in her life that she had not got into Paul Maddison's car, that she had not ruined everything. She tried to say something which would make sense to him.

'Most lads don't make it,' she said.

'I know,' he said, 'it might all come to nowt.'

He looked past her as though he could see the shining future he had planned and made possible and then he looked straight at her, waiting for her answer, waiting for her to say that she wanted to be part of the dream.

There was silence for a while and then he said, 'Come with me, Jenna. Give me another shot at things, give yourself another chance. We can make a go of it, I know we can.'

'I cannot,' she said.

He was silent and then he said, 'I love you, Jenna, come with me, please.'

She knew how much it cost him to say it.

'I cannot,' she said again.

He didn't believe her, she could see, not even then but the shining in his eyes was beginning to dim, he was starting to think that his dream could shatter.

'Why not?' he said.

Jenna knew she owed him the explanation only she couldn't tell him why she had done it. She didn't know, didn't remember why, just that she had had too much champagne. Oh, you couldn't blame the drink, that was what men did, they blamed something else so they didn't have to take the responsibility.

It had not been the drink, it had been other things, it had been the idea of a better time, of some vague notion of the future which had to do with fun. Not even glamour or excitement, just fun, something better, some time when you didn't have to think about every penny you spent and how you could not afford it.

His dream had taken too long to come true, that was the problem and she had become impatient, had ceased to believe in it. She had spent too many nights in the back bedroom at her mother's house and too many days bored in the gloom of the drapery department of the Store, its brown walls and brown counters and fat middle-aged women coming in to buy corsets to contain their overflowing flesh had seen off the odd time that anything pretty had come into the Store.

Even the cheap things she could afford to buy could not fill the emptiness in her. She felt stupidly, like the nuttery at Paul's house, that everything good in her life had long since been torn away and replaced with tinsel.

And the back lane had eaten away at her trust in Ruari, more than anything in the world she had to get somehow beyond the back lane in her mind which she never really had done in spite of moving and maybe there was a part of her that had known Paul Maddison could do that for her.

If she were to be with him there would be

no more back lanes ever. She would not escape just as far as Wesley Road but much, much further. She had not known until that moment how much she wanted to get away and if she had waited Ruari would have done that for her but somehow she had not been able to wait. She had settled for something far short of what she had wanted, like the girl who took the cheap engagement ring because it was offered now rather than waiting for the diamond she might get later when things were better, and there had been a part of her which had never believed that things would ever get better, that she and Ruari would go on and on in the grinding every day of the dark little houses until they died. She had panicked. She had learned in life that there was no point in waiting for what would never happen and that learning was costing her so dearly now.

'Oh, Ruari, I'm sorry.'

'Sorry?' He looked so hard, so accusingly at her.

'You shouldn't have assumed–'

'I didn't assume anything.' He was beginning to sound a little desperate, his words ran into one another at speed as though the more of them he uttered the more he could impress upon her that they had to get away. 'We... we're a pair, you and me, we belong together, you know we do. What has it all been about otherwise? I can't do it without

93

you, Jenna. I'm not saying we'll ever be rich but it would be a chance of a good life.'

'I cannot,' she said. It was the third time she had said it, so it was almost like a chant now, the only thing protecting her, like in church when the more you prayed the better you felt, only she didn't.

His gaze finally wavered and she saw the defeated look come across his face though he fought with it. Ruari had always been a fighter.

'Why not? Tell me why you can't.'

And that was when Jenna thought she owed him some kind of explanation so that he would not go on hoping.

'I love Paul Maddison,' she said.

'You love him?' He couldn't accept that and why should he, he had always come first with her but now she had to make him believe it, it was the only thing left she could do for Ruari.

'Yes,' she said clearly, 'I do.' Like you said 'I do' in church when you were getting married. 'He can give me everything I want.'

He stared at her.

'What is it that you want?' he said.

And she couldn't remember, that was the stupid part, she didn't really care about Spanish holidays and gold taps and how many cars you could get on the drive and where your clothes came from, it was just sticking plaster for the wound and it wouldn't hold but it was too late now, she could never have Ruari and he would go away and she would be left.

He had so little conceit that after the first seconds of disbelief he gave up, she could see it. As though he had never thought he could have somebody like her, that it was a dream too far, that somebody was bound to break it, it was like those dreams you had just before waking, near the surface, with the sunshine butterscotch in the early morning, after the horrors of the night and suddenly you were relieved and you just knew everything was going to be all right only this time there was no relief from it. The dream tore in the half truth of what she said. It broke, she heard it somehow.

He knew that Paul Maddison could have her, why should he not, he had everything else. That was it, she could see it in Ruari's eyes. He didn't try any more. She had convinced him that she didn't want him. He didn't look at her. He walked away and she couldn't bear to watch him.

'Who offered more?' Sorrel Maddison had said.

'Teeshaven.'

Sorrel swore.

'The bastards,' he said. 'They can't afford it. What the hell are they playing at? They're bottom of the division, they have nothing

95

but crap players. What is it, a last-ditch attempt? Hodgkin's losing his mind.'

'Gallacher'll never make it,' Harry said, 'he's just another stupid Geordie lad. He's not that good, I've seen him play. We've lost nothing. I heard Stan Robson left because of what happened.'

'Why couldn't he be loyal?' Sorrel said. 'How can a young lad like that up sticks? He's mad. And to think I tried to help him.'

And then it occurred to Sorrel that if Ruari Gallacher was really leaving he might take the girl with him and once rid of the lass Paul might meet somebody classy, somebody who could talk properly and knew which knife and fork to use when she sat down to dinner with folk like them. He had watched Jenna hesitate and tried not to despise her because it was something he had had to learn but he wanted for his son a girl who knew automatically such things. Was it such a lot to ask? Yes, it would be worth the sacrifice of a not terribly good footballer to get rid of the girl his son thought he was in love with. Sorrel was almost satisfied.

Nine

Jenna went on seeing Paul and it was as though her instincts propelled her towards him. The burden of not telling anybody about the baby was starting to get to her and although they had not so much as kissed again she was panicking. He would bring her home from his house and leave her there and wave and smile and he seemed quite happy about it. One night in the early autumn when he had gone she turned to walk up the stairs and had only got two steps up when her mother's voice, strained somehow, said from the hall, 'Are you all right, Jenna?'

She stopped, about to say that she was fine, and then she heard the worried note in her mother's voice. Her mother didn't often show concern, Jenna had thought her mother was not sensitive at all to how she felt, caught up in her husband and her home and Jenna knew that her mother had been pleased she and Paul were going out together, even proud that her daughter knew the son of the football-club owner, the businessman who was so important, and Jenna had been pleased but her mother had realized something was wrong and the tears threatened.

'Is there something the matter?'

She did not realize she had not answered and her mother had enquired again.

'It's not that other lad, is it?'

Jenna turned. She felt really sick not just at her mother mentioning Ruari but as though he ought not to matter, as though she could not remember his name. It was almost as though Ruari had died, and he might as well have done, Jenna thought, because the chances were she would never see him again.

He had gone, she didn't know exactly when, and her gaze had searched the streets for him day after day for fear that he should leave because once he was gone everything was over in a different way than it had been and then her father had come back from work one day with the news that Ruari had left and since then Jenna had had to stop herself from running to Teeshaven to him, searching the streets and finding wherever he was lodging no matter how long it took and pleading with him to take her with him. She knew now that she couldn't go to him or after him. She would have to stay here and face the consequences of what she had done. She knew that she deserved it.

'No, it's nothing to do with him.'

'You were so very keen on him all that time that I did wonder... You are going to go on seeing Paul?'

This was the point, her mother was worried that the dream would not come true, that Jenna would not go on seeing a boy who was rich. Her mother, Jenna could have laughed, thought that if you had money things were easier, Jenna was beginning to realize that it set up a whole new kind of problem, it certainly had for her.

If money was not the root of all evil, then the love of it, the desire of it, certainly had been. Jenna broke down and then she sat down on the stairs. Her mother stood there at the bottom like it was something out of a film and could not possibly have anything to do with her.

'Has he finished with you?' she said faintly as though the knowledge would be too much to bear.

Jenna said nothing, she sat there, wondering how on earth she was going to tell her mother.

'I'm expecting,' she said.

She did not know how she had got the words out, she had lain awake night after night trying to think of how to coat the pill, of how to tell her mother so that something so hard to swallow would not sound quite so bad. She felt relief that she had said it, even that baldly.

Her mother stood there for so long that Jenna thought maybe she hadn't heard her except that her mother's face drained of colour and her eyes were fixed on Jenna's face as though the ceiling had just fallen in.

'You what?' she said.

'I'm having a baby.'

For a few moments it was as though her mother could not believe such luck, as though she would deny it or run into her newly decorated bedroom and shut the door and shut out Jenna and what was happening.

'Oh God, Jenna, you stupid girl,' her mother said in a breathy voice quite unlike her own. 'And he's gone. Well, he'll have to come back here now and you'll have to get married.'

Jenna sat up slightly. Her mother actually thought that the baby was Ruari's even though they had not seen one another all summer. Her mother really didn't know anything about her life, was not interested, her mother was only interested in illusions, the idea of her daughter marrying above her socially. Perhaps it was the only thing her mother had left to dream about, she had married a man who worked in a shop, she had had only one child, and her sole triumph was this awful house in a terraced street, no wonder she had hoped for better, felt short changed, her life was so dull.

'No,' she said, 'it's Paul's.'

Her mother stood there as though she would never move again. Then she straightened and her lips sounded stiff as though she could not get out the next thing she said.

'Are you telling me you went with two lads at once?'

Her mother made it sound as though they were having an orgy, the kind of threesome you read about in dirty stories.

'I did nothing of the kind,' she said, 'and anyway...' She had been about to tell her mother that Ruari always used protection, that he was careful, that was Ruari, cautious. He had not been cautious about his career. Why had he been so careful with her? If he hadn't been she might have been with him now, fat-bellied and full of hope for the future, instead of which... Instead of which what?

She didn't know. His career, his bloody beloved football, it had meant more to him than she had and then she thought, that was not fair. He had asked her, begged her to go with him. I love him, she thought, I should have said yes, I should have deceived him and told him it was his and gone anyway What am I doing still here? She wanted to get up and run out of the room and down the street after him, screaming his name. She had thrown everything away and she didn't seem able to retrieve it.

'It wasn't like that,' she said. 'It was just the once with Paul.'

And her mother was pleased. Jenna felt

bitterly amused. Her mother could believe that she was not a slut and that was important, that perhaps even she had never gone with Ruari, that this was just a single slip and although it was shameful they would get through. Her mother, Jenna thought, did not live in the real world.

Jenna should have left it there, she knew but she couldn't.

'I loved Ruari Gallacher,' she said.

'So how do you know it's not his? Is this just wishful thinking, Jenna?'

Why did her mother not understand? She didn't love Paul Maddison, she would never love him, she thought his dad was a braggart and his mam was the kind of woman who knew nothing but how to spend money. And she had gone with Paul, like any fool.

'No, it isn't,' she said, 'me and Ruari had fallen out. It's nothing to do with him.'

Her mother sighed. 'Why do things always happen to us? I know women who have lots of children and things like this don't happen.'

'You're exaggerating,' Jenna said, drying her tears with the back of her hand.

'Have you told Paul?'

Jenna shook her head.

'You have to get married.'

Jenna couldn't go on. Her mother was wrong, she didn't know what Paul would do or say. It was such a disgrace to be pregnant when you weren't married. She felt so guilty. Besides, her mother hadn't met Sorrel Maddison.

If he decided there was no way Paul would marry her then there would be no marriage. And thinking about fathers brought her uncomfortably to her own. How would she even tell her father?

He would never think the same about her again and if Paul refused to acknowledge the baby as his she would be an unmarried mother. Her mother, and maybe even her father, would never recover from it. She imagined herself pushing a pram down the street and everybody talking about her, the whispers. She would have no life, she would be almost hidden away, there would be no future of any kind.

'I have to go and talk to Paul,' she said. 'There's no point in putting it off any longer.'

Her mother seemed pleased about this and then she looked at Jenna.

'However will we tell your father?' she said. 'He'll be so disappointed.'

He would wish she had done better, behaved better. He would never get over it, Jenna thought. Being the manager at the Store everybody saw him every day and he would have to face the whole community.

'We won't tell him,' her mother said. 'We won't say anything at all.'

Ten

Teeshaven was not a top club any more though it was still in the First Division but its reputation had suffered, it had almost been relegated to the Second Division at the end of last season. Ruari hadn't thought about it or cared though he knew the position of every club in the First Division, it was the money that had got him, he thought cynically now, and he was slightly uncomfortable about it because Teeshaven was not doing well because it had bought the wrong players. Was he another bad buy?

They had found digs for him, a house in the heart of the town where three other relative newcomers were housed so he couldn't make a fuss over it but Ruari thought he had died and gone to hell. He had thought his mother's house was poor but it was poor and clean. His landlady, Mrs Johnson, was a slut.

She sat in her front room and smoked all day and ate cake, she was so fat that it hung in layers from her middle-aged body and even though her clothes were the kind of tent which covered up such things nobody could be deceived. She wore her hair up possibly because she didn't have to wash it that way, she wore a lot of make-up which was orange. She watched television most of the time, the rest of it she spent talking to her neighbours, hanging over the back gate to catch anyone who would spend the time of day.

The house was not exactly dirty, it was grubby, that was the word, the sheets on the beds were creased and worn, the mattresses were lumpy, dead spiders and flies sat in cobwebs above his bed and he didn't think the carpet under his bed – if he lost anything and got down on the floor he tried not to look – had ever been hoovered. The towels were thin and grey and the bathroom was cold and unfriendly even in summer it never dried out and everything above eye level was lined with mould.

There was no fire in the back room where he would have sat had he ever sat in the house, which he tried not to. Meals were served in there, it smelled of limp cabbage and that was another thing. He was not used to bad food. Mrs Johnson couldn't cook. Everything tasted and smelled the same and it was all cheap.

There was margarine for your bread in the morning and jam so awful it had no fruit in it. The tea was watery and the milk was generally off so that he stopped using it. At night the meat on his plate was grey and anonymous and the vegetables were cooked to wilting. The potatoes were dark and hard and the crumbles that were pudding were not well enough done so that they were soggy and he couldn't tell what the fruit was.

His room was tiny and boasted no wardrobe. All there was for his clothes was a set of shelves open on the wall and sometimes he found mouse droppings on them. He told Mrs Johnson but it was obvious she did nothing so after that he kept most of his clothes in his suitcase beside the window and ignored what he thought was the sound of rodent scufflings in the night.

His window looked out over street after street and it was a noisy area. When it was windy his window rattled because it didn't fit properly and when the autumn set in the wind howled through his bedroom so that the curtains moved. Nightly people got drunk in the pub across the street and spilled out on to the pavement when it was late, shouting and swearing and often fighting. Windows got broken and sometimes the police arrived and in the mornings the pavements were covered in vomit and people had pissed up against the corner walls so that it stank.

Even so he could not be entirely unhappy. He didn't have to go to work any more and although he had not hated it, being able to be in the football world and to be paid to do it was enough. And having to do nothing but play it made a difference to his game, he could see right from the start.

He was full of energy now that he had no work to do, did not tire in training no matter how much was demanded of him and the coach started to praise him and he soon knew that he was the sort of person who did better on praise than on criticism.

There were several areas where Teeshaven was not as good as North End. Sorrel Maddison might have been an awkward bastard, Ruari thought, but he was a rich awkward bastard and he had put a lot of money into North End, Ruari had heard the stories about the wonderful dressing rooms and the training facilities.

Here they did not seem to have very much money and it meant that there were no particular training facilities and the facilities such as showers were basic. You had to take your own soap, even your own towel, and the kit was for everybody, chucked in the middle of the room in a heap so you just picked up what you could.

The pitch itself was reasonably well looked after but the rest of the place was near to falling down, the gates, the fences, the walls, and he soon saw why. There was no money. They had a lot of players who had been good but were now too old and they could not afford to buy experienced players so he could see right from the start that a lot depended on him.

The young players they did have were very young indeed and it showed. The club had taken a huge risk paying so much for him that he lay in his gritty bed at night and wondered whether they might not have made a mistake. The chairman and directors of the club were businessmen, not like Sorrel Maddison, they were not slick bastards, just ordinary people like solicitors and accountants, and while people like that made more money than a lot did it was not the kind of money which made for a rich football club.

He did not miss his home town though he did miss his mother and worry about how she was managing. From the start he sent her money and although she protested he insisted. He learned not to miss Jenna. A girl who did not want you was not somebody you wanted to think about so he shut her from his mind.

Once the football season started up and training began he got to know some of the other players, in particular the goalkeeper for the first team, Jack Eliot, who was from Carlisle.

He had moved here with his family when he was a little kid but he still retained a thick Cumbrian accent which comforted Ruari. Jack was big and solid and had been playing for the first team for two years and he had a reputation as a good goalie. He was determined that things would be better and helped Ruari by showing him around the grounds and introducing him to the other players. He asked Ruari to his home which Ruari thought was very good of him.

They lived in a pretty semi-detached house and he had a wife and two little girls, one three, one just a year old. His dad and mam lived nearby. They had come down here to work in the dockyards and his mam obviously missed Cumbria and talked longingly about how beautiful the Solway looked with the sun on it in the summer evenings. Ruari found himself envying Jack who appeared to have everything and made Ruari imagine how things would have been if Jenna had come with him. Maybe in time they would have had children and his mother could have moved there and ... the idea faded. His mother would never have moved and Jenna was in love with someone else.

On Fridays nobody was allowed to go out, it was the rule, Saturdays the footballers went out together after the match. It wasn't Ruari's problem, as he couldn't drink and didn't anyway, and he wasn't playing for the first team. He would have to wait for his chance. In the meanwhile he trained hard and watched and listened and did what he was told and prayed to get into the reserves so that he would at least be there at the matches and might be asked to play, it was every reserve's dream.

Thinking about it, this was not what he had envisaged and he could see now that lots of the apprentices had been around since they were fifteen and some of them thought he was old for starting and some of them resented his being there at all, especially when he was almost but not quite local, the teams close to one another hated rivals.

They didn't talk to him but huddled in little groups when he was around, though it could have all been in his mind. He thought they didn't like his accent and would pretend they didn't understand him and he had the feeling that they imitated him when he was not there. They didn't like him coming in like this and being better than they were – and he was, it was not just wishful thinking, he could outplay them all, it soon became obvious. At first he was embarrassed and then he was just pleased and within months of getting there he could even outrun and outmanoeuvre some of the top players.

Under the coaching he began to shine at every session and people began to notice him. He had been haunted that he might get here and not be good enough, show up badly in front of other professionals, but he hardly dared to think that his dream might come true except that he did, there was a slow-burning excitement about him, there was a little bit of him which was convinced he would fulfil the ambitions he had set himself and make his mother proud of him and also that he would be able to show North End and Jenna Duncan what they had missed.

He could see that a great many lads never got a game, never got any further, didn't make it as far as the first team or even into the reserves, and his nightmares were full of his failure. What would he do if he didn't make it? Almost everybody, he realized now, didn't make it. He would have to go back and find some kind of job.

He decided then that he wouldn't go back, no matter what happened. He promised himself that he would be as good as he could, train as hard as he could, and hope for a match. The more matches he played the more he would be paid and then his mam could give up her job as a cleaner and he could afford to keep her even at a distance. He had to succeed here.

Eleven

Paul looked surprised to see Jenna.

'You said you were busy. You're always saying you're busy, though what you have to be busy about I don't know.' His voice was a degree or so above freezing because he felt neglected, he had begun to want to see her often and it made her hope that what she had to tell him would not be badly received, she could only pray.

'Could I talk to you?'

He drew her into the sitting room. Sitting room. Even drawing room wouldn't have covered it, Jenna thought. It was massive and over the eight hundred years that it had been there it must have seen a lot of domestic drama. It was hushed somehow and yet she felt comfortable as though you couldn't surprise it at all, it had seen everything.

Jenna tried to ignore the room. Somehow this house was all caught up in her behaviour towards Ruari, she felt like a traitor, she had cared that the house was beautiful and it seemed so stupid now, so shallow, so pathetic, she hated herself. But there was no way round this, she might not tell her dad but she had to tell Paul so she looked straight at him and took a deep breath like a swimmer and then she plunged.

'Paul, I don't know how else to say this. We're having a baby, I know that it was only once and I know that it shouldn't have happened and I know you probably think it's got nothing to do with you, but I thought I should tell you. It seemed fair.' She looked up at him.

Paul frowned. He went on frowning for

quite a long time so that Jenna grew impa-
ient but she couldn't say anything. Then he
looked uncomfortable.

'A baby?' he said. 'Are you sure?'

'Yes, I'm certain.'

'I thought there was something the matter,
all these weeks you've behaved like I was a
leper and then recently you just seemed
plain weird.'

She said nothing. Paul looked almost
apologetic.

'Jenna, you let me have you once and it
was weeks and weeks ago–'

'I know that–'

'So you'll excuse me if I'm being blunt but
Ruari bloody Gallacher must have had you
hundreds of times. There's no point in you
pretending you were a virgin when I had
you because I know damned fine that you
weren't–'

'I never said I was!' Jenna declared, stung.

'Now he's not here and I am so I get the
blame. Does that seem fair to you?'

'I know it seems unlikely but ... it wasn't
like that with Ruari.'

'It wasn't like what?' Paul said, staring
white-faced at her. 'Don't tell me you didn't
do it with him because I know you did and
you and him have probably been going at it
for years.'

'We always used something.'

'And it couldn't have gone wrong?'

'It isn't that.' Jenna couldn't believe he thought she was lying. 'I didn't go with him at the same time. We fell out, at least...' She didn't like to say that she had been teaching Ruari a lesson, that he couldn't take her for granted, that she had felt she should come first, that for weeks and weeks they hadn't touched one another. 'Obviously I didn't go with him.'

'It isn't obvious to me,' Paul said. 'The very idea that you went with both of us doesn't bear thinking about but I put up with knowing you'd been with him. I didn't think you were going with us both but now... now I think you must've done, you're just that sort of girl.'

Jenna was suddenly very cold.

'It is your baby, Paul, it really is.'

'You think I'm an idiot,' Paul said and he was angry, she could see, and she could hardly blame him for that.

'No–'

'Yes, you do. You went with me because I'm rich, you didn't think about the fact that you were already going with somebody else, which shows what a cheap little turn you are–'

'That's not true! How can you say something so horrible?'

Jenna could feel anger and it was strange because she hadn't felt entitled to anger, she felt guilt, she felt ashamed, so where was the

114

anger coming from in Paul's rich, posh bloody house where his father had so little taste that he had destroyed everything that was good about the place, taken out the lovely old things, cut down the nut trees and tarmacked the old-fashioned garden which had the herbs and lavender? She hated Sorrel Maddison, she really did.

'So why did you, then?'

'I don't know. I was fed up.'

'Oh, fed up,' Paul said. 'Well, in that case we won't worry. You were fed up with Ruari Gallacher so you went with me. You had nothing better to do, after all.'

She could hear the anger too in his voice and she wished she could have handled this better, God knew she had rehearsed it often enough, she wasn't getting it right and it made her panic. She couldn't think what to say and then he goaded her.

'Go on, tell me you love me,' he dared her.

Jenna couldn't say it. It wasn't true, it never would be true. She stood there in the enormous room which had no books, no nice ornaments. The curtains were like something in a hotel, right from floor to ceiling and shiny like silk and so full it was almost indecent with those flash cord things in gold around the middle of them, in fact the whole bloody place looked like a hotel.

'I didn't go to Teeshaven with Ruari because of what I'd done—'

'Well, that's noble,' Paul said.

'Stop it!' she said. 'Just stop it!' and her words echoed around the room. She shouted so loudly it seemed to her it must have gone back all the hundreds of years to when the house first had people living there. Rows were like that, they didn't disperse, all the awful things that were said, they stayed in places like that and haunted it and gave it what it was and once things were said they couldn't be unsaid and she didn't care, she didn't care at all. She had tried to be honest with him and it wasn't working.

'I'm having your baby and I'm trying to tell you about it and you have no right to say that I'm bad and a liar and that it isn't yours because it is and I wouldn't say it was otherwise. You can't get out of this by denying it, the baby's a fact and if you don't choose to believe it's yours that's your problem.'

'If you don't want it I'm sure we can get rid of it,' Paul said.

'Get rid of it?' She stared into his narrowed eyes and she thought how cruel he sounded, his mouth like a straight line. He didn't want her or the baby.

'Yes, that's what people do in this enlightened day and age. You don't have to have it, if you are pregnant.'

'What do you mean?'

'I think you just think you're on to a good thing and that because I'm who I am that you can get me to marry you. Well, you can't. I never had any intention of getting married and if I did have any marital intentions it would be because I chose and not because a little slapper like you thinks she can blackmail me into it.'

'Paul—'

'Tell me you love me,' he said again, 'and make me believe it.'

She didn't move or speak.

'I don't want you here,' he said, 'get out.'

Jenna went.

Paul had always been afraid of his father though in a way, gazing at him now, he was not quite sure why. Outside of the house there were stories about him and Paul had heard a great many of them, about how his father and mother had run away from a slum where his father lived on the Tyne when he was fifteen and made money on the markets in Newcastle and gone into various kinds of business and been successful where more educated men had failed.

He was sitting alone when Paul came to him. It was, Paul knew, his favourite time of day. If he was coming back at all it would be early evening. Often he would eat and go back out again but mostly he didn't come back before one or two in the morning so this was in a sense his treat. He was perusing the newspaper, a whisky and soda on a small table beside him. The French windows were open to the sunshine of the evening. The evenings were cutting short. It wouldn't be long before autumn was here for real and the leaves turned.

As Paul hesitated in front of him Sorrel folded his newspaper, put it down and regarded his son from steady eyes.

'Now then,' he said, smiling, 'what is it?'

'I've got a bit of a problem,' Paul said, sitting down and trying to remain calm.

'Right.'

He looked surprised, as well he might, Paul thought. Most things were sorted out without Paul coming to him like this. Paul wished with all his might that this would have sorted itself out in a less complicated and undignified way. He couldn't see why it had to happen to him, how unlucky was that? He had considered ignoring it, he had told himself over and over it was nothing to do with him, that it was Jenna's problem, that Ruari Gallacher had done it. He could take that way out, there was nothing Jenna could do, but the more he thought about it the less happy he was.

Paul couldn't think what to say. Time went by. He didn't want the open look on his father's face to die away and be replaced by anger. His father was scary when he was angry and Paul didn't know how to look at him, not because he was scared but because he knew that his father was disappointed in him, had wanted him to do something splendid with his life and so far he had done nothing but lounge about all summer. His father, to be fair, had said nothing so that Paul felt guilty and he was about to make it worse.

'If you don't tell me I can't help you,' Sorrel said.

'It doesn't have to be a problem. At least I don't think so but... I just had the feeling that if I didn't tell you, you might find out and...' he tried hard to smile into his father's set look, 'you wouldn't be very pleased with me.'

Paul remembered in detail the other times when his father hadn't been pleased with him. To be fair his father had never hit him, not like a lot of fathers, not like the majority and Paul thought that was strange. His father had never even shouted at him, but Sorrel had such presence that he didn't need to. Paul knew too much about him for Sorrel ever to need to do or say anything.

His father had lived with violence. It was never spoken of but it was there. He had vague memories of being somehow in the street when something had gone wrong, somebody tried to take his mother's bag and his father had knocked the man to the ground, so efficiently that it had been a shock.

His father knew of such things and had, during the last few years, managed to keep them from his home and presumably from his life but Paul was afraid of the very air his father breathed when Sorrel was angry. He was unpredictable, that was it.

Sorrel waited and Paul reflected that his father very rarely lost his temper and that in a way it was his forbearance that people were afraid of because that forbearance held his temper at bay and only for so long, Paul had the feeling that men had gone beyond that forbearance in the past and paid dearly for it.

Paul shook his head. He couldn't say it.

'Come on, spit it out.' Sorrel's voice was softer.

He was so practised at these things. Paul was beginning to sweat and think of the house when he was a child resounding with the timbre of his father's voice, not at him and not at his mother, at other men in other rooms. Sorrel didn't look like a man who could be violent but Paul remembered him as a very young man, coming home bleeding, angry and resentful. He did not let people get away with things.

Paul sat there, wanting to cry like he hadn't for years. He was so embarrassed he could feel his face suddenly burn. He mustn't cry in front of his father, yet the water in his eyes stung so much that only shedding it would help. How had he managed such a mess? He felt more stupid than he had ever felt before.

'I'm not going to clip you round the lug, you know,' his father said, trying to smile. 'It can't be that bad.'

Paul vainly tried to smile, to ease the way, but to him now this man was not going to like what he had to say and his memory was providing him with the sounds of furniture smashing and loud voices and almost certainly cruel laughter.

'Look, Paul, anything you think you've done,' his father sat forward and his voice was gentle, 'whatever it is I've done worse myself and I'm not going to judge you, I'll try and help you.'

'I don't even know whether it's ... whether it's anything to do with me.'

'It can't be so very terrible, then.'

Still Paul said nothing.

'The dinner's going to be ready if you don't hurry up.'

It was true, he could smell meat cooking even in here.

'Jenna's pregnant,' Paul said and he let go of his breath and sat back and waited for his father's temper to fill the room and make him want to be a hundred miles away

Sorrel didn't say anything for so long that Paul began to think his father hadn't heard him but when he had the courage to look into his father's face, he had been right. The light had gone from his eyes. There was nothing but darkness and a kind of strange puzzlement.

'Jenna?'

'Yes. She came over to tell me.'

His father seemed completely taken aback. 'I thought she'd gone.'

'Gone?'

'Yes, with Gallacher. He has gone?'

'Yes, he's gone.'

'And so?'

'So.' Paul took a deep breath. 'She says the baby's mine.'

His father stared at him and then frowned.

'Does she now?' he said slowly and he looked as if he wanted to kill somebody. He sat back. Paul couldn't breathe at all now, he was so afraid.

'Right. I didn't realize your ... relationship had got that far. You don't seem to me to be more than friends.'

His father was shrewd, Paul thought. That was exactly how it was.

'It was just once,' he said. 'We had too much champagne and...'

His father nodded.

'And Little Miss Duncan was as pure as the driven snow before you, was she?'

'No.'

'I didn't think so. She went with Gallacher, yes? They were very thick, isn't that the case?'

'Yes.'

'You know that lad's turned out to be something of a pain,' his father said shortly.

Nobody spoke after that. Paul didn't know how to go on or what to say to make things any better.

'So, is she a devious little cow?'

That was exactly it, Paul thought and then was obliged to be honest.

'I don't know. How do you tell?'

'He could be foisting it off on to you because he'd already decided to leave and didn't want the encumbrance of a woman who wants to marry him because she's pregnant. He has his way to make, his future to think about.' Sorrel sighed. 'I think the odds are that it's nothing to do with you.' He sounded comfortable with the notion, Paul thought.

'That's not what she says. She says she didn't go with him at that time, that it could only be mine.'

'It didn't occur to you that she was having you on or that now he's gone you're all that's left?'

'Of course it occurred to me,' Paul said, a trifle impatiently. He wasn't quite as stupid as his father thought.

'What have you said to her?'

'Nothing.' Paul couldn't look at his father.

'Have you said you'll marry her?'

'No, I told her I wouldn't, that it was nothing to do with me, and then she left.'

His father looked so relieved that Paul got up, he felt faint and needed some air. He went to the open doors and stood there and he felt sick.

'There's nothing more she can do,' Sorrel said. 'She can't force you to marry her and neither can her parents so you've got nothing to worry about. Why don't you just forget about it?'

'I don't know that I can.'

That was the trouble, Sorrel thought. The poor sod was in thrall to Little Miss Loose Knickers.

'Let me tell you something, Paul. You can have any woman you want, you can have more than one if you like, as long as you have plenty of money. They're simple creatures, you see. They're only any good in the kitchen or the bedroom—'

Paul gazed at the garden.

'I love her,' he said.

It was exactly the response Sorrel had waited for, had purposely evoked by his own words. At last he thought they were at the crux of the matter.

'You love her?'

'Yes.'

'How can you love a lass like that?'

'What do you mean?'

'She's a little scrubber from a pit row.'

'She's nothing of the kind.' Paul had turned around and was almost glaring, which was

124

brave of him, Sorrel thought idly

'But she doesn't love you?'

'She loves that bastard Ruari Gallacher. I've been trying for months to get someplace with her and I never did apart from that once and it was just because I got her drunk. I know it was stupid but it was the only way and if it was his she would have gone with him, I know she would.'

'What if he didn't want her?'

'He did. He never came near her after I went with her and the look on his face when he was around...'

'Maybe his instincts were better than yours.'

'I don't think so. I want her and I think ... well, obviously we have to get married, as soon as we can.'

Now they were getting to the heart of it, Sorrel thought. Paul, typically wanted what he couldn't have, or what he thought he couldn't have. Maybe Jenna Duncan was clever and had played him and was ready for a second round with Paul since she had not got him to say that he would take her on.

'Have you considered other answers?'

'What?'

'You could get rid of it.'

'I don't really want her to have an abortion and she doesn't want it either and – and you can't. It would be ... your grandchild, you couldn't want–'

'No, of course not,' Sorrel said smoothly, wishing Ruari Gallacher in hell.

'She says it was nothing to do with him.' Paul didn't seem able to get the words out without pain and he had read his father's mind which surprised Sorrel. 'She wouldn't lie to me and do you know why? Because she loves him. If it was his she'd have told him. She would even have gone after him.'

His father sighed.

'You have to consider this very carefully. There will always be girls who will try it on with you, who will know who you are and whose son you are and that you have money. Is that what this is? Because if it is then you want nothing to do with it. And if she doesn't love you...'

'I want her. I've wanted her since the minute I saw her,' Paul said.

'Aren't you going to shut the doors?' Faye said for maybe the fourth time. 'I don't want to put the lights on because the insects will come in but I want to read. Sorrel, are you listening?'

Sorrel was standing by the open doors beside the upstairs balcony. It was one of his favourite places. He loved the sound of the waves. He wished he was there now on the beach. Always there was another problem. He never got a day off, never a day free, he didn't suppose anybody ever did.

126

He was more disconcerted now than he had ever been. He was worried about Paul. Paul was in love with Jenna Duncan and whatever kind of awful lass she was he would not stop loving her.

He had never stopped loving Faye even though it was obvious that she didn't care any more about him, if she ever had which he doubted. He was lucky they were still in the same bedroom. She had long since insisted on single beds and he thought the worst way to spend the night was like this. What was the point in having somebody in the same room but not warm beside you? It was worse than having a room to yourself, lying listening to somebody sleeping, someone you had loved for so long and aware that you couldn't get into bed with them either for sex or for comfort.

All he could think of was the day they had bought the cottage in Tynedale, on the edge of a pretty stone village. It was the first thing they had bought, the first place he had taken her to after they were married, their first holiday, only it didn't belong to him then, he had bought it for her later, knowing how much the place meant to her. He could remember stopping the car at the bottom of the lane and walking up. She had slipped on the wet grass and he had caught her and they had laughed and he had kissed her.

The garden was overgrown and the wall

which bordered it was falling down and he thought, That was the day I realized I would always love her, it was the worst feeling of my whole life because I knew she didn't love me and however many cottages I found for her and whatever I did to please her it wouldn't matter.

The cottage had tiny windows, two of them in the upper storey were rounded, so beautiful, and the stone was grey and square and regular and had been well put together. The cottage was high up a twisting narrow road which had no footpath and the houses clung to the sides of the hill as you ascended and it had a view of the village below and of the river ribbon silver in the bottom of the valley.

Beyond it the sheep huddled on the moorland where there was nothing but a few trees and the stone walls turned this way and that to accommodate the landscape and the cart tracks petered into nothing.

A lapwing rose up crying at them for fear they should disturb the nest. It came, divebombing them, unafraid or so afraid that it would do anything to distract them from what it had to lose, swooping over them endlessly and putting forth its pitiful cry until they had retreated sufficiently far so that it was not afraid of invasion.

He had lost everything he held dearest that day in some obscure way she had found her freedom from him there and he had always hated the cottage from then on. Faye had not been able to understand why he never wanted to go there. He felt as though it belonged to her, it was full of things he didn't understand, open fires which she had to get going, a little pot–bellied stove which always went out when he touched it, books like *Moby Dick* which he found boring. There was no television, no telephone, it drove him mad, he felt out of control, he couldn't remember who he was.

The garden grew rhubarb and goose-berries, blackcurrants, great swathes of nettles and big purple buddleia bushes which the butterflies decorated in red and orange and black spots, wings fluttering as the summer progressed, and in late July the willowherb was three feet high on the roadsides and covered in dark pink flowers.

Every summer she would go there and cut him out of her life. She spent all the school holidays there until Paul objected when he was about fourteen and then she found him a friend to go with and that took care of that for another couple of years, she even wanted to go at Christmas when he wanted to fly away to somewhere warm. She could spend hours reading a book and ignoring him and more than anything in the world he hated being ignored. She made it so obvious she would much rather be alone.

She was rushed from there to hospital

when she lost their second child. They had to send an ambulance down the blasted unmade rutted lane because she was too ill to go by car. He had begged of her to stay at home in the town but she wouldn't because the weather was fine at the cottage and she loved to sit by the fire and read.

I can see Paul about to make all the same mistakes that I made, he thought, and the only thing I can do is to stand around making what I hope are the right noises.

'Sorrel!' Faye sounded exasperated.

Sorrel drew back, turned around, closed the windows.

'You've been standing there ages not saying anything. What's the matter?' she said.

He hesitated. He didn't want to tell her, though she had a right to know.

'Paul thinks he got Jenna Duncan pregnant.'

'Oh no.' She put down the book she was holding and looked anxiously at him and his instinct was the same as always, he would have given anything to take that look away. 'The one who came to the house? She's not the kind of girl I wanted for him.'

'I wasn't going to tell you because I don't know what's happening. He hasn't exactly been frank about it and I didn't want you upset.'

'But they'll have to get married,' and then she read his face. 'No, you can't do that, you can't start insisting that he pretends it's nothing to do with him if he cares about her. This is his life.'

'That's why. Look at us.'

She stiffened, he felt her. He was sitting on her bed by now and wished he hadn't done so. He shifted a little.

'It was worse then. People felt obliged to get married,' Faye said. 'I suppose some still do. Does Paul feel like that about it?'

He wanted to say to her, 'Would you have married me otherwise?' but it was a pointless exercise because he knew that she wouldn't have and he thought if only he had bought Ruari Gallacher none of this would have happened. Jenna might not have gone with Paul and even though Paul cared for her Gallacher would have got in the way and everything would have been different. He had made a basic mistake. He couldn't tell Faye, she wouldn't understand.

'You have to stay out of it,' his wife said.

'He's going to spoil his life over it.'

'Yes, well, each of us does that in our own special way,' she said and that was when he got off the bed.

Twelve

Paul couldn't rest. He had put forward all the hateful things he could think of about Jenna but it didn't help. The following day was Sunday He stayed upstairs until mid morning. Then he ventured downstairs to find only his mother standing in the kitchen reading the *Sunday Express* and drinking tea.

'Where's Dad?'

'He had to go out, something went wrong. Are you all right?' She looked sympathetically at him. At that moment the back door opened and Sorrel came in.

'What was it?' Paul said.

'The betting shop at Easton, somebody broke into it. As though I would leave money in there on a Saturday night.'

Faye poured coffee and made toast and then she went upstairs and Sorrel opened the Sunday newspapers as he sat at the kitchen table.

Paul thought back to various Saturday nights when he was younger and his mother would count piles of notes on the kitchen table and they were broken into every few weeks over the weekends because people thought his father kept cash at home on

132

Saturday nights that he had siphoned off so that the taxman would not get his hands on it. His father would buy jewellery for his mother with crisp notes, diamond earrings, ruby or sapphire rings. The groceries were bought with cash, his father would go around with great rolls of fivers in his pockets.

'I want to marry Jenna Duncan.'

'Oh God,' his father said, looking up from the newspaper and his toast. 'Look, Paul, you've seen what happened with your mother and me–'

'It isn't like that.'

'The more I think about it, the more I realize how like that it is. She didn't want to marry me, they made us get married because you were on the way and I knew that it was the wrong thing to do and now you are going to do the same thing.'

'She's having my child. Weren't you glad you had me? I'm going to ask her to marry me.'

'You'll be making a mistake.'

'I already made the mistake, now I have to try to retrieve what I can of it.'

His father said nothing but his disappointment was thick in the air.

'Maybe this is the right time to consider your future. What are you going to do with your life now that things are changing?' he said and Paul could hear the resignation in his voice and for the first time ever he felt sorry for his father. It was so important to Sorrel that his son should be a better man than he was, that he should not be involved in underhand doings or take part in the business. His father wanted other things for him, worked so that Paul could live differently.

Paul understood but he no longer wanted to move away from what his family did, he didn't know why just that he wanted Jenna and he wanted to stay here with her and to carry on what his father had done and to work with him. He didn't want to go away and try new things.

'I thought I'd come and work for you.'

'Paul, you have brains. You don't need to have brains to do what I do, any idiot could do it.'

Sorrel's background and lack of education was privately a sore spot for him which was why he had wanted Paul to do something else and it was a stupid thing and he knew that you couldn't live through your children even though you might try. It never worked, they were the people that they were and it had very little to do with you.

'I wanted respectability for you,' Sorrel said.

Paul stared, not very surprising, his father thought. He had never said such a thing to him.

'I know it sounds silly but you've lived with me all these years and I've done a lot of things I'm not very proud of because I wasn't clever and I had to do what I knew in order to survive at a good level. I wanted to be rich. It isn't everything. You don't have to do that, you can have anything you want. Don't throw away the idea of trying something else before you've thought really hard about it.'

'I wanted to do something which would please you,' Paul said.

Sorrel felt worse then, he hadn't realized that.

'You shouldn't do it for anybody but your-self,' he said.

'Then I'd like to work with you,' Paul said.

'You changed your mind?' Jenna could not believe it.

'Well, no, I didn't really. I just stopped doing what I thought I should and did what I wanted instead,' he confessed.

'You want the baby?' She could not believe that either.

'I want you.'

Jenna was inclined to burst into tears, into song, anything which would be better than the way that she had been feeling over the past few days. She could not believe that Paul had come back. She had sat in her room and been unable to imagine what the coming months would bring, what the rest of her life would hold and she could not understand the mess she had got herself into.

There was nobody else to blame. She would have to work in the drapery department until she was fat and people stared and stopped talking to her and then she would have to stay in her mother's house until the baby was born and there would be no celebrations, no joy, her parents would not be able to talk about the baby and be glad. She was becoming very depressed at such thoughts when her mother had come into the sitting room, trailing Paul behind her and looking wooden-faced, as though she did not know whether to be pleased or not.

'The trouble is...'

'What trouble?'

He looked at her.

'I know you don't love me. I know you think you should do this but, Jenna, if you don't want this baby we can do something about it. We don't have to go through with it.'

'I would never consider getting rid of my child. Don't you want it?'

'I want it to be what we both want, it's not going to work if it's one-sided. That's what my parents did. It's not the way that I want to live. I know that if it hadn't been for the baby you would have gone with Gallacher.'

Jenna looked at him and she knew what she wanted.

'That's over now.' She stopped and decided to be completely honest with him. 'I don't think Ruari ever wanted me as much as he wanted football. I know it sounds silly but I think subconsciously I was aware of it and perhaps it was the reason I went to you. I think we could have a really good marriage. You're the person I want now and I want our baby,' she said. 'I want it more than I've ever wanted anything or anybody in the world so if that's what you want too let's get married.'

The weight looked as though it had lifted from Paul. He grinned and looked exactly like his father and then he hugged her and promised her he would make it work.

Thirteen

Paul thought he was going to like working for his father and for the first few weeks Paul followed him around while Sorrel explained how everything worked and Paul began to enjoy being there. He was not interested in football but he found he was quite interested in how the club was run from a business point of view and once he had stopped thinking of it as a game and regarded it as a commodity he liked being there.

Sorrel spent almost all his waking time at work. It occurred to Paul that his parents did not give one another much time but he had no illusions about their relationship.

They had been married for almost twenty years and presumably in that long the novelty wore off. His mother was good at spending money, his father at making it. His mother had lots of friends and went out every day, his father worked and never went anywhere socially.

Best of all, Paul discovered, his father loved the football club, he would have said it was the most important thing in Sorrel's life, and sooner or later every day they ended up there, usually in the evenings where Sorrel was content to be until nine or ten o'clock and often after that he would go to the night-clubs to check that everything was running smoothly.

Paul liked this too, he enjoyed seeing people spending money on roulette wheels and in slot machines and at bars and he liked the lights, the music, the way that the girls dressed up, the sight of notes being handed in and the thought that he was part of this.

The office at the football club was very flash, all pale expensive wood and modern chairs and desks in chrome. Drinks were hidden in a big cupboard and in there too was a large refrigerator for champagne, ice and vodka. The tea- and coffee-making facilities were of the best and his secretaries were young, beautiful, blonde, long-haired and neat-fringed with very short skirts and very tanned legs. They wore low-cut tops which showed off their breasts, and they had neat waists and slim hips.

His father had lavished money on the ground, on the buildings, on the new training area, on baths and showers for the players, everything he could think of was done so that the team would win. The pitch itself was immaculately kept and everything around it was spotless, his father was a stickler for perfection, it had to be right, the groundsmen kept it so and the first team played in white and each time they played everything was new. He only had one level, Paul thought with some pride, the top as far as the club was concerned.

When he had taken it over some five years earlier it was in debt but it was not in debt any more. His father did not back losers, not that he was aware of. He had a great manager, he had bought good footballers, they had finished near the top of the division at the end of last season.

It was mid-evening and they should have been at home having dinner but his father was bored at home and Paul had got used to doing without dinner. Sometimes midweek he would be there for Jenna's sake or he would take her out but weekends were the most important for work.

Sorrel poured more whisky for himself and thought. It was autumn, his favourite time of all. He had been born in November and had always imagined that this was why he preferred the autumn, otherwise it seemed silly, the dying back of everything, the onset of winter, and then he realized that it was nothing to do with any of that, it was because it was the beginning of the football season.

He liked the idea of starting new things, especially somehow at this time of the year. Because of the football he looked forward to the leaves falling and the nights darkening. To him it was the excitement of the new football year. Each year was a new opportunity and he had made some good purchases over the summer and he had a good team and with enough encouragement, training and general pampering of the best kind they might make it all the way this time.

One of his friends, Cecil Meredith, who was as unlike him as any man could be, Sorrel thought with a grin, had introduced him to a new club. It was not far from where he had been born and brought up in Newcastle.

It was strange how he loved to go back there, he liked to recapture the idea that his mother was still living there, waiting for him in the tiny house by the river, in his mind she was always there, she had not died and left him when he was ten. Thinking about her was a painful process and yet the familiarity of it brought comfort to him.

Many of the streets had not changed and he would leave his car and walk around a little, remembering the smells of the river and the sounds which came from the houses, the accents and the women in the streets were just like his mother had been. He did not think that he would ever stop missing her. She had been dead for over twenty years yet the sound of her voice and the prettiness of her face were as clear in his mind as they had always been.

Cecil was a well-respected businessman. The new club was just the place for tired men to retreat. There was a billiards room, a bar and other rooms where if you were keen enough you could lounge in a big leather chair and read and smoke and drink brandy. There was good food and great wine and best of all there were girls who danced for you and there were several bedrooms, discreetly away from the rest of the place.

In particular was one girl called Joanna. She reminded him of a girl who had lived near him when he was a small boy, she would put her nose in the air and not speak to him because her dad was something important, or she thought he was.

Living in that street, Sorrel reckoned, he couldn't have been anything very much. Anyway he liked Joanna. She had red hair and blue eyes and small perfect breasts which were high and tilted and when she undressed for him her body was creamy in the lamplight. He liked the way that she sighed when he had her. He didn't pretend to himself, the sighs cost him money but he didn't really mind.

Jenna had to be married in white, that was the custom and nobody said anything and in fact she wasn't getting any fatter. Faye Maddison had suggested that she and Vera and Jenna should go shopping for a bridal gown. They went to Fenwick's French Salon in Newcastle and various other expensive shops.

Jenna lost all sense of reality there because it appeared she could have anything she liked, nobody cared about the money. Although it was traditional for the bride's parents to pay for their wedding, since her parents had no money and Paul's father had plenty of the stuff he and Mrs Maddison were not mean about providing for this wedding.

She was beginning to learn that once you were involved with them the Maddisons took you for theirs and everything was looked after. It might feel slightly uncomfortable in some ways but Jenna thought she might as well enjoy what she could. She put all thoughts of Ruari away from her and concentrated on what she had and the wedding dress which they chose could not have been more beautiful.

It was a miniskirt as was the fashion with long sleeves and a neat veil. Mrs Maddison ordered flowers, they went to the top hotel in the area and booked almost the whole place and Jenna realized that even though she and Paul were getting married in a hurry he was Sorrel Maddison's son and everything would have to be of the best.

In the end her mother invited all the family on both sides. Who Paul invited, other than a couple of his school friends, she had no idea. The other people there were the business people of the area and there were a great many of those.

They were married in the local parish church within sight and sound of the sea and it was full though neither of them had set foot in it other than Easter, Christmas, weddings, christenings and funerals for years.

The vicar was very nice about it in the circumstances, Jenna thought, but she noticed him afterwards talking to Sorrel Maddison so perhaps there was more to it than that and Mr Maddison had given them some money towards a window or such. Certainly the church seemed very grand that day and it was difficult not to be happy

Each pew had a posy of roses at the end of it, she had a bouquet of the same, the wedding meal was a sit-down do though buffets had become fashionable. It was lavish, lots of champagne, the hotel decorated from top to bottom, they had a holiday booked in the Seychelles, she had enough clothes to last her for months and she managed to get Sorrel aside and thank him for what he had done.

He seemed embarrassed which was a strange emotion for such a man, she thought. She didn't like him. He didn't seem to her like a father at all, she felt dangerous when she was near him but not for herself, she was inside the castle walls. Beyond them there were troubles but she was safe because she was now a Maddison. She didn't think he liked her, or it was worse than that, she was beneath his notice, but she kissed him and thanked him. Loyalty she thought, that was what he was good at.

Sorrel could not help thinking back to his own wedding that day. Perhaps because this was the first wedding since which had mattered to him.

They were both Catholic back then so it had to be a church wedding. Nobody had any money, they were very young so nobody came except her parents, and two local people as witnesses. The baby had already showed and there was no meal, no celebration, they went back to her parents' house and then he went to the market stall where he was selling clothes to make his living.

They had run off to begin with but her

father had somehow found them and persuaded them that a wedding must happen but Faye was eight months gone with Paul when it took place. She was seventeen and he was just sixteen.

He would have preferred Jenna to be married from their house but it couldn't be. He couldn't deprive Jenna's mother of the occasion. She had bought a blue outfit which Sorrel thought looked appalling but then Faye wore something very much the same except it was in cream and the women wore hats and Jenna's dad was all done up in morning dress as they all were.

He was glad to get it over with. It was not what he wanted for Paul, he was worried that Paul's marriage would go the same way as his parents' had, he wished Paul could have chosen somebody with a bit of class, had some other kind of life, but there was nothing you could do about such things and regretting it would not make anything different.

Fourteen

Jenna would have preferred a little house of her own. She didn't realize that to begin with, she was so impressed now that she was married with the lovely old house where the

Maddisons lived that she thought it was something she would find easy. She had bad morning sickness and it could last all day. She tried various things, the best was supposed to be somebody bringing you a cup of tea and a biscuit before you got up but Paul was always gone early.

There was nothing to do. Mrs Maddison ran the house so that other people cleaned, cooked, washed and ironed and most of it happened without anybody noticing which was amazing, Jenna thought. Mrs Maddison also went out every day.

She played tennis, she went downstairs to the gym they had, she had coffee with friends and she somehow assumed that Jenna would get on with whatever she was getting on with and it was so lonely that Jenna could not believe it. She found herself going back to see her own mother for something to do but her mother was decorating the lounge and the place was upside down. Also the smell of paint made her morning sickness worse.

Because the business was concerned with the football club there was always a lot to do at weekends and the clubs and hotels took all Paul's time during the week. It did not stop in the evening like normal men's work. She didn't like to complain. Everything they had was of the best, she could have gone out and bought whatever she liked, the trouble

146

was she didn't need anything except things like baby clothes and a pram and a cot and she would have been happier if Paul had gone with her for these things.

She spent a couple of happy days choosing things and thinking about what they would do with the nursery.

Sometimes Jenna would be in bed when Paul came home. One night she awoke as he got into bed and the clock beside her said three.

'Wherever have you been?' she said sitting up.

'We had some trouble at one of the clubs. There was a big fight.'

'Are you all right?' She sat up as he peeled off his clothes, wearily, threw them on a chair and climbed into bed as though he had been thinking about sleep for a good long time.

'It's nothing to worry about, we have bouncers, it just got a bit out of hand, that's all. The place got smashed up and we had to get the police.'

He didn't seem worried. He turned over and went to sleep. Jenna lay awake for ages afterwards, thinking about what would happen if Paul was hurt.

He got up at the same time to go to work, though, it was just after six. He rushed about having a shower.

'Could you make some tea for me? I feel

sick,' she said as he came into the bedroom.

'Haven't got time, sorry. I'm late.'

'How can you be late? You just came home and no club is open this early.'

'I have to make sure everything is all right from last night. I dare say my mother will make you some tea if you ask her.'

'That means I have to get out of bed, which defeats the object,' Jenna said,

'Sorry,' Paul said and pushed on his jacket. As he was about to leave she said,

'Aren't you ever going to have a day off?'

'Yes, Sunday. Dad's taking me out somewhere. It's a surprise,' and he smiled at her and was gone.

Jenna felt even worse after this. Had he no time to spare for her at all, even on his one day off?

On the Sunday morning off he went and she felt resentful that he should leave her. She felt very tired that day not wanting to do anything in particular. Faye was at home and Jenna felt better knowing that somebody else was there even though they didn't do very much together. They had lunch and then Jenna lay down on the sofa by the fire and fell asleep. When she awoke she lay looking at the lawn which was covered in autumn leaves. It would be Christmas in no time, her first married Christmas. What did they do at Christmas? She supposed they would be busy, hotels and clubs were the places people went to for entertainment, especially at such times.

As she lay there Faye came in.

'You've been asleep ages. Are you feeling all right, you look awfully pale, would you like some tea?'

Jenna sat up when the tea arrived and let Faye give her a piece of chocolate cake. Halfway through the tea Jenna dropped both cup and saucer she had just picked up. Tea spilled all over the turkey rug, the cup and saucer bounced and she was gasping for breath beyond the pain.

Faye was not the kind of woman who went around assuring people it would be all right. She moved just as far as the telephone which hung on the wall and within seconds she had called an ambulance. Jenna waited for the pain to ease and when it didn't the tears fell unbidden down her face. At the same time she felt the warmth between her thighs.

'I'm bleeding.'

'Oh God,' Faye said and put an arm around her.

Faye left her briefly to throw on some clothes. She seemed to be gone such a long time but it could have been no more than a minute or two and the ambulance came shortly afterwards. Faye put the rug from the sofa around Jenna and then the men came and they would not let her walk anywhere. She felt stupid but beyond anything she felt pain.

Sorrel had told the office that nobody was to bother him, he had planned a special outing for Paul. He had not expected Paul to be competent in business, he had been so pleased that Paul listened to what he said, did as he was told but was ready to move on in so short a space of time to projects of his own. Sorrel had said nothing so this new car was his gift to Paul to acknowledge that he was doing so well and he wanted nothing to get in the way of this moment for them both.

'Where are we going?' Paul had said.

'Wait until we get there.'

Paul said nothing, just sat and they drove up the coast and towards Newcastle and beyond it to a certain garage and there they got out of his father's car.

'Are you buying something new?'

'Not exactly.'

'Is it something for Mum?'

'She would be here,' Sorrel pointed out.

'A surprise for her?'

'No.'

'Well, it can't be for me, I've got your MGB and the old Volvo for when the baby comes and I don't want Jenna to learn to drive until after the baby is born, I think it's too dangerous, so what is it?'

Sorrel took him inside and there the

manager was waiting, smiling and there stood a Ferrari 250 GTO, red as only Ferraris are and sparkling and new with that wonderful smell. The smell was the best thing about new cars, Sorrel thought. He took the keys from the manager and handed them to Paul

'Congratulations,' he said, 'welcome to the firm.'

Paul's reaction satisfied Sorrel. The boy obviously couldn't believe it.

'But, Dad, I haven't done anything yet.'

'You've shown that you have a lot of ability and that's the most important thing of all. Get in, let's take it for a spin.'

They did. They drove all around the coast and when the cold night drew in Sorrel took his son to the club in Newcastle where he had first met Joanna. He went there often, they knew him, in fact only people they knew were allowed in.

He didn't think until he got into the bar and then Paul stopped. Sorrel didn't know why he stopped at first and then he realized and grinned. Dozens of beautiful women stood around the bar, tall, shapely and blonde most of them, models, actresses, would-be actresses, women with ambition. Paul stared.

'Just choose what you want,' Sorrel said, 'it's yours.'

Paul looked at him.

'Do you mean...' he said and stopped.

Sorrel knew why he stopped. He remembered when Faye had been pregnant. It had never been the same somehow after that. The idea of another person taking over his wife's body had nauseated him and after she was a mother he found that he wanted the person that she had been, the person who was all his.

He was shocked by his reaction but he wanted a woman with a flat stomach and high breasts and slender thighs. Faye had put on weight when she was pregnant with Paul and had never lost it. Here he could choose the body that he wanted and so could Paul and undoubtedly as he saw the light go on in Paul's eyes his son would struggle and then decide.

'Well?' he prompted.

'The one on the left at the end,' Paul said and Sorrel looked at her. The girl at the end of the bar was an excellent choice, long yellow hair and a gorgeous figure. This one looked unattainable. She was the one he would have chosen.

It was an illusion of course. None of the women who came here were that. They wanted men with money and men with money wanted them. The gamble was for how long, would it be just for the night, would it be a week, a month, would there be jewellery in it for them, perhaps a car, maybe even better than that, a flat in a good area and a monthly income so that they could give up the shitty little job they were paid to do and in return all they had to do was be available occasionally? It was not much to ask, he thought, though he had never settled for one girl like that. He didn't see why any man would when there were so many.

Paul went to the girl. She did not seem to be looking at them but that too was false, everybody in the room knew who Paul was, who his father was. She smiled. Paul knew what to do instinctively, Sorrel thought, and he watched Paul order champagne.

Sorrel left him to it. He went to the back of the club and to the room where Joanna was waiting for him. Their arrangement was such that he would see her on certain nights and this was one of them. He knocked softly on the door and she opened it and then she flung herself into his arms.

From the hospital while she sat waiting Faye tried to get her husband and Paul on the telephone but there was nobody at the office and it was growing late. She even tried Sorrel's secretary at home but she had no idea where he was, she said she hadn't seen him, he had left, he had just said he and Mr Paul were going out, he didn't know when they would be back and they weren't to be disturbed.

'But I must find him,' Faye said. 'It's a family problem, very important, and he must be told.'

'I'm sorry I can't help you. I don't have a number for him.'

'But you must have.' Faye was sure her husband had to be available in case something went wrong at any of his numerous business concerns but all she got from his secretary was a stony silence and she realized that the woman would not help her no matter what the circumstances.

She kept ringing the house but there was no certainty that Sorrel would answer the telephone, he rarely did so as though it was nothing to do with him and most of his business acquaintances would know better than to ring him there. Surely if he went back, seeing nobody there he would do so but the telephone rang out every time she tried it.

Faye didn't want to go back there for when he did arrive home, she wished now that she had had the presence of mind to leave a note but at the time she had thought of nothing but Jenna, she felt that she was some kind of talisman, that as long as she was there this would prove to be a false alarm, that Jenna would be all right, that the bleeding was something that happened to lots of women, as she was sure it was and that in the morning it would be better.

Rain was starting to fall. She had telephoned Jenna's parents as soon as she got to the hospital and tried to explain as well as she could and of course they insisted on coming to the hospital and she was glad of them. She had not thought she would be but somehow when she saw them coming up the hospital corridor the relief which flooded her made her want to cry.

They were so badly dressed, they were so poor. Mrs Duncan was a short fat woman, amazing how some people had beautiful children. Mr Duncan was terse-mouthed and he was little too and stocky, probably his ancestors had all been pitmen. Mrs Duncan was white-faced and crying and Mr Duncan didn't look directly at her so she went to them. Mrs Duncan insisted on seeing Jenna and went in, Mr Duncan hovered and then said, 'Is she going to be all right?'

Faye didn't believe that she was when nobody was reassuring, when there were no sighs of relief, she knew exactly what this was like, this was what had happened when she was having her second child. She tried to force the memory away from her while she reassured him. Why should she not? He sat down with a sigh.

'I knew nothing about this, you know,' he said.

Faye tried to look across the corridor where other people were sitting waiting and looking much the same.

'Nobody told me.'

'Would it have helped if they had?'

'Did you know?' he said.

'I think Jenna was so ashamed and she cares about you so much–'

'Her mother knew.'

'That's different.'

'Aye, well,' he said bitterly.

'I think she wanted to do better for you.'

He looked at her.

'Better than your family?' he said.

'Definitely,' Faye said and smiled dimly.

'Aye, I wish she had too, she was going with a nice lad when your son happened along with his flash car and his flash suit.'

And his flash father, she added silently.

She had been amazed at how personally Sorrel took it when their second child had died. She hadn't thought men ever reacted like that. She hadn't thought he would, as though it was his fault, and in a way it was. He was never there, he was always out making money he was obsessed with the idea of security, of making enough so that he could look after his family like he could hold everything off with cash and she had a very small child and no help. In some ways they had not got past it. Would Paul and Jenna get past this?

The evening wore into night, the rain poured down and they sat and waited. Faye had always thought that three o'clock in the morning was the worst time but she realized tonight that it wasn't so. Jenna lost her baby at four o'clock in the dark, when there was no prospect of light for months to come and then she wanted her mother. Faye went home.

The windscreen wipers were of some comfort somehow, something normal. The house was empty. She didn't realize until she got there that she had hoped he would be there, she hadn't really thought he would but she had hoped. She sat in the car, unable to get out somehow and then managed to open the car door and walk across the gravel and open the door.

She went into the sitting room and put her feet up and dozed on the sofa. She was awoken by the slamming of the outside door. It was daylight. Nobody came into the room and why would they she thought sitting up, dazed but beginning to remember?

It was early morning, light filtered through the clouds. She soon heard her husband's footsteps upstairs, there was a long pause and then he came back down again and he shouted her name and then Paul came down and they came into the sitting room.

'Where's Jenna? What happened?' Paul said.

Faye stood up, collected her shoes from where she must have kicked them off and said, 'She miscarried.'

There was silence. She didn't question them, she didn't ask anything, she just walked slowly out of the room and into the hall. Paul went after her.

'Miscarried?'

'That's what I said,' and then she walked up the stairs and into her bedroom and closed the door behind her.

'Dad–'

'No, you go to the hospital, I'll talk to your mother,' Sorrel said.

He followed her upstairs. She was standing in the bedroom, not doing anything, just standing.

'Did you have to do that?' she said.

'Do what?'

'I'm too tired for games. I know very well now where you were, you were at some wretched club in bed with some floozy. You must have been, you didn't come home at all. Did you have to introduce your son to such...'

He said nothing and she looked at him and she sat down on her bed.

'I just wish I had known, could have got in touch. Your secretary was of no help though I'm sure–'

'She didn't know where I was.'

'Well, all I can say is you have a strange sense of priority.'

158

'The girls there are clean,' he said.

'Clean?' Faye looked at him. 'That's not a mind you have there, Sorrel, it's a sewer.'

'At least I'm realistic. Don't you see what is happening? It's the same thing all over again–'

'It is now. They stood a chance–'

'Oh, come on. It was all over when she said "I do".'

'If Jenna can't have any more or she doesn't want him there'll be no grandchild. Have you thought of that or don't you care about that either?'

'Just because we lost our child...' he said and his voice faded as she turned away from him. 'Lots of women miscarry and go on to have other children.'

'He wasn't there,' Faye said. 'She went through all that without her husband. I just hope whatever girl you were screwing gave you a good time.'

'It's more than you ever did,' Sorrel said before he could stop himself and she got up off the bed and came across the room so fast he didn't have time to move before she cracked him over the face. It was the first time she had touched him in fifteen years.

Jenna had never felt so ill and when it was over, when they told her that the baby had died, she felt nothing. She lay in her hospital bed and watched the autumn rain pour

159

down the windows. She was in a room of her own. Sorrel had come to the hospital and made a great fuss and she was now in this palatial place with flowers everywhere at the very time when she would much rather have had some company. It was so clean and so white that only the heat saved it from being close to a refrigerator but she had already learned that there was no point in arguing with Sorrel, he didn't listen to what anybody said.

Paul had been pale-faced when he came in.

'I'm so sorry I wasn't there. Dad insisted on taking me out and we just forgot the time, got carried away.'

'It doesn't matter,' Jenna said, not caring whether he was with her now it was too late. She felt so bad, she was so tired she didn't even want to talk. 'It wouldn't have made any difference.'

'I will never, ever leave you again, I swear it.'

Why was he beating himself up about this, she thought, it was not his fault that his father had tried to give him a treat, even though she thought he could have let her know?

He was inconsolable, she was touched, she hadn't thought of him like that. She thought he had taken the baby for granted but now that there was no baby – how would she get used to the idea? – he was grief-stricken.

Sorrel also seemed most concerned. She didn't realize he wanted a grandchild so much but then he would, a man like that who was concerned with business wanted people to carry it on and no matter how unimportant she might think that, it was obviously a big part of his life, and then she remembered how keen he had been that Paul should go on and do something other than go into business with him and knew he was just upset.

He sat down on the bed and kissed her hands. It was a strange gesture, as though he was acknowledging his responsibility and that wasn't fair, she thought, it wasn't his fault, he had done everything he could to help once he had known she was pregnant.

'Is the room all right?' he said looking about anxiously as though there might be something wrong or a speck of dust somewhere.

Stupidly he made her feel better, he was so out of place there, in his expensive suit, watching the door as though some dragon might come for her and he would slay it in an instant. Jenna couldn't help but smile.

'The room is fine.'

'Jenna, I'm sorry we weren't there,' he looked her straight in the eyes and his eyes were so very blue, so very dark, 'especially I'm sorry that Paul wasn't there. I wanted to

161

buy him a new car, he's worked so hard lately.'

She could vouch for that, Paul had hardly been at home for weeks. She had grown used to it.

'And then we went to this club in Newcastle and ... well, you know.'

'I know,' she said.

It was odd. He was like a little boy, charming, repentant.

'We came in with the milk bottles,' he said and pulled a face. 'You won't leave, will you?' he said.

And then she realized. Sorrel was used to being left, perhaps his parents had done it, he expected people to leave, even lived his life taking for granted they would and moving on in case they did and before they did. How odd and how very uncomfortable.

Jenna wanted to look away but she couldn't because somehow he held her there.

There was a flash of understanding between them and then she said softly, 'I have nowhere else to go.'

Sorrel smiled at that and he kissed her forehead and then he got up.

'I should go to work. If you need anything just tell them,' and then he was gone and somehow she felt cocooned by his concern and it was a very warm feeling.

Paul was only amazed that his guilt didn't

fell him, that God didn't strike him dead. He waited for his sentence and when nothing happened he sat by Jenna's bed and burned like somebody condemned to the stake.

The trouble was the blonde girl was experienced and he had never had anyone but Jenna. Now as the guilt began to wash, to move from him a little, he tried to justify to himself what he had done and his memory gave him Trudie on her knees before him, her blonde hair hiding who she was. He had imagined Jenna like that. He had even tried to push her head down so that she would take him into her mouth but she had always refused just by shaking his hands from her head.

Had she not done that with Gallacher? Was the boy genius a prude? Was he sexually naive, unimaginative or was it just that Jenna gave as little as she could to her husband because she didn't love him and only her sense of duty had got her to him. She had married him because she could not bear the talk and her poverty and the look on her parents' face.

Whatever else it was it was not love. And even while he assured her that he would never leave her again he remembered the look in her eyes when they had sex. She would turn her face away and wait until it was over, as he was convinced she had never done with Gallacher. She never said anything, she never took the lead, she never caressed him or kissed him voluntarily.

He knew now that his father had been right to take him to that club or he would have done what he had seen a great many other men do of a Friday or Saturday night, pick up a prostitute from the street or get drunk and stupidly pay just anybody for what they weren't getting at home. The truth was that he was gagging for it. Last night had been the best night since he had been married and he could not bear it. When Jenna finally slept he went out into the corridor and cried.

Sorrel didn't expect Paul to go into work that day he should stay with Jenna, but Paul turned up mid morning, lurching into Sorrel's office at the football club as though he was drunk. He probably had a hangover, Sorrel thought, but surely he hadn't been drinking again this early in the day.

He slammed the door.

'I feel dreadful.'

Sorrel lifted his head from the figures he was studying and looked up.

'It's mixing your drinks that does it. You should stick to one type.'

'Not about that.' Paul sounded irritated. 'I feel guilty.'

'You're married, get used to it,' his father said.

Paul said nothing for so long that Sorrel was inclined to think he had left the room and was back to looking at the papers in front of him and then he saw that Paul was at the window. It was a fine view, he had built it that way so that he could see the sea.

'You couldn't have done any more than was done for Jenna.'

'I could have been there!' Paul was shouting. 'I was shagging a blonde in a back room while my wife lost our baby. Doesn't it matter to you?'

Sorrel didn't answer.

'I love her,' Paul said. 'Don't you understand?'

'And does she love you?'

Paul didn't answer for a few seconds and then he looked down at the floor and he said, 'We're married and...'

'Last night had nothing to do with your marriage and you had a good time.'

'I shall never do it again,' Paul said.

'Yes, you will. Lots of times. You were just unlucky, that's all.'

There was silence. Then Paul said softly, 'I feel so awful, so guilty.'

'Yes, well, that's how most men feel most of the time,' Sorrel said.

Paul felt like a drug addict or an alcoholic. He lasted that night until about half-past nine and then he couldn't stand it any more. Jenna was still in hospital and his parents

165

were at home and he was alone so he got into his new car and drove to the club and there he had Trudie and a bottle of Scotch to himself all night.

When Trudie finally slept he made a decision. If she would let him he would rent Trudie a flat, somewhere pretty so that he could go to her whenever he wanted. It would be something completely separate from his marriage, he would be a better man for it. He would not always be bothering Jenna for sex and things would be much easier.

Jenna could not believe that she had lost her baby. Her first instinct was to get out of bed and run away, preferably as far as Teeshaven and tell Ruari Gallacher that it had all been a mistake, that the time between now and when she had gone to bed with Paul was just a nightmare, because that was how it felt. She wanted to cry, she wanted to wake up, she wanted Paul not to sit on the end of the bed like a man who is about to be executed and doesn't really care at the outcome but most of all she wanted to go back to being pregnant, she wanted her baby.

She felt as though she would never come to terms with her guilt and that she was being punished for what she had done. She felt that she owed Paul for getting him to marry her when she was pregnant and now the reason for it had gone. When she felt better, when she could think more clearly, they must try harder, they must work at their marriage and maybe in time she would give him a child and they would be happy. She went home and there Mrs Maddison looked after her.

She had not been looked after in such a way before, her mother hated it when people were ill, she did not know what to say about the baby and would come to the bedside for a minute or two in the hospital, pat her hand and tell her the next one would be all right when all Jenna could think about was the child she had lost and how it was her fault and how much she missed Ruari. After she went home her mother did not visit at all as though everything was said and done and they could move on.

Jenna thought about what her life could have been, she dreaded going on with this one but Faye was good to her and she got out of bed the day after she reached home. Faye was sitting in a chair in the conservatory and got to her feet.

'You shouldn't be up.'

'I'm bored.'

'I was just going to bring you some tea.'

'I can't face any more tea,' Jenna said and made her smile but she liked the way that Faye fussed and made her drink warm milk and she sat in the conservatory watching the flowers and was astonished to think that it was still autumn in the garden. A few leaves had drifted on to the lawn. Faye came back to find her in tears.

'My baby. I was making plans.' Faye cuddled her.

'I know, I know,' she said.

'All the things we bought...'

'I've put them in the attic. You won't see them.'

'I feel like such a lot of time has passed but really it's nothing and yet such a lot has happened to me. I feel like one of those twigs that gets caught up when there's a lot of rain and the river rushes away to Sunderland. What on earth can I do now?'

'Drink your milk,' Faye advised her.

Paul came home early and Jenna wondered for how long the look on his face would persist, like his guilt had overwhelmed him. She determined to put Ruari from her mind and to go forward and make Paul happy.

Fifteen

There was training at the ground in the morning, just running and stuff like that, it wasn't difficult, in fact it was so mindless that Ruari was bored, he would have been a lot happier if it had involved work with a ball rather than this idea of general exercise, it didn't suit him but he did it because that was what they did at this club.

He went with some of the others to a local billiard hall and played snooker in the afternoons. Other lads when they began to make money playing football bought themselves a car but Ruari spent nothing, he got the bus to the ground and saved his money. He wanted to pay the deposit for a house as soon as he could and for his mam to be able to stop cleaning.

One autumn day his mam came to see him. He had told her that he would travel back but she knew that he didn't want to do that so she got the bus, it must have taken ages, he thought.

He didn't want to meet her at his digs, he knew she would be concerned because it was not clean and he was not being fed properly as she would think of it, so he met her in town and took her out for a meal and she chatted and tried to look happy but he could tell that something was wrong, so after she had been cheerful and asked him about his playing and he had said everything was fine he gave in to the look in her eyes.

'What is it?' he said.

'What's what?'

'Oh, Mam, I know you too well. Summat's the matter.'

'Nothing,' she said and she drank her tea.

'Summat up with somebody?'

The look on her face didn't bode well.

'Ruari...'

'Hell, I wish you wouldn't say "Ruari" like that and then stop. What's happened?'

'You did know that Jenna married Paul Maddison?'

He wished he could say that he didn't want to know, didn't want to hear but it wasn't true.

'She was pregnant, Ruari, and she lost it.'

The words were said in such a rush that there was no way he could shut them out though he dearly wanted to. It hurt more than leaving her had done. It hurt more than anything had ever hurt before. It made him think of Jenna standing in the rain and how she had told him about Paul and how awful it had been.

'Don't you see,' his mam said, 'that was why she married him. It didn't mean she cared about him.'

'And you think that makes it better?'

'Wouldn't you rather have her a better person, than to think that she left you for him because he had more money?'

'She did! She did go with him for his money.'

'It was a mistake. Everybody makes those.'

'You don't know that. She was impressed with them, she liked the way they lived and

170

I couldn't do that for her, I couldn't provide things like that.'

His mam said nothing.

'I will now, though,' he said. 'And one day I'm going to go back and better them because of what they did to us, the way they tried to take advantage, the way Paul Maddison took my girl. I'm going to go back and sort them out.'

'You mustn't,' his mam said. 'That would make you just like them.'

'And I'm going to save up and buy you a house–'

'Ruari, I don't want a house. I don't want anything except for you to live your life and find something which matters to you and I think you're doing that. I like being among people who know me, I can afford the rent, I go and play bingo, I have tea with my friends. There's nothing I want. Don't save your money for me, buy yourself a car, find yourself somewhere to live. I know you don't like your digs even though you've kept quiet about it and I know how unhappy you've been. You'll meet somebody else, believe me you will.'

He felt like saying to her that she hadn't, that she hadn't gone on to meet somebody who cared for her. She had got tangled up with a hard drinker and married him and look what had happened to that but he couldn't say anything to her, he knew what

171

she meant, that he must get on with his life and try for things. Well, he would now.

When his mother had gone home and he had gone back to his digs he couldn't stop thinking about what Jenna had done and how she had let Paul Maddison have her without any kind of protection. How could she have been so stupid? And why? Maybe she had never cared about him really maybe she hadn't wanted the idea of a child with him whereas with Paul, because he came from a family who had money and because Sorrel Maddison could do anything he wanted, she had felt safe giving herself to him and not minding whether there was a baby.

It wouldn't go from his mind for the next day or two so he was almost pleased when Mr Hodgkin told him he would be a reserve for Saturday's match against Liverpool.

Ruari had not realized that he was going to go immediately into a cold sweating panic over such a thing. He wanted to run away. The chances were that he wouldn't get to play anyhow, nobody had told him he was any good but some reserves didn't get a chance like this. Also it meant he could be replacing a first-team player, John Simons, who had been injured a few games back and had been playing badly.

Ruari thought he had got used to being involved in the club, that he was used to the

noise that the fans made, sensed the antici-
pation, but it was not like that in the end.
He wanted to throw up.

Jack sat with him in the dressing room, it
was an away match which made it worse, all
that having to travel and a strange place and
another ground. Jack was encouraging and
Ruari couldn't believe that Jack could be so
calm, that they were not all getting up and
running away. He had never imagined it
would be like this. There was another
reserve going with them, a player who had
been with them for two years and had
played several times already that season but
when it came to it he was terrified.

The wait before going out on to the pitch
was one of the worst times of Ruari's life.
Somebody was actually throwing up in the
toilet, he could be heard, another was walking up and down, sweating, one or two talked
quietly and Jack, seemingly unconcerned,
listened to the manager's pep talk and then
waited silently so Ruari did the same.

He had not known that Mr Hodgkin
would make him feel good before he went
out. Mr Hodgkin told him he could do it,
talked to him using his name a lot, smiling so
by the time they were ready to go Ruari had
stopped being nervous. When he was on the
pitch he was almost numb with amazement.

There were thousands of people around
watching and he felt aware of each one of

them. The noise was deafening, the pitch was huge and he was only too well aware of the other side, the other players, in particular one little man, whom in his terror he didn't recognize, coming to him and telling him that if he touched the fucking ball he'd break both his fucking legs. Ruari believed him.

And then the game began and it all changed. He had never even as a little kid imagined it would be like this. He had come home. He was meant to be there. How extraordinary. The football field had seemed so big and now it didn't and he could see where he was meant to be and it seemed to him as though the fans, even on the other side, were there for him.

Suddenly it was the simplest thing in the whole world. All he had to do was get the ball and pass it to the player who was nearest the goal and even at one point when he was just outside the penalty area he could see Phil Wilson was in a better position and he passed it cleanly and swiftly and Wilson scored.

The place erupted. His ears couldn't take the noise. Phil was clapping him on the back and Ruari realized that even though Phil had made the goal he had made the goal possible and every player on his team knew it and every player on the other team knew it too and they were scowling at him.

He had never thought to be a part of anything so exciting and to be a part of something like this, it made him aware of all those minutes and hours and days in the back lane, all those years had come down to this moment and as he stood bathed in glory it began to snow small hard white flakes which turned the scene into one of those ticker-tape parades he had seen on television when people celebrated a great event in an American city. It was only for a few moments as though the very weather was pleased with him.

At half-time Mr Hodgkin had turned into Father Christmas, jolly, glowing, red-cheeked, full of praise. It had been the only goal scored.

'We need another,' Mr Hodgkin said. 'One's not enough, you know it isn't. There's nothing worse than a team that's one goal ahead and relaxes. Absolutely nothing.'

Ruari sat in a daze until they went back on and almost immediately and to his disappointment Liverpool scored and the crowd went up again screaming and the screaming and shouting and swearing and bawling seemed to crash and echo all around the ground.

He took it personally. He was very upset that they had scored and that the little man who had threatened him kicked him hard on the shin and the anger moved him forward. It seemed to move him forward faster than other people, he could get past them somehow and even though there seemed to be a lot of them in the way he wouldn't have it, he could dribble and swerve around them and he could get ahead of them and from way down the pitch he could see the goal.

He had heard people talking of footballers who could see the goal clearer than other players did, that it seemed a shorter distance, that the goal to the best players was a huge thing, that it was very big indeed and that the distance between the goal posts was as big as the heavens.

Suddenly there was nothing in the way that couldn't be got round, there was nobody in view between him and it and when he had run far enough and outrun them he paused to see which way the goalkeeper thought he was going to go and he turned his body so that the goalkeeper took his dive one way, he twisted his body ever so slightly and turned his foot and the ball, not wet, not leather but suddenly about as heavy as a balloon, soared like a coloured kite on a beach into the sky.

It seemed to him to go in slow motion from his foot, across the top beyond the grass, beyond the green, into the sky which was blue behind the big white flakes of the snow which had started up again and were square and momentarily dazzling. He could taste snow in his mouth and he could see the ball, like a bird, like one of those seagulls which soared high above the North Sea, and then it began to fall ever so slightly and while the world stood still and the goalkeeper went the other way towards the ground it buried itself in the back of the net as accurate as the gull that dived and lifted its trophy, the shining silver fish from the sea.

It seemed to Ruari that the world had stopped completely. The players didn't move and for seconds together there was silence and then the whole arena erupted and it was ecstasy. He had never in his whole life felt anything like it. Great waves of feeling came off the crowd and lifted him so high that he was weightless.

It was the final goal.

When they came off the pitch Ruari couldn't believe what had happened. He hadn't thought you could feel like that about anything other than Jenna. It was exactly the same thing, he had felt it before but he had forgotten and now it hurt because she was not there and she should have been there to see what he could do with the gift which he had worked so hard to improve and it was bittersweet, the gift which had cost him the girl that he loved.

Already he had begun to come down but once in the dressing room with the other players laughing and teasing him and Mr

Hodgkin, who looked like he was going to cry, he was so pleased that the image of Jenna was wiped momentarily from his mind.

He had a bath and got changed and when he came out to get on the coach his mother was there and his mother really was crying and she came over and cuddled him and kissed him and she said, 'I knew you could do it. I'm so very proud of you.'

He hadn't known she was going to be there, Mr Hodgkin had organized a car and paid for a hotel room and Ruari was pleased so the good feelings started all over again. They went back to the hotel and Jack ordered champagne and Ruari could hardly speak for the feelings.

Later, when Jack had gone off and his mother had long since gone to bed the other players were drinking in the bar and they came over and offered to take him to a nightclub.

They weren't supposed to do this after a match but he thought Mr Hodgkin would turn a blind eye because it had been such a good day. He didn't want to go but he didn't want to stay there and go to bed, he didn't want the evening to end because he was convinced there would never be another like it and indeed there wouldn't, it would never be his first match, his first goal, the crowd on their feet like that in recognition of what he could do.

'The newspapers'll be full of you,' Phil said as they walked out of the hotel.

'Of you,' Ruari said.

Phil smiled.

'You're the new boy,' he said.

'It doesn't necessarily mean I'll get to play again, though, does it? When John comes back–'

'He won't be back for the next game, I shouldn't think,' Phil said.

'There are other substitutes.'

'There are but they didn't just make two goals against a fantastic side,' Phil said.

Ruari had never been to a nightclub, but he was recognized on the door and nobody was going to deny him anything that night.

Liverpool was the place of dreams where the Beatles had been discovered playing at the Cavern. It had more atmosphere, he thought, than anywhere he had ever been, and there was no antagonism against the visiting players, at least as far as he could see and if there was fighting in the streets between the fans he was shielded from it completely.

The place they went to was very high class, he could see that because it was quiet, hushed, thick–carpeted, low lights and at the bar were the kind of girls that most lads only dreamed of. He thought about Jenna then and resented so much what she had done to him.

He didn't drink very much though some of the others did. He now felt as though he had a responsibility to look after the body which had given him pace and strength and vision but he was beginning to come down, to lose the high which the game had given him. He kept running it back through his mind but each time it played a little duller and a little further away and he understood then that there had to be another time and another game.

The girls at the bar seemed to know what he had done and were there, talking to him, and one in particular looked a little bit like Jenna though she had a Scouse accent, he liked it, it sounded so sexy, so gravelly. He danced with her. She smelled of expensive perfume, just a little so that you wanted to get nearer, and later, when it was very late and his so wonderful day was almost completely gone, he kissed her in the shadows and she was not Jenna and the day slid slowly to the floor where it crashed around him.

He went outside. It was still snowing. Phil for some reason followed him. Ruari was surprised. They had not been friends before now and only Jack ever thought about him.

'You all right, kidder?' he said. 'You haven't had too much to drink, unlike the rest of us?'

Ruari shook his head.

'It'll happen again.'

'What will?'

Phil waved a hand.

'The goals, the crowd, the feeling.'

'It's nearly gone now.'

'It won't ever go completely. You're lucky, think of all the thousands of daft sods who wish they were you tonight. They all hate you.'

It made him laugh.

'Maybe it was just a one off,' he said.

'Well, it had better not be, because Hodgkin will have your balls if it was,' and they laughed again, 'and thanks.'

Ruari looked at him.

'What for?'

'For the goal, you daft sod. You didn't have to pass it, you could have taken it yourself. You'd never scored before. Who would give up the chance?'

'I didn't think.'

'Yeah, you did. I saw you look at me before you passed it.'

'You were in a better position.'

Phil smiled.

'Dozens of other footballers would have taken the chance on themselves. It takes a particular kind of unselfish player to do such a thing, or just somebody so gifted that they see the whole team as one.'

'Bloody hell,' Ruari said, 'what did you have to drink? You sound like a teacher.'

'Come inside,' Phil said. 'A piece of advice before then. Take the little blonde to bed before you explode.'

'I don't think she wants me to.'

'Yeah, she does,' Phil said.

And sure enough she did. They went to his hotel. In a way it put Jenna back a pace, several paces, in fact. There had never been anybody but Jenna and stupidly he had thought, there never would be. What lad only ever had one woman? He had been daft, he had been naive. He had thought they were going to spend their whole lives together but Jenna hadn't thought that, Jenna had gone to Paul Maddison.

Ruari actually cried. He hadn't done that since he was a little kid and Stan had belted him for something. He couldn't even remember what now but it must have been something bad because he remembered it.

The blonde girl touched his shoulder. He was buried in the pillows and he didn't think she knew, or maybe she did.

'You all right, Ruari?' she said.

'Aye, I'm grand,' Ruari said.

And he knew why he had cried because the blonde was not Jenna, nobody ever would be Jenna, and the only way he could create the same feeling was on the football pitch, scoring goals, and he didn't know whether he would be able to sustain that.

The flat which Paul rented for Trudie was only ten minutes away from his home. He had not intended that, he had thought he might find something in Sunderland on the sea front or in the middle of Newcastle so that it would be well away just in case somebody saw them but in fact the flat that she liked was the top floor of an old building which looked out across the countryside and she liked the view there. It was nothing like he would have chosen but he could see how pleased she was so he agreed to it and they even spent wonderful stolen time furnishing it. He had not thought he would like buying a bed or a sofa or wine glasses and several times in Bainbridge's or Fenwick's in Newcastle they had to hide to avoid seeing people they knew, friends of his parents or neighbours, his father was so well known that it was difficult to avoid being caught. That was part of the pleasure. Half a dozen times they emerged from a shop giggling.

All he did there was go to bed with her and drink wine. There was nothing domestic about it after the furnishings. He kept her, they went to bed. She didn't cook, they had fish and chips or cheese and biscuits. Sometimes he watched television. He didn't want to be part of her life, he never asked her what she did when he wasn't there, he didn't care. He didn't know whether she had family or friends or who else she spent her time with.

The sex with Jenna was something they began doing because she wanted a child. He didn't care any more about such things, he was starting to think that he had never really cared, that he had married her out of guilt.

Babies were horrid wet things which shrieked and he avoided small children, he was not interested in them. He made sure that Trudie was on the pill so that there would be no complications and he did nothing more than service his wife because she seemed to become obsessed with the idea that they might have another child. He found it boring but necessary, perhaps everybody's marriage was like that. He had stopped regretting that he had married her, he had ceased blaming himself for her miscarriage, he just got on with his life.

He left the club and was not very surprised when his father commented on it.

'No, well, I've been busy.'

'Doing what?

Paul did not meet his father's gaze. It was half-time on a Saturday afternoon. He had begun going to the football with his father though he still couldn't see the point of running up and down a pitch, back and forth chasing a bloody leather ball but because his father was so involved it was difficult not to be and his father insisted on his being there at least most of the time so Paul endured it.

This day was mid-season and it was raining hard. That was the trouble with football being a winter game, the weather was usually foul and he would sit there thinking of how he could have been huddled over the fire at Trudie's and when the game was done he would go there, pretending he was somewhere else. His father didn't seem to mind if he took time off because God knew they worked almost all the time.

The home team had scored, they were a respectable two goals up at half-time and his father was in a good mood. They had left their seats and gone back into the office as Sorrel had an important telephone call to make and he said,

'I want to talk to you,' so Paul had no option but to follow him.

'You don't go to the club any more,' Sorrel said when the telephone call was over and he looked directly at his son.

Paul was not confused. He did not pretend that he did not know what his father meant.

'I've set Trudie up in a flat,' he said. 'Why are you asking when you know?'

'Because I don't know. I haven't been spying on you–'

'You guessed it, then. It's a long-standing affair. Plenty of people have them. She gives me what I don't get at home. You do the same–'

'I haven't set anybody up in a flat.'

185

'No, well, I expect it's because you get bored quicker than everybody else. I'll bet you've lost count of the women you've had over the years.'

He had said something significant, Paul thought, when silence followed this remark.

'I kept looking for ... whatever it was when I saw your mother. It never happened again. I've grown used to the idea that it will never happen now.'

Maybe he was right, Paul thought, frightened, that falling in love was only really something you could do when you were young, that if it went wrong you could be alone for the rest of your life in that way. And since the mood seemed right he asked what he had never dared ask before.

'Why hasn't she left?'

'I don't know. I used to think she didn't want me because she had a lover, I waited for your mother to leave after we lost the baby but there was never another man.'

'Maybe it was the money.'

'She could have had any amount she wanted and really she's never been much of a spender. She's had the same car for six years. Nobody could call her greedy. I don't even know why I care about her so much. It isn't as if she's especially interesting.' Sorrel smiled against himself. 'I think it's something to do with the way she turns her head. Nobody else does that. It was the first thing

I noticed about her. She was fifteen and I was just a kid and I was working a market stall and she was walking across the Market Place with a friend. And she turned her head and looked at me. Things were never the same after that. I wanted her so much as a part of my life.' He sighed. 'Well, I certainly got that.'

Ruari played again and then again and each time he was on the pitch he scored. When they won they got extra money and they got extra money every week until he came to expect it and he determined to leave Mrs Johnson's, buy a house and a new car, but at the moment it all went satisfactorily into his bank account aside from what he sent his mother.

It was funny when she did come to see him – because he didn't go home, she insisted on spending the money he had sent her and would take him out to tea at lavish hotels and buy him supper in Italian restaurants and he would put her up at good hotels. She didn't want to give up her job, she said she would be bored, she was thrilled at his success and he was pleased that she seemed happy at last.

Whether it was tact on Mr Hodgkin's part or because Ruari had not much experience when they played against Dunelm North End he was not included in the team. He thought probably Mr Hodgkin judged it would be very difficult for him to go back there so soon after leaving under a cloud and that he wouldn't play well because he wouldn't be able to concentrate so he didn't go.

He wanted to tell Mr Hodgkin that he had grown up a lot and that it wouldn't affect him to do it but he hadn't yet the confidence to be sure and since Mr Hodgkin was the one making the decisions it would have been awful to have let him down, so he didn't say anything and it was a relief in a way not to have to do it so maybe Mr Hodgkin had judged it well.

It wasn't the only time he didn't play, there were other people who had to be given chances, but Ruari gradually began to play more and more often and every time he played he scored and Teeshaven began to do better and better.

The money worries were disappearing completely and all he had to do was play football. It was so simple really.

The newspapers were full of Ruari's name by then and of his girlfriends and of his social life. He and his team mates very often went up to London and stayed there and went to clubs. He learned how to dress fashionably and then he bought himself a car and the fans started to recognize him, shouted for him.

It seemed to him, all of a sudden, when he had played a particularly good match against Arsenal and scored three times, that the street was always full of people, staring in at the windows, hanging around the door, and he decided to move. He was tired of the awful room, the bad food.

He tried to talk his mother into going with him but she was determined to stay where she was. She let him pay so that she could go on a modest holiday with a friend and that was all and he would lie in bed at night and wonder what on earth he was doing when he had nobody to work for, nobody to come home to.

In the end he bought a modest house, it was a cottage in a tiny village on the Yorkshire moors, nothing like anybody else had but he had lived in a town all his life and he liked to go back to it when the day was over and he could take taxis or stay at a hotel if he didn't want to, but once the novelty had worn off he was lonely there and hardly ever went, he stayed in hotels or with friends, he couldn't bear the silence when he walked into the house. There was something so impersonal about it that he came to dread being there. It was the idea that he liked of having somewhere of his own, the cottage did not matter to him at all.

Ruari began to take for granted that he

189

would play even when Simons came back on to the team during the first season. He only came back for two games that season and both times he didn't score. Ruari hadn't thought much about what it was like when you failed. Simons had a wife and two small children, Ruari had seen them and already there was talk of a transfer. He felt bad for Simons. He hadn't realized until then that when somebody won somebody else lost, sometimes several other people.

The reserve who had been with him somehow quietly melted away during the second year and the next they heard he had gone to Guildford to be a butcher. The very idea made Ruari lose sleep and shudder. He could end up as a butcher, getting up at five, starting at six, finishing at seven in the evening, spending three hours a day washing out fridges, chopping up lambs. It was enough to turn you into a vegetarian and that wasn't funny at three in the morning.

He was injured soon after that, it was his knee, a weak point, and then he was afraid. Every footballer feared injury it was such a rough game, but he was only out for a couple of weeks and then back and fit so he didn't worry about it. From time to time it bothered him but as long as he was careful and trained well and kept fit it didn't stop him losing more than the odd game.

He was no longer the new boy. By the

third season he felt confident and sure of himself. The first time they played a game that season he didn't score, and it was against Sheffield Wednesday at home so he should have, he felt the responsibility and even Mr Hodgkin said to him, 'Having an off day are we, Gallacher?'

It was faintly ironic, Ruari knew, but the truth was that they relied on him and the pressure was beginning to feel heavy. Mr Hodgkin saw his face.

'I'm only teasing you, son, you're doing brilliantly,' he said, 'and we won.'

That was it, they had won without his help somehow. Ruari was unhappy about that, he was used to being the best, he didn't like not coming top, he hadn't thought until then that he was so competitive but he trained harder, ate properly, slept properly and didn't drink and in the next game he scored.

Everybody knew who he was by that time and he went out one weekend after Christmas in London and in the pub a big young man came to him and called him 'a fucking Geordie' and Jack had to pull Ruari outside because Ruari turned around, fists clenched.

'You don't hit him.'

'I wasn't going to hit him.'

'Yes, you were. You can't afford it. He was probably paid by a newspaper.'

Ruari stared.

'Paid?'

'What wouldn't they give to see you fall from grace, to see you in a national rag socking somebody in the gob and ending up in court. Mr Hodgkin won't stand for it, so you don't do it.'

'I'm not that famous.'

'Hey, you almost are,' Jack said. '"Wonderboy Strikes". You have to be aware of it, OK? The newspapers don't mind seeing you with a different girl on your arm every week or the fact that you go clubbing in the big city, they'll accept that but they won't accept you being aggressive.'

'It would have been self-defence.'

'It doesn't matter. The public doesn't remember that, it only remembers the pictures of him bleeding and you going into court.'

'All right. I'm aware of it.'

Jack hesitated.

'I said I know.'

'Aye, I know you did.'

'So?'

The street was dark, it was late and Ruari resented Jack. It was like having a bloody older brother, always interfering and then he caved in.

'I'm frightened.'

Jack moved back slightly in surprise, Ruari thought.

'Of?'

'We're going home next week.'

Jack nodded, Ruari could only just see

him in the shadows of the town.

'I want never to go back to play and now I have to.'

'Yeah, well, you knew that.'

'I told meself it wasn't going to happen.'

'She's married,' Jack said, as heavily as if he was carrying a sack of coal.

'If you tell me there are plenty more fish in the sea I'll hit you,' Ruari said.

Jack laughed and his laughter bounced across the street at the buildings opposite and re-echoed at his side.

'It had to happen sometime and you can count on it that Hodgkin knows the time is right. You can go back there and show them,' he said.

'I want to but what if I don't score?'

'Oh, Christ, yes,' Jack said, 'the end of the world is nigh.'

'It's all right for you,' Ruari said. 'You don't have to score.'

'No, I just have to stop ten other blokes on the far side from scoring. Neither do you, not every time.'

'It's what I do.'

'Well, then, go back there and score, do it for the bitch who left you.'

He pretended that it was just another game, that it was nothing to do with Jenna, or Paul Maddison or Maddison's bastard father or Harry Philips, but the funny thing was that

193

when Ruari saw Philips as they came on to the pitch he went cold with temper, remembering how he had tried to manipulate Stan and how Stan, who was never the strongest man on the planet, couldn't handle it, and he thought Philips had known how weak Stan was, how poor they were and had done it on purpose to get Ruari cheap.

The anger had lasted him through seeing his home town again – actually he didn't see it, he just looked blindly through the coach windows, he didn't really see the fans or the town or the flash dressing rooms, all he saw was that rainy day when Jenna had told him that she had gone with Paul Maddison. He saw it over and over and it was silly really because it was what passed for a spring day in the north, freezing cold and very bright.

He just sat there in the dressing room and waited for the game. Other people were nervous, other people paced, threw up, couldn't eat. He was focused, he didn't even hear what Mr Hodgkin said, he just waited.

He went out on to the pitch and the home crowd reacted. Nothing had ever happened like that before. They booed and shouted and swore and even threw things on to the pitch and shrieked his name and called him traitor and arsehole and bastard and a good many other things which thankfully he couldn't make out and the home team grinned or glared depending on what they thought of him, and Ruari stopped at one point and wanted more than he had ever wanted in his life to run away, to go back down the tunnel and into the dressing room and hide against the huge roaring and spitting and cursing of the angry fans.

It was one of the scariest things he had ever experienced, so many of them, like a tidal wave. He couldn't breathe, he wouldn't be able to play and then he managed to look up and there was a single seagull soaring. He thought, stupidly that it was the same seagull which turned up all the time somehow, like a lucky mascot, a charm. Ridiculous how your thoughts just carried away.

There it was up in the blue sky all elegant and white and perfectly in control, and all he had to do was to follow it, to take control and he went cold and knew that he could do it. He had come back here to show Sorrel Maddison, to show them all what he could do and he was not going to waste the chance, he was not going to be intimidated by a lot of sheep or by any of the North End players who were more experienced. He could feel the hate coming off them and coming off the crowd and suddenly he didn't care.

He thought about Jenna and how she had let him go and none of it mattered any more. He was here because he was good, he had a right to be here and it was his home, it belonged to him. He could own this place, this pitch.

He could remember as a small boy hoping that one day he would be allowed to play here. This was not what he had envisaged but he knew that this was how it had been meant to be. He was master here and nobody was going to get in his way and spoil it, he had sacrificed too much to make a mess of it.

The kick-off came, the match began, the players moved and he could see that he was going to have the whole thing all to himself like a great big box of sweets that you got at Christmas, a selection box, that was it, where you got a Mars Bar and a Crunchie and a tube of Smarties and a bar of Dairy Milk and on the outside you got a game and his mam would sit with him by the fire on Christmas night and play snakes and ladders or whatever game it was with a dice and the back of the box and they would sit at the kitchen table and do the jigsaw she had bought.

He was just as happy here as he had been during those Christmases which had been the best of his life. Just him and his mam. Stan was never there, he was always out drinking and Ruari realized now that nobody could take such things away and nobody was going to take this. His mam was there watching, and no doubt she had bragged long and hard about her lad to her neighbours and this was his chance to make the whole thing memorable in all the best ways. He wouldn't let his mam down now.

Phil got the ball after a bit of scuffle and passed it to him and after that he just ran with it, like he had done so many times before. He knew how to do it, he knew the others couldn't get anywhere near, he was too far from them, too far in front, too far away and the goal was as big as the North Sea, it was the biggest space that he had ever seen. The gull didn't even flap its wings when he scored the first goal. He sank it not just neatly but totally, the goalkeeper didn't even see it coming past him.

The second was just before half-time and the two players from Dunelm North End who had been sent to see him off didn't get anywhere close before he netted it. The third was just after half-time and was a gift to another player, Selby, who acknowledged it afterwards with a clenched fist.

The fourth was another Phil goal, they did it so often that they almost took it for granted now and were, Mr Hodgkin had said, grinning, 'the well-oiled machine of the side'. The opposing team didn't score at all. Teeshaven were too fast and Ruari was too quick and too accurate.

The triumph Ruari felt made his head reel and spin but there was something bitter in it too and he could not help looking for Jenna in the crowd. Had she thought about him, was she aware that he was even in the game or did she care so little that she no longer noticed? She would not be there, he decided, why on earth should she be? She must know he was playing and that would be enough to keep her away and even though she had married the chairman's son it would not bring her there.

That night the others went home, but Ruari stayed and after he had been partied at a hotel by his mother and her friends he bedded a blonde with a local accent. He liked the way that she said his name, it sounded just like Jenna.

'We lost.'

Paul practically howled when he got home. Jenna already knew. She had known and dreaded Ruari coming back to North End even though she told herself it was not a proper homecoming at all, it was just as part of a team, for a few hours and would affect nothing and she tried not to let it get to her but it was hard.

She was hearing stories about how good he was. There were photographs in the newspapers of him all the time now, looking older and well dressed and always with a girl on his arm. He was 'a rising star'. She tried not to listen to the tide of publicity which began to follow him but it was impossible not to notice.

198

'Four goals,' Paul said, 'four.'

Jenna was about to point out that Ruari hadn't scored them all himself but it would have been a pointless exercise. He had set them up so it was the same thing really.

'We lost four-nil. My father is furious. Ruari Gallacher could have done it by himself, in fact he just about did. He made our players look like little lads. Harry was catatonic by the end of the match. He may never recover.'

Jenna wished she could have gone somewhere to get away from this. Paul had obviously forgotten all about her connection with Ruari. Paul, since they had lost the baby was also very attentive. Jenna could no longer accuse him of neglecting her. If he couldn't come home he telephoned and she could hear by the clearness of his voice that he was being honest with her. Two or three nights he would come back at three or four in the morning but she knew that it was part of his work to be at the clubs late and sometimes to socialize and she did not complain.

They were trying for another baby but nothing had happened. Month after month Jenna bled with monotonous regularity. Paul even took holidays. They went to Spain and sat on beaches and ate good food and swam in big blue hotel pools, it was the kind of life she had thought she wanted, the best of everything. Now it meant nothing, now that she could not conceive the idea of never having a child seemed to fill her whole life. She had lots of other things, of course, everything, as the saying went, she thought, that money could buy It was cold comfort.

Her clothes were expensive, she learned to drive but the trouble was that nothing held her attention now that she was not pregnant with the child which had cost her Ruari Gallacher. She had thought she would despise it but she ached for a baby and nothing had happened. She had to try to think of other things because she had the feeling that when you wanted something so badly nothing ever did happen.

'I could go out and get a job,' she suggested one night when she and Paul were alone in their bedroom. That was another thing, they were rarely alone. If they went out Paul liked a crowd though she did not become friends with any of his friends somehow and in the house his mother was often there and sometimes even his father and he would bring friends back and drink. Jenna privately thought that Paul drank far too much but at least he didn't drive when he drank.

'I pay enough tax as it is,' Paul said, 'it wouldn't be worth it.'

'Could we move, then?'

'Whatever for? I thought you liked being here.'

Just when she felt her mood slipping into self-pity Paul, who had just got into bed, looked at her.

'If you really want to move we can.'

'No, I don't, I was just...' I was just the spoiled kid, she thought but there was a part of her which thought they might manage a lot better if they didn't live with his parents but he so obviously liked being there and since they could not have a house like this on their own it seemed small-minded to insist.

'We could buy a place to go at weekends.'

Jenna kissed him for the thought, she was so grateful. Really she thought, she only had to ask and she could have anything.

'Your busiest time is the weekend. We'd never go.'

'We could, though. We could buy somewhere abroad, if you like. Spain, maybe?'

'Spain?'

'Why not?'

'It isn't practical, I can't go there by myself and I don't see the others coming and you don't even have time to take a weekend off.'

'I will,' he promised, 'and we'll go somewhere nice.'

Sorrel and Harry didn't speak after the match. They each tried not to blame the other. Sorrel knew that if he had behaved differently they would have secured Ruari for the team and Harry just felt stupid at the way that he had attempted to manoeuvre Gallacher and had failed and they both blamed Ruari Gallacher for being so much better than anybody had ever dreamed he would.

'I never saw a lad come from nowt at seventeen, going on eighteen, like that,' Harry said two weeks later when their team had finally won against Newcastle and they thought the balance was somewhat restored.

'They must do it all the time,' Sorrel said comfortingly.

They were sitting in his office and this was the first time they had spoken of it. He had had the board to contend with and had made polite noises. Footballers came and went, he had said, Gallacher was just having a good season. He could be injured – in fact in his best dreams that was what happened. Gallacher got hurt and was consigned to the wilderness with a team in the Third Division and his career was over.

Neither of them said that they wished they had done differently, that was football, you couldn't win them all, you had to use what judgement you could and you made mistakes, it was just that to make such a mistake in their own back yard was seemingly stupid. There was worse news the following week. Ruari was chosen to play in the under-23s for England. They didn't talk about that, it hurt too much.

'Would you like some Scotch?' was what Sorrel said and Harry looked gratefully at him.

Sorrel poured generously into short squat glasses and then he said, 'I've thought of a solution.'

'What's that?'

'We should buy him back.'

Harry took his glass carefully and looked above it at his boss.

'He's worth a small fortune.'

'They have no money. He's the only really decent player they possess. If they could get sufficient money for him they could buy two or three mediocre players and that's what they are, a mediocre team.'

Sorrel took a good slurp out of his glass. It was ten-year-old malt and excellent.

'It would make up for a lot of things,' Harry said.

'And the lad would be back where he belongs.'

'What would the fans think?'

'At first they would hate him, they wouldn't forget that he left here when he could have played for us but after he scored his first goal wearing our colours he would become their hero. You know what they're like, fickle, and they have short memories. And in a way we'd be getting our own back on what he did to us, in the nicest possible sense, of course,' Sorrel said and he grinned.

Harry sipped appreciatively at his Scotch and sighed.

'They need to sell him before their whole bloody ground falls to pieces,' he said. 'And we could win with a player like that, we've already got half a dozen good people, all we need is a really good striker, somebody who never misses.'

'I'll talk to the board about it, get them to agree,' Sorrel said.

Sixteen

Mr Hodgkin looked narrowly at Ruari as he came into his office and Ruari thought back and wondered if there was anything he had done wrong because Mr Hodgkin never looked like that at him and then he realized it wasn't exactly at him it was in spite of him somehow because Mr Hodgkin's eyes were still warm on him.

'Sit down, Ruari,' he said.

That was a bad beginning. You never got to sit in Mr Hodgkin's office. Mr Hodgkin sat down too. That was even worse. Mr Hodgkin didn't look at him for several seconds during which time Ruari tried to think of all the awful things that could have gone wrong and of anything he had done lately which might condemn him to criticism.

'We're in debt – the club, I mean, the club's badly in debt. We've been losing money for a long time and we need more good players. We have one or two but we don't have enough of the right quality. The ... management doesn't have enough money, we need a very big influx of cash from somewhere.' He stopped there.

'I know things are difficult,' Ruari said, trying to better it.

'Yes, well, the top and bottom of it is that we've had a very good offer for you. We didn't seek it though to be honest we were thinking about it.'

He stopped there. It had never occurred to Ruari that he could be sold and now that Mr Hodgkin had said it he sat there and his whole body turned cold. He felt as though the office floor was giving way and there was an endless chasm beneath it and it made him feel dizzy and sick. He couldn't even say anything, he had to concentrate on trying to keep his breath even.

'You're worth a great deal of money and although we don't want to get rid of you we can't think of another solution to our money worries.'

There was silence. It was almost on Ruari's tongue to say that they couldn't but of course that wasn't true, he was a contract to them and they could do what they liked. He wanted to get up and run out of the office, to run home to his mam like he was a little kid who had just been bested in the school-yard.

He could object, of course, he could complain, he could say he wasn't going but these were good people and they had given him his chance when nobody else saw the potential, they had looked after him, had paid him more than anybody else would have and they needn't have done that.

This man had seen his ability and put money behind it such as nobody else had or might have and they had looked after him. He could think of lots of clubs he might have gone to where his talent would have been spoiled or neglected or just not come to fruition as it had here. They had treated him like valuable china and because of it he was now worth a lot of money and because of it he had to go.

'Can I ask where?'

The question seemed to make things even harder. Mr Hodgkin looked down.

'Dunelm North End,' he said.

Ruari didn't believe it.

'I can't go back there,' he said, unable to stop himself. 'I won't. Do you know what this means?' but of course Mr Hodgkin didn't, how could he?

'Ruari—'

'I can't go back there, it's ... it's a horrible place, it... I've got a house here and friends and ... and a life. I'm not going. You can do what you like to me, I'm not going.' He got up from his chair and slammed out of Mr Hodgkin's office. He didn't think anybody had ever slammed out of it before but then maybe Mr Hodgkin had never given anybody such a reason.

He tried to talk himself into it, he would get good money out of it, it was time to move on, did it really matter so very much? But it did.

He didn't say anything to anybody he had the feeling that if he didn't talk about it he would wake up from the nightmare, it couldn't be true or real, not when they had all tried so hard and had managed to establish something so good.

Nobody said anything more for several days, none of the directors, or the chairman, an accountant who was a decent man and fatherly and the least like Sorrel Maddison that any man could be and Ruari was glad and grateful for that. They didn't even send him to talk to Ruari and Mr Hodgkin said nothing more.

Jack was more to the point when Ruari drove over to his house and they were by themselves. Jack's wife, Nora, had taken the two little kids away, she was a tactful young

207

woman and she could see there was something the matter and that it was something Ruari didn't want to talk about in front of her.

'You're bigger than the club,' Jack said, moving around awkwardly on his new white leather sofa.

'What do you mean?'

'I mean all the stories are about you, every time anybody breathes out it's about you. The whole thing is about you. The club has to be more than one player. You have to go.'

'Well, thanks very much, Jack,' Ruari said really annoyed. He had thought Jack would be horrified, would be sympathetic, might even talk to Mr Hodgkin for him, though now he came to think of it, it was a long shot and even daft for him to think such a thing.

'Oh, come on, you know it's true. You're the only really good player we've got.'

'That's not so, you're good and Phil and Pete and–'

'Yes, but not like you. Players like you come forward once or twice in a generation. It wouldn't matter what position you played, nobody can teach you anything, you were born knowing it and it shows. You make everybody else look slow and daft.'

'That's not true,' Ruari said.

'You're good with both feet, you don't have a weak foot like other people, you play like some men paint and some men write, you've got it all, you bastard. You're faster than everybody else, more skilled with the ball than anybody else, sometimes in a match you hardly touch the ground.

'I've never seen anything like it. I've seen you come down the field from nowhere and leave everybody standing watching, like they didn't have legs, you're so fast. They don't know where you're going or how you do it, it's a natural God-given thing, it can't be taught. You outplay everybody so that they don't understand. You were born to do this and now you have to move on because this club cannot sustain you, it hasn't got the players to match you any more.'

'They'll be able to afford to buy other players when I go.'

'Yes, they will.'

'I have good reasons for not wanting to go back there.'

'I know you do,' Jack said, 'but you're going to have to go.'

'How will I manage? I can hardly go and live back with my mam, can I?'

'I don't suppose she expects it.'

Or wants it, Ruari thought. His mam had got used to being on her own and he thought she liked it, knowing he was doing what he wanted, where he wanted. He felt like he would be intruding if he went back to the little terraced house.

'The fans hate me.'

'They won't hate you when you belong to them. They resent you for having left but once you get back there it'll be different. You're one of them–'

'Not any more. I hate the place.'

'How can you hate it?'

'I do. I never wanted to go back there and live. I thought if I was being sold it would be to Manchester United or – or Arsenal–'

'In fact anywhere else would have done.'

'Even bloody Newcastle would have been better than this.'

'Oh no, it wouldn't,' Jack said. 'You couldn't go to Newcastle, some poor Geordie bastard would bang you over the head.'

Ruari couldn't help smiling slightly at that, which was what Jack had intended all along.

'You won't be there to moan over,' was Ruari's other complaint.

'No, I know. Just think how I'll feel when I play against you and I have to try and stop you putting the sodding ball into the back of the frigging net,' Jack said.

Paul stood in the doorway of his father's office in the football club. Sorrel hadn't heard him and looked up almost instinctively

'Oh, I didn't see you there.'

Paul didn't come inside, he stood there but Sorrel could see that there was something very wrong.

'What's happened?' he said.

'My father's turned into a sodding idiot,' Paul said.

Sorrel sat back in his chair. There had been a time when his son would never have said such things to him and he was amazed even now that they had been working together for some time and worked well together.

'I had to find out from Harry,' Paul said and he came inside and slammed the door so hard that it shook and he stood there glaring at Sorrel. 'Why didn't you tell me?'

Sorrel understood now.

'It wasn't anything to do with you. You aren't interested in football.'

'I'm interested in my wife.'

'Oh, don't be soft,' Sorrel said dismissively and would have gone back to his papers.

'You're bringing him back here?'

'I've bought him.'

'You didn't consult me.'

'Why would I? Paul, you know a great deal about how to run the clubs and the betting shops by now. There is nothing you know about football which is valuable in spite of having spent most of your Saturdays at the ground for the past two seasons.'

'It can't mean that much to you that you would buy him and bring him back here.'

'I've always wanted to,' Sorrel said. 'I've always regretted letting him go. It was a mistake and as far as football was concerned it was a major mistake and I flattered myself that I knew talent.

'I was mean and because of that for the sake of a few quid a week I could have had him and didn't. Now I can, it's that simple. They're broke and I can afford him even though it's costing me so much more than if I'd signed him up to begin with that it makes me want to retch. Now is there anything else?'

'You don't like him, that's why you want him back, because he bettered you.'

'He did, yes, and he was a lad. Men with brains, influence and vast experience have tried to better me and they've never done it but that little bastard ... he was seventeen and he got away.'

'And do you think you're bettering him now?'

'No, I'm big enough to admit that I made a mistake. I want his talent for my team. I want my team to win. Is that basic enough for you?'

'This club cannot matter more to you than your family. You don't like him.'

'No, I don't like him, what I know of him, which is nothing personally. I think he's a jumped-up little shit for the way that he behaved in the first place but he has magic feet and I admire that. I know it's nothing but instinct but I like it. And for that I'm prepared to put up with him and I feel like

I've won because I know that he doesn't want to come back here and I can make him so I'm feeling a little bit powerful and if it's pathetic I will learn to live with myself.'

'But Jenna—'

Sorrel looked patiently at him.

'That lad has had more lasses than you've had hot dinners. What the hell makes you think he remembers a nice little lass like Jenna?'

'A nice little lass? Your daughter-in-law is a nice little lass?'

'Aye, she is,' Sorrel said. 'She's a grand little lass and it's more than could be said of most others. And you should look after her better.'

Paul said nothing to this, he walked out.

Ruari drove home through the rain in the early summer. It wasn't a long way but it certainly felt like it, like another world, like he was going back and things would be just as bad or even worse than what he had left.

There was a wind behind the rain but the E-type Jaguar, which he had finally bought because he had fallen in love with it, was low and long and most of the wind and rain went above it and it was a good car so it cut whatever didn't go over the top as it had done on other nights when the weather was vile. He had long since ceased to notice such things but tonight because he was coming home the car seemed buffeted as though in some peculiar way it wanted to turn back just like he did.

It seemed to him the least public way of returning. He had told his mother he would wait a day or two and now he had changed his mind, there was no point in putting things off so he had announced his return only to Sorrel Maddison's secretary and she had booked him in at a hotel.

It was evening but not yet dark when he reached the outskirts of the town and although he tried very hard not to he could not help driving into the area which had been his home.

The houses were still there, long rows of them dropping down steeply towards the sea. He left the car some way off and walked. It was dusk and he was glad of that. Even here or maybe especially here there was a possibility that he would be recognized. In the near darkness he was just another tall slender young man, rather better dressed than everybody else but nobody could see and he kept his head down and stayed in the shadows as best he could.

It had not altered as much as he had thought or even hoped and the details of his childhood came back at him, the fish shop on the corner was still there and the un-made back lane where he had spent so many evenings. He was still able to imagine he

214

could hear the sound of the children playing in the street as he dribbled the ball up and down the lane.

He had reached their house now, the back of it, the yard. It seemed smaller but it was not really and the lights were on in the kitchen. He stood outside until it was quite dark and even the dogs had gone home in the rain and then he walked slowly back to his car, trying not to think about Jenna. He had promised himself he would not. There was nothing to be gained from it.

He wasn't going to go and see his mother tonight, he had wanted to see the place privately so that he could come to terms with how he felt and he was not going to go and stay there, she had not even tried to talk him into it. She understood perhaps better than anybody how his fame could ruin things and neither of them wanted it to spoil the little house which was her home. She would come and see him at the hotel when he let her know that he was there.

He began to walk back up the street and was suddenly confronted by a gang of boys. In the lamplight he could see that one of them had a knife and the knife was pointed at him. It was almost funny he thought that he had to be attacked for the first time in his life in the street where he had been born and brought up and left years ago. There were half a dozen of them so it was far too many for him to handle. The one with the knife clicked his fingers and Ruari was in the act of taking his wallet from his jacket pocket when the boy next to the leader said, 'Bloody hell, it's Ruari Gallacher.'

This was not necessarily good news, a lot of people round here hated that he had left, did not know or care that his choices had seemed slight, they regarded him as a traitor in the war between the different clubs.

There was nothing more important than cash in his wallet so despite the fact that the knife disappeared and the boys moved with the excitement of nervousness and were not as far as he could judge hostile any more, their eyes beginning to shine, he pushed the wallet at the leader.

'Here, take it,' he said, surprised and rather pleased at how they had reacted, watched them hesitate, shoved it into the boy's hand and then he strolled off as nonchalantly as he could manage just in case they recovered and decided they wanted to damage him. He waited until he got to the end of the road and then he ran, reaching his car by taking several short cuts down narrow alleys. He had long since lost them when he reached his car.

'Jesus,' he said, grinning in derision and breathing heavily, 'and you call yourself fit.'

He drove through the middle of the town. It was still raining. You never forgot how much it rained here, how even in the summer like now it rained so very often that if there was more than one fine day together people got excited and sat outside their houses, those who had no garden would sit on the front street rather he thought as Americans sat on their porches except that here you were right on the pavement but it was a sociable thing to do too because people passing would stop to chat. There was no chance of that tonight, the rain was relentless and gave the town a cleaner look than he felt sure it normally had.

It wasn't a big town, he had forgotten that too or maybe when you were younger it looked bigger. It wasn't as big as Newcastle or as small as Durham, as industrial as Middlesbrough or as busy as Sunderland but it had pits here, though a lot in similar places had closed. These were the big coastal pits, some of which employed thousands of men.

The town was big enough to boast a very classy hotel and it was here that he was staying. He would feel safe from the crowds and as anonymous as he could be. It was set in big grounds and had a long winding drive so had been some kind of country house in the century before this one, he thought. Somebody had lived here lavishly at one time.

He parked neatly at the end of the building

and walked inside and there was a reception desk and the usual dog-leg staircase. He had been in lots of hotels like this one. The receptionist looked up with a ready smile, recognized him and smiled even more.

'Good evening sir,' she said and pushed the register towards him and when he had signed it she gave him a key. 'If you would like dinner–'

'No, thanks, I'm fine.'

'Room service?'

'Possibly, later. Thank you.' Ruari took the key and his suitcases and made off swiftly towards the lift while she was still offering help with his luggage.

When he opened the door of his room he let go of the suitcases, closed the door and sighed. It was the biggest room in the hotel, he had no doubt. It was massive. Sorrel Maddison had ordered it. Best of all when he went over to the window it had a great big balcony and not far beyond it was the sea and the moon was out there giving light. He had forgotten how beautiful it was.

It was the sound of his childhood, he thought, opening the doors, the best sound, the one he always went to when things were wrong and even when they weren't, and now the sea was wonderful. He missed it. There were a lot of things he didn't miss but he missed this, it was the only thing which was better here than anywhere else on earth.

The waves were parading up the beach in spectacular style. The rain had stopped and he stood there in the darkness and watched the sea.

He had thought he had left nothing here but he was wrong. Somehow everything had been left here, all the things he had wanted to forget, all the things which he had thought he had bettered returned to him as though the time in between had counted for nothing. He was tired, he told himself, that was all it was and he missed everything and he wished he had gone home except that he didn't want to burden his mother and her tiny house with reporters and people looking through the windows, it wasn't fair and he knew she had been relieved when he had declined her offer.

The following morning Ruari awoke and couldn't remember where he was for a few seconds and then knew. He was back in North End. From beyond the window the seagulls were kicking up a fuss and in the next room a couple were shouting at each other. He phoned down and ordered tea and toast and bacon and eggs then went into the bathroom and stood under a warm shower for a long time.

When he had eaten he felt better. He opened the windows. The sea was calm, the seagulls had stopped squawking and you

219

could see way out to the horizon. It made him feel like a little lad again. The Farne Islands were not a long way off. He could remember being taken there in a boat and being sick and the wonderful birds, the kittiwakes fighting in the sea, the puffins were his favourites, soundless, their wonderful wings beating in the air and how he had loved their spectacular orange beaks.

St Cuthbert had lived on Inner Farne. Cuthbert had been his favourite saint as a child, who could live in such a place and survive and yet it was so beautiful on a day like this? What would Cuthbert have done for warmth, sustenance, when it was comfortless as it so often was here in the north? It had always seemed to Ruari that the Farnes and Lindisfarne in particular were full of God somehow.

Maybe when you really had God you didn't need all the rest. He had long since given up on God. He couldn't remember his last confession. He was ashamed. He didn't want to go anywhere that day, officially he was not there but the newspapers would soon know and after that there would be no peace so he did nothing, he sat on the balcony, it was a beautiful day, warm and almost still, he read, he had meals sent up and he talked to his mother on the telephone.

In the early evening the telephone shrilled.

He left the sunshine and went back inside and picked it up. Tony Evans was in reception. What the hell was he doing there? was Ruari's first reaction. Tony Evans was North End's best striker, a tall good-looking confident young man. When they had met in matches Ruari had always wanted to knock his teeth down his throat, he was such an arrogant little shit.

Tony came up, smiling, holding out his hand and saying, 'Welcome to North End.'

'I'm from here,' Ruari reminded him.

'Are you really? I thought you were from Manchester. I was going to show you around.'

'That's nice of you but I'm sure I can find my way.'

'I was only being friendly,' Tony said. 'I tell you what, I'm going to a party tonight. Why don't you come along?'

'I don't think so.'

Tony looked at him in a curious manner.

'Oh, I think you might want to,' he said, 'I think it's probably expected of you.'

'Really? Why would that be?'

Seventeen

Jenna had gone over in her mind many times the way that she and Ruari would meet again but none of it stood up to what actually happened. It was early summer. The trees were bright green from all the rain and the dark stones of the house were covered in sunshine. They had been looking forward to a lovely day. It was Paul's birthday.

It started off misty and then the sun got out and was hot. There was to be a party at the house and all their friends had been invited. Faye and she had gone to London for their clothes and Jenna was happy with what they had chosen, Faye had a pale pink dress with flowing sleeves and a square neck and she was wearing yellow and orange with thin velvet ribbons.

The food was laid out in the garden on big tables and people flocked to the front of the house. The guests had arrived. Jenna could hear the sound of champagne corks popping and then she heard Tony Evans's Lotus Elan as it roared up the street. He was late as usual.

When it stopped she could even hear the sound of the engine dying away and of

Tony's voice, always louder than everybody else's. He was North End's playboy lots of girlfriends, drank champagne and had aspirations to be rich. He owned clothing shops in Newcastle and wanted to open a nightclub. Sorrel thought he was a very enterprising young man and encouraged him in his business ventures and even invested in them, Jenna thought.

As Tony idled up the path toward the house she caught sight of him moving through the garden and beyond the beech hedge. He was wearing an expensive cream suit. He had somebody with him. No doubt one of the other footballers. Everybody had been invited.

The other man was taller than Tony, black haired, Jenna could make him out now. He was wearing a grey suit and a white shirt, he had cream skin and there was something about the way that he moved, flowing and yet contained, that she recognized in that instant from the way he had spent his childhood learning to control a ball in the unmade back lane among the puddles outside their houses. Her head told her it couldn't be, that he was still not home and she had been safe from this, but her heart knew him in an instant. It was Ruari.

She panicked. Had he been invited? He wasn't supposed to be here yet surely. They came into view, chatting, Tony smiling like an idiot. He would not know how very embarrassing this was going to be for everyone, or had he done it on purpose? She began to think that he was just stupid but whichever way it was it was unacceptable. Sorrel would have a fit.

Tony was gesturing with his hands. Everybody was looking now, had stopped talking. There was silence throughout the garden so that she could hear the birds singing, feel the slight breeze which came off the sea.

The people gathered here were used to footballers but Ruari they thought of as some kind of traitor because he had been a local boy genius who sold his talent to the highest bidder. He had left and gone to their deadliest rivals and now had deigned to come back.

From the corner of her eye she could see Sorrel, the way that he brought his shoulders up and then let them back down; he watched without blinking as Tony brought Ruari across the garden and into their midst. Sorrel ignored Tony. He didn't care how rude it looked, she could see. His gaze went to Ruari like an arrow and she knew then that he had expected Ruari back, had even perhaps planned it like this.

'Mr Gallacher,' he said, 'how nice that you could join us.' His voice was like early morning frost.

Ruari smiled. It didn't go anywhere near

his eyes, it was the thinnest smile that Jenna had ever seen. They were, she thought, the nearest thing to gladiators out of a Roman arena, eyeing one another. How strange.

Worse still somehow Ruari had changed almost beyond bearing. He was not a boy any longer, she looked in vain for anything beyond his appearance which was familiar and could find nothing. That was a shock. He had always seemed so young to her and vulnerable, it had been one of his best qualities. It was gone. He was taller, she thought, and his eyes were like iced puddles in the back lane when they were children, so blue that they were almost black with a silver sheen.

'Mr Maddison,' he said, 'good evening.'

He didn't even sound the same. There was no local lilt to his voice, it was cool, flat, nothing like the footballers she was used to. He looked and sounded so classy, Jenna thought, pleased, and then realized that she was on the other side. How strange, she hadn't known. And the boy genius carried an aura with him, she had seen it slightly in other men but it was so well defined in Ruari, as though he knew exactly who he was, that he was the best, sure of himself, so confident.

She had observed it many times watching him play on television, he saw more than other men, he saw the goal, he saw the ball, he saw the spaces where you would not think there were any and he could move very fast, it left other footballers rooted, it brought the crowd to their feet.

He was poetry she could see, not just on the field but off it as he moved and did not move and every woman present knew it and there was something about it which was devastatingly attractive. She was horrified. He had been hers and she felt cheated somehow. He had gone and this man was in his place, famous, objective somehow calculating. There was nothing left of the boy she had loved.

It was difficult even to take your eyes off him and he knew it though he didn't mind or didn't care, he accepted that other people were drawn to him, looked at him, it had become part of who he was. And he was successful and if there were women in the room who weren't aware of the attraction of all that, Jenna couldn't see them. They were staring.

Then Ruari saw Jenna and he smiled and the second smile held no more warmth than the first. He covered the space between them in a second. Funny that. All that time and yet he was in front of her.

'Hello, Jenna,' he said, 'how are you?' So simple, so direct, so cool as though he wanted everybody to see that he no longer cared for her or for any of them.

Somehow it broke the spell, the music started up, trays of champagne were carried around, people began to talk. Jenna extended a hand and he took it in slender fingers. His grasp was light but firm as though he shook hands very often and didn't think about it.

'Ruari,' she said, 'how nice to see you. How's your mother?'

'She's fine.'

Ruari looked beyond her, as though he was bored. Jenna felt a pain cross her chest that was almost physical. And then, to her relief and also to her alarm, she saw that it was the band he was looking at.

'Perhaps you'd like to dance,' he said.

Jenna wanted to run away but she did not know how to refuse and he took her by the arm. He had such a good grip on her that she would have had to make a fuss to get away. The music was slow. He took her into his arms and Jenna wanted more than anything in the world for Paul to come across and claim her. She was so humiliated.

'How's your marriage?' he said, looking her in the eyes.

This was taking frankness too far, Jenna thought, and she was amazed that he should say such a thing. Had she been wrong about the way that he looked? Was it all a show? Did he not realize how bitter it made him sound? Did he not care?

And to her horror she realized that it proved how he felt about her. That he felt anything at all amazed her. She had thought he was a different person but underneath the gloss and the success he was just the same. She was uplifted at the idea that he even cared and downhearted for him that he had not moved on. She wanted him to find somebody else but dreaded it.

'Fine. What about you?'

'Oh, I didn't marry. The girl I loved gave me up for a clown with a nice car.'

She concentrated on not crying, on not running away though she badly wanted to. People would talk, Paul would be angry at such a display. She had been right, he had not got over it. Her heart beat hard and she wanted to grab his hand and run out of there with him. That made her want to cry more.

She had worked so hard to be Paul Maddison's wife, to greet him with joy when he came home and be pleased, and her world had shattered in those few minutes since Ruari had walked into the garden. It made her want to weep, as though everything she had gone through with Paul and with the baby and with his family counted for nothing at all, her marriage evaporated like early morning summer mist.

She drew back slightly and his fingers stopped her from going any further from him. The trouble was she liked the feel of his hand on her back just as she had always done, the pressure, as though it was the only thing which mattered to him, having her there so near. It made her wonder why they had been apart for so long. Did he feel again that incredible attraction or was he taking revenge here? She didn't know and she didn't want to know, she wanted to run away, to run back to Paul, to have Paul rescue her. Where was he?

'I have a nice car now. Maybe I could compete or does my background get in the way?'

'Don't.'

'Are you happy?'

'Don't you want me to be?' She looked up at him but she couldn't see him very well because her eyes were wet. 'When you love people don't you want the best for them?'

'I never heard anything quite so stupid,' he said. 'Paul Maddison is an idiot.'

'There are worse things for men to be,' Jenna said.

'You're right,' he said, 'to be called a genius is much worse.'

'It's what you are.'

'Einstein was, Mozart was. I play a game for my living. It makes people feel better to think they've seen genius, but it's just a talent. I'm very good at it and so are a dozen men every few years and people always think they're the best because they want to be close to something like that, they want to be part of history, to have seen the best even when there's no such thing. It makes them feel good, makes them feel part of something. I'm just a football player. I don't even enjoy it any more.'

Jenna hadn't thought of this.

'Why not?' she said.

'Because when I play badly they curse me and scream and spit and when I play well they think it's them doing it, that they make the difference, and they don't. I have to score goals, I have to do it all the time and I'm told what to do. I'm here because I was told to be, I'm Sorrel Maddison's puppet. He bought me.'

'But you're ... you have so much.'

'I would have given it all to have you. I wish I had known what it was going to be like. I would have stayed in the shipyard.'

Jenna stopped dancing and when he let her go she moved back a little way. She wanted to run like she had when she was a young girl but everybody was watching so she smiled and pretended nothing was wrong.

She felt like she was burning, as though nothing in her life mattered any more. She wanted so badly to go back to her room now but it was not late enough, people would remark, maybe they would even remember.

She remembered, only too well, and it seemed to her as though neither she nor

Ruari would ever escape the back lane. Maybe nobody ever did escape the first years of their lives, they spent the whole time trying to get back there to whatever joy or misery they had first known, perhaps wanting to change everything. She wanted to change what she had done so much, more now than ever.

Paul appeared as the music ended and he looked straight at Ruari and he said in soft tones, 'Keep your bastard hands off my wife.'

'Paul!' Jenna said in a loud whisper even though nobody else was within earshot.

Ruari said nothing. He was in no position to take on the Maddisons. He was miserable. There was nothing to bring comfort to him on cold wet Saturdays, when the fans, full of brown ale, were screaming abuse at him because he hadn't scored.

It had been a very long day. When Paul put an arm around Jenna and led her away he was only glad at the idea of going back to the hotel. It was almost like going home, going back there, it was such a relief. He was looking forward to seeing from his balcony the place where he had been born and brought up and the sea and then he would remember what it had been like when Jenna had been his, when she had loved him.

It would not have been so bad if he had not

been able to remember and stupidly it was not really to do with how she felt under his hands, beneath him, it was to do with her voice calling him down the back lane. There had been other girls much more beautiful beneath him and in other ways, girls with silken limbs and warm eyes, and he had liked them all, had even, he thought, been in love once or twice but they were not Jenna.

As he went back to his hotel, when he drove through the town, he saw the fish shop on the end of the road and suddenly he could smell the chips and the vinegar running through them and the warm acid smell was the best in the world, he knew.

He was that boy again, making music with a football and avoiding the way the road went up and down in the back lane, the puddles with rainbows in them and Jenna coming back with the fish and chips for her family and the day dark with rain and the sea behind it all crashing to the shore. It was never like that any more and if she didn't know it then at least he had the memories.

When it was late he stood there on the balcony thinking of how when he was young he would watch the sun go down, the sea darken until you couldn't see the beach any more and the sand grew cold under your feet if you ventured down there. He and Jenna on the beach with the bitter North Sea which even in August had not warmed through but it was theirs, the beach and the sea and the little town and the back lane and the lights coming on as the day drew towards its end, he in his little house and Jenna next door, never together but never apart. It had not been as good as that again and now he was beginning to believe that it never would be.

Maybe it was all you could expect. Maybe some people never had that. Why should they? Maybe he had been lucky in that Jenna had loved him once and he had had so much since. He had been able to help his mother, the little she would let him, with nothing more than a stupid ability in his feet which somehow connected to his head. It was not intelligence, it was not education, it was nothing more than instinct. It had not given him what he had wanted, what he had planned, but maybe it wasn't supposed to.

He went back inside, the air was chilled even in early summer here, he thought fondly. He opened a bottle and poured himself a glass of wine and he stood inside with the doors shut. Even then you could hear the sound of the sea. It was enough to comfort him, enough to sleep by.

Jenna was so angry with Paul that she left him at the party and went upstairs. It was not long before he followed her into their bedroom.

233

'How dare you do that?' she said.

'I don't trust him.'

'What about me? Don't you trust me? People are going to talk if you behave like that. You've got nothing to worry about. I don't care about him. It was finished a very long time ago.'

'Was it? It didn't look like that.'

'Then what on earth did it look like? We danced.'

'He couldn't take his eyes off you and you ... you watched him from the minute he arrived.'

'I didn't know he was going to be here, it was a shock, that's all. Somebody could have told me.'

'The bastard wasn't invited.'

'I imagine he would feel obliged. All the other footballers were here, after all, and your father looked to me as though he knew.'

'My father turns everything into business.'

'I think he likes them, wants to invite them. Your father's very sociable,' Jenna said.

Paul laughed. 'I've never heard it called that before.'

'What do you mean?'

'You don't know what my father's like, you don't see anything. He doesn't care about anybody, all he really cares about is his bloody football club. He can't stand Gallacher but he had to come back because he's

234

so good and because it was the best thing for the club.'

'And isn't he right?'

'I don't care. I don't want the bastard back here dancing with you and coming over all smarmy and clever.'

'It means nothing to me,' Jenna said and even as she said it she realized what a lie it was. Ruari would always matter to her but he, like Sorrel and Paul, cared more for other things and she was not about to make any more mistakes with men, she had learned her lesson. She had the feeling that Ruari only wanted her now because she belonged to somebody else and he had to have everything he wanted, he had always been like that, maybe they all were. It was easier in some ways because he was nothing like he had been and that was the feeling that lingered with her. Between them she and Ruari had destroyed the boy and girl they had been.

It was only two days later that Ruari telephoned her at home in the early evening. She was alone. She was nearly always alone. Faye went out with friends and did not ask her and anyhow they were older and Paul was never at home at that hour. She had taken to drinking gin and sitting in the garden and reading and she was just coming in for her first gin and tonic when the

235

telephone rang and she answered it.

'It's me,' he said, 'can I see you?'

She was astonished at his nerve.

'Certainly not,' she said.

'Why not?'

She didn't answer that, she was suddenly so frustrated.

'Are you busy?'

'No, not really.' She cursed herself instantly. Could she not lie to him, could she not manage? She tried to remind herself of how remote, how different he had looked and even the sound of his voice was different but there was enough of her that cared so that she wished the telephone call would never end.

'Come to the hotel. We could have a drink. It's been such a long time.' When she said nothing he said, 'I'm sorry for the way I behaved, I haven't seen you in so long, it would be nice.'

'How can I do that, everybody would see, and besides...'

'There's nobody about and you could come in the back way. Please. I just want to talk to you. There's no harm in it, Jenna, please.'

She went. She tried not to but it was no good, she could not help it somehow. It was a lovely summer's evening and she was quite alone as she almost always was. All the friends they had were couples, most of them by now had children and in the evenings they went home to one another or to their babies and it hurt, the being left out, the wishing she had the same kind of thing. She was starting to think she would never move on from where she was now, so she went.

Reporters were camped out at the front, she could see half a dozen of them lounging in the shade, chatting, bored no doubt that nothing was happening. She parked her car around to the side in among the trees in the shadows and she met no one and slid around by the side of the building and up the back stairs which the staff used and nobody saw her. She held her breath trying to remember which floor and which number and she prayed that there were no cleaning ladies about or any of the guests in the long corridor, thickly carpeted, which she had to negotiate. She banged on the door and he opened it. She took a deep breath and tried to keep her face in a polite smile.

It was the first time she had tried to look at him objectively. It wasn't simple. He wore expensive clothes and wore them well and easily and he was tall and in very good shape as a sportsman would be at his age. His hair was as black as a raven and his eyes were icy blue. His voice was soft and only a slight lilt betrayed his northern origins. He was sure of himself but in a polite way. He wasn't loud or boastful or difficult. He didn't greet her with kisses or try to get hold of her or launch into explanations, he just asked her to come in and it was a lovely room, full of light which it would be from the long day and clear sky. It was the best time of the year.

The first thing she noticed in the room was the double doors which led on to the balcony and the view he had of the beach and the sea. It reminded her of a good many things she thought she had long since forgotten, she could smell the beach and because of it the back lane somehow and all the things that they had forfeited. How on earth, she thought for the thousandth time, had things come to this?

She went out on to the balcony and watched the view and wished that she had not come here and thought of how she had nothing to stay at home for, Paul was never there and ... if only we had had a child, if only the baby had lived, everything would have been different, she thought. Paul would have loved a baby and I would have had something so positive in my life I wouldn't be standing here like any idiot wishing to have back the past when I know very well that I can't do anything about it. He didn't follow her out, he stood inside and she could feel him hesitating as though he was nervous, as though he half wished he hadn't asked her there or wasn't there himself and yes, he must wish that, that he was back at Teeshaven where things must be less complicated.

Still he didn't say anything and the silence went on until finally she felt irritated that he had got her there and apparently for no reason and she grew tired of the view and turned and he was standing behind her watching her carefully and he said, 'Would you like a drink? There's champagne.'

She shook her head but, maybe just for something to do, he went over and took the champagne from the fridge.

'Don't open it for me,' she said.

'Don't you like champagne?'

'Not particularly.'

'Only rich people dislike champagne,' he said.

'You must have drunk gallons over the years.'

'I have.'

She watched him open it expertly with a quick twist of the bottle and like good champagne it popped discreetly and he poured it into two tall glasses and then he handed her a glass. Jenna moved into the room and took it. She sipped it. It was very good, cold. The summer evening light spilled in at the window. She didn't know what to say and she thought how strange that was, whatever had they talked about, it had always been so easy.

Ruari smiled slightly

'Come and see the view.'

'I know the view and I've just seen it.'

'That's why,' and then he went out on to the balcony. Jenna followed him. A warm wind was coming off the sea, most unusual. It made her think of how things had been when they were very young and it was the last thing she wanted to think of. She tried to concentrate, looking out to sea as though there was something interesting on the horizon.

'How's Paul after seeing me yesterday?'

'Oh, don't let's do that,' she appealed and he looked at her. 'You didn't really ask me over here to resurrect it all, surely. You must know why I married him but I do care for him now, I do love him.'

He turned and Jenna saw the anger in his face in spite of the way he tried to hide it and then his eyes sparked and he said, 'How dare you talk to me about love after what you did to me?'

Jenna was astonished. 'You're still angry? After all this time? We're different people—'

'Rubbish,' he said and he looked at her.

'You're very different,' she said.

'You know nothing about me other than what you see in the gutter press. I'm exactly the same as I was. Talk about ruining things for people. How is your marriage?'

Jenna had to stop herself from throwing

her champagne at him.

'You already asked me that. There's nothing wrong with my marriage,' she said.

'No? Where are the children?'

The pain that went through her was physical and she had to put her glass down on the little table beside her.

'I lost my child after you left. Didn't you know? I miscarried late and badly and I don't seem able to have any more. You hate me?'

'I did know and I'm sorry. You could have come to me then,' he said.

Jenna stared at him.

'You knew?'

'Of course I knew but I thought you'd married Paul because you wanted him. You told me that was why. I wish I could hate you,' he said evenly, still looking at her and he looked all over her face as though he wished to imprint the look of her on his mind. 'I've always loved you. After a while it becomes bitterness, that big empty nothing that nobody else can fill. It's sort of like gangrene. And I always think with every woman that comes along that she'll rescue me. Do you love Paul now have you sort of grown into it? I think you must, you're still with him.'

Jenna could hardly breathe.

'Certainly,' she said.

'You bloody liar,' he said and that was

when she threw the champagne over him and she thought, Yes, I did it on purpose so that he would get hold of me because that was what he did. He kissed her until she wanted him so much that she pushed hard from him, breathing as though she had been running a long way He let her go. Jenna wanted to cry the tension between them was so taut, and while she stood, fighting for breath so that she would not disgrace herself, he realized how upset she was and that was when for the first time since he had come back she saw a little glint of the boy that he had been because he tried to defuse the situation. He smiled slightly into her eyes and said softly, 'Stop chucking champagne at me, it's expensive.'

It made her laugh, which was what he had intended all along she thought.

'You taste wonderful,' she said.

'Is that an invitation?'

'Of course it's not.'

'Anybody would after Paul,' he said.

'You're being nasty about him. I'm very fond of him.'

'Oh God,' he said.

'He's nicer than most men. A lot of women would kill for a husband like Paul.'

'You sound like somebody forty,' he said. 'Comfort, what you're used to, when in fact you lie in bed at night and——'

'Don't,' she said, 'it isn't true.'

'Isn't it?' he said, idly. 'There goes another of my dreams.'

Jenna looked at him.

'I have missed you so much.'

He took her into his arms again and this time she let him hold her because that was all it was as though he had divined it was as close as she would allow him. She felt right for the first time in years, her eyes closed against his shoulder.

Nobody was like him and though she had tried to make Paul as important if not more so it had never worked. She cared about Paul, she would not have betrayed him, but this man was her soul mate. She knew it was a stupid expression and trite but she felt that she would have wasted her whole life if they had not known one another.

'You think I can't love anybody else?' he said, when she made as if to let go.

'That would be ... conceited and...'

'Yes, but it's true, isn't it? You don't want me to.'

'I wouldn't act like that.'

'You were pregnant, that's why you let me leave.

'I had to.'

'You could have pretended it was mine.'

'I wouldn't do that.'

'I would never have known. If the baby had looked like Paul would I have known? He has the same colouring as you.'

243

'I would have known. I couldn't do that to you.'

'No, but you could do worse and you did just by staying there instead of coming with me.'

She stared at him.

'That wasn't how it was.'

'Oh, I see. You did it for me. You let me go and stay away from you and you married somebody you didn't really care about that much and you kept us apart all this time because you thought your kid might look like Paul.'

'It was his child.'

'Parenting isn't just biology you know, Jenna.'

'I would have deceived you.'

'Honesty is a very overrated thing,' he said.

Jenna smiled and drew well away from him.

'What?' he said.

'You're so intelligent.'

That made him laugh.

'Oh yes? It was my body you wanted me for.'

'It was indeed,' she said. 'Can we try to be friends?'

'Friends?'

'It's all that's left. I married Paul. He's ... attentive and kind and I have no right to betray him. He did nothing wrong, he married me because he cared about me and because he wanted our child. It isn't his fault it went wrong. As far as I'm concerned this is for life.'

'Things aren't for life any more, everything's changed.'

'I will never leave him, so don't go thinking it. Please let's try to be civilized about this. I don't want you and Paul at loggerheads. There's no reason for it to be. Now either we are friends or we never meet again, I never speak to you again. Which is it to be?'

She watched the fight go on as his face worked and he looked down to hide it and then away for distraction. She waited for him to make the decision and then she said, 'We were friends first. You were always my best friend.'

And then finally he said, 'All right, I'll try.'

Jenna did not see when she pulled out of the hotel gates the car that was parked there, nor did she notice the camera which was taking photographs of her in the car park.

Ruari was awoken by the sound of the telephone. He fumbled, half still seeing the dream, he was at his little house in the country by himself and wishing Jenna was there. He took a deep breath and said hello and Jack's voice, angry and loud said back, 'What the hell are you doing?'

245

Ruari sat up. The clock by the bed said half-past nine. He squinted at it thinking it must be earlier than that, he was still half asleep and wasn't reading it properly

'What do you mean? I'm not even out of bed yet.'

'You're all over the newspapers. I told you, how many times did I tell you, to be careful?'

Ruari sat up further.

'I don't know what you're talking about.'

'You and Jenna Maddison. There are photographs of her leaving your hotel. The owner's son's wife. Are you completely out of your mind?'

'Jack...'

'They are having a field day with you. Do you know what Sorrel Maddison does to people who cross him? What on earth were you thinking about? No, don't answer that. It's perfectly obvious what you were thinking about and it wasn't football.'

'I don't...' Ruari couldn't imagine what he was trying to say 'Hang on a minute.' He put down the receiver, got out of bed and padded to the door. Outside were a whole pile of newspapers which he had automatically ordered the day before, he always tried to know what was happening. Now he had made a mistake. He turned over one after the other, there were thick black headlines, things like 'LOVE TRIANGLE' making it sound smutty and photographs of

246

Jenna looking so beautiful as she walked to her car, her long blonde hair, her expensive clothes, her small serious profile.

'Oh shit,' he said.

'You went to him?'

Jenna was trembling. Paul was angrier than she had ever seen him.

'I just wanted to sort it out. I don't want you and Ruari fighting–'

'Fighting? Look at the pictures of you.'

'Paul, this is the nineteen-seventies, women are allowed to go to men's hotel rooms without everybody thinking they're going to bed together. Or is that just your mind? I can see that the tabloids are happy with it but I didn't think you were that foolish.'

Paul had come back from work. He looked dishevelled, Jenna thought. He had been out all night, something had gone wrong somewhere, she couldn't even remember what and he had not been home to shower and shave and change as he so often did. But he had seen or been shown the newspapers and he had come back to accuse her. Jenna only wished that Faye was there, not that she would have been much help but at least she would have diluted Paul's presence. She didn't get up on Sunday mornings and rarely put in an appearance before lunch.

Jenna had been sitting in the conservatory eating tea and toast and thinking how well she had handled Ruari and thinking how right she had been, it was all any of them could hope for now and it wasn't much but in some ways she had got Ruari back and if it could be kept as she wanted then they would be able to meet and be friends, and in some ways stupidly she had thought it would be like it had been when they were very young and there was the shore, the sea, the sun and his presence.

She had seen flashes of his kindness and who he had been and all she wanted was to see him, to be around him, it would be enough. She was almost happy until Paul came in and threw the newspapers at her. She sat there, gazing down at them, and she wondered why everything had to be spoiled. She could not even be friends with Ruari, somebody had turned it into a circus, the newspapers were making yet more money from something which wasn't true.

'You went to him,' Paul said again as though she hadn't spoken at all and his voice was very loud and raised. 'How could you be so bloody stupid?'

She resented his language and the way that he shouted at her but the look on his face was frightening. She had never been afraid of Paul before but he was glaring and she was uncomfortable and wanted to get out but she had the feeling he would not let her past if she even got up.

'He asked you to go there, didn't he?' Paul guessed. 'He wants to start things up again.'

It was unfortunately the truth but Jenna wasn't having that, it wouldn't help.

'No, he didn't,' she said calmly, 'he just wanted to sort things out so that we could be friends.'

'Friends? Look.' He waved yet another newspaper under her nose. 'What on earth do you think my father will say now?'

'I think your father has more sense than the tabloids.'

'How it looks matters.'

'And doesn't how it is matter? I want this to work out, I want us to be happy.'

Paul started to laugh. It wasn't a good sound, it was low and harsh and upset her.

'How can you be so naive?'

'He's here, Paul, it's a fact and I wanted us to get round it and I went to see him to sort things out and we did, he's quite happy to be friends—'

'Is he indeed? Oh, well, that's all right, then.'

'It will be,' she said but after Paul had finally been appeased and shut up and even sat down and had some coffee without spouting off again like that Jenna knew that he was right and that it would be difficult for the two men ever to be civil to one another because of her.

Sorrel was so angry when he saw the newspapers that he couldn't think. He didn't like his family being caught up in his business ventures but when he got home and saw Jenna and Paul sitting in the conservatory his better sense stopped him from going in there and then Faye had appeared and he was able to go into the kitchen and hide there while he calmed down.

'Yes, I've seen it,' she said before he had a chance to say anything. 'Let it be, it's for the best. Shouting at her isn't going to help.'

He sat down and she buttered toast for him as she hadn't done for years and put it in front of him and poured coffee.

'We don't need the scandal,' he said.

'You should have thought of that before you brought him back here.'

'I did it for the club.'

'Of course you did but even you must have known there would be repercussions. He was her childhood sweetheart, what on earth did you think would happen? If you don't fuel it and Jenna doesn't see him in private again it will die down. All you have to do is wait.'

Sorrel could see the sense to this but he was furious. He felt as though the whole plan had been ruined by a bastard like Ruari Gallacher and he couldn't think what to do. He had just paid out the biggest fee he had ever paid for a footballer. He had no doubt that in time Ruari would be worth it, he had already made more column inches for the club than anyone before, but the price of his son's marriage was too high for him to stomach. He wanted to kill Gallacher.

He knew that Ruari wasn't stupid. He had not forgotten how Ruari had turned down the original offer and gone to Teeshaven for a better fee, how he had not taken any notice of anybody and he had seen Ruari in front of a camera and he was just as articulate as any other man. Sorrel had come from a back street himself, he knew that such places could make success and intelligence run hand in hand as well as any university. Neither did he believe that Ruari would purposely cause problems here. You never shit in your own nest, he knew. So had he or hadn't he? The sight of Jenna sitting in the conservatory with Paul made him feel slightly better but he was not a happy man.

'You asked to see me?'

Sorrel looked up. Ruari Gallacher stood in the doorway of Sorrel's office and it was like a bad dream. Of all the millions of men in the world that Jenna could have chosen to have an affair with surely she didn't have to choose this one, Sorrel thought. Was she or wasn't she? He didn't know and he wished he didn't have to care.

He felt weary. Not just tired. For the first

time in his life he understood how old people felt. It was the feeling constantly that just one more small thing would push you so far over the edge that you would end up in the kind of hospital bed from where the only direction was the crematorium.

Paul's apparently working marriage had been the single bright spark of ambition left in his life and this bastard had caused it to break down and then Sorrel thought, No, this is partly my fault, firstly for not taking on Gallacher originally and secondly for insisting on having him back because although he had what was undeniably the finest footballing talent of his generation Sorrel knew that his own motivation had been partly – he didn't like to think what percentage of it – revenge.

He didn't like to be bettered and Ruari Gallacher had bettered him at the age of seventeen. To be bettered by a lad who although he showed promise had given no real indication of how brilliant he would turn out to be had made the bile rise into Sorrel's mouth. He had never forgotten it. He had been ready to better the lad and now the lad had bettered him for the second time.

He was not a lad any longer. He was still very young but Ruari Gallacher stood in the doorway of Sorrel's office so self-confidently that Sorrel wanted, for the first time in his life to say 'All right, you win.'

'Ruari. Come in.'

Sorrel got to his feet. He usually did it because that way he looked down on people but he found himself looking straight into Ruari's eyes which was a shock, had he seemed so tall at the party or was it just that Sorrel was noticing different things and he had to stop himself from saying stupidly 'You've grown,' like he was Ruari's father and was seeing his offspring fully fledged, and it was even worse because they had not met properly and known one another when Ruari was a boy. For the first time Sorrel wished they had and that somehow he could have helped and he had the most horrible envy, which was ridiculous, since Ruari Gallacher's father was long since dead down the Black Diamond pit, of a man who could produce such a son. So as they stood there facing one another like soldiers Sorrel was moved by the idea and held out his hand.

'So, are you settled nicely into your hotel?'

Ruari took the hand and smiled though the smile never moved above his mouth.

'I'm fine, I'm used to being on my own,' he said and it was so obviously untrue that Sorrel wanted to break his neck.

'Do you play chess?'

'No.'

'What a pity. You would be a grand master by now.'

Ruari said nothing. He didn't even move uncomfortably like any decent man would who had done such a thing to anyone, not to the man who employed him. It occurred to Sorrel that Ruari Gallacher was not a decent man, that he had none of that left, fame and success had taken it from him and he cared for nothing. He could look Sorrel straight in the eyes like this and it was Sorrel who broke the gaze.

'I got you back here to play football, not to play silly buggers.'

Ruari looked angry. Really Sorrel thought, he was a first-rate bastard.

'I know that you ... you had some kind of relationship with Paul's wife but it's a long time ago and I wouldn't have brought you back here if I had thought you assumed you could ... pick it up where you left off, so to speak.'

'Relationship,' Ruari rolled the word around on his tongue, 'is that what you call it?' His look was unblinking as though he had waited a long time for this. And in that moment Sorrel thought of Jenna.

She had that starry look about her, the bright shiny look that women had when they were involved with a man other than their husband and he couldn't stand it. He thought of the possibilities. Was there anything he could offer Ruari to go away, to leave her alone?

Sorrel was tortured with the idea of Ruari running off with the woman his son loved. It would be like somebody running off with Faye and dreadful as their marriage was he did not think he could go on if she walked out and left him.

That was what men like them did, they got women to marry them and then left the marriage like it was a deposit from a dog on a doorstep. Marriage, he thought savagely who had ever thought it was a good idea, it was nothing more than control, a way of herding people into little houses and closing the door on their lives.

And men fought past it and some women did too and some gave in and some ... some loved so hard, so truly well that they endured it. Was Jenna like that, would she give up her life and her freedom for this bastard and he felt as though it was all his fault.

'You made the tabloids and you've made me very angry. I've dealt with better men than you. If you don't leave her alone I will make sure you do. Do you understand me?'

Ruari frowned.

'Mr Maddison—'

'She's married to my son and it may not be a marriage made in heaven but it's legitimate and he cares about her. I don't care how many women you have but leave Jenna alone for all our sakes.'

'I haven't—'

'I don't want to know about it, I just want you to stop.'

'We had a drink—'

'I don't care what you had. It's finished, do you understand me? Well?'

Ruari's shoulders went down.

'She told me we might be friends—'

'No. You don't see her. If you see her at a function of any kind you keep your distance. If you ask her to your hotel or you try meeting her on the quiet I will know. I'm watching you. Now get out.'

Eighteen

The football season began in September and from the very beginning Ruari hated it. There were some parts of it he should have liked, he should have liked the immaculate training facilities, the way that the ground was kept perfectly, that the changing rooms were almost newly built. Everything was of the best but he had to face Harry Philips, who was still the manager. When they came face to face for the first time he said, 'Now then, Gallacher. Home at last, eh?' Harry was the worst thing a man could be, Ruari thought, he abused power, he might even enjoying hurting people if he held a grudge and he held a grudge here. His eyes were almost starry that he had control of the young man who had turned him down, he had gone away and become rich and famous when he could have done that at Harry's beloved North End. Harry, Ruari thought with an inward shudder, would never forgive him. Would he take revenge? What could he do? Ruari didn't think he could legitimately do much and it would be a fight between his base instincts and his love of the football club because if he upset Ruari too much would he then not get the goals he so badly wanted, the way that North End might do so well, so much better with such a striker?

'Yes, sir.'

Philips' eyes widened.

'You called Hodgkin sir?'

'Isn't that what you get called?'

'They call me Boss. Quite different.'

'Yes, Boss.'

Ruari didn't smile. He wouldn't. This man had treated him badly and now he felt as though he was in his power though it was a different game. This man had seen him as a beginner and maybe as somebody to break before he moulded him. Now it was too late, the mould was set and who had set it had made a good job. He would do what it took to mollify Philips, obey him, listen to his advice, show respect but if Philips went too far...

Philips looked down and Ruari thought, with some relief, Yes, he cares more about the game than about what we did to one another. Finally after a very long pause Philips looked him in the eyes and said, 'I wanted you back here and not for the reasons you think. You think I'm going to hang you upside down and shake you until you drop and I could but I'm not going to. You're the most naturally gifted player I've seen in a long time and I was a fool not to secure you long before I did and then a bigger fool not to make sure of it.

'I think we've both changed. I brought you here to score goals. I'm not going to say I don't care how you do it because I care how all my team conducts themselves on a football pitch. We don't do mucky, we don't do underhand like a lot I could name—'

Ruari wanted to interrupt here and say that neither did the team he had left but he didn't want to sound defensive or like a kid crying for home so he didn't.

'You're a clean player, a good lad and you're a bright spark. I underestimated you. I didn't realize some lads are adults at seventeen. I should have remembered your father.'

'You knew him?' Ruari was interested now he couldn't stop himself.

'Aye, I did. We were mates, we played football on the same team when we were school kids. You didn't know that?'

'No.'

'There's a lot of things about me that you don't know. I'm a disappointed man so I'm going to say this to you, Gallacher. Don't let me down, don't disappoint me, because if you do then you'll look back on this conversation like drowning sailors look on a mill-pond.'

'I always do my best.'

'I know you do, that's what you're doing here. You didn't want to come back?'

Ruari was surprised by the question.

'We paid a lot of money for you, Gallacher, and we expect to get our money's worth, so no pressure, eh?' He gave a ghostly grin, it woke Ruari up from his sleep with a shout that night when he dreamed it.

'I said I'll do my best.'

'You'd better,' Philips said. 'If you don't I'll make you wish you had.'

It seemed ironic to Ruari that the first game of the season should be against Teeshaven. Last year he had scored three times against Dunelm North End. Now he was in different colours and working against them. It was lucky that he didn't see his former team mates though he and Jack had already met several times in the past weeks as Jack was determined to sort out what he called 'this mess'. Ruari in what spare time he had kept going back and staying with Jack and Nora because he didn't want his mother to see how difficult everything was because she would worry, but he needed support of some kind and he could go to Jack and Nora's when he had time off during the week, even stay overnight and take the kids to the park with Jack and sleep in a bed which was not in a hotel. He didn't go to his house, somehow he couldn't bear to, and when he thought hard about it he realized that it was because in some remote part of his mind he had seen himself there with Jenna. What an idiot he was.

'It isn't a mess,' Ruari insisted when Nora had taken the children to bed one night that autumn and he and Jack were sitting over a beer.

'You should have refused to go there in the first place,' Jack said unhelpfully.

'How could I? You encouraged me, even.'

'I don't know,' Jack admitted, 'but I wish you'd found a way. I don't like how this is going.'

'It's nothing to do with you.'

Jack glared at him.

'It's to do with me when you're all over the bloody newspapers. Are you stupid or what?'

Ruari didn't answer. He wished they were somewhere other than Jack's, anywhere that Jack couldn't shout at him like this. He wanted to remind Jack about the children upstairs but Nora had gone up to read them a story and besides it was a lovely house with thick walls and ceilings so they probably couldn't hear anyway.

'You don't know what it was like leaving here,' he said now.

'It's over,' Jack insisted.

'No, it isn't,' and it was then that Ruari acknowledged for the first time how much Jenna still meant to him and how much he had hoped. 'You know nothing about it and you've never...' His voice trailed off there.

'I've never what?' Jack said, still glaring. 'I've never lost the girl I loved? No, I haven't, and do you think you're going to get her back this way?'

'I'm never going to get her back,' Ruari yelled.

'Well, at least you know it. She's married to somebody else, man, she married him because she was having his kid and it's nothing to do with you. She chose him and she stayed with him. When will you ever get over it?'

'Do you think I haven't tried?'

Jack was silent for a few moments and then he said more softly 'You cannot go on like this, hating Sorrel Maddison. He did what he did for his club. And he was right, wasn't he? In a way he was right, because he knew what he'd lost. It was defeat, Ruari, he hated you in defeat. You got the better of a powerful man like him and he didn't like it

261

but you're still here and you're still bettering him. You won and now you've gone back there and you're battering the shit out of him–'

'He made me go back!'

'Aye, he did, because you're the best and he knows it and you wanted to be the best, nothing less would do. When other people had given up and gone home you practised. Second anything wouldn't do for you and a lot of it was to show him what he had done, what he had lost. Those years you spent at Teeshaven you and I both know those are a footballer's best years.

'You're a North End boy, you should have been there in the place where you were born and where your dad died and where the girl you loved lived but you couldn't. He took it off you and he took it off himself and there's no way back. People will never forget the way that you have played and you did it for another club and he has had to put up with the fact that he did that. But he didn't cause you to lose Jenna.'

'His son did,' Ruari said bitterly.

'No,' Jack said, 'you did it yourself, you even told me. For Christ's sake, admit it just once. You wanted to play football, you wanted everything that comes with it, and you sacrificed the girl that you loved so that you could have it. You know it's true. I think you've always known it and you can't live with the person you are and you go on playing up to him, behaving like a bastard.'

There was silence. It was one of those silences as thick as bricks.

'No.'

'Yes, you did.'

There was another silence during which Ruari would have given anything at all to get out of the room but for some reason he couldn't move and had to listen to the long silence which followed and put up with Jack, saying the things that nobody should say to him.

'I thought I could have everything.'

'Yes, well, you cannot,' Jack said.

'You have.'

'No, I don't. I don't have that talent that destroys everything it touches. You have it and I've seen other people brought down by it, it ruins people, it sends them to drink and to drugs and to people they shouldn't trust and it eats up everything else in their lives until they're obsessed with it, until nothing else matters. And they believe their talent is invincible and unstoppable and that it will carry them through their lives and it doesn't and won't.

'And you know it doesn't and that's really hard. People don't understand what this game is really like and the pressures that we put up with for it, being owned and being spat at by the fans and being vilified in the press week after week and being criticized over and over and the managers standing shrieking abuse when we get something wrong.

'You're not going to go back there and have Jenna and have everything come right, Ruari, it's not going to happen.'

This time the silence was complete and it was only when Ruari could bear it no longer that he said, 'You're wasted as a goalie, Jack, you should've been a vicar.'

'I know. Me mam always said I was too clever for my own good,' Jack said.

That Saturday the pitch was muddy like it was December. In really bad weather in winter the green was nothing but a big patch in the middle and it was reminiscent of it now, black and thick and slippery and hell to play on. The rain never stopped. Ruari didn't mind that, a wet pitch could be an advantage, all that sliding around made it even, it was almost like being an ice-skater.

It was strange to be against the team he had played with for so long. There were vague nods and looks but nobody said anything and within moments of the game starting Ruari had completely forgotten they were anything to do with him. He was not confused at the white strip, he was playing in blue now and he knew which way he was going. The rest was automatic.

He scored in the first five minutes and the crowd went wild. It must be odd, he thought, for the fans who had travelled all the way to watch the footballer who had been theirs score against their team. The rain came down even harder until it was difficult to see the ball but he put another one past Jack before half-time and it was satisfying after Jack had shouted so much at him.

He heard Jack curse as he hit the ground the opposite way that the ball went into the net. When he got up he was covered in mud. He wasn't the only one. They went back into the dressing rooms at half-time pushing the wet dirt from their faces and hands.

'You could have passed that to me,' Pat Smith said.

'It went in the net, didn't it?' Ruari said.

He was undeceived. Nobody said anything else but he knew that the other strikers would resent him if he kept all the glory for himself. He could be a one-man team but they all hated a selfish player. It was not just about scoring goals and he had his way to make here but suddenly he was tired and didn't very much care.

The dressing room was soon steaming from the wet heat of everybody and Philips was down there telling them all the things they had got wrong instead of, Ruari thought, telling them all the things they had got right and he resented it. He ignored everybody and sat by himself as much as he could in such cramped quarters, drinking his tea and not thinking about what Philips was saying.

He thought about the other side. Mr Hodgkin would be in there telling them now how wonderful they were, even though they were two down and how in the second half they could defeat the phenomenon that was Ruari Gallacher because they knew him so well, they knew his moves, the way he played, they could defeat him, he was just one man, he was only one player, he could not win here and he was reminding them of what Ruari would do now inspiring them, assuring them. Ruari couldn't help smiling at the idea. He knew them equally well and was defeating them almost single-handedly.

They came out for the second half and his former teammates did everything they could except stamp on him and hold him down and still he got past them and put another one into the net. Jack was taking it personally by now and swearing horribly, Ruari could hear even beyond the crowd.

It was nearly over and he was glad, he had not realized until then how difficult that first game was and to have the first game against Teeshaven was anything but what he would have wished, any other team would have been easier but it was almost done and it would never be the same again, from now on

266

everything would get easier. He was almost happy he had shown both sides and the fans what he could do and the North End fans could not doubt his loyalty. He could hear them shouting and singing his name and he thought it might work out here after all.

He would make friends, he could put up with Paul and Jenna being together, he would be near his mam and he might even sell the little house in Yorkshire and buy something here. He could at least persuade his mother that he could buy her house for her and he would take her out for wonderful meals and buy her holidays in warm places in lavish hotels.

Very soon it would be back to the dressing room for a hot bath, into clean clothes and the joy of the victory and then, and he didn't understand what happened, there was no-body near enough to have caused it – he turned suddenly and the wrong way to inter-cept the ball. There was an agonizing scream from somebody and to his surprise he went down.

The ground came up all over him like a blanket, the very pitch where he should have been playing during those years as his own covered him in inches of cold mud. It was in his eyes and in his mouth, he could taste the gravel, the grit, the grass. Philips was bel-lowing at him from a long way off to get on his feet.

He couldn't see, he wasn't sure he could breathe and then he could because he needed to breathe because of the pain. It was him, it was his scream, he relived the whole thing instantly and in amazement, it had sounded so far off like nothing to do with him but the pain was coming at him in increasing waves like a great tide over the beach until he had to hold his breath almost all the time because the waves of pain were going into a long line, there was no let up between them. He couldn't see for the pain, he couldn't think for it, he would have given years of his life for relief of any kind. He couldn't bear it but he had to somehow because it didn't stop.

Then Philips was screaming louder, he was nearer and the game had halted, he could see boots, legs and then Philips was near, so near that Ruari could feel his warm chewing-gum-fresh breath.

'You bastard, Gallacher, get up,' and then the voices of his former teammates.

'He isn't pretending,' somebody said.

'Ruari, where does it hurt?'

The trainer came on with his magic sponge while Ruari clutched at his knee, although the pain by then was coming from his whole leg so nothing seemed to make any difference and he couldn't make out what the trainer was saying, it hurt so much and then he could hear Jack's voice close.

And after that Philips's voice screaming in his ear, 'You did this on purpose, Gallacher, you bastard,' and the pain went on and on.

Jack got down beside him. 'Ruari?'

Ruari shook his head. The tears of pain were running down his face.

It didn't get better and he didn't think he could stand it for another second. The trouble was when there was nobody and nothing to better it you didn't have any choice. The game was halted, the rain poured down and after a short eternity a reassuring voice said something into his ear and after that they moved him away from the pitch, beyond the shouting and the noises changed. They put him into an ambulance and put a needle into him and the pain started to ease up a bit.

He had never been so thankful for anything, he remembered afterwards thanking the ambulance man over and over and the way that he began to be able to take breaths so that there was a little space between the pains, they began to even out a little and as he went on they evened out further and further. He had never liked hospitals but oh, he was so glad of it now, grateful to be lifted down and taken inside and through the long corridor and then eventually for the doctors to put him beyond pain and into a hospital bed. He was so glad he could have cried.

It felt so comfortable, smelled so clean. He

had thrown up with the pain and was covered in mud and vomit but he was cleaned up and put into bed and filled full of whatever dulled the pain and he went thankfully into oblivion.

The first thing Jenna wanted to do was dash off to the hospital but she couldn't because Paul came home to tell her about what had happened and it would have been too much for him to stand.

'Is it serious?' she asked Paul when she heard him clash the front door and she ran into the hall. Paul didn't look at her.

'For God's sake, tell me!'

'He twisted his knee somehow or other.'

'It doesn't sound bad.'

Paul grimaced.

'People have done less and not been able to play. It's an accumulation of injuries with them, every time they get on to the bloody pitch... Do you realize how much he cost? He could be out all season. I think the bastard did it on purpose.'

'Why would he do that?'

'To get even with Dad and me because of you.'

'That's ridiculous,' Jenna said. 'He loves his football, he loves it more than anything. Why don't you still understand how these things work?'

'He might.'

'And how could he, anyway?'

'I don't know.'

'Oh, Paul, I don't think he would.'

Paul brushed her off because he obviously didn't want to discuss it. She followed him through into the sitting room while he stood in the middle of the floor, shaking his head as though he couldn't believe this had happened. Finally he looked across the room at her.

'You think he's still the kid from the back lane, don't you? Your little friend has changed quite a lot.'

She was about to say 'I don't think he has,' and then she remembered that Paul couldn't bear this and anyway he was right and she had flashes of guilt because she felt that she had caused all of this, it was a strange feeling, she had upset so many things, set so many events in motion just by betraying Ruari that once with Paul. All these things had started then and all the hatred and resentment was because of her. She wanted to try and make it better but she didn't know how, she thought of what she might say and came up with, 'Surely he wants to play. That's what footballers do.' And as she said the words she knew it wasn't so, she wasn't sure that Ruari cared any more and then she began to doubt him. She wanted to see him so badly, to see herself whether he was going to recover quickly. He must, this was his whole life.

There were varying reports on the news and in the papers which she scanned but she could do nothing but wait and fret. She didn't sleep she was so anxious and when finally Paul went out the following day which was the first opportunity she had she drove to the hospital.

There was nobody about, it was not visiting hours, but he was in a private room in a private wing and she thought any of his friends could go in at any time. She didn't ask anybody she dodged people in case she shouldn't be there and made her way past reporters inside and outside the building by taking another route and then slipped quietly into his room. Nobody was expecting her so she wore a hat and pushed her hair up inside it and looked as though she was confidently going to visit somebody else and finally she reached him.

The dark September day had already given itself up and rain besieged the window. In here all was quiet and a single light burned near the bed. He was still, he was asleep but as she sat down he murmured, 'Mam?'

'No, it's me.' She spoke softly He looked exhausted, white, with great dark shadows on his face. He didn't answer so she said, 'Ruari, it's me, Jenna.'

'Oh.' He opened his eyes. They were full of pain, Jenna thought, but lightened a little when he saw who it was. 'She was here a minute ago, I think she went to get a cup of tea.'

'How do you feel?'

'Oh ... you know. Won't be playing much football for a while. They had to operate to try and put it right.' He put out a hand to her and Jenna moved nearer and clasped his cold fingers in hers.

He went to sleep and then the door opened and his mother stood there, her face white, her lips thin when she saw who was there.

'It was good of you to come,' she said stiffly as though he was her private property, Jenna thought, hurt, and then remembered she had no rights here.

'What did they say?'

'Nobody tells you anything.'

They sat by the bed for a while but Jenna was uncomfortable now that his mother was there. She had to stop herself from apologizing. His mam knew exactly what had happened. She didn't say anything more, she didn't even look at Jenna, she just watched Ruari, afraid no doubt for what the future would hold. His mother had seen things go wrong before, perhaps even expected them to all the time. Was that what being middle-aged taught you?

'He only twisted it,' was all she could think to say.

'Apparently there have been other injuries, they all have them, and this was the final kind of straw.'

'What do you mean?' Jenna said, stopping and remembering what Paul had said.

'He might not play again. Wait until Sorrel Maddison finds that out.'

'Not play?' Jenna couldn't imagine a world where Ruari wouldn't be able to play football, it was his whole life, he had given up everything for it and even though he was bitter now she knew that when he was on the pitch it was the only thing which mattered to him. 'Have they said that?' she asked, trying to make things better.

His mother looked as though she was about to cry.

'Not yet but they haven't said anything positive either. I wish it didn't matter so much. I can't imagine what he would be like if he couldn't play. What on earth would he do and ... his whole life would change? How would he ... make a living? It's not as though he's good at anything else, when did he ever give himself a chance to be?'

Mrs Robson seemed agitated, which was hardly surprising, Jenna thought.

'You must be tired,' Jenna said, 'why don't you go home for a little while? I'll stay with him.'

'He keeps asking for me. I don't like to leave him and besides I would only worry more there, I don't have to go to work, they've been ever so good, that was one thing, they covered it for me. They know who Ruari is, everybody at work is so proud of him.'

Jenna didn't want to leave him either but she made herself go home when his mother would not be moved and he went on sleeping. The anaesthetic did that for you, she thought, put you into an easier, more comfortable place.

The photographers had another go at her when she left the hospital but she no longer cared. She kept her head down and didn't give anybody a decent picture and although they threw questions at her, some of them very rude she thought, she didn't answer. At least she had learned that much though she knew that now she had been to the hospital the speculation, the columns and the photographs would be all over the place by evening and even more so by the next day.

Paul came home late, Jenna was in bed.

'So,' he said, flicking on the bedside light at his side, 'you went to see Wonderboy.' He sounded exasperated.

Jenna wanted to ask who had told him but she didn't. Paul smelled heavily of drink, so much so that when he got into bed she wanted to turn away.

'Gallacher may not be much of a prospect any more,' Paul said, 'six months from now nobody will remember him. Except Dad, of course. He'll never bloody well forget.'

'Aren't you getting a bit ahead of yourself?'

'I managed to get the doctor to speak to me. We aren't talking about something which will be better in six weeks. It might not be better in six months.'

'Have you told your father?'

'No, I thought I'd leave it to the doctor,' Paul said calmly. 'He was at the hospital with me. I came out and left him to it.'

'Does Ruari know?'

'I think he does,' Paul said. 'Did you not think about the tabloids? Did you have to go? Did you not think about me or my family or yours?'

The truth was that she had not and she was not about to get into a discussion about it so she just turned the other way and pretended to go to sleep. She had the feeling that Paul did exactly the same. He turned over a lot during the night and even got up a couple of times and was gone from the bed for a long time.

'I won't play again, is that what you're telling me?' Ruari stared at the doctor. The sun was pouring into the window of his private room. He was coming to hate that room, the silence of the night and the uncertainty of the days, it felt like months since he had last been on the pitch but the trouble was when he thought about playing now he associated it with pain and that was something you didn't forget.

'I'm not saying that,' the doctor said. They didn't deal in definite things, Ruari had come to realize, they would put off saying anything for as long as they could. Medicine was an inexact science and the trouble was that people needed it to be exact, needed to be assured that things would get better, that they would recover, that they would always be here to greet the sun tomorrow, that the world could be patched up and made well, even perfect.

"Then what are you saying?' Ruari tried to insist though he wasn't feeling strong enough either physically or mentally and he was afraid that once they told him he couldn't play that the most awful thing in the world would happen and he would never play, he would never get better, he would have the future to face without football and it was not a thought to be borne.

'I'm saying it's very unlikely that you will play in the immediate future. It will certainly take a very long time to heal.'

'I thought weeks.'

'Think months or ... even longer.'

'You don't know, in other words.'

The doctor didn't comment. He was not going to fall into a hole of saying he didn't know. He left and Ruari lay there, frustrated, afraid for the immediate future and a lot more afraid for what might happen after that. It was like looking into a black hole.

It must be bad because his mother had walked into his hospital room some time later so she must have been talking to them and he could see that she had been crying though she was doing her best not to now. He thought he had never been as glad to see anybody.

'Don't worry,' she said, 'as soon as we can we're going to get you home. You'll be better there.'

'I can't just do that.'

'Ruari, you can't walk,' his mother pointed out. 'You aren't going to be much good to Mr Maddison like this.'

'But...' She couldn't want him there but he could see that she did, she expected him to go back with her and he couldn't tell her that the very last thing he wanted was to go to the little house in the back lane where he had started, in case he should finish there, that his career would really be ended and he would have nothing left but the back lane full of puddles and his dreams dashed and over. Whatever would he do? It made him panic, the big beating wings of uncertainty flapped around inside him and his hands shook. He tried to hide all this from his mother but she knew him too well, she was not deceived.

'They said what?' Harry stared at Sorrel. They were in Sorrel's office at the club. 'We've just bought the little bastard. He has to play.'

Sorrel shook his head, 'He can hardly stand. He did it on purpose.' Sorrel thought his head would explode he was so angry.

'You cannot do summat like that on purpose, Mr Maddison. I saw him go down. He's torn all his leg up—'

'I saw it, I was bloody there, you know.'

'Didn't it look real to you?'

'I know what it looked like, it looked like money down the drain,' Sorrel said and came to rest and sat down in his chair and sighed.

'He's finished,' Harry said. 'If he was a horse they'd shoot him.'

Sorrel could not believe the Almighty would treat him as badly as this. He had paid more for Ruari Gallacher than he had ever paid for a player, he had wondered at the time whether any footballer was worth that much but if Ruari couldn't play then he couldn't be sold, he was a liability. He had cost a fortune. Sorrel sat there for a very long time while he tried to take in the enormity of what had happened. Eventually of course they wouldn't have to pay him but every penny now was money wasted, money

279

he could have used to buy other players, and worst of all he didn't think the team could get to the top without its star player so it was not just the money, it was prestige and excitement and the club's future over the next two or three years because he wouldn't be able to buy anybody else for a long while.

He retained a faint hope that Ruari would play again but in the meanwhile he would be stuck at home and the team would be doing badly and Sorrel would have to sit through it all and there was nothing he could do. He was not used to feeling helpless, it made him angry. There was only one thing which would help. He would go to the club and see Joanna and he would drink some whisky and take her to bed and try to forget his troubles for a while.

It was odd to go back to his mother's house, it made Ruari feel like a child again, as though he had fallen in the back lane as he did often when he was a little boy and bloodied his knees. It was one place he had thought he would never go again except as a visitor and when the front door shut behind him it was like a prison closing.

Coming in the front way was something else he wasn't used to. His mother twittered on about leaving his expensive car outside the house as they must move it from the hotel so that Ruari telephoned Jack and asked him to come and collect it and keep it for the time being. Jack had plenty of space at his house.

'Maybe somebody might buy it,' Ruari said.

'I think you should hang on to it.'

'Why? I'm going to need the money and it isn't as if I'll be able to drive for a while.' He didn't say if at all, he couldn't face that idea and indeed it was a very black way of looking at things but coming back to the little terraced house which he had left so hopefully brought his mood almost to despair.

His mother had got from somewhere a put-up bed so that he could sleep in the front room. He was only glad the bathroom was downstairs, it had been put on some time ago as an addition to the house beyond the kitchen, there having been no bathroom since the house had been built in the early part of the century when coal was the most important thing and workers were needed. Lots of the houses around did the same.

He wanted to suggest to his mother that they should go to live in his cottage for now but he couldn't do that, she had her work, her friends and her own life and though he knew she would go with him if he asked he couldn't ask her to leave here so he put up with it.

From the beginning it was difficult. The people he had hoped to make friends with were no longer interested in him, none of the other North End players even came to see him and he heard nothing from the management. Jack was busy as the football season was now at its height and he had his family to consider so although he rang Ruari told him there was no need to come up, everything was fine and he was feeling better by the day.

He told his mother that she must not alter her life for him, he would manage, but she ended up doing so much that he felt guilty and would try to get up and help. It was difficult in such a small space with crutches and often his efforts to assist were worse than if he had sat down and let her manage by herself.

She worked every day, she still cleaned at the school and she also did offices so she was at home during the day after her early shift and went out each evening. The evenings went on forever and there was nothing to do but read or watch television. He did manage better on his crutches after a few weeks but there was no more progress.

One dark November evening when it had begun raining in the early afternoon and his mother had been gone for about three hours Ruari got so far down in mood that he thought he would never come back up again.

He breathed carefully, tried to think

positively about anything at all and when nothing presented itself he ended up imagining that he would be stuck here like this for the rest of his life and then there was a noise in the back yard, in the rain. He gazed through the back window and saw the person come to the door and lift the sneck and then he heard Jenna's voice say, 'It's only me.'

Paul had told her not to go to Ruari, had made her promise she would not see him.

'Why should I not?'

'Because I'm asking you not to. He's caused enough problems. My father has had to try and find another player to replace him and we can't afford it, do you realize how difficult this is making things?'

Jenna did know. It seemed to her that Sorrel blamed her, he wasn't at home much but he rarely spoke to her when he was, though perhaps he just didn't notice, he had so many business problems on his mind.

Faye went to the cottage even in the bad weather. Jenna wished she would not. She hated being in the house by herself all the time and even tentatively suggested one time when Faye was at home that she might visit.

'Oh, you would hate it, there's nothing to do.'

'There's nothing to do here either,' Jenna

pointed out.

'Paul's here.'

'He's never in.'

'You should go out and make friends, take on charity work, play badminton, join clubs.'

'Is that what you did?' Jenna said and then wished she hadn't. Faye looked at her.

'That's exactly what I did. I was like you, I wanted to have children and after we lost the second and Paul went to school there were hours and hours of leisure.

'Sorrel made so much money we bought this place and could afford cleaners and ... and he changed the place to suit him and I didn't care for any of it so I no longer wanted to be involved. I like the cottage now. I build up the fire, read, drink whisky and thank God I'm not here waiting for that bastard to come home.'

Jenna was astonished at her mother-in-law's frankness but she didn't think it was much of a fate. Besides, Paul did come back. He arranged for them to go dancing with his friends the first weekend after Ruari's accident and they went to a very exclusive club, not one of their own, that would have been like being at work, he said.

In the ladies' room there was another rich young woman, who had a diamond in each ear and one around her neck and an expensive silver dress and high heels. Jenna was looking in the mirror putting on more lipstick, when Kate said,

'And how is Wonderboy now? What a comedown for him and by implication of course for you.'

'What do you mean?' Jenna stopped applying lipstick and looked at her.

Kate laughed. 'Oh, don't tell me you weren't having an affair. Paul must be relieved even if his father is upset.'

Jenna was about to deny this hotly but realized that that was what most people were thinking and denying it would not change that. Kate was looking enviously at her too as though Ruari was some kind of superior animal who had had his uses and didn't any more.

She put the lipstick back into her bag and walked calmly into the darkness of the club where Paul was waiting for her. He was already drunk. He had come home and had several whiskies before they left, had assumed that she would drive.

When he got to the club he went on drinking and stumbled when they danced so that she insisted on sitting down. The music was too loud for conversation and then he suggested to the men they were with that they should go downstairs and play roulette so she was stuck with Kate and Kate's friends, none of whom seemed to have anything to say to her, though perhaps she

285

should have been glad of that.

One girl, Susan, came and sat down with her.

'I'm glad to get rid of Gary, honestly I wish they wouldn't drink quite so much,' she said. 'How's Ruari?'

'I haven't seen him.'

Susan looked at her.

'There was a picture in our paper of you coming out of the hospital.'

'Oh, yes, well, his mother was there,' Jenna said as though that explained everything. 'We were children together, lived next door.'

'Were you? I didn't know that. I thought the romance was something new.'

'It's not a romance, Susan.'

'Isn't it? I gained the impression you were very thick and certainly at Paul's birthday party Ruari looked as though he was happy dancing with you. Paul didn't seem very happy about it but then men are all alike, aren't they ... they always want what they think they can't have.'

'Do they? I don't know.'

'You don't know much, do you?' Susan said. 'Well, I'm going to the bar, it doesn't look like any of the men are here to buy me another drink. Can I get you anything?'

'No, thanks.'

'New boyfriend maybe? There are certainly lots of good-looking types there, I might see if I can get one for myself,' and off she went.

The evening was endless. At one o'clock in the morning Paul still didn't want to go home and when they left at two he sang for the first part of the journey, snored the rest and had to be helped up the stairs to bed but when they got into bed he reached for her.

'No, you smell of whisky.'

'You wouldn't say that if I was Gallacher, though, would you? Tell me, Jenna, why do you never do for me the things you did for him?'

'I don't know what you mean.' She pushed him off but Paul got hold of her. He didn't exactly force her, Jenna thought afterwards because she gave in, because he was drunk and wouldn't listen to anything she said and because it was going to be a big struggle and then maybe he would shout and swear but he made her very unhappy because he didn't seem to care that she didn't want him or was it just that he was too drunk to understand any protestation short of physical defence?

She let him have her. She didn't cry either then or afterwards, it was brief and Paul was too drunk to be violent. He went straight to sleep after that and she thought it was probably no worse than what thousands of men did to thousands of women on Saturday nights when they had been to the pub.

She told herself that it wasn't worth getting upset about but she lay awake all through the night and listened to the rain on

287

the window and thought again that if they had had a child it would never have come to this, they would have had more to focus upon than Paul's business. She spent several minutes rerunning her marriage as something perfect with two small children, holidays, Christmases, christenings, Sorrel and Faye would have been involved too and would have been pleased. Sorrel would have come home in the evenings and Faye would not spend all her time at the cottage and...

The rain had not stopped even halfway through Sunday morning when Paul awoke and came downstairs into the kitchen.

'Make me some breakfast, eh?' he said, slumping down at the table.

Jenna tried to move away when he touched her shoulder and he got hold of her and pushed her up against the cupboard and said, 'Don't do that.'

'What?'

'Like you can't bear me touching you.'

'You were drunk,' she said.

'It was Saturday night,' Paul said but he didn't meet her eyes and he let go of her in a fashion which suggested to her that he was ashamed of himself. Then he said softly, 'Just tell me one thing.'

'What's that?'

'Whether you slept with Gallacher.'

She said, 'Oh,' impatiently. She was going

to try and brush it off as unworthy of an answer and ask him what he wanted to eat but he stood in the middle of the floor and he looked so pathetic somehow that she went on, 'Of course I didn't sleep with him, how could you think that I would?'

Instant relief held his eyes and she remembered uncomfortably how he had been when they had first met, how much he had loved her and how the circumstances had chased the better feelings away.

'You gave the impression that you did.'

'I did nothing of the kind. People jump to conclusions and the newspapers... You and I are married. As far as I'm concerned that's it. I would never sleep with anybody else, don't you know that?'

He didn't answer but when neither of them said anything or moved he eventually said in a low voice, 'I didn't hurt you, did I?'

'No,' Jenna said stiffly, 'you didn't hurt me, I just wish you wouldn't get drunk like that. I didn't want you and you didn't care.'

'It's your fault.' His eyes flashed with temper since he knew he had been in the wrong but wasn't about to admit it. She wanted to deny it had been her fault but couldn't because she thought they were both to blame and in the end she just asked him what he wanted for breakfast.

'I would like bacon and egg and some toast and marmalade and some freshly ground coffee and some orange juice and I'd like it in the dining room.'

Sunday was the only day they had no help so she could hardly object, it was his mood she objected to, but at least making the breakfast would get her out of his way She went into the dining room and laid the table and when she came back into the kitchen he went in there and sat down and read the newspapers. She was eager to have something to do so that she didn't have to put up with him any further.

Ruari was staring at her now as she walked into the little pit house. She was trembling. It wasn't because she was breaking her promise to Paul, it was because she too had thought he would never come back here. In some ways there were too many memories, she could think of being a little girl here and of Ruari's mother having taken them to the beach and as they came in the back door she would take their buckets and spades from them after they had spent all the afternoon building sandcastles on the beach.

They would come back quite late sometimes because they would want to wait for the tide to come in and for the water to fill their castle moats. Jenna always put flowers on her castles and Ruari would search the beach for shells for her. She liked razor shells best and sometimes he would find some which were quite unbroken and bring them proudly to her so that she could put them into the top of the middle of her castle. Her dearest memory was of trying to stop the incoming waves from destroying the castles. She and Ruari would build back furiously the destroyed walls which the tide was reducing to wet sand.

His mother would toast teacakes for them when they got home and sometimes she would buy them ice cream while they were on the beach though they only took sandwiches once because Ruari dropped them. Jenna had thought it very funny how sandy they were after that.

She ventured inside very carefully now, over the back step and down the step from the pantry into the back room and he was sitting at the kitchen table like somebody who had nowhere to go and he looked so unlike the brash young man who had entertained her with champagne in his lavish hotel room that she was aghast. He had lost weight, his eyes were uncertain, but the look turned to pleasure when he saw who it was and said her name and she went over and hugged him as best she could considering he was sitting on a kitchen chair and she was bending down to him.

'Oh, it's so lovely to see you,' she said, 'it's like really coming home, all my best memories are of here.'

He hid his face against her for so long that she was disconcerted.

'My back's aching,' she objected and heard his muffled laughter and when he drew back he said,

'I would ask you into the front room but there's nowhere to sit except my bed.'

She saw now that the sofa was in this room so that it was crowded now that it did for dining room, kitchen and sitting room. She was also surprised at how she felt, she had forgotten how poorly they had all lived, how small the rooms were. There was nowhere to get away from anybody even when there was just two of you.

In the end they sat on the tiny sofa side by side and she half expected to hear Stan come clashing in at the back door as he had done so many times when they were children, she had never been afraid of him because he was such an amiable drunk, smiling at her and waving his arms and staggering up the stairs to bed to sleep off the midday drinking session on Sundays so that he would be fit to go back to the pub when it opened later. How had she and Ruari come to this and lost everything which mattered?

Ruari's house had always contained a certain kind of comfort which her own home had lacked. There was always the smell of paint next door as her mother put layer upon layer to hide whatever she could not bear and she was always too busy to go anywhere or take Jenna anywhere.

It was Ruari's mother who spent time with them even though she went out to work. Jenna could remember the evenings, being alone there with Ruari in the house as they got older and his mother was happy to leave them by themselves but she would come in with gossip and a warm greeting and the fire was always banked up when the weather was cold and she would hug Jenna as though she didn't live next door and see her every day. It was the on-goingness of it which made Jenna ache for the past, that casual way they had always had, the security of not even thinking that things might be any different.

She got hold of Ruari's hand now, tentatively laced her fingers through his and he let her. He didn't say anything but he didn't move from her and Jenna wished she could hold the moment because soon his mother would come back from work and the spell would be broken and she hadn't felt like this in so very long that she couldn't remember the last time she had sat still and comfortable so that the only thing that broke the silence was the sound of the coals shifting a little in the grate.

She didn't want to go now, she felt as though she never wanted to leave, as though Paul would come to collect her and she would cling to the nearest piece of furniture like a child and be dragged, protesting, from the one place where she now felt safe and happy.

She turned to him, waited until he looked at her and she kissed him full on the mouth, her hands deep in his hair and she realized that it was not for him, it was for herself, it was to rid her mind of Paul's possession of her, of his harshness, of the way that he felt threatened and when she kissed Ruari she knew that it was not surprising Paul was worried, there was something to worry about.

It was the best kiss she could remember and in some ways that made everything just that little bit harder and she didn't know how much more she could bear. Guilt held her, remembering Paul's eyes when he had accused her of having an affair with Ruari.

She heard footsteps up the yard and his mother came in. She couldn't hide her surprise either but it was uncomplicated.

'Why, Jenna,' she said, 'how lovely to see you. Has our Ruari let the kettle boil dry again? He'll never learn,' and Jenna thought his mother was enjoying having him at home despite the circumstances. That was what she was like, used to making the best of a situation however awful it seemed and this was truly awful.

Her eyes were not lit, she felt her son's disappointment, his frustration, his boredom but she would not make him think she was worried. She went through into the pantry and put more water in the kettle and when it boiled she made tea and gave Jenna some sponge cake with raspberry jam in the middle and they sat over the fire while she told them about the people at work and who she had seen and which girl of her acquaintance had just had her first baby.

The kitchen fire, even though it was the only warm room in the house, beat any other kind of heating and they watched the flames until Jenna knew she must go.

'Here, Ruari, see the lass out, it's dark,' his mother said and she protested.

'No, I left my car out the front and walked round. I'll be fine if I go out the front way.'

He got up and limped through into the front room and his mother came and put the lights on and kissed her goodbye and told her not to be long in coming back, it had been so lovely to see her, and Ruari insisted on seeing her to her car though he needed both crutches once he was out of the door. His mother had gone back in. Jenna got hold of him and kissed him again.

'I'll come tomorrow.'

'No, you mustn't.' His voice had taken on a serious note.

'But–'

'It isn't fair to Paul.' He stopped there and then he said, 'It isn't fair to you and me either and if the newspapers see you we'll still make news, in spite of how things are. Don't come back. Please.'

'You don't understand,' she said, 'this is for me.'

'Not even for you,' he said, 'I'm finished, Jenna, I'm done here. When I can I will leave but it won't be like before.'

'What makes you think I want it like before?'

'No, well, you know what I mean. I don't think I'll ever play again. I'm not being downhearted,' he said as she tried to interrupt, 'I'm just trying to be realistic. I don't know what I'm going to do or where I'm going to go when I can but...'

'Have you somewhere to go?'

'Aye, I have a cottage.'

'Have you really? Where?'

'Yorkshire moors.'

'I didn't know you had a house.'

'It's just little,' he said, 'in a village and when I'm well enough I'll go there.'

'Wouldn't you like to go there for a visit?'

'Above everything, but–'

'I'll take you,' she said.

She wouldn't be talked out of it, Paul's bullying was at the front of her mind and she was determined not to think about it any more, she insisted that she would come over on the first fine day provided she could, and they would go over and they would have lunch at a pub or she could bring a picnic and they could eat at the cottage. He said it would be too cold to go, much too cold to eat there but Jenna didn't listen. She waved and left and it was only when she had driven away that she began to cry.

She had done all the wrong things, she shouldn't have gone there, she shouldn't have kissed him, he was right, it wasn't fair, it wouldn't do, it would only make things worse.

She should not have said that she would see him again, that she would take him to the cottage, that they would spend time together and then she thought back to how he had looked when she had first opened the door and it was despair, loneliness, she could see it. She couldn't leave him to his fate, she just couldn't do it.

Ruari stood there in the cold darkness long after she had left, alone on the front street, wishing he could go after her, wishing everything different, until his mother came out and said, 'You'll catch your death, on top of everything else, come in,' and he followed her inside. He did so, closed the front door and went from the chilly front room which was his bedroom into the kitchen and closed that door to keep in the heat because the stairs went up from the kitchen and warmed the upstairs and his mother said, in quite a different tone than she had used when Jenna was there, 'What on earth is that lass doing here?'

He didn't answer. She was right and he had been right to try and persuade Jenna not to come back. Not that he realized it had done any good or she had taken any notice.

His mother let the silence increase for a few minutes so that he could feel her gaze and her agitation but when he said nothing she said, 'No good will come of it, Ruari. She's married and they're a rich and powerful family and you have no right encouraging her.'

'I didn't.'

'You must have done. I knew it was a mistake when you came back here.'

'It wasn't my mistake.'

'No, well. That Sorrel Maddison, he's nothing but a troublemaker,' his mother said as though Sorrel was still in the schoolyard.

'Will you stop worrying?' Ruari said.

His mother said nothing and from her saying nothing he realized how upset she was and finally she said, 'You should have been married, I always thought so.'

'Aye, I always thought so too.'

'I don't understand why things never work out.'

He heard the quiver in her voice and went

to her where she was laying the table for breakfast as she always did mid-evening and she turned and smiled at him and then she kissed him on the cheek and he knew they would talk no more about it.

The following day there was a letter for him and when he opened it it was from the *Northern Echo*, the newspaper based in Darlington, asking him if he would write an article for them on the state of the football league. Ruari had never thought of such a thing but since they were offering to pay him and he had nothing else to do he sat down and spent the day trying to and when it was done his mother asked Cissie next door if her daughter might type it out for him as she was a clerk at one of the local factories. This done it was sent off and that weekend was published.

It had not occurred to Ruari that he could manage to do such a thing but lots of people wrote letters to the newspaper that week enthusing about it so the newspaper asked him if he would do another and when that was done if he would do one every week and he was so enthusiastic at having something to do that it made the days shorter and less grey.

Just after that he heard from a national newspaper and they too wanted him to write for them and he had now to keep up with football for a good reason and not just as something he was not part of any more. It brought a whole new dimension to his days, gave him something to look forward to, a new angle, and he liked the writing, he liked the precision of it. He even bought a typewriter and taught himself the basics so that he didn't have to rely on anybody else.

It was about this time that Jenna began to feel different about everything. She had thought was it Ruari, the gladness of seeing him, but after a week or so when the feeling did not go away she realized that it was physical, she felt almost like a different person. She began to wonder whether there was something wrong, she was so very tired, so moody. It couldn't be Paul, he had not touched her since the night he had got drunk, as though he was trying to make up for everything.

She felt like crying so very often, it was ridiculous. She thought that it was the time of year, the lead-up to Christmas when every day was dark. She had promised Ruari that they would go to the cottage but the trouble was there was no fine day, the rain and sometimes sleet poured down day after day until she barely wanted to go over the doorstep.

She went to the doctor in the end, telling him that she thought she was depressed. He looked severely at her.

'Depressed?'

'People do get depressed. I feel awful, tired, like I don't want to get out of bed and like I can't take an interest in anything.'

He asked if he could take a look at her and when she lay down on the bed tested her breathing and felt her stomach and generally made her feel as though she wished she hadn't gone there. When she had put her clothes on and sat down again he said, 'You're pregnant.'

Jenna stared at him.

'What? Are you sure?'

'Well, I would say so. Tiredness, no periods, feeling very different–' Her bleeding had stopped some weeks since but she had just thought that she was down and nothing was going right and her body was responding accordingly.

'You've been trying for a baby for a long time. You must be pleased,' he said,

Jenna was stunned. She didn't go home. She sat in the car outside the surgery for a long time and tried to take in what the doctor had said. The sleet was turning to snow and what light there had been was already gone and it was only mid-afternoon. Slowly she made her way back and spent the rest of the afternoon sitting over a log fire with a book on her knee trying to take in the idea.

Ruari didn't like to say anything to his mother but he wanted to leave and one night when she had fussed more than usual trying to do everything he said abruptly, 'I'm thinking about going and living at my house, I'm managing my crutches much better now and I've got lots more energy.'

They were sitting at the table, drinking tea, having just finished eating and she was about to protest, he could see, and then she looked down and she said, 'Yes, I think you should.'

He was so relieved and he realized then that his mother found it difficult having her house turned upside down by somebody moody and difficult and needing looking after.

'You've been grand,' he said.

'I'm your mother, Ruari, that's what mothers are supposed to be. I think you'd be better in your own home and away from here. I think the timing is right and in a lot of ways it would be better for both of us. You need to move on and if you can get sufficient newspaper work it'll be a big help.'

She didn't say 'And away from Jenna,' though she might just as well have done. Jenna had not come back and he had not seen her but he thought about her every day and had no doubt that his mother was right.

'I shall miss you very much,' she said.

'You can come and visit,' he said but he

knew she wouldn't. She hated being away from home and having never lived in the country she felt like it was a different world.

The following day was a change at last, the sun came out and although she wasn't sure she wanted to go Jenna remembered her promise to Ruari. Although he denied it, it was obvious that he had been hoping she would remember and he put up objections only because he felt guilty about dragging her all the way to Yorkshire.

It was not really a long drive but it felt like one. She had never driven with Ruari and was expecting that he would be like Paul who criticized her driving to such an extent that she tried never to drive with him in the car, but Ruari looked around him with increasing interest as they left County Durham and into North Yorkshire and the scenery was lovely, the up and down of cliffs on the coast, the industrial bits interspersed with neat little market towns and small farms.

She followed the coast and then cut across to where the little villages were all stone cottages and had narrow streets and he directed her to the place that he had chosen to live. It was not a big village but it had a stream running through the middle of it and a stone arched bridge at either end. There were three pubs and a village shop and post

303

office and the terraces were short. One of these was his. She parked outside. It had a little front garden and a white front door and small white windows.

Ruari went first and opened the door and he let Jenna inside. It was so cold that you could see your breath. The door opened straight into the sitting room where there was a wood-burning stove in a neat fireplace, baskets of logs at either side, a sofa and two armchairs and further over a table and chairs.

The walls were thick and the room was square. Across the tiny hall was a kitchen, quite new, and a downstairs cloakroom. Jenna ran upstairs and there were two good-size bedrooms and a bathroom and the back windows looked out over a neat garden.

'It's beautiful,' she said.

'It's absolutely bloody freezing,' he said, 'let's go to the pub.'

'Certainly not. I've brought a picnic.'

When she came back he had lit the wood-stove. The room began to warm up straight away and Jenna, interested in his tiny kitchen like she had never been interested in a kitchen before, went in there and put the kettle on and made tea. She liked that she had brought tea and milk, she felt so orga-nized and domestic as she didn't need to be at home. She had made beef sandwiches with horseradish and there were bags of

304

crisps and a fruit cake so as the house warmed they sat by the wood-burner with the doors open and had their picnic and several cups of hot tea.

'I've got a job,' he said. 'Writing about football.'

'I didn't know you could do things like that.'

'Neither did I until a newspaper asked if I would write a column for them. I've done it a few times now and I've had other offers so I must be getting something right. The thing is…'

She looked at him. She didn't want to because she hated the direction in which the conversation was going but she felt that she had to even though there was a sick feeling inside her which was nothing to do with the baby.

'I'm getting better, I mean I can get about with crutches quite well now and…'

Ruari didn't look at her.

'I'm going to move down here. I can manage and I think it's time I did.'

Jenna didn't say anything. She leaned over and put another log on the fire and closed the doors.

'It's almost an hour and a half away.'

He didn't say anything to that.

'It's a long way for me to come and visit.'

'I didn't think you would,' he said.

'You don't want me to?'

'No. No, I don't want you to.'

He said it slowly and with emphasis as though he was not quite sure, as though he didn't want to believe it, and he watched the flames flickering through the little square glass doors instead of looking at her. There seemed nothing more to say somehow, she felt panicked, as though everything was finished, as though she was going to lose him again for the second time and that this time it might be for good and maybe he had another reason for moving.

'Do you have somebody here?'

'Of course I don't.' He turned his face to her then, in surprise she thought with joy and so quickly that Jenna looked carefully at him.

'You did have a lot of girlfriends,' she said.

'I never wanted anybody but you,' he said and kept his voice steady.

It was the thing she most liked hearing and in some ways the worst. Jenna thought about the baby. She thought of how she had cheated Paul of his first child. She hadn't loved him, she hadn't wanted him, and in spite of all that he had taken her and married her because of the child and he had loved her in spite of it all and then she had lost the baby and the whole reason for their marriage was gone and that was why it had failed, she knew.

'And it isn't right,' he said, 'going on like

this when Paul doesn't know and doesn't like me. You're married and as far as I'm concerned that's all there is to it. So, I wanted to see you and I wanted to show you this place and…'

'It seems stupid that you should be here by yourself and I should be there like that.'

'It's the right thing to do, though, isn't it?'

She wanted to say, 'Why should we do the right thing?' but she understood what he meant. It wasn't fair to Paul now that she was pregnant to spend time with Ruari, she knew that it wasn't, that none of it could ever work if she betrayed him now, especially when she had such good news. She had never belonged more to Paul than she did now so she didn't argue with him, she washed up and put the cutlery and crockery into the right places and then she packed up the remnants of the picnic and then she came through and said, 'When will you move here?'

'For Christmas, I think. Jack and his family would come over and it would be nice to settle in then. I don't know whether my mam would come, I'll have to try and talk her into it.'

It seemed such a long drive back somehow and nobody spoke as she hurled the little car forward through the darkness. It was stupid, she thought, and so typical that she should be pregnant now. She imagined her marriage

307

getting better because of it, she thought of what Christmas would be like with a baby and how pleased Paul would be and how Sorrel and Faye would become involved.

Things would get so much better, the whole house, all their lives would be altered by this child but she also acknowledged to herself that if she had not been pregnant she would have begged Ruari to take her with him. It was like a replay of what had happened the first time and so unfair that she could not believe it was happening again. It was as though the gods did not choose to let her be with Ruari, as though the time never would be right.

She dropped Ruari off at his door. He said he could manage perfectly well, thanked her for the day and neither of them even hugged or offered another word. It was a frosty night and once she had seen him in at his front door without slipping she set off again.

She had to go through the town to get back to the manor house. She was not looking forward to it. Paul would not be home until two or three at least, it was one of his late nights and there would probably be nobody at home at all. The place would be in darkness.

She half wished that Ruari had asked her in but it was so awkward between them that she didn't think it would have helped. She was glad that he was trying to do something

308

with his life, to change things, she was glad he had such a lovely little place to live and she thought of him sitting there by the fire with his mother on Christmas Day.

She pulled up at the traffic lights on the edge of the town because they were on red and she had to wait and as she did so she saw Paul's car. He still had the red Ferrari his father had bought for him the night that she had lost the baby. It was sitting outside the fish-and-chip shop and it stuck out like a sore thumb she thought, nobody else had a red Ferrari. She could see into the fish-and-chip shop and Paul was standing at the front of the queue next to a young blonde girl.

It seemed strange that he should be having fish and chips, had his father had a sudden craving for such a thing? She didn't think so, Sorrel was too conscious of his waistline to eat things like that on impulse and in the evenings he was too busy to eat most of the time.

At clubs or in meetings she didn't think he would have done such a thing. Paul was probably just hungry, it was not surprising, she thought in sudden affection, because his father never stopped and Paul had probably had nothing to eat all day and was on the way to one of the clubs and had smelled the salt and vinegar and frying chips on the wind.

She imagined stopping the car and going into the shop and getting him to buy fish and chips for her, the smell was so good, and then she would tell him about the baby and then she thought she should wait until he came home because doubtless he wouldn't have time now for such things and his having to go back to work would ruin her surprise. How pleased he would be, how very glad. Maybe her Christmas would be good too.

Paul, his fish and chips wrapped now, came out of the shop and the lights turned green and Jenna didn't go. She just sat there. The blonde girl was coming out with him. It must be one of Sorrel's beautiful secretaries, Jenna thought, there were so many of them. She had to go before people started pipping but a small worm of doubt troubled her almost immediately and she turned off and waited. Within a few moments the Ferrari had turned down the same street as she had somehow known it would so she set off and followed it.

He was making for the coast road where the old Edwardian houses were on the edge of the town. She had sometimes thought, when she was a little girl, that she would love to live there. They had always looked so glamorous with their three storeys, their gardens which fell away at the back and from the front looked out across the sea. It was where the rich people had lived in olden times, she thought. Now they were flats, some of them really nice from what she could observe from the outside.

Paul's car pulled up here. She was surprised when he stopped. She had to go on of course though she doubted he would have noticed anyway. It was dark and there were various cars about. She pulled up again further along, conscious of her heart beating though still not quite sure why she was here. Was he giving somebody a lift home?

She turned around. His car was very handily parked under a street lamp and she could see now that he was leaning over. Was he going to let her out, opening the door for her, a compromise between getting out and opening the door which would have been ludicrous and letting her get out by herself which might have seemed to him rude?

And then Jenna stared. He was kissing the girl, and there was nothing polite about that, she was getting nearer and had both arms around his neck and the kiss went on and on. Finally they drew apart and then they got out of the car and tripped away into the house and Jenna was left, numb. She should have driven away she should have gone home, but she sat there, telling herself that she had not seen what she had seen.

The car became cold and she was just reaching that temperature when it seemed too much of an effort to start the car up, to get warm again, and then she thought of the baby and then she thought of Paul kissing the other girl but she started the car up then and drove back to the house. It was in darkness and suddenly she was driving away again, she was driving through the town and towards her mother's house.

She parked outside and hammered on the front door. There were lights in the back room. She had to bang harder and when she did so she still had to wait a long time. Even here, she thought, people did not come to the front door and eventually she heard her mother's voice and saw the curtains twitch and said impatiently, 'It's me, Jenna.'

'Who?'

'Jenna.'

She heard the bolts go back in the front door and then her mother cautiously opened the door.

'What on earth are you doing here at this time of night?' she said as though it was two in the morning.

'Can I come in?'

It was not much warmer inside and her mother closed the door quickly and ushered her through, shutting the sitting-room door firmly.

'Is there something the matter?'

There would have to be, Jenna thought grimly, her mother might be pleased she had married Paul but they hardly ever saw one another. There was the smell of paint in the hall, her mother must have been decorating the stairs.

Jenna didn't know what to say. She couldn't tell her mother about Paul. She couldn't tell her mother about the baby. In fact she wasn't sure why she had come here just that she could not think where else to go.

'Where's Dad?'

'He's at a darts match. Is everything all right?' Her mother's face was concerned and not sympathetic, she didn't want her evening interrupted, Jenna thought, she didn't want bad news. I always bring bad news with me, no wonder she looks so worried.

'No, I ... I just wondered how you were.'

'We're fine. I mean your dad's sciatica's playing him up a bit and my knees aren't too good but... You look peaky.'

Jenna longed for her mother to be the sort of person you could confide in, somebody who would care. No, that was not right, her mother did care she just wished things to go well and there was nothing wrong with that.

'Shall I make you a cup of tea?' her mother offered, getting up.

'No. No, really I have to go.'

'But you've just got here. Is there really nothing the matter?'

'No, it's all fine, it was just that ... it was

just that we wondered what you were doing for Christmas and I thought I'd come and ask you. Maybe you'd like to come to us.'

Her mother looked well pleased, she loved the few invitations she ever received to the Maddison household.

'Well, we did plan to stop here but I'm sure your dad wouldn't mind.'

Her father always liked his own fireside best, Jenna thought with affection. He was not prepared to give it up for the grand setting of the manor house but her mother would persuade him, he would do anything for her mother.

'That's good. That was all it was. We're having goose stuffed with apricots.'

'That'll be lovely,' her mother said, knowing that her father insisted on turkey.

The house had become insufferably hot somehow, she hated the constant smell of paint and in her condition it was making her feel sick. It was just like the last time, she thought, she trying to tell her mother, only this time she couldn't and not telling her father and having to face up to things she didn't want to face up to.

She had always hated this house, the little castle which her mother loved so much and lavished all her time and affection on. It never looked any different, it never looked any better, Jenna thought savagely and suddenly she couldn't bear being there any more, so far away from everything she cared about and even as her mother protested that she had just got there she left, slamming her way into the little car.

Once she was away she tried not to drive too fast, she didn't want to have an accident, not the way she was. Did she really want Paul's baby? She wished and wished it could have been Ruari's. Were things never going to go right for her? She almost gave up caring.

She almost thought if she could crash into a tree or a lamppost and finish the whole thing how much would it really matter to anybody but somehow the little car found its way home to Back Church Street and she managed to get out of it and found herself hammering once again on the front door. She had to wait, the wind was screaming past her now and the hail was sideways.

'For God's sake,' she implored, 'open the bloody door,' and when he did, and it was Ruari, she had been afraid it was his mother, she cast herself on him even as she saw his astonished face and then she broke down in tears.

He gathered her into the house and his mother was there by then.

'Why, lass,' she said, drawing her away from Ruari and inside, 'what is it? Come in, come by the fire.'

In the back room, which she realized now

315

she had left such a short time ago, they sat her down and he held her hands and she tried to stop crying and his mam said, 'It cannot be as bad as that,' and she said,

'Oh, yes it can. It's just as bad as last time and I've got nowhere to go and I don't know what to do.'

Mrs Robson gave her tea and though she didn't drink it somehow the warmth of the cup in her hands and the warmth from the fire and how safe she began to feel made the situation easier and then she remembered quite how awful it was.

'What is it, Jen?'

He hadn't called her Jen in years and his soft reassuring voice made her want to tell him but if he found out she was pregnant he would urge her to go back and she couldn't do that.

'Can I stay? I don't want to go back there, I don't ever want to.'

'Nobody's going to make you go any-where,' Ruari said as his mother nodded.

They didn't question her any further. Mrs Robson ushered her into a freezing bedroom and gave her a thick full-length nightdress with long sleeves, Jenna hadn't been in a cold bedroom for so long that she was amazed at how awful it was but when she had undressed and climbed into the bed there was the joy of an electric blanket and she was so exhausted that she curled up into a ball, glad of the warmth and the darkness where nobody and nothing could reach her, and she went to sleep, she couldn't manage any more.

Paul got home as he usually did at about three in the morning to discover his bed empty. He thought that Jenna had a cold or some such and had gone into the other room but when he ventured in she wasn't there either. He went back downstairs and searched in the sitting room, perhaps she couldn't sleep – and then in the kitchen. Maybe she had got up to make some tea, he thought, but she was nowhere to be found and he began to worry and when he put on a coat and went outside her car had gone.

He ran quickly back into the house and up the stairs and banged hard on his parents' bedroom door. There was a short wait and then his father appeared, wearing a pair of expensive blue pyjamas. He peered into the light of the hall, looking bewildered.

'Where's Jenna?' Paul said.

Sorrel looked blankly at him.

'She's missing. She isn't here,' Paul explained carefully.

'Missing?'

'Was she here when you came in?'

'I was late,' his father said as though he should have known and Paul could hear his mother's voice and she came to the door, tying a dressing gown around her.

'What is it?' she said.

'Was Jenna here when you went to bed?'

'I don't know. I presume so. I'd been out playing bridge. I thought she'd gone to bed early.'

'Well, she hasn't; she's not here.'

'She probably went to see her mother and stayed. Is there a note?'

They searched the whole house, all the lights on.

'She probably knew you'd be back late and stayed there,' his father said impatiently.

'She never stays with them. She doesn't get on with her mother,' Paul said. 'I'll have to go and see.'

'You can't go there at this time of night,' his mother protested but he was already halfway down the stairs and collecting his car keys from the hall table.

It was snowing by now. He slipped as he stepped out of the front door and cursed his expensive shoes which were not meant for such things. He tried to go carefully to the garage and then backed the car out, turned it around and drove across the town to where Jenna's parents lived in the little terraced house which he had hardly ever been in and hated, it was tiny and claustro-phobic and Jenna's mother was always fussing with bloody wallpaper and paste that stank. He didn't know how her father stood it but then her father was a pathetic little man who wouldn't say boo to a goose.

Paul tore down the roads in spite of the thickening snowflakes so that the windscreen wipers would barely take it and pulled up with a jerk outside their front door. The street was dark and silent as it would be now that it was half-past four. He got out and brayed hell out of their door. He seemed to wait for ages, the snowflakes falling on to his hair and his coat and he cursed under his breath, trying not to panic. She could not have gone far but why had she left the house at all, what was going on?

After he had done knocking hell out of the door twice more, after a short forever lights came on above and so he did it again and after a very long cold period when he became covered in snow the downstairs lights came on and the door was unlocked and Mr Duncan peered out. He wore striped pyjamas and a grey woollen dressing gown and he looked surprised. Paul didn't blame him.

'I need to speak to Jenna.'

Mr Duncan looked at him.

'Jenna?'

'I'm worried about her. She didn't leave a note. She is all right?'

'Isn't she with you?' Mr Duncan said with all the vagueness of somebody who had been sound asleep ten minutes ago.

'She's here. I want to speak to her.'

'She's not here,' and the idea suddenly seemed to hit her father.

He let Paul into the house, or rather he stood back as Paul, tired of being cold, outside and confused, pushed his way inside. By then Mrs Duncan was hovering in the background and when Mr Duncan explained Paul could see the concern on her face. She began to cry. Paul was very embarrassed, he wasn't used to tears. His mother never cried and Jenna had shed few tears except when she lost the baby. Thinking about that time made him feel very uncomfortable.

'She came here earlier,' her mother said.

'When was this?'

'Oh, in the middle of the evening. About nine or something like that. You weren't back from the pub then,' she said to her husband. 'I didn't know there was anything the matter, though she didn't look well. I thought maybe you'd had words or something.'

'Did she say anything?' Paul's patience was almost at an end.

'She invited us to your house for Christmas. I asked her what was wrong, and she didn't look well but she wouldn't stop.'

'So where is she?' Paul said and then he knew and he was angry and hurt and confused. He could see that her parents had no idea where she had gone so he didn't say anything to them. He tried to be reassuring.

He made his apologies, he told them he would let them know when he found her. Mr Duncan offered to help, Paul said brusquely that he didn't need any help and then he urged the car forward through the snow the few streets until he got to Back Church Street and yes, there it was, her car parked so obviously outside Ruari Gallacher's door. He cursed her as he pulled up behind it.

What the bloody hell was she playing at and as for that bastard Gallacher... He wrenched on the handbrake, got out and slammed the door and then again began hammering on the wood of the front door. At least the snow had stopped. It gave everything such a strange and almost eerie look. Total silence except for his efforts which seemed huge, big enough to reverberate off the houses opposite.

Here again he had to wait but eventually the door opened and there stood Gallacher, propped by crutches but not looking very surprised.

'Hello, Paul,' he said.

Paul pushed past him, it wasn't difficult, when a man's on crutches he doesn't take a lot of getting past. He saw the small put-up bed and then he looked back at Ruari and he said, 'Where's my wife?'

'She's in bed upstairs.'

'You didn't think to let me know?'

'My mother doesn't have a telephone.'

Paul couldn't believe it. Everybody had telephones. He was about to say there was a public call box on the corner and then he stopped himself. It was ridiculous. Gallacher had had no intention of letting him know his wife was there, didn't care enough to put anybody at their ease, least of all somebody of his family.

'What's going on?' he said.

'I don't know,' Ruari said so convincingly that Paul believed him. 'She was upset when she got here and it was late and she was tired and she wouldn't go home so my mother made up the bed in the other room.'

'I'd like to see her.'

'Maybe you should wait until the morning.'

'I don't think you're in any position to tell me what to do,' Paul said, indicating the crutches.

'Possibly not, but–'

Ruari stopped as both Jenna and his mother appeared behind Paul, who was standing with his back to the room. He turned around. His wife was wearing the most unbecoming nightclothes he had ever seen. They were undoubtedly Gallacher's mother's, long and washed-out looking and she was washed-out looking too. He could not help comparing her to the lovely armful he had left, Trudie in black and cream satin, warm and willing.

Jenna's blonde hair was lank and her eyes were dark and empty and she clutched the front of the shapeless garment she had been offered for warmth, her hands were thin and her face was pale and she stared. And yet he thought she had never looked more beautiful, more appealing, and he had never loved her more. He could have shrieked with frustration. He could see now that what he felt for Trudie would never equal the love he had had for Jenna and went on having in spite of everything that had happened. Trudie was like having one glass of cheap brandy when what you really wanted was two good measures of Rémy Martin.

'What are you doing here?' Paul said. He noticed how his voice was soft with relief but rough with anger. He was glad to find her but hated that she was here in Gallacher's mother's bloody awful little house.

'Ruari,' his mother said, 'I think these people need some space.'

Ruari hobbled off into the kitchen and his mother went with him and closed the door behind her. In some stupid way Paul wished they wouldn't go. Whatever reason Jenna had for coming here he had the feeling he wasn't going to like it and he wanted to put it off for as long as possible.

He also wished he could just whisk her

away back to the manor house where he thought she was safe and his and waiting for him, no matter what he had done, he needed her there for him to come back to, he felt it was the only real thing he had left somehow. He tried to keep his voice low so that she would not run off into the other room. At least she and Gallacher were not sleeping in the same bed, it was respectable, his mother was there, he had had the horrible feeling, which he had kept to the back of his mind, that Jenna and Ruari had run away together, though run was perhaps a little generous, considering Gallacher could barely walk.

'I got home and you weren't there,' he said slightly accusing. 'I've searched everywhere, I've even been to your mother's. Are you all right?'

Jenna seemed to take a breath and then she sat down. She didn't say anything for so long that Paul wanted to prompt her but he knew it wouldn't help, he just had to sit there and give her time. Jenna was not the kind of woman who didn't answer questions, she had been brought up to respond no matter how difficult things were, he knew. Eventually she shifted her weight about and then she said honestly and with a sigh, in a way he had always loved, 'No, I'm not all right. Nothing's right in my life at all.'

It was what he was expecting in some

ways. He knew nothing was right, he just didn't know any longer how to make it right, because he had tried and tried for so long to make things up to her that he had long since given up and not known how to go on. Muddling along, wasn't that what most people did?

'You could have told me.'

'I think you knew,' she said.

'What did I know?' He sat down on the awful little bed which creaked under his weight so that he thought it might tip up and land them both on the floor.

'How unhappy I was.'

'I didn't know you were unhappy.'

'I've been unhappy for a long time now and I think you have too otherwise why would you have somebody else?'

So that was it, that was what she was doing here. At first he could only be pleased that it was something so unimportant, at least to him, but then she had run to Gallacher. He thought of the awful house which her parents had. She had run there first but had not had any help. Maybe she had had nowhere but here to go. Paul didn't know what to say, she seemed so sure.

'I saw you,' she said, 'tonight, with her. I saw you come out of the fish shop and I saw you kissing her in the car and I saw you go into the pretty Edwardian house.'

Paul didn't know what to say doubly now.

He thought about explaining it away but it seemed so pointless. He imagined how it looked to her, how tawdry, how stupid, him acting like a teenager, like he had no wife, no commitment, no comfort. And then he thought that really that had been the problem, there was no comfort with Jenna. That was what Trudie provided. How odd.

He had thought it was the sex, the sexy underwear, the illicitness of it all, the badness, something he thought that most men wanted, for excitement in their lives, when in fact it had been stupid things like the fish and chips, the way that he had been able to go home to Trudie as he had never been able to go home to Jenna.

He had got it wrong, he should have given her her own home, he should have been able to come home to her, and to their child, rather than staying with his parents in a house which he thought, honest now with himself, he had never liked. It was nothing to do with them and the failure of his parents' marriage was so evident in the way that his mother ran to the cottage and his father to that awful club and the young woman he bedded because he wasn't getting any at home. It was no way to live, Paul thought, and yet he had accepted it as inevitable somehow. It was apparently the best they could do, but it shouldn't be.

'And you blame me?' he said.

'I don't blame anybody any more,' she said and there was a weary note in her voice.

He got up. He didn't think the bed would take his weight for much longer.

'Has it been going on for long?' she said.

'Yes, quite a while.' Paul walked about the room, he couldn't sit still or stand still and he didn't know what to say. He could not explain it away because it was his own doing. 'God, it's cold in here. How do people live like this and what made you come here?'

'I tried going to my parents but ... you know what my mother's like. Do you love her?'

'No.' He felt like a traitor at both sides now. 'I like her a lot, she's fun and she ... gives me things you don't and...' Paul laughed shortly. 'I didn't think I'd turn into my father quite this quickly. I wanted us to be a family but after we lost the baby and in such a way everything seemed to fall apart. I'm sorry Jenna.'

In the kitchen Ruari's mother brought the fire back to life. He loved how she could do that, she raked the still warm ashes and put on a few sticks and within seconds they burst into flames. He should have been re-assured by it, it was what she had been doing for years, and he sat there while she fussed because there was nothing else for either of them to do and he tried not to listen to the conversation which was going on next door. It wasn't easy. The houses had been thrown up by the pit owners years ago, they were not well built and you could hear everything in every room, there was no escape.

The voices were low and even and Ruari thought he didn't know Paul well, was he the kind of man who shouted and threatened or was he more like Sorrel would be, devious and cunning? Jenna hardly spoke at all and his voice was thankfully, most of the time just a low even sound which became more difficult to discern as the fire crackled and burned and his mother put on coal and the flames licked around the blackness of it.

'I knew it wasn't right her coming here in the first place,' his mother said. 'Once people are married everything's different.'

'Not these days, Mam. People get divorced.'

'Divorced women have a very bad time in places like this. They get called names and people think less of them. If she doesn't want to go back with him what will we do then?'

Ruari didn't know what to say. Jenna was all wrong here now. Even in his mother's old nightwear she looked so appealing, like an orphan from a Dickens stony she should have had a house of her own and... He thought of her at the cottage and how at home she had looked there but it wasn't right when she was another man's wife.

In the living room Paul said, 'Come back home and we'll sort this out. You can't want to stay here, it's awful.'

Jenna didn't know what to say, what to do. She was half inclined to tell Paul about the baby but she thought, We've been here before and look what happened to us. She hadn't been invited to stay here, Ruari and his mother had just taken her in because they could think of no alternative, she could see, she didn't belong, hadn't belonged here for a very long time. She only wished her parents had been the kind of people who would look after her for a few days until she worked out what to do. And as they sat there the front door went. Paul got up and opened it and there stood her dad.

'I worked it out,' he said, 'it wasn't too difficult,' and he stepped past Paul and into the living room. There he hugged Jenna as she got to her feet. 'I don't know what's going on but I think you should come home with me for a day or two,' he said.

Paul tried to protest but for once Mr Duncan wasn't having any of it.

'No, Paul,' he said so that Jenna was proud of him and he looked Paul in the face and he said, 'This needs sorting out but I don't think it'll be done here. The place for Jenna

329

is back in her own home for the moment.'

'Our house is her home,' Paul protested but even as he said it it sounded all wrong.

Mrs Robson came through and even while Paul was still trying to argue she said, 'Come upstairs, Jenna, and collect your things. I think your dad's right, you need your family now,' so Jenna went into the back room, nodded at Ruari who smiled reassuringly at her and then she went upstairs and changed into her own clothes and picked up her handbag and thanked his mam for her help and then she followed her father's car back to Wesley Road.

It didn't smell of paint any more, either it had dried or she just didn't feel the same about it. Her mam was sitting up in her big blue candlewick dressing gown and she looked so white and worried.

'I've made the bed up for you in your old room and I've put a hot-water bottle in,' she said and Jenna thanked her briefly and for the second time that night got into a bed other than the one she shared with Paul. She had thought she was too upset to rest but she was exhausted. Once again she undressed and this time got into one of her mother's flannelette nighties which wrapped itself comfortingly around her and the moment she cuddled the hot-water bottle to her she closed her eyes on the sweet-smelling pillow and fell asleep.

Paul couldn't believe that the situation had been taken away from him. He wanted to shout and bluster and make a difference like his father would have done but short of violence which had no place here there was nothing he could do as other people did things around him. He wanted Jenna back very badly indeed, wanted to shout that he would give up Trudie, that everything would be like before, and then he remembered what things had been like before and knew that there was nothing he could offer Jenna that she would even consider.

He wanted to blame Gallacher and shout at him and maybe even knock him down but he couldn't do that either, he could only stand by while Mrs Robson fussed and put an arm around her shoulders and talked softly to her like he wished somebody would do to him, anybody to make it feel better and then wait while she went off upstairs.

Her father stood there like a terrier, glaring at him from time to time in a way that Paul had never expected, as though Paul was about to insist she went back to the manor house, as though he could insist on anything any more.

She came back, dressed in clothes he recognized, looking more like herself so that there was a part of him that did not believe she was going to her parents' house, that she would turn around and change her mind and go with him and tell him that she had forgiven him and everything would be all right.

She didn't even look at him, she went off without a word to either Gallacher or himself and once her car had driven off down the road there was nothing left for Paul but to go home. He stepped out into the street and watched the brake lights as she took the corner and then the road was empty and Gallacher had shut the front door of his house, turned the key and put in the bolts and even turned off the lights, he was obviously not taking any risks in that direction in case Paul decided to go back in, though what point there would have been in it Paul could not think. Now he wanted to go home, it was all that was left.

His father and mother were drinking tea in the kitchen. He assured them that Jenna was fine and that she would be back in a day or two, she had gone to her parents. He didn't say anything about Gallacher or his mother.

He thought his parents would accept what he said but they looked at one another and, still sitting at the kitchen table, his mother said baldly, 'Is she leaving you?'

'No, of course not. Whatever gave you that impression?' How on earth had his mother got that far?

'I didn't think it was much of a match right from the beginning,' his mother said. 'I thought you could have done a lot better but there was no point in saying anything. It was never right for you, marrying her like that...'

She didn't call Jenna names though she sounded as if she would have liked to and felt such words appropriate, Paul thought.

'Was she at her parents'?'

Trust his father to ask the difficult question. He evaded it.

'She's staying there for a few days, I said. We just need to sort things out, it'll be all right.'

Neither of his parents looked as though they believed him but they got up to go back to bed as though they thought they had done everything they could whereas in fact they had done nothing. His mother put the tea cups in the sink, his father didn't even speak and Paul didn't trust himself to say anything more to him because he had the impression that his father knew exactly what was going on but didn't think it would help to talk about it any more.

Paul escaped to bed but he wished he could have gone to Trudie. He wasn't ever alone in bed, he wasn't used to it and he didn't like it. He was so used to having Jenna there, breathing evenly beside him. He was no good on his own, he panicked by himself, there was too much space in which to think and it was the last thing he wanted to do.

Ruari's mother sat over the newly burning-up fire with him for a while and she said, 'You never did get over that lass. I dare say you never will.'

'Maybe not.'

'It was good her dad came for her, they didn't do enough, at least he managed that.' She got up with a sigh. 'It's just as well you're going,' she said and then she went to bed.

Ruari didn't want to go back into the freezing front room. He lay down on the sofa with a thick blanket over him and a pillow which his mother had brought in, having already read his mind. He thanked her and he didn't even try to sleep. He couldn't help but imagine what it would have been like if he and Jenna could have gone to live in his lovely little cottage. He wouldn't have been lonely then. He thought of them buying a Christmas tree, maybe hanging decorations, sitting over the fire and even going to bed together, something they had never done. Why could he not accept that things like that didn't happen?

She would go back to Paul, he was her husband, why should she not? He wished he could have heard their conversation properly. He still didn't know why she had left, though she must have had a very good reason. He wished she had been able to tell him what was going on, why she was so very upset. Paul seemed equally as upset. Could it be that they had just quarrelled and she had taken it badly and run away and he had got frightened as to what had happened?

Ruari tried not to think about it. He tried to think about the future. His leg was getting better. He thought he could just about manage with a stick. He needed to be more confident, he had got so used to crutches but with a stick he would be able to get about much more easily, he would be able to manage by himself at the cottage.

He would be so glad to go. He could hire a taxi to take him there. He would even be able to go to the shops in the village and if they delivered the groceries for him he thought he would be able to manage the rest. He couldn't wait to leave. He would have his writing to do.

The following morning while he and his mother were having breakfast the post arrived and she went through into the front and picked up the letters and there was one for him. When he opened it at the kitchen table it was a letter from a publisher. They wanted him to write his autobiography. His mother laughed.

'At your age?' she said.

'It's about football, Mam.'

'Well, I never,' she said, 'and do you think you can do it?'

'I don't see why I shouldn't.'

'And are they going to pay you to do it?'

'They are.'

'Well, that's wonderful,' his mother said and she sat down and buttered her second piece of toast.

Jenna awoke in the back room at her mother's house. It brought back all the memories of being there when Ruari had left and she had been pregnant and Paul had agreed to marry her. Now she had another problem to sort out. She was not prepared for Paul to turn up just after nine.

She wished her father had still been there but he had gone off to work. Her mother was no defence. To her Paul was still the white knight who had rescued Jenna from Ruari, he was the best thing that had happened to her and if she couldn't keep it together it was most likely her own fault though she had been relieved to see Jenna back under her roof. She greeted Paul like he was the cavalry, Jenna could hear her ushering him into the front room where Jenna sat over the fire. It was a banana colour these days in there, it was hideous, she thought.

'I've come to take you back with me,' he

said when her mother had ostentatiously left them as though they were lovers about to be reconciled.

He was wearing the same clothes he had had on the day before, which was not like him, Jenna thought. He looked dishevelled, as though he didn't care about such things, as though he had not slept, and he kept avoiding her eyes.

'I think I might stay here for a day or two, Paul, if it's all the same to you.'

'It isn't all the same to me. My parents are worried about you and you belong with us.'

He was still trying to bully her, she couldn't believe it. Jenna wanted to say not as long as you have somebody else but she had started thinking about this and she realized that it was not the point. She was having Paul's child. She didn't imagine that somebody would wave a magic wand and he would give up the blonde girl for her and even if he was to do that she thought that in time he would probably do the same thing again.

She had no illusions about babies bringing people together when their marriages were rocky. She had the feeling that another person taking up her time and needing her attention so very much would make Paul feel so insecure that he would not stay with her any more than he had to but it was his child. She didn't want to go back, her instincts were to run away once again to Back Church Street, but she knew it was not fair on Ruari or his mother and especially it was not fair to go to Ruari when she was carrying Paul's child.

Her father came back. She was astonished. She thought he had gone to work but maybe he had known what would happen and that if he wasn't there worse would follow He didn't give Paul a chance to say anything, he just came into the room.

'Jenna isn't going back today, Paul,' he said. 'She needs a rest from all that.'

Paul was not, Jenna thought with dry humour, about to enquire what 'all that' was but her father for once was not giving in and he didn't even go out of the room so that they could talk by themselves so Paul had no alternative. He could hardly insist and look like he was forcing her,

'I was so bothered last night, Jenna,' her father confided when he had gone. 'I wish I'd been here when you came and hadn't let you go. I wish you'd told me what the problem was. I'm not saying I could have done anything but I would have listened.'

Jenna didn't say anything.

'Is it that lad? You went there. How could you do that? Are you doing something you shouldn't?'

'No, I'm not,' Jenna said.

She was so pleased when her dad came

back again at tea time and that it was Sunday the following day and he would not be going to work. It was a fine bright day and cold and he took her for a walk on the beach and she put her hand through his arm. Her mother made a Sunday dinner and she quite enjoyed that day sitting over the fire when the darkness fell in the late afternoon, but come the following morning when he went to work and she was left with her mother she didn't want to be there any more and she thanked her mother for having her and left. She didn't go home, she went to Ruari's.

When he opened the door he was using only a stick and she was so pleased that they didn't talk about anything else. His mother had gone shopping and Jenna was only pleased to have him to herself.

'I wanted to talk to you,' she said as he showed her into the back room.

'I was hoping you would come. Can you tell me what's going on or would you rather not?'

She told him about what she had seen after she had left his house, about Paul and the blonde girl and that he had had someone else for some time and then she said, 'I don't want to stay with him. If I have to I'll find a little flat and get a job, I'll manage something. I'm not going back to my parents, my mother doesn't really want me there and I couldn't bear it but I'm not staying with Paul now. I can't go and live there knowing that he has somebody else.'

'Wouldn't he give her up?'

'He might but the reason he has her is because we have such an awful marriage. There are no two ways about it, it's horrible,' she said. 'The thing is...' She wanted to say it but couldn't. 'The thing is...'

'Jenna, look,' he said and then he stopped and then he said, 'Will you come with me? I haven't got much to offer any more but I've always loved you. It might be very difficult and Paul might kick up a bad fuss but if you want to you can come to Yorkshire. I've got the cottage and I can change the car for something more sensible, I don't think I could drive it anyway like this, I don't feel as if I could but I got a good offer from a publisher to write a book about the football I've played and I think I might get more work in journalism so it could turn out to be all right. What do you think?'

It was such a long speech on his part that Jenna could only stare. She didn't know whether she could afford to be honest with him and then she knew that if she was going with him that she had to be.

'I'm having a baby,' she said.

Ruari stared for so long that she wished she hadn't said it, yet what else could she do?

'Does Paul know?'

Jenna shook her head. 'I was ready to tell him. After that lovely day we had at your cottage I wished I didn't have to but I thought I might be able to have some kind of a life without you if only we had a child but I don't think it would matter, that it would make the difference. What's spoiled our marriage is that I never loved him like I love you, I couldn't do it and though I tried it didn't work out. In some ways I shouldn't blame him for going to another girl. I should never have married him. He did the right thing but then ... he cared for me and I think he hoped in time that I would care for him but after the baby died...'

'You don't think it might happen now?'

'I want you,' she said.

'I want you too but ... his kid.'

'You wouldn't want it?'

'Of course I would want it, didn't I say that I would have taken the first?'

'Well, then.'

'But for him not to know.'

'If I tell him we'll never get out of here,' Jenna said.

'It doesn't seem right.'

'It's the only way.'

'So what are you going to tell him?'

Jenna looked Ruari straight in the eyes.

'I'm going to tell him you and I have been having an affair ever since you got here and it's yours.'

341

'That doesn't seem right either.'

'I know but again, I've thought a lot about it over the last couple of days and I think it's the only way we'll ever have any peace. I don't want him and his family to have rights over our baby and it'll be ours if we bring it up. The Maddisons have never bothered with me, I was always in the way.

'If Paul and I divorce at least he would have the chance to marry somebody they might like or at least approve of. I was never good enough for them. I don't want them connected to us or Paul having rights to the baby while he's been out sleeping with somebody else all this while.

'I'm not going to put up with it so if you don't want to be part of this, Ruari, just say so because I will leave anyway and I will manage. I'm not stopping here to have the Maddisons run my life any more. Do you want me to come with you or not?

'Make up your mind because that's what I'm going to tell him, regardless of whether you let me come with you. You can deny it of course but I'll blame you and nobody will believe anything else by the time I'm finished. I'll make sure the papers get it.'

She thought Ruari looked astonished but that he could see she meant it. She waited and finally he said, 'I want you. I've always wanted you.'

She came to him and put her arms around

him and then she kissed him.

'I'm going back there for my stuff, just the little that's mine, and when your mam comes back you can tell her and we could go to the cottage today because I can look after you.'

Jenna got into her car and drove back to the manor house. Only Paul's mother was at home. Jenna didn't bother with her, she just took her suitcases, opened them on the bed and began putting her clothes and make-up and toiletries into them. After a while she noticed Faye standing in the doorway

'You are going, then?'

'I am, yes. You must be glad.'

'Well, I have to say that I was never very happy about it.'

'I'm taking nothing that isn't mine,' Jenna pointed out.

'Take what you want,' Faye said. 'Is it Gallacher?'

'Yes.'

'He's nice,' Faye said. 'I hope you find what you're looking for,' and she turned around and walked out.

Jenna didn't even say goodbye and Faye didn't offer to help. She was so obviously glad to be rid of Jenna, no doubt thinking that her son would find somebody else soon, men like him always did and that possibly she would have grandchildren. It

343

was quite ironic in some ways, Jenna thought. She carried two suitcases downstairs and put them into the car. She considered whether to tell her mother and then she thought she wouldn't bother. She would ring so that they wouldn't worry but she didn't want to see them, she didn't want anybody trying to talk her out of this when her mind was made up.

She was just about to leave when the red Ferrari pulled up in the driveway. The sickness that Jenna felt was nothing to do with the baby but then she thought, I couldn't really have gone without telling him, it would have been cowardly so she stood there.

Paul got slowly out of the car, his gaze fixed on this evidence of her leaving.

'You're back early. I was going to come to the office and tell you,' she said.

'Jenna, I can make it different, honestly I can. I'll give up Trudie and we'll start again, we'll buy a house of our own and–'

'I don't want to live like this any more,' Jenna said.

'It won't be like this–'

'I'm having Ruari Gallacher's baby,' Jenna said.

She held her breath to see whether he would accept this but she thought that in the trashy world where the Maddisons lived this was what people did, how they behaved, perhaps even expected it. They betrayed one another without thought, what mattered to them most was money and power and football, not the decent things of life like giving time and effort to the people they said they loved.

Paul stared at her but she could see that he was ready to think she had done exactly what he had done only worse and she didn't care. She thought of all the evenings when he had left her, the nights she had been alone, the days when he hadn't even bothered to ask her what she was doing or where she was going or whether she was lonely. Paul had been taught by selfish self-indulgent people in a selfish self-indulgent world such as football was and it had taught him to be ruthless and self-seeking. She had never managed to be part of it and in some ways neither had Ruari.

'We've been having an affair ever since he got back.' She looked Paul straight in the eyes when she said this and there was a small sense of satisfaction in it somehow even though she knew it was cruel.

'Couldn't it be mine?' It was the one thing she had known he would ask but she had not counted on the hungry look in his eyes when he said it and her insides twisted when she went on watching him and she told him the lie.

'It's Ruari's,' she said and she knew

345

immediately that he believed it, they had had sex so very infrequently.

That was when he lost his temper and shouted and called Ruari names and called her names as though he had done nothing wrong himself and she thought back to the night she had lost her first baby All she could remember was that he hadn't been there and that was the point somehow. Paul was not and never had been there for her, he wanted her waiting at home so that he could not come back to her like she was a prisoner, like the girl in the tower who let down her hair. Well, she had finally let down her hair and escaped. It was through a lie and it would never be right but she thought just this once she would do what she wanted to do or she would never have any real say over herself.

He tried to stop her from leaving, he got hold of her when she was about to get into the car but his father had turned up by then, maybe his mother had telephoned, Jenna didn't know, just that Sorrel's car came screaming up the drive in a shower of gravel and he got out and got hold of his son and he said, 'Let her go. Let her go, Paul.'

Paul turned around, suddenly realizing that his father had hold of him, and for the first time that Jenna could remember he turned with sudden resignation into his father's arms and to Jenna's horror he began to cry huge agonizing sobs. She stood, rooted. She now had nothing to stop her but she couldn't move.

Over his son's head Sorrel looked at her, nodded towards the car. He didn't say anything and somehow Jenna got her feet to move, slammed shut the boot, got into the driver's seat and very slowly forced herself, trying to remember how the car worked and telling herself that if she didn't go now she would be sentencing herself to a lifetime of the Maddisons. Once she had stayed and told Paul the baby was his she would never escape. She managed to get the car into gear and it began to move slowly away down the drive. She got to the gates and turned into the road and a little feeling of relief and freedom began to edge its way into her mind.

When she walked into the little house in Back Church Street, Ruari's mother hugged her.

'Oh, Jenna,' she said, 'I wish it didn't have to be like this but there isn't any other way and I do want my Ruari to be happy.'

'I think I might promise you that,' Jenna said.

She stood there shaking while Ruari came to her. She couldn't quite meet his eyes but he loaded suitcases into the back of her car without speaking as though somehow the decision between them was so tenuous that conversation would not hold it. Nobody said anything and though it could only have taken a few minutes for Jenna it was a lifetime during which she somehow expected everything to go wrong as it had gone wrong so often, as though she never would get to spend the rest of her life with the man she should have been with always but nobody screamed around the corner in a car, nobody shouted, nobody suddenly appeared calling her a liar. She didn't think she would ever forget how Paul had turned stricken to his father, she would live with it. Her baby would become Ruari's and they would have other children.

He finally looked at her when he had loaded his belongings and then he hugged his mother and she nodded at Jenna and then they got into the car and Jenna ignored her shaking hands and started up the car and began to drive slowly down the road away from Back Church Street, away from the little town which had been her life towards something new. She brought to mind the little cottage and a slow wisp of excitement began to edge its way through her. She would have the little cottage and Ruari and the baby all to herself, nobody could stop her now.

'I just hope that lad Gallacher goes a long

way away from me,' Sorrel said that evening when Paul had gone back to work and he and Faye were for once sitting over the fire together. Sorrel had insisted that he should go and sort out the problem at one of the clubs, it would give him something to do, he thought. 'He's caused me more bloody trouble than anybody else I ever met and as for Jenna...'

'I'm just glad to see the back of her,' Faye said.

'Maybe if he found somebody else we might get a grandchild out of it,' Sorrel said and he poured himself a large whisky and soda and sat down with the evening papers to read before going to bed.

Books used for reference and information

The Football Man by Arthur Hopcraft, Aurum Press Limited.

England Managers by Brian Glanville, Headline.

England! England! The Complete Who's Who of Players Since 1946 by Dean P. Hayes, Sutton Publishing.

The Glory Game by Hunter Davies, Mainstream Publishing Company.

Blessed by George Best, Ebury Press.

Shearer: My Story So Far by Alan Shearer with Dave Harrison, Hodder & Stoughton.

A Photographic History of English Football by Tim Hill, Paragon.

Fashion Sourcebooks: The 1960s by John Peacock, Thames and Hudson.

Fashion Sourcebooks: The 1970s by John Peacock, Thames and Hudson.

White Heat by Dominic Sandbrook, Abacus.

Sunderland: The Complete Record by Rob Mason, Breedon Books Publishing.

The publishers hope that this book has given you enjoyable reading. Large Print Books are especially designed to be as easy to see and hold as possible. If you wish a complete list of our books please ask at your local library or write directly to:

Magna Large Print Books
Magna House, Long Preston,
Skipton, North Yorkshire.
BD23 4ND

This Large Print Book, for people
who cannot read normal print,
is published under the auspices of

THE ULVERSCROFT FOUNDATION

The making of the
Soviet state apparatus

Olga A. Narkiewicz

Manchester University Press

Published by the University of Manchester at
THE UNIVERSITY PRESS
316–324 Oxford Road, Manchester M13 9NR

International standard book number: 0 7190 0401 2

Printed in Great Britain by
Butler & Tanner Ltd., Frome and London

Contents

CONTENTS

Preface

This book does not attempt to formulate any new theories nor to prove any hypotheses. It is merely an account of the problems facing the ordinary people of the Soviet Union and to some extent their rulers in the period of the New Economic Policy. I have purposely avoided any involvement with the intellectual classes and the central government; they have been dealt with amply by many scholars. Because of this, the book probably suffers from a certain one-sidedness, but I hope that what is lost in historical perspective has been gained in human interest.

In writing this record, I have had occasion to consult a lot of statistics, many economic works and agricultural treatises. This arose from the necessity to acquaint myself and the readers with various aspects of life in the period. If I have committed major errors of judgment in the process, I regret this. My only excuse is that a fuller picture may have been presented in this way than had I used a strict historical approach. It is for the reader to decide whether this approach has been successful.

The sources I have used were very carefully chosen. It will be noticed that hardly any works published during the period 1930-56 have been consulted. I have preferred to rely on sources published during the 1920's, and on the excellent books and documents which have started to appear again after 1956. These publications have been very little used in the West—the former because they had been forgotten, the latter because they are too recent. I have found the agricultural controversies of the 1920's—those written by the experts, not by the politicians—to be of particular interest. I think that on re-assessment they will be judged to be the best body of Russian writing since the controversial literature of the mid-nineteenth century.

A large part of some chapters is taken up by unpublished documents from the Smolensk party archives. The only comprehensive book dealing with these archives is Merle Fainsod's *Smolensk under Soviet Rule*. I have not utilized any documents used by Fainsod, with the exception of one (protocol No. 27 of April 1928), and have therefore quoted some at length, because as far as I can judge they are an authentic record of events in an important region of the Soviet Union which has not been published anywhere else. I first read the documents in microfilm form, though I have subsequently had occasion to check them in the original. Since the microfilm is more likely to be available to other students, I have retained the classification according to the reel number, the year under which the document was entered in the archives (which does not necessarily correspond to its date), the W.K.P. number and protocol number, if extant. In addition, whenever possible, the full title of the document has been added. I found the practice of quoting page numbers almost useless because the pagination is very confused and often faded on the microfilm.

A glossary of specialized terms will be found at the end of this book. I have experienced a great deal of difficulty in producing consistent and semantically correct translations. In the case of one term alone, *zemleustroistvo*, some English works produced such varied translations as 'land confiscation' and 'land distribution'. Even with the greatest care, however, some terms lose their meaning through translation. Nevertheless, I have preferred to translate wherever possible, rather than to use foreign terminology. The British Standards Institute's system of Cyrillic characters has been used to transliterate Russian names, place names and terms, with one exception. All Russian surnames ending in *-kii* have been rendered with the ending '-ky' to avoid confusion between the accepted English spelling and the transliterated spelling.

The opinions expressed in this book are my own, but it owes its existence to a great many people. Professor John Erickson of the University of Edinburgh conceived the idea of returning to the grass-roots problems of the N.E.P. period, and he guided me skilfully through the preparatory work. Professor W. J. M. Mackenzie of the University of Glasgow and Professor Brian Chapman of the University of Manchester have, by their generosity, enabled me to carry out the project. Professor L. B. Schapiro of the London School of Economics and Professor Ghita Ionescu of Manchester University have encouraged me to complete the work in its present form and were a constant source of help and information. Professor R. W. Davies and Professor R. E. F. Smith, both of Birmingham University, have proffered generous and critical advice for a long period of time. Dr Sergei Utechin and Mr Jack Miller of the University of Glasgow supplied rich bibliographical information, supported by personal recollections. I am also indebted to my many Soviet friends who freely discussed the problems of present-day agricultural and industrial life with me, thus allowing me to form a more accurate opinion of the earlier periods.

The William Waldorf Astor Foundation gave me a generous grant to enable me to visit the United States in order to examine the originals of the Smolensk archives. Dr Michael Brooke of Manchester University read the manuscript and made many relevant comments. Dr Barry Hollingsworth of Manchester University read the proofs and offered invaluable advice on transliteration. My husband prepared all the tables and diagrams used in this book, and my daughter took over the task of housekeeping when the pace grew too hot. Mrs Sheila Watt, who typed and rearranged the manuscript more times than either of us cares to recall, has retained her usual efficiency and cheerfulness throughout, and never missed a deadline.

The title of the book and all the chapter headings are taken from Lenin's *Collected Works*.

Manchester, 1969

O. A. N.

1 Introduction

For where the very safety of the country depends upon the resolution to be taken, no considerations of justice or injustice, humanity or cruelty, nor of glory or of shame, should be allowed to prevail. But putting all other considerations aside, the only question should be, what course will save the life and liberty of the country?

Machiavelli, *Discourses*

Every study of the Soviet Union has to start with the study of its founder and a study of the organization which was his brain-child. Though both Lenin and the Communist party underwent major changes after the Bolshevik revolution, and though these changes were of such a nature that Lenin's pre-revolutionary thought and post-revolutionary thought seem to be the work of two different men, yet a discerning critic will see a continuation of certain trends, and a thread which runs through these periods without a break. An eminent historian of the French revolution tells us that:

major social revolutions are like geological faults. The rolling evolution of the historical landscape is suddenly broken and the continuity of its strata interrupted. What follows is conditioned by what went before, but is not a direct continuation of it.[1]

Similarly, the Bolshevik revolution was in many ways a continuation of earlier Russian revolutions, and Lenin was the heir to the rich tradition of Russian revolutionaries. While he himself acknowledged Marx as his guide and teacher, there was also much that he owed to the French revolution; not the one which mostly occupied his thoughts—the Communard movement of Marxist fame—but the Great Revolution. With Robespierre Lenin shared a belief in the healing power of a bloodthirsty revolution, and his demands to shed more blood were like Robespierre's calls for more terror:

Is our government then like despotism? Yes, as the sword that flashes in the hand of the hero of liberty is like that with which the satellites of

1

tyranny are armed. . . . The government of the Revolution is the despotism of liberty against tyranny.[2]

While borrowing his revolutionary philosophy from the Jacobins, Lenin—mindful perhaps of the rise of the Empire and the restoration of the Bourbons—took his administrative precepts from the French commune. Just before the Bolshevik coup, when the revolutionary tide seemed to be receding after the abortive days of July, Lenin wrote a treatise, meant to be a handbook for future revolutionaries. He did not yet know that very soon these precepts would have to be put to test by his own party, and he therefore allowed himself a measure of idealism and a certain degree of mildness which were absent from his later writings till the time when he felt his own death approaching, and when he belatedly tried to alter the balance of his influence on Soviet government.[3]

Cutting across centuries of organized State power, Lenin went back to the simple communal organization of city States and small communities. He forbore to mention that these often had to rely on slavery, crude force and even brigandage in order to retain their small measure of power and wealth.[4] The State, Lenin explained, was nothing but armed forces, which had at their disposal prisons and other instruments of oppression. The breakdown of the State's power would not, however, mean a return to primitive conditions of life:

Without the break-up into classes 'an independent armed organization of the population' would still be different by its complexity and by its high techniques from a primitive organization of a tribe of apes armed with sticks, or from primitive man, or from men united in clans; but such an organization would be possible.[5]

In order to bring about this development, Lenin insisted on the destruction of the whole organism:

. . . the demolition of the bureaucratic military State machine is the 'essential preliminary of every real *popular* revolution'.[6]

The Paris commune's first step in this direction had been the abolition of the permanent army, and its replacement by the power of the armed people. The second step was the abolition of officialdom. To accomplish this, the commune called to office deputies chosen by general franchise: these were responsible to the people and could be recalled at any time. Administrative duties had to be performed for the wage of a working man. The judiciary was similarly elected by general suffrage and its members were responsible and recallable. Thus the commune and its elected representatives were not a parliamentary body, but a working corporation which simultaneously legislated and executed the laws. The real democracy of this lay in the fact that the

Commune exchanged the corrupt and rotten bourgeois parliamentarism by institutions in which the freedom of discussion and judgment did not become a deception, for the parliamentarians had to work themselves, to execute their own laws, to check up their viability, and to be responsible directly to their electors.[7]

Exactly how Lenin expected these precepts to be put into practice in a complicated industrial State he never elaborated. Even in the eighteenth century, when Rousseau paid a tribute to the city State, his

enthusiasm for the democratic city State was an anachronism. The small community with a prevailingly rural economy, loosely federated with other similar communities, which would perhaps have represented his ideals most literally had no importance in Europe and only a passing importance in America.[8]

Naturally, this situation was even less viable at the beginning of the twentieth century. Lenin recognized this, and instead of trying to relate a complex State with a small agricultural community he substituted the theory of the withering State and of a subsequent new social order. If this programme might seem anachronistic, he said, this was only a temporary phase. His plans were not to be equated with 'primitive democracy', though the transition could not be accomplished without a certain return to primitive democracy. Since this would have its basis in capitalism and capitalist culture, however, it would be completely different from a primitive democracy in the pre-capitalist era:

Capitalist culture created large industries, factories, railways, post offices, telephones . . . and on this basis the majority of functions of the old State powers have become so simplified, and can be reduced to such very simple operations as registration, keeping of records and inspection, that these functions are completely accessible to all literate people; that these functions will be completely sufficiently paid for with the wage of a working man; that it is possible (and necessary) to deprive these functions of the very shadow of privilege or of command.[9]

This period would be one of transition from a capitalist State to a socialist one, which would be accompanied by a proletarian coercive

3

organization and designed as that of the dictatorship of the proletariat. Once capitalism was overthrown, the people would have in their hands

a highly technically developed mechanism, which can be put into motion by the united workers themselves, who would hire technicians, overseers, book-keepers, paying them all for work, just as they were rewarding all the other State functionaries, with the wages of an ordinary working man.[10]

It can easily be seen that this programme was both idealized and very nebulous. Under the circumstances, it seems a pity that Lenin had it published, for it provided ammunition for his opposition to the day of his death. It is needless to add that all the postulates expressed in *The State and the Revolution* were reversed *in toto* after the Bolsheviks came to power; what is perhaps more curious is that some of Lenin's own supporters, while clutching power with both hands, yet reproached him incessantly that the unworkable tenets were not being put into practice.

Yet close followers of Lenin's theories from earlier years would not have been surprised by this reversal. They would have remembered that as early as 1902 he wrote another long essay, in which he advocated just such an undemocratic way of governing as he was to introduce into the new Soviet State. It is true that in those days he was speaking of a conspiratorial party, fighting against an authoritarian government; in 1917 he was dealing with a party which was determined to stay in power despite the opposition of almost every enlightened element in the country. Yet the similarities are striking. In 1902 Lenin advocated a

Small, tightly-knit nucleus of the most promising, experienced and hardened workers . . . which will be able to fulfil . . . all the functions of a professional organization . . .[11]

and he continued his argument in a way which proved his essentially Russian approach to every problem. In Russia, he said, the only party which used to have such a centralized organization was 'Zemlia i Volia', a party which became bankrupt not because it was organized in this way but because its programme was not a revolutionary one. The conditions had not changed; since there was no democracy, it would be ludicrous to fight the government with a democratic, open organization. Similarly, the principle of electiveness was condemned. In democratic countries, elective political offices were accepted *ipso facto*. This was impossible in Russia:

4

THE MAKING OF THE SOVIET STATE APPARATUS

. . . no revolutionary organization had ever introduced a wide democracy, and could not introduce it, even if it wished to do so . . .[12]

One by one, Lenin disposed of his adversaries and their pet theories. Democracy, openness, elections, all these were in order for the Germans, for other countries which had had representative governments for a long time. The Russian tradition was that the government was oppressive and relied on a large police force; that the workers were backward and uneducated; that the intelligentsia were woolly-minded and inefficient. To all these ills Lenin saw but one answer: an iron discipline, conspiratorial techniques and telling the people what was good for them. *What is to be done* has been dissected and analysed more than any of Lenin's other works. It is considered to be an aspiring revolutionary's handbook. Yet how can we tell which was the real Lenin—the one who was advocating iron discipline and dictatorial techniques, or the one who proposed a free organization of workers, hiring their own managers? We shall probably never know the answer, but in the following pages I shall try to shed some light on this dilemma, and to show how in the days after coming to power he attempted to square the circle; how the ideas and ideals propounded before the revolution had to give way to the harsh realities of government; how dogmatism gave way to pragmatism, and how the illusions of pre-revolutionary days were still clung to, long after the theories had been discarded.

Some eighteen months had passed since Lenin wrote *The State and the Revolution*. The time had been almost entirely taken up by the difficulties of retaining power, by the German invasion and by the party split over the Brest-Litovsk treaty. Now the position was a little stronger, though still far from secure, and the Bolshevik party met once again to consider its own situation and that of the country. Since the Bolshevik revolution, the country had been run on behalf of the masses, particularly the proletariat. However, the masses were not benefiting by this theoretical right to govern, and within the party opposition to the privileges accorded to the former ruling classes was growing. The most acrimonious debate at the eighth congress of the Bolshevik party centred on the high pay of the bourgeois specialists who were reintroduced into industry, and the decision to change over from workers' control to workers' management of industry. In the debate Lenin himself defended the specialists' high pay, though he admitted it was causing great discontent, as it was contrary to socialist principles. But he stressed that

5

the specialists were needed to run industry and that they had to be given good material conditions in order to do it productively.[13] The rest of the apparatus also required the services of the old bourgeoisie:

The Soviet republic had nothing against the working masses taking part in the government of the country, but the low cultural standard of those masses proved to be an obstacle to this. Because of that, the *soviets which were planned as organs of government through the workers have become organs of government for the workers*—by way of a proletarian stratum, but not through the masses [my italics].[14]

The proletarian stratum to which Lenin was referring was, of course, the party. The party found it necessary to supervise all the decisions of the State machine in order to make certain that they were in accordance with its policy. The difficulty of these operations lay in the fact that the new State (not unlike the old tsarist State) did not provide for a proper division of functions, nor indeed for a division of offices. Thus at a meeting of the organizational section one member seriously suggested that centralization of the government could be effected by making the majority of the members of the Council of National Commissars members of the party's Central Committee as well. In this way the council would have the most responsible political workers, and the Central Committee would be informed of all the decisions on the spot—there would be no necessity to call separate meetings. This proposal was condemned by Zinoviev, who stated that already in the provinces the chairman of the party committee was often also the chairman of the soviet, of the Cheka, of the revolutionary tribunal and of other institutions. Such accumulation of power was wrong, and it reinforced the tendency of the executive committees to replace the soviets and of party committees to replace the party organization. In addition one question occupied Zinoviev's mind—the fact that relations between the soviets and the party organizations were often strained. This arose from a lack of a definite ruling on the exact grading of the importance of these organs. The question was often put: which is superior—the party or the soviets? There was no reply to it: it could only be countered with another question: which is superior—the proletariat or the party? There was no reply to this either; one could only decide on the correlation of the organs by observation. It has already been noticed that the trade unions were gained for the Communists through infiltration; the soviets would have to be won over in the same manner. Thus, just as the party had become the guardian of

6

the trade unions, without replacing them, so it should become the guardian of the soviets.[15]

This discussion showed not only the amorphous state of the new government machinery, but also the serious difficulties which the Bolsheviks were now encountering through the creation of new, official and often powerful bodies which had no special functions but nurtured ambitions to become governmental organs. The position of the trade unions was particularly delicate. Up to the revolution they were voluntary organizations, protecting the workers from the employers. They were also pressure groups, acting on the workers' behalf in such matters as taxation or labour laws. In addition, after the 1905 revolution, the Russian trade unions became in a great measure revolutionary instruments, working for the overthrow of the government. This long experience of revolutionary work, coupled with the fact that the trade unions were a Menshevik stronghold, was very worrying for the Bolshevik government. But even without this complication, their position was anomalous enough.

There were several questions in connection with this. Were the trade unions to remain voluntary associations, pursuing the general aims of socialism? The trade union leaders, Tomsky and Rudzutak, were inclined to adopt this line. There was a proposal, supported for a time by Lenin, that they should be included in the State apparatus, with the leadership forming the commissariat of labour. Or they could become political instruments, providing Communist education for the workers. The left wing seemed to think this was the best solution. The eighth congress was prepared to grant the trade unions quite wide functions—indeed it was suggested that they should take a major part in the running of industries:

Being already . . . participants in all local and central organs of industrial administration, the professional unions ought to arrive at a factual concentration in their hands of all the administration of national economy as a single economic whole. The participation of professional unions in the management of the economy and drawing in of wide masses in the same is . . . both the chief means of fighting bureaucratism of the economic apparatus in the Soviet government, and gives the possibility of real national controls over industrial production.[16]

By the time the ninth congress met, this policy was condemned as syndicalist. Krestinsky, speaking for the Central Committee, stated that it was against party policy to introduce such vertical organization; normally all trade union party fractions should be subject to local party organizations. In addition the Trades Union Council (VTSPS) should be subject to the Central Committee on all questions of labour. If the council was allowed to discuss questions which the Central Committee had already decided upon, it would undermine the correct party line. The council had too many non-Communist members, who would acquire vital information at an early date, and might oppose the Central Committee's decisions. To take a recent example: it had cost the Central Committee a lot of trouble to delay the opening of the trades union congress so that it would not take place till after the party congress. The delay was essential, for if the trades union congress had adopted resolutions which were contrary to the party line, it would have been impracticable for the party congress to adopt completely contrary resolutions so soon afterwards.[17]

Lenin supported the relegation of the trade unions to a very secondary role. The demands for non-party mass participation in the collective running of industry were particularly strongly criticized, for if the demands were granted the trade unions would also demand participation in economic and political policy making, and this would create an impossible situation. Naturally, Lenin had an ulterior motive in his criticism of the trade unions' demands. At the ninth congress the most burning question of the day was the proposed militarization of labour. This was a solution proposed by Trotsky as an answer to the problem of disciplining such remnants of the proletariat as were still left, and of providing fresh labour forces where and when they were needed. Trotsky expounded his policy thus. The trade unions would carry out the direction of labour; therefore they would have to be put on a military footing, so that every worker would feel that he was a soldier of labour and had no freedom of choice. Militarization of labour was necessary in order to save the cities, to stop the disappearance of the workers to the countryside, to improve the transport of food, fuel and raw materials to the cities. This part of the programme he called the first period of militarization. The second period, which would last for months or even years, would be devoted to building machines for transport, for producing raw materials and food. The third period would mean building machines to produce consumer goods. Finally, the fourth period would be devoted to producing consumer goods. Productivity of labour would not fall under militarization, Trotsky thought; it was a bourgeois axiom that forced labour was uneconomic. What

8

was true in a bourgeois society was not true in a socialist one, where forced labour was a necessity and therefore would not be objected to[18]

There were many opponents of the policy advocated by Lenin and Trotsky. But the opposition had a complicated task: they were faced not only with the proposed militarization of labour and the changed role of the trade unions, but also with the introduction of single management into industry. In general, those leaders who favoured militarization—Lenin, Bukharin, Rykov—were also in favour of some 'stratification' (for want of a better word) of the trade unions in order to reduce their independence, as well as of single management. The opposition numbered such people as Osinsky, Tomsky, Smirnov and Shlyapnikov. Tomsky was particularly scathing about the militarization of the railway services, which, he said, were working despite Rykov's dictatorship and thanks only to collective management. There was no statistical proof that single management was more effective than collective management, but the congress was asked to believe in it as though it was 'the kingdom of heaven'.

The position was summed up by Bukharin in these terms: there were two groups in existence; one of them wished to give all rights to the trade unions, while the other wanted to annihilate the unions. He submitted that the problem could be broken down into these questions: the change of trade union functions under the dictatorship of the proletariat; the character of problems facing the trade unions at present; and the relationship between the trade unions and other organizations under the dictatorship of the proletariat. The Central Committee's view was that while, under the capitalist system, the trade unions were the working classes' main organ of economic and political struggle against capitalism, under the dictatorship of the proletariat they should become part of the ruling apparatus. Trade union functions should become organizational, economic and pedagogical, and should be directed at educating the working classes for building Communism, where previously they were directed at fighting the system. As the party was the vanguard of the proletariat, it had to fulfil its role by leading the unions. Every trade union cell should have a party fraction to direct it. This fraction must be subject to the party organs, not to the trade union organs, otherwise the party would have no influence over the trade unions or, through them, of the masses.

The relations of trade unions to the soviets were more complicated. The soviet State represented a workers' organization, just as

9

the trade unions were a workers' organization. Thus it was nonsense to say that the soviet apparatus was less proletarian than the trade unions, and there should be no objection to the trade unions being subjected to the soviets; the only problem was the timing of this operation. The Central Committee thought that great care was needed not to start conflicts, and therefore the matter would take rather a long time. It had not been settled yet in what manner to include the trade unions in the State apparatus. They could be declared State organs, without any other changes, and could then function independently both as trade unions and as State organs. Or they could penetrate the soviet organs, so that they would become the basis of the soviet economic-administrative organs, with no independent functions. This solution would be the most Marxist one because, according to Marx, 'revolutionary association of the working class' lay at the basis of Communism. Thus they would automatically become the foundation of the Communist system.[19]

It can be seen from this discussion that the Central Committee was determined to undermine the strength of the trade unions but was not yet ready to do so openly and by violent means. Trotsky was more honest when he bluntly demanded the introduction of military discipline into the trade unions; Bukharin's programme was subtler but more deadly in its implications.

The discussions at the ninth congress showed conclusively that the party leadership was not prepared to grant any degree of autonomy to the proletariat, as organized into trade unions, or to the workers, who had in many cases been running the nationalized factories quite efficiently. The triple fear of the Menshevik opposition, loss of productivity, and any show of independent organization on the part of the proletariat were the mainsprings of this disappointing policy. The results were soon apparent. The disappearance of the proletariat in the following years, the fall in productivity per worker and the industrial unrest which lasted for years until it was disciplined by draconic laws, were all caused at least in part by the party's rigid and uncompromising stand on this issue. It may be that the policy saved the Bolshevik government at this particular juncture, though this would be impossible to prove. It is far more likely that it sowed the seeds of industrial discontent which persisted for many years, and that it deprived the new State of the support and willing labour of many thousands of workers—a loss which the government really could not afford.

10

It need hardly be repeated here that the problem of the peasants and agricultural policy was the one which exercised the party's ingenuity more than any other, and with good reason. What is perhaps less well known is the fact that, with the exception of the immediate post-revolutionary period, this policy was seldom pursued along socialist lines, and that the leadership was fully aware of the pitfalls of a serious disagreement with the majority of the population until such time as it would have sufficient forces to subdue the peasants. The peasants had three valuable things to offer the new government: support against the restoration of the old order, agricultural produce, and a new industrial labour force in place of the old organized proletariat. While the government needed all three it had at the same time to pay lip service to the socialist tenets which were the theoretical basis of its rise to power. In the realm of agricultural policy, therefore, the conflict was not so much between a bourgeois and socialist ideology (though it appeared as such in official party documents), but the classic conflict between the city and the countryside; between the non-productive exploiting government apparatus and the productive but unorganized peasants.

The first official signs that the party would have to acknowledge the existing situation appeared early in 1919, when Lenin gave his opening address to the eighth congress of the party. He stated that neutralizing the small peasants was no longer enough—the party had now reached a stage where it had to work out a stable alliance with the medium peasant. This task, which could not be accomplished by force, consisted in convincing the peasants that the Communist party was the first party to dispossess the landlords and to set up a real democracy. In theory the medium peasant was not an enemy, but the party's tactics would have to be very careful. It would often be necessary to give with one hand and take away with the other (this policy may be said to have been faithfully followed by the leadership from that day onwards until the present time— a strange confirmation of how far Lenin's guidance on most important matters has survived changes in leadership over fifty years). It had to be borne in mind, said Lenin, that though the Russian peasants could not be devoted to socialism, because their economic interests lay elsewhere, they would accept it if there was no other way out. The party's main task was to assure the peasants that there was no wish to expropriate them; only afterwards could measures be taken which were consistent with the dictatorship of the proletariat.[20]

11

Lenin reminded the congress that the peasant question had to be linked with the problem of food supplies. Since the revolution had to be carried out with the peasants' help, it was a bourgeois revolution. It was only since the formation of the Poor Peasants' Committees in the autumn of 1918 that the revolution became a proletarian one. But it was thanks to the help of the peasants that success had been relatively easy. Nevertheless, the Poor Peasants' Committees could be regarded only as a transitional phenomenon (in fact, some of them were already disbanded as early as November 1918) necessary to save the population of the cities from death by starvation. It was now up to the party to evolve a proletarian organization in the countryside and to find support there. The Poor Peasants' Committees were a start, and possibly the soviets could also play a part —but at present many Communists' behaviour antagonized the peasants. The party's measures designed to injure the rich peasants were often applied to medium peasants, with the result that they bore the party a grudge. The situation was grave, for the Soviet government had nothing to offer the medium peasant; therefore it was necessary to change the administrative practice, to improve the apparatus and to remove the mass of abuses. The party line must be amended to point to an alliance with the medium peasants. Lenin warned all party members that though revolutionary force and dictatorship were wonderful in themselves, they must be used only against enemies, not indiscriminately.[21]

Lenin's advocacy of a policy of concessions to the peasants met with strong criticism from many party members. The most telling speaker reminded the congress that as long ago as 1889 Plekhanov had warned that any revolutionary movement in Russia would either be successful as a proletarian movement or would not succeed at all. Russia was a predominantly peasant country, and if the party made concessions to the peasants the Soviet government would end up as a peasant government, indifferent to the interests of the international proletariat.[22] But the party line was already decided upon, and the protests were of no avail. There were, of course, sound reasons for the 'softer' course in the countryside. Apart from the food supply situation, the government had to contend with a war on several fronts, an almost complete stoppage of industry, and localized peasant revolts. In addition, the more realistic elements in the party had come to the conclusion that the policy of 'War Communism' was bankrupt. Such a policy presupposes several factors: that a

12

large part of the nation supports it; that it is carried out by a body of highly disciplined men; and that their discipline must, in a large measure, be reinforced by idealism. In addition, a reserve of capital is absolutely necessary, since the outlay is quick and the returns are slow. When all these factors are lacking, this policy is almost bound to turn into a simple matter of looting and robbery. This was happening in the new Soviet Republic, and Lenin himself pointed out that the main reason for the abuses was the lack of cadres, allied with the upheavals of the civil war.

The civil war was also responsible for another phenomenon: large numbers of men were needed to stop the White forces. These had to be called up in the countryside, and the problem of desertions by disaffected peasants was worrying the army authorities. That this was an extremely serious problem is shown by reports from commanders at the front. One of them wrote:

We needed an entire quarter of a million men in order to get the upper hand of Judenic's 15,000 White Guards. . . . The total number of deserters for the second half of 1919 was about 1,500,000. . . . The political measures taken to win over the middle peasants contribute towards the reversal of this trend; nearly one million men voluntarily reported for duty during the second half of 1919.[23]

In view of such an essential need for the goodwill of the peasants, it is not difficult to see that Lenin was right in changing the agricultural policy.

Nevertheless, even the above factors do not constitute the whole picture. The most important factor was the growing conviction, expressed clearly by Lenin at the eighth congress, that the peasants would not voluntarily become socialist, and that without their support, or at least passivity, the government would be unable to retain power.[24] A decisive anti-Bolshevik peasant rebellion would tip the scales in favour of the White forces. Because of this the policy of concessions to the peasants was the end of War Communism, and the beginning of the New Economic Policy—though the latter would not be presented to the party for another two years.

The policy of relaxation and a partial return to capitalism were finally presented to the truncated tenth party congress, which passed them with an unverified majority.[25] The resolution had the support of the Central Committee, but a similar course had been advocated earlier, apparently by Trotsky.[26] It was not till the Krondstadt rebellion had finally forced the government's hand, however, that

13

it was thought necessary to introduce such measures officially, in order to pacify those sections of the population which were suffering most under the indecisive policy which was no longer War Communism but had not yet become the New Economic Policy. While the Central Committee could count on the support of the majority of the population in thus officially renouncing Communism (even if the policy was described as only temporary), it found itself in great difficulties with the party members themselves. The left wing of the party was particularly strongly opposed to the New Economic Policy, and Lenin voiced his annoyance with the opposition when, at the tenth congress, he bluntly refused to discuss the complaints, branded the opposition as treasonable and invited it to 'discuss it [the New Economic Policy] with rifles, not with theses'.[27]

The opposition was finally silenced by the introduction of the famous resolution on the 'Unity of the Party', which outlawed all internal party discussion on controversial topics. It was only then that the new measures were quietly introduced at the end of the congress, under the name of 'replacement of food requisitioning by food tax'. Further measures were announced after the congress was over, and were followed somewhat later by the changed agricultural legislation (see chapter 2). All these changes were not so much a return to pre-revolutionary policies as a legal endorsement of what was already practised illegally in many districts. As such, they did not change the nature of the new State—which had not yet been formed, in any case, on the other hand they did change the aims of the party, and they undermined its idealistic elements almost completely.

The organization and composition of the party have been analysed by many authors in recent years;[28] so has the intricate network of interlocked institutions which grew up in the Soviet Union as a result of inexperience, lack of trained administrators and the reluctance of the Central Committee to delegate any of its powers.[29] Nevertheless, one problem still needs some elucidation. This is the vexed question of why the rank and file of the party allowed themselves to be manipulated in such an obvious way by an autocratic Central Committee. Apart from the trade union leaders, the representatives of the Democratic Centralism and the Workers' Opposition (which was in part a trade union bloc), the rest of the delegates remained passive, particularly during the crucial tenth congress, and voted for the Central Committee's resolutions without discussion.

14

It was a very different picture from that envisaged by Lenin, in which the new parliamentarians would have freedom of discussion and judgment, and would be fully responsible to their electors. Increasingly, the party congresses were trammelled and forbidden to discuss any controversial questions (just as discussion had already been stifled in the congress of the soviets, on the pretext of the delegates' containing too many non-Bolshevik elements), to be finally silenced for good in 1921, at the tenth congress. The answer to this puzzle lay not only in the imposition of an authoritarian organization, but also in the changed party membership. It must not be forgotten that up to the revolution the party was an underground organization, and that its numbers were never known exactly. After the Bolsheviks came to power, attempts were made to collate a register of members, but in 1919, at the eighth congress, it was pointed out that registration was still far from complete. According to one authority, the number of members was reduced to about 150,000 (or a little over half of former membership) by the autumn of 1919, and a drive was launched to recruit new members. By the time of the ninth congress, in March 1920, the size of the party was given as 611,878 members.[30] It must therefore be estimated that from half to three-quarters of the members were new by the time the ninth congress met.

At this congress strong protests were made about the weakness of the party membership and the autocratic rule of the Central Committee. One delegate even demanded that the Central Committee should be completely re-elected, in order to choose members who would feel bound to abide by the congress's decisions.[31] This opposition was stifled by Lenin, who pointed out that any show of division in the congress would reinforce nationalistic tendencies on the part of the provincial organizations, and formulated his own interpretation of the term 'democratic centralism' as follows:

Democratic centralism means only that local representatives gather together and elect a responsible organ, which must govern from then on.[32]

Once again, the Central Committee won its point and the delegates approved the official list.

A year later, the Central Committee for the first time felt strong enough to exclude members of the opposition from the presidium of the congress (a purely honorary status).[33] The verbal lashing to which Lenin then subjected the delegates had a strong tinge of

15

exasperation; his tone was that of an angry schoolmaster berating naughty children rather than that of a party leader discussing party policy with his followers. Here again, the composition of the congress may have had something to do with the tone of its discussions. The newly published voting lists show that out of 717 delegates with a vote, 183 (25·6 per cent) had joined the party only since 1918; 130 did not fill in the date of joining, and there is reason to believe that they were completely new members. This supposes a congress almost half of whose delegates were inexperienced members and very new Communists.[34]

The dilution of the Communist elements through purges and new admissions was accompanied by a growth of the party bureaucracy. While the secretariat had a staff of thirty people in 1919, the number had risen to 602 by 1921—a twenty-fold increase.[35] Unfortunately, the efficiency of the augmented staff left something to be desired; it now handled 3,000 documents each month, but the standard party card, which was to have been issued a year earlier, had not yet been introduced. The proliferation of institutions did not stop there; only recently the Central Committee had created the Organizational Bureau and the Political Bureau, with the secretariat to serve both these offices. But they did not prove sufficient either, and between the ninth and tenth congresses a new body had been created: the Control Commission. There was some confusion about the commission's actual functions. Finding itself in a quandary, the commission decided to work on its own initiative, and to fight the low moral tone of the party. This course derived from the need to stem the desertions from the party's ranks of its most valuable elements.[36]

Thus one can see how the gradual tightening of discipline changed the party from a comradely organization, much addicted to discussions and even arguments but composed of men who had similar aims, into a body of passive, assenting members. This situation aided the growth of bureaucracy, from which both the party and the State have suffered ever since. As early as 1921 Lenin said at the tenth congress:

We know ourselves that we have a bureaucratic stratum, and we ourselves [the Central Committee] who happen to deal with this bureaucratic apparatus most closely, suffer from this. We sign a document, but how will it be executed? How can we check this, when the bureaucratic apparatus is so enormous?[37]

The complaints about bureaucracy have changed little since those

16

days. The bureaucracy was built into the system from its very inception, and unfortunately it was a very inefficient bureaucracy. This combination of several factors—government by a party which had lost its best men and most of its ideals, a large and amorphous State apparatus, lack of a determined policy—produced manifold problems. Some of them will be discussed in the following chapters.

NOTES

1. N. Hampson, *A Social History of the French Revolution*, p. vi.
2. Robespierre to the National Convention, February, 1794, quoted in G. H. Sabine, *A History of Political Theory*, p. 591.
3. Lenin, *Gosudarstvo i Revolyutsiya*, Sochinenya, vol. 25, pp. 355–6.
4. Lenin's views on this non-State, as expounded in this work, had always been severely criticized. One commentator described them as 'This preposterous caricature of an industrial economy and its transformation from capitalism to socialism is from every point so extraordinary that it calls for comment'. The author calls in question Lenin's sincerity, which was 'out of character for Lenin, who was usually pretty hard-headed' (G. H. Sabine, op. cit., p. 852). Another says: 'By discussing Marx's views of the State without reproducing Marx's ideas of the Asiatic State and the Oriental despotism of tsarist Russia, Lenin wrote what probably is the most dishonest book of his political career': *State and Revolution* (Karl A. Wittfogel, *Oriental despotism*). Yet it must be remembered that Lenin was still the theoretician of the revolution, not a practical politician, while he was writing this work; and that an idealized picture of new political institutions in 1917 was not to be despised. The fact that these could never be brought into being is another matter.
5. Lenin, *Gosudarstvo i Revolyutsiya*, op. cit., p. 361.
6. Ibid., p. 388, Lenin's italics.
7. Ibid., p. 396.
8. Sabine, op. cit., p. 593.
9. Lenin, *Gosudarstvo i Revolyutsiya*, op. cit., p. 392.
10. Ibid., p. 398.
11. Lenin, 'Chto delat' in *Izbrannye Proizvedeniya*, vol. 1, p. 200.
12. Ibid., p. 216.
13. Eighth congress of RKP (b), March 1919, Protokoly, pp. 18 and 58–60. Lenin pointed out that at present all salaries and wages ranged from 600 to 3,000 roubles, whereas before the war a specialist received twenty-five times the pay of an unskilled worker.
14. Ibid., p. 62.
15. Ibid., pp. 187–225.
16. Ibid., note 42.
17. Ninth congress of RKP (b), 1920, Protokoly, p. 82.
18. Ibid., pp. 91–115.
19. Ibid., pp. 211–26.
20. Eighth congress of RKP (b), op. cit., pp. 5–6 and 13–16.
21. Ibid., pp. 20–23.
22. Sunitsa, ibid., p. 86.
23. *The Trotsky Papers*, vol. 1, pp. 797–8.
24. At this stage in the development of 'peasantism' Lenin's remark is remarkably penetrating. Lenin saw behind the peasants' 'greed for land' a far deeper

17

involvement with the need to own land, though he did not see fit to analyse it. Fifty more years of peasant movements have taught us the lesson better. Ghita Ionescu has commented on it very cogently in his essay on populism and peasantism in Eastern Europe. The private ownership of land became one of the articles of faith of peasant movements in Eastern Europe between the wars. Ionescu says: 'Most peasant parties were . . . adamant in their belief that the right of private ownership of the land and of other goods was one of the foundations of the good society' ('Eastern Europe' in *Populism, its Meanings and National Characteristics*, ed. G. Ionescu and Ernest Gellner, p. 108). It will have been noted that towards the end of his life, in his essay 'On co-operation', Lenin expressed almost a similar point of view.

25. Tenth congress of the RKP (b), 1921, stenograficheskii otchet. The resolution on the change-over from requisitioning to tax was announced by Lenin (pp. 403–15), and the vote was taken. Apparently no count of delegates was kept (see ibid., p. 445); there is no record of this either in the minutes or in the voting lists appended to the 1963 edition.

26. See Max Schachtman, *The Struggle for the New Course*, pp. 135–6. When Trotsky was already in exile, he claimed that he had suggested the New Economic Policy before proposing the measures for militarization of labour. These were introduced only because the Central Committee had rejected his former plan. We know that at the time of the militarization measures a partial policy of relaxation was already practised, so it is quite possible that he was right in his claims.

27. Tenth congress, op. cit., p. 118.

28. E.g. L. Schapiro, *The Origin of the Communist Autocracy*, and R. V. Daniels, *The Conscience of the Revolution*.

29. See E. H. Carr, *The Bolshevik Revolution*, op. cit.; M. Fainsod, *How Russia is Ruled*; L. Schapiro, *The Communist Party of the Soviet Union*.

30. L. Schapiro, *The Communist Party of the Soviet Union*, op. cit., p. 231.

31. Ninth congress, op. cit., p. 45. Yurenev was the opposing delegate. Yurenev was a relative newcomer; he had been a *mezhraionets* till the sixth congress. He held responsible organizational posts in the army, and later became a diplomat, only to perish in the 1937–38 purges. See *Trotsky papers*, op. cit., p. 122.

32. Ninth congress, op. cit., pp. 84–5.

33. Tenth congress, op. cit., p. 2.

34. See tenth congress, op. cit., voting lists of delegates.

35. Tenth congress, op. cit., p. 56.

36. Ibid., Solts' report on the work of the control commission, pp. 57–65. Solts said, in connection with the setting up of the control commission, that 'It was not clear even to the Central Committee what the control commission ought to become. . . . The work at the beginning consisted in that the commission received complaints, investigated them, turned to party members and to organizations with appeals of the following kind: "The control commission asks everybody to turn to it in case of incorrect behaviour on the part of party members, as it has the task of investigating these" ' (p. 58).

37. Tenth congress, op. cit., p. 121.

2 'The Soviet state has inherited many of the worst features of capitalism'

The brief introduction in chapter 1 is intended merely to show that the government of the new State (and by this term we mean the top party and government officials) was in no way as rigid, or as decisive, as might be expected from its early policies. It may help us to understand why, at the period with which we are concerned in the following chapters, government policy veered in many different directions, and how this reduced the government's claims to rule the country to a mere underwriting of an already existing situation.

The new government, composed in the main of city-bred intellectuals, had many problems to contend with. The most crucial was that of governing a predominantly agricultural country in which the majority of the population were poor peasants. How to come to a working arrangement with this majority, without endangering its own rule, became the main difficulty of the administration. It must be stressed that the Bolsheviks had had little practical knowledge of agricultural issues, since they were basically a city party. Hence many of their mistakes were simply the result of a lack of understanding. But there was more to it than that. There were clear indications that even with the greatest amount of goodwill (which the Bolsheviks did not exhibit), and with a great deal of capital investment (which they did not propose to undertake), the agricultural question was insoluble. Students of nineteenth-century Russian agricultural writers can see this clearly. So can the scholars who nowadays concern themselves with under-developed countries such as India. It

19

would have been odd if the Bolsheviks, with their lack of practical and emotional equipment and faced by constant crises in every realm of government, had suddenly found a philosopher's stone to solve this problem.

It is impossible to stress too often the great complexity of the agricultural problem; its involvement with social questions on the one hand, and administrative difficulties on the other—though, of course, the crucial question had always been one of food: would the countryside grow enough food to feed itself, to feed the towns, and to provide a reserve fund as well? We are not claiming to have covered all the ground here, since that would be impossible even in several volumes; we are concerned merely to shed some light on the lesser known aspects of agricultural life and the relationship it bore to the Soviet administration. To do this, we must first take a brief look at the historical background.

The Stolypin reforms, introduced after the terrible fiasco of the Russian–Japanese war and the 1905 revolution, were aimed at bringing the Russian peasant into the twentieth century, and creating a class of prosperous peasant farmers. How preposterous such hopes were can be seen when it is realized that little more than a generation had passed since the Emancipation Act, that hardly any civil rights had been conferred on the peasants up to 1905, and that none the less from 1906 they were suddenly expected to become mature citizens, allowed to dispose of property, forced to make their own decisions and forced willy-nilly into the competitive world of trade and industry. As was to be expected, the peasants could not cope with such radical changes in their status. Mavor, writing a few years after the reforms, had this to say:

... whereas previous legislation had been on the whole favourable to the maintenance of land-holding in community as a characteristic Russian institution, the new ukase was apparently designed, along with the encouragement of 'separation', to break up not only the community, but the family. The full effect of this ukase remains to be seen.It is, however, clear that it endows the heads of peasant families with considerable powers which they did not enjoy under previous laws. . . . He [the head of the family] may alienate it [the land] practically at will. . . . There is thus created with one hand a peasant proprietary, and with the other a peasant proletariat. . . . It is true that extreme sub-division of peasant holdings may, by these means, be avoided; but it is also true that peasant heads of households who wish to do so may sell their lands to speculators. Unaccustomed to the possession of ready money and unacquainted with the means of turning it to advantage, the peasant is unlikely to benefit by this
20

arrangement. He and his family come to be separated from their customary means of livelihood, and they necessarily swell the ranks of the proletariat either in the villages or in the cities.[1]

Further, Mavor comments on the bankruptcy of other government measures, such as the operations of the Peasant Bank, which, owing to the landowners' pressure, accumulated in its hands a fund of land at high prices and made an overall rise in the price of land possible, while at the same time poor peasants were crying out for more land. The situation of the poor peasants seemed in fact to have improved slightly, but as a result not so much of the reforms as of the economic conditions prevailing in 1900–5. Stolypin's measures, which had as their prime concern the creation of a class of prosperous peasants, worked to the detriment of the poorer rural elements. While the richer peasants found it easier to pay the high prices for land and keep up the high rates of interest charged by the Peasant Bank, the poor peasants, seeing this rising prosperity in their own villages, became even more embittered with their fate. Perhaps it might be well to remind the reader of conditions obtaining in rural Russia at the beginning of the twentieth century.

Cottages having no chimneys are still very common, the smoke being let out through a hole in the roof . . . the walls are generally covered with dung to keep the place warm. Earth floors are the rule because in cold weather lambs, calves, pigs, and even cows are brought into the cottage. . . .[2]

Other details show that the peasants did not use soap, had no washing facilities, and existed all the year round on a diet of bread, kvass, cabbage and onions. The Stolypin reforms, Florinsky asserts, went both too far and not far enough. The legal measures coerced the population into obedience to official policy, while the agricultural measures had little effect in improving the methods of agriculture, where the three-course system was still, in the majority of cases, in operation up to the outbreak of the first world war. The low standard of agriculture had for many years resulted in rural over-population.

In this respect, the outbreak of the first world war had a beneficial effect on agriculture, in so far as the call-up removed a great many mouths to feed from the countryside. This made many women take up work on the land; in 1916, when 36 per cent of the male population of working age was under arms, the acreage of land under cultivation rose by 13 million dessiatinas (47 million dessiatinas under cultivation in 1909–13, 60 million in 1916).[3] An incidental effect of the war was that the peasants began to eat better, since they were producing more foodstuffs and were reluctant to sell them to the government in return for inflated currency. A report made by the Zemstvo committee stated that:

On the surface, the situation appeared to be fairly normal. In fact, as far as the condition of the individual peasant was concerned, there seemed to be even something like an improvement. On every hand it was observed that money was flowing freely into the villages and it was found that, whilst the cities were already beginning to feel the pinch of a food shortage, rural districts, upon the whole, were living better than ever before, for the peasants were now consuming more and more of their home produce and were becoming increasingly averse to selling grain.[4]

However, it was but a temporary improvement. The ill effects of the war began to be felt when the drain on manpower continued (the Zemstvo report states that in 1916 there were 158 women for every 100 men engaged in agricultural work), and the agricultural implements began to wear out. The combined effect of these two factors, added to the primitive agricultural methods practised, proved catastrophic. The Zemstvos attempted to come to the aid of the peasants by loaning them machinery, but it was found that:

It was not always possible to obtain a sufficient number of the required machines; or again, the peasants found themselves absolutely incapable of operating them, and besides, the compulsory rotation of crops due to communal tenure and scattered strips placed obstacles in the way of efficient use of steam ploughs, harvesting machines, binders, and other agricultural implements. Expensive and heavy machines were of little use on the narrow strips of land owned by soldiers, which were simply lost amidst the strips belonging to the other peasants of the village.[5]

There is little evidence of research into the situation in the countryside later than 1916. This is only natural, for the first revolution broke out early in 1917. What were the causes of the peasant rebellion which accompanied this and the later October revolution? Even if the position in the countryside was not very satisfactory, there seemed to have been some increase in peasant prosperity. Moreover, those who survived the war might look forward to an even greater prosperity, for the population would be depleted, and foodstuffs more in demand after war-time rationing. One does not have to look to Bolshevik propaganda to know why this happened. Expectations of some gains after a war were historically grounded in the peasant mentality. After the Napoleonic wars, the peasants fully expected to be given their freedom; after the Crimean war the same sentiment

22

prevailed, and was followed by the Emancipation Act; after the Russian–Japanese war the Stolypin reforms were designed to satisfy the peasants, if only in part. These piecemeal concessions only whetted their appetite for more; and presumably, by the middle of the first world war, the peasants were psychologically prepared to take what they had long regarded as theirs. It is worthy of note that land was being seized long before the Bolshevik revolution (though it is not clear whether this was before or after the March revolution):

... official reports agreed that in rural areas, as early as the spring of 1917, 'war was often almost completely forgotten'. . . . The impending redistribution of land was uppermost to the peasant soldier when he turned a deaf ear on combat orders, threw away his rifle, and deserted by the thousand.[6]

Despite their overriding passion for land, the peasants were still afraid of retribution:

The peasants, . . . proceeded at first cautiously and by quasi-legal methods: wages of agricultural labourers were raised to prohibitive levels; refugees and prisoners of war employed on large estates were withdrawn . . . there was much trespassing and wanton destruction of timber and woodlands. When . . . life on the estates came to a standstill, peasant committees took over arable land, meadows, forests, machines, and livestock on the ground that the owners were incapable of managing their properties.[7]

It is not difficult to see the hand of the Social Revolutionaries, that most nihilistic of Russian political parties, in such proceedings. Their programme included both the wanton destruction of estates and the division of estates into small holdings. The bitter irony of this programme and its resultant action was that it was almost useless in the circumstances. What the Russian peasant needed more than anything else was not more land, but consolidated land.

The cultivation of fragmented holdings is often extremely wasteful of labour, of capital (especially in the form of storage facilities and transport equipment) and even of land as well. In these circumstances economy in the use of resources and a consequent increase in total output could be secured from the consolidation of holdings into contiguous properties. In other words, consolidation could raise output, and a division of the consolidated holdings is possible which in principle might improve the position of each cultivator.[8]

This quotation comes not from a Stalinist tract but from the work of two well known contemporary economists. Once consolidation had been accomplished—and this operation required ingenuity but little capital—the use of improved machines could be introduced

c   23 gradually. Since the second greatest fault of Russian peasant agriculture was lack of livestock, the improved machinery would rely on mechanical power, thus eliminating the need for draught animals and enabling the peasant to concentrate on breeding animals for food. Naturally, it is easy to give such advice nowadays, with our growing knowledge of the needs of under-developed territories. The Russian peasant in 1917 would have paid little heed to such words, and he proceeded to divide up land which had previously been consolidated (i.e. the large estates), thus forcing the Bolsheviks to abandon the only sensible part of their programme—agriculture on a large scale—and to take over the wasteful and wanton Social Revolutionary motto of 'a little more land for everybody'. The results were unjust, deleterious, and carried the seed of forced collectivization in them as early as 1918.

It is almost impossible to gain a clear picture of the state of land distribution up to 1917. Certain statistics exist, but since they apparently include territories which the Soviet Union lost after the revolution (that is, the Baltic States, Poland, parts of Bessarabia), and since these do not seem to have been compared with the amount of land in Soviet possession after 1917, it is difficult to make an exact assessment. To obtain an insight into the acreage and the size of population, some figures are quoted here, but they have to be treated with caution, as some are out of date and it has proved impossible to check the others.

This was how land was distributed among the owners in 1890, according to one source:

	Acres
State lands	376,024,924
Crown lands	17,419,350
Peasant lands	328,431,142
Private lands	233,452,925
Church, sundry	21,431,555

[G. Drage, *Russian Affairs*, p. 86.]

As to distribution of land among individual owners, Lenin made the following estimate:[9]

	Average per owner (*dessiatinas*)
Poorest peasant	7·0
Medium peasant	15·0
Rich peasant and medium landlord	46·7
Big landlords (including Church)	2,333·0

24

However, land was changing hands all the time. Florinsky shows that while 2·4 million dessiatinas were sold to the peasants with the help of the State-owned Peasant Bank in the years 1883–95, 8·5 million dessiatinas were sold in 1906–13. Moreover, land was acquired by the peasants without the help of the bank as well.[10] But this land ownership was very often more apparent than real, for a lot of the land was heavily mortgaged:

In 1913 somewhat less than one-half of the non-allotment land held by the peasants in 47 provinces was mortgaged to the State Peasant Bank.[11]

The proportion of the landowners' land which was mortgaged was even greater.

The numbers of peasants are equally difficult to establish. Lenin estimated that the number of poor peasant owners was about $10\frac{1}{2}$ million, and that of rich and medium peasants about $2\frac{1}{2}$ million. The division into arbitrary classes, without attention being paid to other factors besides land ownership, renders these figures almost useless.

This fluid position probably explains why the law on nationalization of land, promulgated on 19 February 1918, was very vaguely worded. It simply stipulated 'the abolition of all private property for land, . . . forest, et al.' and stated that 'land is to pass without any . . redemption payments into the use of all working people'.[12] The Bolshevik idea of a just distribution was that it should be done on the 'equalization–labour' principle, which Lenin called the 'soul of the law'.[13] The peasants took very little heed of this principle, and proceeded to divide the land as they saw fit. The socialization of land was

not accomplished on a general scale. . . . In practice land was appropriated by the local population. . . . Equalization in the villages themselves was done strictly, in townships [volosti] this was done rarely, in regions [uezdy] still more rarely . . .[14]

The 'equalization–labour' principle requires that land be put into a common pool, and then distributed equally among the people. According to Prokopovich, this happened only in some regions of the Orlov and Tula guberniyas.[15] On the whole, the peasant action was regressive; particularly so in cases of commune peasants, who often tried to put back into communal use plots rented out to individual peasants.

However, the 'equalization–labour' principle was insufficient on its own, and was to be used later only as a guideline.

25

Each working peasant ought to receive the same amount of land (according to the number of dependants) as his neighbour in the village.[16] But land allocated should be of equal fertility; or poorer land made up by a bigger acreage. The same must apply to pasturage, forest and other integral elements of agricultural usage. This task obviously required a great deal of thought, experience and, above all, many skilled and impartial surveyors. Needless to say, Russia in 1917 could dispose of none of those factors. As a result, the distribution of land was disorderly, harmful to agriculture as a whole, and failed to solve any of the outstanding problems. Unpublished records show that as late as 1920 repeated land inventories were made by apparently semi-literate people, in a vain attempt at least to assess the acreage.[17] Though there were attempts to dispossess richer peasants by armed action—Snegirev quotes one example, in which an armed detachment of villagers pointed guns at rich peasants for half an hour, till they consented to part with their land[18]—this was by no means the rule. But even peaceful distribution was inadequate; in Novgorod guberniya only a rough and temporary division of land was possible, reported soviet authorities.[19] It is most likely that this position was true for many other guberniyas. The peasants, left to themselves, proceeded to distribute the off-cuts (*otrezki*), and then the landlord's estate. This again brought some difficulties, for often two neighbouring villages would vie with each other for the possession of the same estate:

Three communes of the village of Ksisovo had pasture on the other side of the river Don, by the village of Vvedenskoe. Vvedenskoe wanted to mow the hay on this pasture land. Ksisovo set up machine guns on its high shore— the threat worked, and there was no shooting.[20]

Elsewhere, the distribution was carried out on other principles—for instance, according to the number of livestock held, or the number of farm buildings. It would appear that such division usually favoured the richer peasants.

Since the division of land was so clumsy, it is hardly surprising that the left wing of the Bolshevik party started to press for real socialization of land. Presumably under the pressure of left wing elements, the Commissariat of Agriculture began, at the end of 1918 and the beginning of 1919, to take land away from individual peasants and to allocate it to State farms and agricultural communes. On hearing about this, Lenin sent a telegram to all the regional offices (*gubzemotdely*) telling them that land belonging . . . to working peasants . . . cannot be forcibly taken away to organize State farms, communes, or other collective establishments.[21] The same attitude was adopted by Stalin, then Commissar of State Control. The assertion of private ownership by Lenin almost coincided with the decision to make an alliance with the medium peasant, announced by Lenin at the eighth congress (see chapter 1). The results of the redistribution would appear to have been startling. According to Soviet sources, in 1919 the peasants owned individually 96·8 per cent of the land under cultivation; agricultural co-operatives owned 0·5 per cent and State farms 2·7 per cent.[22] Unfortunately, the same source points out that these figures may well be incorrect. The basis of these percentages is the figure of 150 million hectares formerly owned by the gentry, Crown and State and supposedly given to the peasants for their use. This figure was quoted by Stalin in *Voprosy Leninisma*, and it has been found to be incorrect. Research workers using the figures have arrived at varying results, the range being from 20 million to 100,000 million dessiatinas.[23] Such new data from post-Stalinist period may put the whole question of land distribution in a new light. In the meantime, we still have to base our conclusions on Kritsman's *Geroicheskii Period Sovetskoi Revolutsii*, in which he estimated that in 1920 there were 86 per cent of farms with arable land of up to four dessiatinas, 6·5 per cent farms with arable land of between four and eight dessiatinas, and only 1·7 per cent farms with land above eight dessiatinas. If this is compared with Lenin's estimate of peasant holdings earlier in this chapter, it will be seen that over 90 per cent of peasant holdings were now well below Lenin's line for the poorest peasants, which was up to seven dessiatinas per household. It would be interesting to follow this argument, since many conclusions have been based on these figures. For instance, E. H. Carr concludes that there was 'a striking equalization of the size of the unit of production'.[24] But it would be a hypothetical exercise until the actual size of holdings, the number of households and other details can be established for certain. For the time being no more can be said other than that which has been noted above: the distribution of land was neither complete, nor fair, nor beneficial in the long run either to the State or to the peasants.

While the agricultural situation was fluctuating in these early days of Soviet power, and agricultural output declined almost to zero, what of that other concomitant of a modern State—its industrial

27

potential? In order to understand this and the relation of agriculture to industry fully, we must consider the following points: the organization of Russian industry before the revolution, the composition of the proletariat at the outbreak of the first world war, and the developments in industry during and after the civil war. It is unfortunate that we are confined, by lack of space and of satisfactory material, to a very short survey of these questions, for the subject had an important bearing on the industrialization debate of the 1920's, and consequently on the whole agricultural policy. Although the debate itself has been brilliantly and fully treated,[25] the conditions leading to it, while described in general histories of the Soviet Union, still await a monograph.[26] The tendency has been for Western scholars to concentrate on the economic aspects of the problem and for Soviet scholars to take account of political and social developments, allowing officially released figures to speak for the economic aspects. It may be that it is not possible to envisage a study blending all the economic data with the social data underlying it; in this and the following chapters of this book, I have merely tried to highlight the multilateral nature of the problem, and to assess, in a small measure, its implications for the general policy of the government. If the attempt is unsuccessful, perhaps I may be forgiven for making it when the reader realizes the difficulties.

Russian industrial conditions before and during the first world war have been treated very fully by such eminent economists as S. O. Zagorsky and S. G. Strumilin,[27] and it would be difficult to add much to their exposition. However, certain features of contemporary industrial organization have to be summed up here, since they had a direct bearing on the post-revolutionary development of Soviet industry. One of the most important was the tendency of the newer industries to concentrate in large-scale units of production. In 1913 there were 17,877 enterprises belonging to different branches of industry, of which 2,366 employed 0·7 per cent of the total labour force, while 894 employed 54·4 per cent of the total labour force.[28] This comparison shows in a striking way the contrast between the small cottage industry and the big enterprises, few in number but employing a majority of workers. According to Strumilin, the percentage of workers concentrated in large factories was 47·6 per cent of the total as early as 1902.[29] This concentration of workers in large factories seems to have been a distinguishing feature of Russian industry, as compared with the West. In Germany in 1907 there were

28

655,000 workers in factories with more than a thousand employees; in the United States in 1914 there were 1,255,000 workers in factories of this size, while in Russia the number of operatives concentrated in such factories was 980,000 in 1902 and at least 1,300,000 in 1914. Even as far as the size of the factories went, Russia had the biggest units of production. The average number of workers in large factories in Germany in 1907 was 1,980; in the United States in 1914 it was 1,940, but in Russia the average was 2,490 workers in 1902. The same applied to factories employing over 5,000 workers; there were twelve in Germany in 1907, with a total number of workers put at 119,000, while in Petersburg alone there were fourteen factories of this size, with a total of 132,000 workers. In the whole of Russia there were thirty-five such factories with a total of 270,000 workers.[30] In other words, to quote Strumilin's florid language:

Capitalism fought its way into under-developed Russia clad in full armour, thus destroying any ability on the part of small industry to rival it.[31]

This is not, of course, quite accurate. The big enterprises supplied the national needs for technically advanced manufactured goods, while the smaller industries were mostly local, had a small output and relied heavily on seasonal peasant labour. The difficulty lay in distinguishing between the small producer who worked for a big capitalist, and the large industrialist. For instance, there was a tobacco trust in pre-revolutionary Russia which controlled 60–70 per cent of all tobacco produced in the country.[32] But there must have been many small manufacturers who belonged to the trust. Were they to be counted as big industrialists or as small producers? As Zagorsky says, the formation of trusts resulted directly from the late development of Russian industry, and its dependence on and close connection with foreign banking and capital. As an example, the metal industry syndicate had as its chief shareholder a Russian bank, the Azov-Don, but the other shareholders were French, German and Belgian banks.[33]

Conversely, small industries sprang from traditional Russian crafts and depended little on foreign capital, though there is some evidence to suppose that by the time of the outbreak of the first world war they were already being organized on the lines of the English 'domestic system' and were therefore losing their character of true cottage industries. We may therefore suggest that despite the impressive figures quoted above, demonstrating the giant character of

29

the new industries and the minuteness of the old type of industry, the disparity was not as great as some writers (notably Strumilin) would like to make out. The small industries (and often the big factories as well) could augment their labour force by taking on extra workers from among the peasants, for the Russian had long practised interchangeability in that he worked in a factory in winter and on the land in summer.[34] Perhaps on this account, and perhaps by native versatility, the Russian could also switch from work in a factory to work in cottage industry, from mechanization to hand-powered tools, at a very short notice. This habit, which caused a lot of instability in the proletariat, was realized by the Bolsheviks only after it had happened on a large scale. The closeness of the Russian workers to the village is another matter on which it is difficult to be dogmatic, but as a general rule one must affirm that they were on the whole far removed from the English proletarian, who was completely divorced from the soil. Just as one must be careful about the cleavage between large and small industry, so caution is necessary about juxtaposing the 'real' proletarian to the 'real' peasant.

Again, while working conditions in Russian factories were in-credibly shocking to the modern mind, they were just as shocking in small factories as in large ones—indeed, often worse, for the factory inspectors seldom had time to visit the numerous smaller enterprises. The workers were often far more exploited by small industrialists aiming to get rich quickly than by the large ones. This lay at the basis of a lot of post-revolutionary bitterness against the 'kulaks', for while ideologically the Bolsheviks were inclined to hate the big capitalist more—and the foreign capitalist in particular—they knew well enough that it was the small domestic-bred capitalist who had oppressed the workers most in former days.

Another important feature of industry was its dependence on foreign imports, particularly as regards machinery and railway roll-ing stock. It is perhaps less widely appreciated that Russia depended in a great measure on imports of raw materials as well. In the period 1909–13 the percentage of imported manufactured goods was 32·2 per cent while the percentage of raw materials and semi-manufac-tured goods was 48·7 per cent.[35]

Importation of raw materials played a large part in the textile in-dustry, with Russian-grown cotton supplying only half the demand by 1913; cotton and flax yarn and wool and silk imports were all increasing steeply before the war. The position was even more striking in the mining industry, which had not kept pace with developments in the textile industry. Thus iron, lead, zinc and copper had to be imported in significant quantities. Moreover, the necessity for importing foreign fuel to keep the industries going was rising, and all Russian factories came to depend heavily on foreign petroleum and coal.

The geographical distribution of Russian industry also played an important part in future developments. The chief raw material producing districts lay in the south (the Ukraine, the Donets basin), the east (the Urals) or the south-east (Transcaucasia and Central Asia), while the chief manufacturing districts were centred around Petersburg and Moscow. The cost of bringing coal and iron from the Ukraine and the Urals may well have made the import of these materials by sea to Petersburg much more economic. The important part that the industries of the kingdom of Poland played in the period 1880–1914 cannot be discounted. These included not only a thriving textile industry, but chemicals as well as the coal, iron and steel. All were lost to Russia almost immediately on the outbreak of the war. It can be seen from this that Russian industry had many negative features. Concentration made it vulnerable in the event of war or revolution. Dependence on imported raw materials meant that it suffered heavily when imports were cut off. Long-distance transportation affected it when transport became disorganized.

To these handicaps, which might have been avoided by better planning, one must add the inherent disadvantages. It is customary to quote as the first of these the huge and illiterate peasant population, whose mass weighed the country down. The sheer size of the country, which strained the efficiency and speed of communications, is also of great importance. Without minimizing either of these factors, I would put in the first place what I can only (reluctantly) describe as the schizophrenic tendencies which had for some time existed among the two educated classes of the country, the ruling class and the intelligentsia. Of the two, the ruling class was perhaps less torn in its views, for on the whole it had but one aim in view: to preserve the status quo. Even here we find that the means by which this was to be done took two different directions, and that this inconsistency provided a very real obstacle to the retention of power. It was the intelligentsia's position, however, which was made untenable by this mental dichotomy, a dichotomy which proceeded

31

directly from the great nineteenth-century ideological split between the Slavophiles and the Westernizers. The oddity of the Bolsheviks' position (and perhaps the secret of their success) lay in the fact that they attempted to straddle these two movements and could, therefore, at various points in time satisfy the different currents in Russian society.

From the Slavophiles the Bolsheviks borrowed their vociferous condemnation of Western capitalism (the Marxist theory only gave formal clothing to a far deeper Russian belief) and their faith in the social justice of communal farming. The Slavophiles' dislike of capitalism had even led them to despise the very necessary forms of rural and cottage industry, and they are reputed to have been the first people to have applied the term 'kulak' to all richer peasants indiscriminately. It was the Slavophiles also who were the exponents of a specifically 'Russian' solution to all Russian problems, an ideology which made Lenin's reshaping of Marx much easier. On the other hand, it was from the Westernizers that the Bolsheviks borrowed the desire for a quicker development of industry, better means of communication, better education, and many other concomitants of a developed State. If the Bolsheviks' methods were developed out of the experience of modern political parties, the Social Revolutionaries and the Social Democrats, their ideology was far more integrally 'Russian' than they themselves, seduced by their thin veneer of Marxism, would ever have believed. We have seen the split in the ideology manifested strongly in the approach to the peasant question during the 1920's. The situation on the industrial front was both less and more complicated, but here the difficulties can also be traced to a similar duality of thought.

Naturally, the ideological division sprang from the conditions in the country. It would be a truism to repeat that Russia was a predominantly peasant country. But the Bolshevik revolution was launched in the name of the victorious proletariat, the supposedly new force for progress in the world. It was only later that the cost could be counted, and questions asked. Was the proletariat worth three years of murderous and exhausting civil war? Was it aware of the blessings about to be bestowed on it? But the greatest question, one that was never voiced, was: was there a proletariat?

In the year 1897 there were just over two million industrial workers out of a population of 126 million;[36] in 1913, before the outbreak of the first world war, the industrial workers numbered just under

32

three million.[37] Had there not been an intervening war and revolution, one can envisage, without being a statistician, an industrial population in the region of six million by 1921. While the proletariat was relatively small in numbers, it lived in highly concentrated localities. The peasants were amorphous, unorganized and had mainly local interests; the proletariat had developed, despite (or perhaps because of) various oppressive measures, a relatively tightly knit organization, both through the trade unions and through the various political parties. And though their relationship to the land was closer than in Western European countries, there is no basis for thinking that every worker was a peasant at heart.

First there is the fact that the exodus of factory workers during the summer is much smaller than is generally believed. M. Dementieff, after a minute inquiry in three districts of the government of Moscow, found that, excluding the mat factories, only 14 per cent of the workers left the factory during the summer, and of these 12 per cent were absent less than four weeks. In large factories where machinery was used he found the workers were practically a stationary class, whose one remaining link with the soil was the obligation to pay taxes. The same inquiry proved that this alienation from the land is no new thing. Out of some 18,000 persons questioned, 55 per cent were found to be the children of factory workers.[38]

These are the words of a factory inspector at the beginning of the twentieth century. Though Dementiev's survey has been criticized,[39] one cannot dismiss his evidence too lightly.

The conditions of factory life before 1905 were notoriously bad. Even so, many were glad to get factory work, for the alternative might be a slow death from hunger:

The limited extent of manufacturing industries by itself goes far to explain the miserable condition of the industrial population. Industry has not hitherto absorbed more than half the surplus of the agricultural population, and hence the supply of labour is always in excess of the demand, and wages are consequently barely sufficient to maintain life.

. . . even in the smaller factories . . . they are probably dependent on the shop kept by the factory owner for their necessaries. Thus the factory class generally receives some part of its wages in kind . . .

Fines and deductions were until recently imposed entirely at the pleasure of the employer. Indeed . . . a factory owner proposed to his manager that fresh fines should be imposed to indemnify him for a temporary fluctuation of trade.

The Russian worker's wages were 'from one-half to four-fifths less than in England'. On the other hand, his working day was limited

33

since 1897 to eleven and a half hours a day, but very often the conditions of labour required either longer hours, night work following a day shift, or other similar extensions. The rate of accidents was high, productivity per worker very low.[40]

These almost impossible living and working conditions gave rise to a great deal of revolutionary propaganda, which culminated in the 1905 revolution. Incredibly enough, though the working class was the main agent of the revolution, hardly anything was done when order had been restored to remedy the worst evils. The government's chief efforts were concentrated on land reform, and on creating a land-owning class of peasants. This serious misjudgment of the mood of the times (which probably hastened the 1917 revolution) may have been the result of the nationalistic leanings of Witte and Stolypin; or, to put it another way, though Slavophilism was rejected as far as peasant communes went, its other tenets still held good. In fact, after 1905 a great deal of legislation and 'special measures' was designed expressly to terrorise the revolutionary workers into complete submission, and such was the power of the reactionary forces that by 1907 the government was almost completely successful. On the positive side, the trade unions were legalized in 1906, but the provisional rules

limited their functions to vaguely defined activities, such as improvement in the conditions of labor, setting up of a machinery for the arbitration of industrial disputes, inquiry into the wages, educational work, and management of labor exchanges. These provisions, if liberally interpreted, might have led to a fruitful development of the labor movement. . . . Under the stern rule of Stolypin, however, the bigger unions speedily disappeared, and the few smaller unions that managed to survive . . . exercised hardly any influence. The anti-union policy was adhered to by Stolypin's successors.[41]

In this way, at a time of unprecedented growth in Russian industry— a growth which was vital for the survival of the national economy— the government attempted to repress politically, and to eliminate from any influence on national affairs, the ever-increasing industrial population. This short-sighted policy, of course, led only to a strengthening of the more radical forms of revolutionary propaganda.

The outbreak of the first world war, then, found the Russian proletariat better off neither financially nor politically. However, it seemed somewhat pacified:

Deprived of its leadership, and swayed, perhaps, by patriotic emotion, labor appeared to be willing to make peace with the imperial government, or at least to postpone domestic strife until the end of the war.[42]

34

The numbers of the workers at the beginning of the war appear to have constituted a constant puzzle to economists and historians alike, and have not up to now been established exactly. The figure of almost three million, quoted by Zagorsky, has already been given earlier in this chapter. Some Soviet sources, while admitting the impossibility of an exact estimate, say that the figure for the industrial proletariat can be set at three to six million people, a somewhat wide divergence.[43]

This particular author blames the divergence on the bad state of pre-revolutionary statistics, as well as on the fact that no comprehensive surveys were conducted. He adds, however, that it is also uncertain to which class certain categories of workers (such as the railway workers, the road and construction workers) belonged. It would also appear that in some industries all employees were included, so that a proportion of white-collar workers might have been classed as 'proletariat'. Lenin estimated the number of the proletariat at about twenty million, but he obviously meant the rural labourer or *batrak* as well as the industrial worker. Rashin, in his much quoted work on the proletariat,[44] gave a more detailed breakdown of the figures. But Gaponenko is able to prove that in one case alone Rashin under-estimated the number of labourers by some 400,000.[45] Such fluctuation is obviously unsatisfactory; the best one can do is to estimate the full-time (or almost full-time) industrial population at three to four million workers, of whom some two million worked in large mechanized enterprises, while the rest were employed in smaller, possibly semi-mechanized or hand-powered, industries.

The mobilization during the war brought about great changes in the industrial population. According to Zagorsky's figures, there were just under 6½ million men under arms in 1914, and just over 15 million in 1917. Of these 15 million, 10 million were peasants.[46] Gaponenko says that of the 15 million, 11 million were peasants, and the rest townspeople. As to the percentage of workers mobilized in 1914, he says that some authors put it as high as 40 per cent, while others, citing Petrograd as an example, give the figure as only 17 per cent. However, Petrograd was where almost all defence industries were concentrated, and most of the workers there would be exempt from call-up.[47] The figure of 40 per cent called up seems exceptionally high for industries essential to the war effort, but in inessential industries the percentage must have been higher, perhaps 60–80 per cent. Otherwise the sharp diminution of the labour force in the years

35

1914–15 cannot be explained. These are the figures given for factories under the supervision of factory inspectors (which excluded a large proportion of munition factories and mines):[48]

Year	1913	1914	1915
Labour force	2,319,577	1,960,860	1,922,572

Apart from the call-up, there was also movement from inessential industries to essential ones. For instance, in metallurgical and engineering factories in Petrograd, the number of workers rose by 224·5 per cent on average between January 1914 and January 1917.[49] To add to the difficulty, after the initial indiscriminate mobilization, workers began to be recalled to the factories (often under pressure from employers), and those still working were being granted deferment.

Owing to all these changes, the composition of the working class by age alone underwent radical changes in the years 1914–16. These are the age groups for the two years concerned (all figures per cent):[50]

	1914	1916
Up to 17 years old	7·3	21
18–25 years old	38·1	20·9
25–40 years old	43·2	33
40–50 years old	9·6	20
Over 50 years old	1·8	5

According to these figures, while workers of the most desirable age constituted over 80 per cent of the working population in 1914, their number was already reduced by 1916 to barely 54 per cent, with, no doubt, a corresponding reduction in 1917.

While I have been unable to find any overall breakdown of figures for the type of worker employed in Russia in 1917, a list of workers employed in the Donets district in 1917 will give an idea of the change of composition of the proletariat:[51]

Men liable to conscription	126,526
Prisoners of war	75,464
Women	12,185
Boys and children	19,283
Refugees	2,403
Chinese and Persians	1,467

The author comments that almost two-fifths of the total number employed were drawn from other regions. Another conclusion is that only about half these workers could be expected to be in any way politically committed; the women, children and prisoners of war
36

were almost certain to be totally uninterested in politics, though Bolshevik propaganda may have had some effect on the prisoners of war.

Another table shows the changes in composition according to age and sex in private industry in the years 1913–17 (all figures per cent):[52]

	1913	1917
Children	1·9	3·0
Adolescents	8·4	12·4
Women	22·5	38·9
Men	67·2	45·7

These figures illustrate the fact that by 1917 men—the most politically conscious part of the working population—formed less than half the workers in privately owned industries.

Mere numerical changes, however, do not show the full extent of change in the Russian proletariat. Social change played as big a role as the changes in numbers. As the workers in essential industries were exempt from call-up, the factories became the haven of those who wanted to avoid mobilization. The factory workers were so afraid of army service that discontent was stifled and strikes avoided by the government's holding the threat of mobilization over their heads; both Zagorsky and Gaponenko quote several such instances. In this way, many people who would otherwise never have worked in a factory became industrial workers because of the circumstances of the war. Lenin acknowledged this, and reckoned that it made the workers less conscious of their proletarian obligations:

Since the outbreak of war, the industrial workers in Russia became much less proletarian than before, because during the war those who wanted to avoid military service became workers.[53]

According to research based on the 'Materials for the census of the workers' composition . . .', Lenin was quite right. In 1916 75–80 per cent of workers owned some land and a house; these figures rose to 92 per cent among construction workers and fell to 60 per cent among metallurgical workers. Factories became filled by many more seasonal workers, who left them in the spring, only to return to town after the harvest was over.[54]

It is interesting, on reading this information, to find that the pre-revolutionary industrial situation was already in many cases similar to that which obtained after the revolution. The phenomena of great industrial concentration, bad living conditions, low wages, government distrust of the trade unions, peasant influx into towns in search of industrial work, the resultant close ties with the countryside, and of too many people chasing too few industrial jobs—all of which caused such misery among the people and heart-searching in government circles—were evident in Russia as early as the beginning of the twentieth century.

The first world war brought the additional complication of the disappearance of the settled and hereditary proletariat, and of a heterogeneous mass of new workers taking its place. In this connection, the Bolsheviks' claim to represent the proletariat assumes rather different dimensions. They may have represented the poor, dispossessed masses; they were hardly in a position to represent an almost non-existent proletariat. Only a quick and decisive policy of industrial development, coupled with a big educational programme, immediately after the civil war could have produced this class. The following chapters will discuss whether the government's policy was, in fact, conceived on these lines.

NOTES

1. James Mavor, *An Economic History of Russia*, vol. 2, pp. 342–3.
2. Report of the Tula committee on the needs of agriculture in 1902, quoted in M. T. Florinsky, *Russia, its History and Interpretation*, vol. 2, p. 1223.
3. One dessiatina = 2·7 acres. Figures given by Florinsky, ibid., vol. 2, pp. 1353–4. Their validity is somewhat doubtful, since according to Prokopovich the cultivated area shrank by 12 per cent in 1916. Quoted in T. J. Polner, *Russian Local Government during the War and the Union of Zemstvos*, p. 47.
4. T. J. Polner, op. cit., p. 149.
5. Ibid., p. 47.
6. Florinsky, op. cit., vol. 2, p. 1412.
7. Ibid., pp. 1415–16.
8. P. T. Bauer and B. S. Yamey, *The Economics of Under-Developed Countries*, pp. 177–8.
9. Figures quoted in A. Baykov, *The Development of the Soviet Economic System*, p. 13. Baykov himself has some reservations about them.
10. Florinsky, op. cit., vol. 2, pp. 1217–18.
11. Ibid., p. 1218.
12. Quoted by M. Snegirev, 'Velikaya Oktyabrskaya Sotsialisticheskaya Revolyutsiya i raspredelenie zemel v 1917–1918 godakh,' in *Voprosy Istorii*, No. 11, 1947, pp. 3–28.
13. M. Snegirev, op. cit., p. 6.
14. S. S. Prokopovich, *Narodnoe Khozyaistvo SSSR*, vol. 1, p. 129.
15. Prokopovich, op. cit., vol. 1, p. 130.
16. Snegirev, op cit., p. 4.
17. Smolensk Archives, Smolensk, 1917–18, reel 2, WKP 1.
18. Snegirev, op. cit., p. 15.
19. Ibid., p. 17.

20. Ibid., p. 15.
21. Ibid., p. 20.
22. Yu. A. Poliakov, 'Sotsialno-ekonomicheskie itogi agrarnykh preobrazovanii Oktyabrskoi revolutsii (1917–20)' in: *Istoriya sovetskogo krestyanstva i kolkhoz nogo stroitelstva v SSSR*, p. 15.
23. Ibid., p. 17.
24. E. H. Carr, *The Bolshevik Revolution*, op. cit., vol. 2, p. 168.
25. See A. Erlich, *The Soviet Industrialization Debate, 1924–28*.
26. I am, of course, aware of one monograph on Soviet industry, N. Jasny's *Soviet Industrialization, 1928–52*. This excellent book (though I consider it inferior to the brilliant book on agriculture by the same author) is, however, concerned with a later period, and the 1920's are treated very briefly. Margaret Dewar's *Labour Policy in the USSR, 1917–28* and S. M. Schwarz's *Labor in the Soviet Union* are mainly concerned with official policies and central organizations. A newly published study by A. Broderson, *The Soviet Workers; Labor and Government in Soviet Society*, almost completely ignores the early period and concentrates on later years.
27. S. O. Zagorsky, *State Control of Industry in Russia during the War;* S. G. Strumilin, *Ocherki Ekonomicheskoi Istorii Rossii*.
28. Zagorsky, op. cit., p. 10.
29. Strumilin, op. cit., p. 540.
30. Ibid., p. 540.
31. Ibid., p. 542.
32. Zagorsky, op. cit., p. 11.
33. Ibid., p. 11. On trusts, see also G. V. Tsiperovich, *Sindikaty i tresty v Rossii i v SSSR*.
34. A great part of Tugan Baranovsky's classic work *Russkaya Fabrika* is devoted to describing this phenomenon.
35. Zagorsky, op. cit., p. 14.
36. First figure quoted by G. Drage, *Russian Affairs*, op. cit., p. 156. Second figure quoted by Brokhaus and Efron, *Entsiklopedicheskii Slovar*.
37. Figure quoted by Zagorsky, op. cit., p. 5.
38. G. Drage, op. cit., p. 190.
39. See S. M. Schwarz, *Labor in the Soviet Union*, op. cit., pp. 2–3, where he argues that Rashin criticized Dementiev's figures, because Tugan Baranovsky gave exactly opposite results after a survey of a Moscow textile mill.
40. Drage, op. cit., pp. 189–99.
41. M. T. Florinsky, op. cit., vol 2, p. 1228.
42. Ibid., p. 1229.
43. L. S. Gaponenko, 'Rabochii Klass Rossii nakanune Velikogo Okt'yabrya' in *Istoricheskie Zapiski*, vol. 73, 1963, p. 38.
44. A. G. Rashin: *Formirovanie rabochego klassa Rossii*, p. 172.
45. Gaponenko, op. cit., p. 48.
46. Zagorsky, op. cit., p. 51.
47. Gaponenko, op. cit., pp. 55–56.
48. Zagorsky, op. cit., p. 53.
49. Gaponenko, op. cit., p. 77.
50. Ibid., p. 57.
51. Zagorsky, op. cit., p. 54. The statistics refer to workers in coal mines.
52. Figures worked out on the basis of a table given by Zagorsky, op. cit., appendix 26.
53. Quoted by Gaponenko, op. cit., p. 62.
54. Ibid., p. 62.

3 'The people have control of all means of production'

We have seen that Soviet policy as regards industrialization required a great and consistent effort on the part of government in order to make good the mistakes of pre-revolutionary governments and the ravages of war. But in 1917 Russia was a predominantly peasant country and one would have expected that in this field, at least, the Bolsheviks, supported by the new class of peasant land owners, could have produced a partial solution to the problem of the countryside. It was not so.

Nowhere was the government's lack of policy as evident as in its initial support for Poor Peasants' Committees, and its subsequent retreat from them. The Poor Peasants' Committees were supposedly the party's socialist vanguard in the countryside. Lenin had said several times that their creation had changed the revolution from a bourgeois revolution to a socialist revolution.[1] Research, however, proves that these committees were established with nothing more in view than to provide help in requisitioning grain from the richer peasants. The committees were asked to form detachments, and if necessary to get the help of the army or some armed forces. Thus equipped, they were to seek out the hidden grain stores of the rich peasants. The biggest part was to go to the State, while the rest (save the grain needed for sowing) was to be distributed to poor peasants. To help them in their work, the Commissariat of Food allowed the committees a large amount of consumer goods, to be distributed among themselves. This operation the Soviet authorities termed 'barter',
40

though Prokopovich gives it the simple name of 'expropriation'.[2] The Committees of Poor Peasants were extremely unsuccessful in requisitioning grain. On the other hand, being mostly composed of rabble, they managed to rouse the peasants to armed rebellions:

They often took all the expropriated grain from rich peasants for themselves, not sending anything to the starving capitals or manufacturing towns. In provinces rich in grain they were weak; in consuming provinces they were strong, but there they could not apply their strength to any object, for there was little grain.[3]

The only really effective means of getting grain from the peasants were the workers' detachments sent out from the cities. Their strength did not lie in propaganda:

. . . each detachment should consist of not fewer than 75 men, and two to three machine guns, . . . They must be capable of uniting two to three detachments in a short space of time. . . .

read the instruction.[4] When the workers' detachments proved much more effective at grain expropriation than the Committees of Poor Peasants, the latters' fate was probably already sealed. Even so, they might have been allowed to die a natural death had they not reached for more power. At the sixth All-Russian Congress of the Soviets in November 1918, the committees demanded the transfer of all political power from the rural soviets to the Committees of Poor Peasants. The congress swiftly passed a resolution incorporating the committees in the local soviets.[5] It is difficult to imagine how the assumption grew that the Bolsheviks had staked all their hopes on these committees. The main episode lasted barely five months, officially (though of course, pockets of committees may have survived longer in some provinces; in some districts they were revived in 1928, for reasons which will be discussed); apart from Lenin's statements on the role of the committees, there is little evidence that they played an important part in the shaping of the new State. Yet their liquidation (which was envisaged in Lenin's stress on the 'temporariness' of the committees) has been described as a 'retreat from an untenable position'.[6] Had the committees proved useful, they might have been allowed to survive rather longer, though their lawlessness was causing the government great anxiety. They were not useful, however, and they could become dangerous in the long run. There was no hesitation, no consideration of 'revolutionary values' in their abolition. If their creation was hailed as a revolutionary victory, their abolition was presented as a simple administrative measure—a down-grading, which it is doubtful if the committees themselves were capable of understanding. Once again, the party experienced the necessity for some sort of law and order in the State, and it decided to act quickly in defence of the peaceful and hard-working people against the looting rabble.

As has been mentioned, while the policy of plunder in the countryside was slowly being reversed as early as the end of 1918, the real switch towards a positive policy did not come till the eighth party congress, in March 1919. The congress's resolutions point to this clearly:

The Soviet government . . . has already begun to put into practice a whole range of measures directed at the organization of large-scale socialist agriculture.

stated point 10, but it continued:

Taking into consideration that small peasant holdings will still exist for a long time, the RKP tries to carry out a series of measures directed at improving the productivity of peasant agriculture. Such measures are:

1 Rationalization of peasant land tenure.
2 Supplying the peasants with improved grain and artificial fertilizers.
3 Improving the breed of peasant-owned cattle.
4 Spreading agricultural knowledge.
5 Arranging for the agronomists to help the peasants.
6 Repair in soviet repair stations of all objects of agricultural use.
7 Setting up of hiring stations, experimental stations and model farms.
8 Reclamation of peasant-owned land.[7]

This shows that a new spirit of solicitude for the private farmer was entering the party line. Perhaps this was not very surprising, for the food position was getting more desperate every day. But it was not the only reason: another very important one proved to be the bankruptcy of the State farm policy. In 1920 the State farms covered about 1,399,365 dessiatinas of land, a small fraction of the whole cultivated area, but even so they proved expensive to run and suffered from 'hypertrophy of officialdom and strong bureaucratism'.[8] The communal farms did not fare much better. The number of 'village communes' (as they were called in those early days) in November 1919 was 1,921, their membership 320,000 people. Members of the communes were persecuted by their fellow peasants, sometimes even murdered. Because of this, many were disbanded. By March 1920 the number of communes fell to 1,520.[8] The most interesting thing about

42

these early martyrs of Communism is the fact that many of the richer peasants joined the communes very willingly; often the head of the commune was the former owner of the estate. Thus it could hardly be said that the so-called *rassloenie* (class stratification) had produced any results other than a certain change of heart on the part of the richer elements.

Since the measures taken in 1919 were obviously but the beginning of a new course and insufficient in themselves to produce big results, another hesitant step was taken in the summer of 1920. The decree promulgated then proved the government's realization that Russia was an agricultural country, and that only by helping the farmers could the nation be put back on its feet. It stated that:

the working population carrying on intensive farming can keep all the land which it is farming *de facto* with its own work-hands, even if the amount of land is bigger than that fixed for the region by redistribution norms. The same applies to those farms which may develop a more intensive cultivation in the future.[9]

The decree was interpreted thus by the paper which catered for the villages, *Derevenskaya kommuna*:

... [this decree] creates stability in rural farming. It is necessary that every peasant should be convinced that his share will remain his own, that it will not be taken away from him because the majority wish to make another redistribution instead of thinking about better agricultural methods. As the peasants are used to individual labour, and to care for their own land ... it is necessary to influence them not by taking their land away, but by measures which would have a pedagogic effect.[10]

Further measures towards strengthening the private sector of farming were yet to come, but before they are discussed it would be as well to consider the change in the government's policy at this juncture. Did this mean that it realized socialized agriculture could not work under any circumstances? Far from it. It simply meant that under contemporary conditions any attempt to socialize agriculture would end in disaster. As the Bolsheviks themselves were not slow to point out, it was difficult to carry out experiments under conditions of interventionist and civil war. Second, the disastrous lack of agricultural machinery made even traditional farming difficult; any experimental farming on a large scale would require thousands of new machines for use on the land (Lenin expressed the need as 100,000 tractors). But the difficulty was even more fundamental: efforts to change the system were bound to break down in the face of the

43

OLGA A. NARKIEWICZ

traditionalist attitude of the majority of peasants. The poor and medium peasant wanted only to get more land from the commune, to stay in the commune, to keep redistributing in the hope that he would get still more or better land in the next distribution. It was the richer, better educated peasants who could see the advantages of collective farming.

Therefore the first setback the Bolsheviks encountered was the realization that the traditional commune was very far from being a primitive socialist form of agriculture (as had been supposed in the nineteenth century). On the contrary, it was a reactionary, regressive form of farming which discouraged the hard-working peasant and feather-bedded the lazy and stupid.[11] The second shock, which was even more difficult to face, was that prosperity among the peasants did not necessarily mean anti-socialism; in other words, that the more wide-awake a peasant was, the better he could see the advantages of more modern systems. Had the Bolsheviks been allowed by their ideology to ally themselves with the progressive former land-owners, or with the more progressive rich peasants, it is just possible that a success might have been made of the new farming methods. There were many people in Russia who, encouraged by the growth of co-operative farming at the beginning of the twentieth century, were ready to experiment with some form of collective farming. Unfortunately, the slogans on which the Bolsheviks came to power meant that even an alliance with the medium peasant was ideologically doubtful. And in most cases the medium peasant of 1920 had been a landless peasant in 1917: his inability to understand the processes of progressive farming would have been complete. A realistic assessment of the situation led the government to support the private farmer more and more, to the detriment of any experimental forms of farming.[12]

Naturally, the introduction of measures supporting the private farmer was bound to damage the Bolsheviks' image as a socialist party. It is perhaps difficult to imagine nowadays the almost pathological need to justify themselves as socialists in the eyes of the population—and, even more important, in the eyes of the outside world—which was common among Bolsheviks of all shades of opinion. Some of the problems have already been discussed in chapter 1; at this point, all we can do is to sum up the implications of the New Economic Policy and show by what means it was hoped to introduce a mixed economy, yet keep a maximum of State control.

As a recent biographer of Lenin aptly says, 'Soviet Russia would

44

have gone N E P without Kronstadt. The revolt merely swept away a negligible communist minority's doubts'.[13] He supports this by quoting Lenin's remark at a meeting prior to the tenth congress:

The party Central Committee, on 24 February, approved the introduction of a tax in kind to replace requisitions, but Lenin objected to a suggestion that this important news be published immediately . . . 'In my opinion publication should take place before the [sowing] campaign, that is, right after the party congress.'[14]

This supports the hypothesis that the two articles in *Pravda* which appeared on 17 and 24 February, discussing the desirability of changing from requisitioning to taxation, were kites flown to see how the party opinion reacted. The reaction could not have been very good, since on 20 February Lenin was in favour of keeping the announcement back until after the party congress.

The Kronstadt revolt softened up party opinion sufficiently to enable the topic to be introduced at the congress. The decree changing food requisitioning to a tax came out on 21 March (the congress ended on 16 March) and was followed in a few days by the much more significant decree permitting free trade, the sale and purchase of foodstuffs, and the removal of restrictions on the movement of foodstuffs by all means of transport.[15] The second decree was more important than the first, for it restored the legality of trade and the turnover of money. Up to then trade had been a dangerous occupation, and the transport of foodstuffs was forbidden to peasants under pain of confiscation. As a result, trade fell into the hands of desperadoes, who charged extremely high prices to compensate for the risks they ran. The apparent loss of grain the State was prepared to bear was considerable, for whereas the set figure of deliveries for 1920–21 had been 423 million puds of grain, the figure envisaged for 1921–22 was only 240 million puds.[16] In actual fact neither figure came up to expectations. In the first case, only 300 million puds were collected; in 1921–22, owing to the effects of drought and famine, only 150 million puds were collected.[17]

The change of course in agriculture had to be covered by new legislation, and on 22 May 1922 a decree came out which was the direct precursor of the Land Code. This was a law on peasant land cultivation, which allowed the peasants to form land communes (*zemelnoe obshchestvo*—not to be confused with collective farms) and to choose the form of farming they preferred—communal, individual, co-operative or mixed. This law also allowed the renting of land for

45

periods of one to three years, on condition that it was worked without hired hands. However, another clause allowed the hiring of labourers in case of need, thus tacitly admitting that farming without the hire of additional hands is often impossible even on small farms.[18] After this interim decree appeared, work must have been going feverishly on the new Land Code.[19] That long and elaborate document did not appear until 15 November 1922, but even so it shows signs of undue haste in drafting. Many clauses seem to be inaccurate, while others, obviously designed as a compromise, are not very clear. The code suffers from two incompatible tendencies: one, to satisfy the peasant desire for private farming; the other, to prevent the return to antiquated farming methods. These tendencies were irreconcilable in the circumstances.

Several sections of the code are worth analysing, for they explain better than anything else the situation as it obtained, and forecast the future developments. Section IV, entitled 'The Land Commune' (*zemelnoe obshchestvo*; see the glossary for the further use of this and subsequent terms) allowed the formation of a land commune, or an association of several households or village communes. In this way a provision was made for a unit which could be larger than the traditional village commune. The new land commune was to be administered by a gathering (*skhod*) of all those entitled to vote, and by the commune's elective organs. However, the next clause immediately counteracted this unitary aspect of administration by laying down that in cases where the land commune's boundaries corresponded to the boundaries of the rural soviet, the duties normally assumed by the commune's elective organs would be assumed by the officials of the rural soviet; otherwise the elected agent (*upolnomochennyi*) of the commune would act in the normal way. This sort of ambiguity was to lead to land communes trying to set up unnatural boundaries in order to avoid being administered by the rural soviet, and on the other hand it gave the rural soviet an inducement to extend its authority over the land commune. Where neither is strong enough, it gives rise to dual authority.

The 'gathering' of the land commune was to embrace all land holders of both sexes over the age of 18. In this it differed from the pre-revolutionary gathering, which was limited to property-owning men. The gathering's rights within its boundaries were very powerful: it set up the commune's statute and could introduce changes into it; it decided how the common amenities were to be used; it had the right

46

to say who could belong to the commune and who could leave it; it decided on the type of agriculture to be followed by the commune; it divided the land among the peasants; it decided what amenities to build and what to do with unused land. The decisions of the gathering were made by a simple majority of votes, and it was responsible to government organs for the proper use of the land. The commune was given the status of a corporate body: it could buy property, enter into contracts, start legal proceedings or be a defendant in a legal action; it could also make petitions on its own behalf to State organs. It is clear from the above that the drafters of the code still believed (despite earlier experience to the contrary) that the commune in largely its old form was a road to socialism; on the other hand, they were obliged to allow it to acquire wealth, and thus become anti-socialist. If the individual peasant, on becoming wealthy, constituted a threat to the State, what of an association of these same peasants growing wealthy collectively? The drafters refused to face this problem squarely. Stolypin wanted rich individual farmers and said that the government 'placed its wager not on the needy and the drunken, but on the strong'; 'prosperous farmers endowed with full property rights were regarded as a bulwark against the revolution'.[20] Now the Bolsheviks in attempting to reverse his measures were in fact creating new peasant societies, with whose strength they would have to reckon in the future.

In this way, traditional commune farming was being encouraged positively for the first time since the beginning of the twentieth century. But this farming was often an inefficient and wasteful method of agriculture. The drafters of the code took some steps to improve commune farming, but the remedies had all been tried before without much success; none of them could be called new, and none had anything to do with socialism. Section V of the Land Code dealt with part of this question, for it set up some rules for individual households (*dvory*). The difficulty with household allotments had always been that when the children grew up the allotments tended to be divided between them. A fair-sized allotment could easily become six small plots of land. But if fragmentation is forbidden, the head of the household wields near-dictatorial powers over all members of the family. This was well known at the time of the Emancipation, and the conservatives (who in this case included Slavophiles and Populists) were against permitting division of land among members of the family.

47

In a memorandum submitted to the State Council in January 1884, Tolstoy argued that 'the multiplication of dissolutions of households was one of the causes of the impoverishment of the peasantry' because small families 'were deprived of the advantages of the divisions of labor' . . . the breaking-up of a household was not recognized as valid unless it was approved by a two-thirds majority of the assembly. . . .[21]

The new drafters were slightly more liberal than the notorious Count Tolstoy. They did not forbid the division of land among members of a family; they only encouraged its non-division. It was stated that a land commune, farming communally, 'could establish non-divisibility either communally, or by individual households, [all] agreeing to it voluntarily. . . .' In cases of consolidated farmsteads and plots (*khutora* and *otruba*), the ruling was even stricter. Their division was forbidden; if a member of the family wanted to leave, his share had to be paid out in money or movable property.[22] This condition, which gave considerable power to the head of the household, was fully regressive, even though it was designed to keep the economic unit intact. It enriched a peasant whose sons left the land, for he kept possession of the same amount of land; it favoured the bigger farmer, for he would find it easier to pay out his sons' share in money; and last, but not least, it boosted the authority of old men in the commune, something which one would have imagined the government would be very much against.

Despite all these criticisms, one cannot but sympathize with the drafters in their task. Even an attempt to catalogue the various kinds of agriculture practised in Russia produced the systems as varied as communal cultivation with an equalizing redistribution of land; individual cultivation with an unchanged amount of land held either in strips, consolidated holdings or consolidated farmsteads; and comradely cultivation, in which land was worked jointly and used jointly by a commune, an association or an artel. All these different types and sub-types of farming had to have different rules of land tenure devised for them, and in this respect the code made an attempt to assure the individual farmer who had improved his land or his methods of continuous land tenure. If the earlier parts of the code carry strong overtones of the Emancipation Act, the later ones are reminiscent of Stolypin's measures to support the hard-working farmer. But this ambiguous approach to the problems of agriculture was calamitous in its effects.

We have seen in this chapter how the agricultural situation, which had been dealt with piecemeal under successive tsarist governments, was finally utilized by the Bolsheviks for their own purposes in 1917. When it became obvious to the new government that their policies on land distribution were faulty, it reverted to land policies practised before the revolution, though tempered in some measure by the new ideology. The Land Code of November 1922 was the first full expression of this policy. Though the reversion operated from an earlier period in fact, the introduction of communes, permission to use hired labour and various other stipulations were not confirmed legally until the beginning of 1923.

While the government was reversing its policies with regard to agriculture, it is interesting to note that a similar change was taking place in its industrial policy. Frightened by the independence with which the workers were managing some industrial enterprises, Lenin became very explicit on the need to abolish workers' councils and to return to the old managerial system. Naturally, such a complete volte-face was difficult to justify. Lenin called the change a transition from workers' control to workers' management. Rather naïvely, he stated that at the beginning of Bolshevik rule it had been thought that workers' control of industry was a very easy thing, till it was tried out in practice. The industrial enterprises, and particularly the railways, were the biggest expressions of capitalist centralism. After nationalization, all these industries brought enormous difficulties to the Communists. Many blunders were made, which could only be overcome by changing over from workers' control to workers' management.

One point which Lenin omitted from his speeches was that while industrial output had fallen disastrously, this was not so much because the factories had been run by the workers as because workers were leaving industry. If we accept for a starting point the estimated figure of three million workers before the outbreak of the revolution, the numbers declined to $2\frac{1}{2}$ million in 1918, to just under $1\frac{1}{2}$ million in 1920–21, and finally the lowest figure was recorded in 1921–22: 1,240,000 people.[23] This disappearance of the proletariat has been the subject of many investigations. Obviously, the main cause was the civil war, the disorganization in the country, lack of raw materials and fuel, and the wilful shutting down of factories by the owners. But other causes must be mentioned as well.

Some of the 'melting away' is explained by the fact that many workers were casual labourers who were returning home once the high wages of war-time had stopped. Hunger, driving the workers to look for food in the countryside, is often quoted as the principal cause. One factor which has not been mentioned is that as the workers realized that the revolution on which so many of their hopes had been built was producing more misery than ever before, they must have turned away from the factories in hundreds to find a better living in cottage industries in the countryside. This realization must have come at an early stage, for there are reasons to think that despite the great initial emphasis on 'workers' control', the nationalizing policy of the party was not introduced in order to establish a socialist State, but in order to frighten the managers and owners into submission to the Bolshevik government. The punitive stress on nationalization in the first years was clear. Nationalization was carried out slowly and reluctantly, and often resorted to only when no other means of keeping the factory running could be found. Lenin said in April 1918, in a speech devoted mainly to running down the left wing of the Bolshevik party:

And when I see any workers' delegation which comes to me to complain that their factory has stopped, I tell them: you would like your factory to be confiscated. Very well, we have blank decrees, we can sign them in a moment. But tell me: have you managed to take production into your hands, have you added up what you are producing, do you know the links of your production with the Russian and international markets? And then it will be seen that you have not found out how to do this yet, that Bolshevik books on this subject have yet to be written.[24]

Even when we turn to Lenin's earlier work, there is very little to guide us in the matter of his proposed industrial policy. In a 1917 pamphlet he wrote:

control, inspection, accounting, regulation on the part of the State, the establishment of a correct distribution of the labour forces engaged in the production and distribution of goods and husbanding of national resources, a cessation of all wasteful expenditure of resources and economy in the use of them.[25]

All these objectives mirrored the outlook of a moderate Social Democrat rather than of a Bolshevik set to nationalize all industries. None of them seems to leave room for any form of workers' control; it was State control that Lenin was thinking of in this work, and State capitalism that he specifically recommended in his April speech.

The meaning of Lenin's position on nationalization and workers' control has been widely discussed by the Soviet historians in the last few years. One authority states that workers' control was to be associated only with the transitional period till industry was fully nationalized, and was to be used to keep the unruly factory owners in check, in the same way that nationalization—which should at this early stage be called 'confiscation'—was used as a punitive measure:

The main task of the organs of workers' control . . . consisted in repressing the capitalists, in carrying on the production. In the process of carrying out this task, the workers were drawn into the process of production, learned how to manage it. It is understandable that this was a difficult business, and the party constructed its policy in the expectation of a relatively long period of introducing control over industry and transition from capitalism to socialism. But as soon as circumstances required the hastening of industrial nationalization, naturally it was necessary to create and strengthen locally special State organs to manage industry—the soviets of national economy. As to the organs of workers' control—social organs (though in many cases those were temporarily fulfilling State functions)—it is quite incorrect to confuse them with the system of State organs to manage industry which was then being created.[26]

The same author adamantly refutes other historians' views that workers' control gradually changed into workers' management of industry. It merely happened sometimes that personnel from the organs of workers' control were used in the State organs which were then being created.[26] If we accept this point of view, we can establish that nationalization was resorted to only if the owner consistently refused to co-operate with the government; and that workers' control was to be introduced only if it was thought that the management could be induced to co-operate with the government under the control of a workers' council. In view of this, it is not to be wondered at that nationalization was not as wholesale between 1917 and 1921 as had been claimed by the Soviet authorities, and that the introduction of partial private ownership in 1921 was merely a confirmation of the status quo, not a new measure.[27] Even more cogently, we might ask whether full-scale nationalization of industry (apart from the accepted socialist programme of nationalization of the steel works, and other enterprises of national importance, as well as the foreign-owned companies) was contemplated in practice—that is, apart from theoretical statements—till a mixture of disorderly proceedings on the part of various local authorities and the owners' tactics rendered it absolutely necessary. These things are in the realm of speculation, however, until more Soviet sources become available, telling us exactly what happened in the years 1917–21.

51

One thing that is certain, however, is that if the state of industry was bad, that of the workers was even worse:

The British Labour delegation visiting Russia in the spring [1920] noted 'the ragged and half-starved condition' of factory workers, and learned that the peasants employed men at higher wages than the factories, 'plus a plentiful supply of food which the town worker does not get'.[28]

The party congresses confirmed this unhappy situation but, instead of remedying it, asked for more sacrifices. At the eighth congress, the trade union leader, Tomsky, allowed that it would be in keeping with Bolshevik policy to make the workers' lot easier. But the costs of running the State apparatus and the Red Army were immense. A shorter working day when higher productivity was required would be quite unrealistic. On the contrary (that is, despite the risk of higher unemployment) it was necessary to rationalize industry, to cut down uneconomic enterprises and concentrate on those which could pay their own way. Before allowing the workers a higher standard of living, the party ought to see to it that welfare measures already granted were being carried out. It was a sad fact that the workers' condition was lamentable at the moment. They had even started to set up funds for self-help again—a shameful thing in a socialist State, Tomsky thought.[29]

It is possible that the disastrous economic condition of the workers at that time made them oblivious to the repressive policy of the State. On the other hand, some show of goodwill on the part of the government, such as giving them even a partial share in the administration, might have made them slightly more interested in the productive running of industry. But Lenin's almost hysterical insistence on single management (and why should he, who always claimed that the party was run by collective management, object to the same in industry?), coupled with the senseless wholesale dismissal of those workers who had somehow survived the war—confirmed by Tomsky's statement that uneconomic enterprises had to be shut down—must have put an end to the proletariat's hopes of better times to come. It is difficult to envisage the sheer lack of vision in dismissing the only trained proletarian cadres the State had at a time when industry would have to be started up again. There seems to have been enough money and foresight to take care of the technologists, but they could not run factories without skilled workers. The effects of this policy were to make themselves felt throughout the 1920's, and will be discussed later. For the time being, we must examine the most controversial issue of the time: the management of industry by factory committees.

If one is to believe Gorman, the factory committees were doomed from the start, and later many reasons were advanced for their liquidation. It was claimed that they were inefficient, slow, technically unprepared. One cannot blame Soviet historians for trying to justify their disappearance for reasons other than Lenin's dictatorial tendencies, but one should look at Western historians' uncritical acceptance of this justification with some caution. Doubtless it is true to say that during the period of workers' control the state of industry was abysmal and productivity very low. Would it have been otherwise under the control of the former owners, with all the wartime shortages of raw material, fuel, machinery and labour? Fairly recent Soviet research shows that, in some cases at least, the factory committees were neither so stupid nor so inefficient as has been generally thought. A study of the textile industry in 1917–20, while paying lip service to Lenin on the inadequacy of factory committees, gives a rather different picture of the situation.[3⁹] The textile industry was one of the most important of pre-revolutionary Russian industries. It employed 28 per cent of all workers, and the new Soviet organs formed in it were therefore typical for a large part of industry after the revolution. Nationalization in the textile industry proceeded more slowly than in the heavy industries. Up to June 1918, of 512 nationalized or confiscated undertakings, 218 were mining or metallurgical concerns, and only 26 were textile mills. It was not until after the decree of June 1918 on general nationalization that the nationalization of textile mills began to move on. Towards the end of 1918, 71 mills were nationalized; this figure reached 468 by October 1919 and 629 by November 1920, out of a total of 847 mills.[30] However, by June 1918, 'the workers had already acquired some habits of factory management'.

It was quite normal for the textile workers to start up factory production where it had been stopped. In November 1917 the Fairman mill in the village of Rostokino was put into operation, thanks to the efforts of the Moscow Textile Trade Union. The old management was dismissed and the union turned to the Moscow soviet to arrange for the confiscation of the mill, as it did not want to assume the role of ownership itself. The workers at the mill asked for a State controller to whom the mill could be handed over. After the

53

nationalization of the mill, on 4 January 1918, the factory committee sent a telegram to the Sovnarkom in which all the personnel

promised to support the activities of the national commissars, and to use all their strength to develop the mill, which had now become the property of the Russian republic, as a national heritage for the use of Russia and her people.[31]

There was not a trace of anarchism in the activities of this committee, stresses the author. Anarchistic tendencies did occur, but not in proletarian factories, only in mills where the work-force consisted of at least 50 per cent peasants; particularly in cottage industries.[32] Neither did the workers seem to be bent on undermining productivity. The Likinskii mill was the first to be nationalized. The workers sent the old management away and set up the first workers' management in the textile industry. The Moscow Textile Trade Union took an active part in this undertaking. The new management consisted of three representatives of the factory committee, one engineer, two representatives from the Moscow Textile Trade Union and one representative from the National Commissariat of Labour. This management was confirmed in office by the Moscow commissar for labour on 24 November 1917.[32] Though the new management lacked sufficient technical skill, it performed its task better than could have been expected. The workers gave a written undertaking to the National Commissariat of Labour to the effect that they would work to raise the productivity of labour, guard the mill's property, hand over the manufactured products only to State organs, and fix their wages according to nationally set levels.

Despite the counter-action taken by the dismissed administration and the mill owners of the Orekhovo-Zuebskii raion, as a result of the energetic action of the new management the mill received a big quantity of cotton; the necessary quantity of oil and four months' supply of raw materials was collected, as well as fuel and other materials. . . . The workers showed a truly revolutionary enthusiasm in preparing the mill for starting up production; they repaired machines and looms and cleared up the grounds.[32]

Measures were taken to strengthen labour discipline and fight wastage. In the first seven months of its operation, the mill paid off its big debt and earned more than $10\frac{1}{2}$ million roubles profit. It seems to have been a real success story. Unfortunately, we are not told what happened at the mill once workers' control had been abolished.

Though several other such instances of success can be found, it must not be assumed that all factories were similarly fortunate. The

54

Bogorodskii–Glukhovskii mill remained in its owners' hands until the nationalization decree of June 1918, but a rather large factory committee had been set up as early as February 1918. For some reason, possibly because the former owners were still managing the mill—though the report stresses that the management was helpful in every respect—the workers, and particularly the white-collar workers, took little interest in the work of the factory committee. The mill had financial and raw material difficulties from the beginning of the Soviet regime, and it would appear that the factory committee was rather relieved when the final nationalization measures were taken. It is not known how long the mill had to wait for the actual nationalization; at the time the report was being compiled (not earlier than August 1918), the take-over by the State had not yet been completed.[32]

Enough has been said here to show that it was not simply a question of inefficiency on the part of the workers as against efficiency and eagerness on the part of the State. Had the State allowed the factory committees to take at least a part in the management, the whole history of Soviet industry might well have been shaped differently. This was not to be.

As we have seen from this short account, in the first stage the functions of the factory committees were not divided from those of factory managements in textile enterprises. By December 1918 this state of affairs had changed when the All-Russian Textile Union decided to divide these functions. From then on, the managements were to decide on questions of production, and the factory committees were to watch after internal order, to supervise wage rates, labour discipline and cultural work; in other words, they were to act as primary organs of the trade unions.[33] It will be seen that the 'workers' control' period lasted barely a year after the Bolshevik revolution and cannot be said to have been given a fair trial at all. Soviet writers acknowledge that this was the end of an experimental period which had many things to commend it.

This decision did not exclude, but on the contrary demanded, creative initiative on the part of the workers organized in the textile union in perfecting production and forms of management[34]

comments one author. Coming as it does at the end of a long work describing the success of some factory committees, this statement can be ascribed only to the writer's need to conform to the tradition that

E

what was lost was not a valuable experiment in co-operation between the workers and management, but simply a bit of revolutionary utopianism.

The factory committees were not abolished, therefore; they were merely incorporated into the general trade union structure, and thus lost all their importance. There were some exceptions to the rule, however. Where a factory committee was particularly useful, or zealously Communist, it carried on under the new name of factory management. The new management of the Voskresenskii mill, for instance, installed in October 1918, had seven members, four of whom had been members of the factory committee. The other three were the former manager of the mill, the former sales manager and the former timekeeper. In this way, old specialists were added to the factory committee (their choice speaks for itself) and made up a new management. Three of these old factory committee men were Communists; their role was also plain. Where did this leave the workers?

The creation of the new socialist discipline of labour presupposed the use not only of persuasion but also of repression and punishment for those who broke discipline. In the summer of 1918 disciplinary workers' tribunals were created everywhere in the textile industry. Depending on the worker's misdemeanour, the workers' tribunal could give the guilty person a warning, print an announcement in the press, suggest that he should be put in a less well paid job, or sack him; if the misdemeanour was of a criminal nature, he was sent for trial by the national tribunal.[34]

Whether such measures were introduced thanks to the presence of the former manager or because of governmental pressure, they differed little in intent from, and were rather harsher than, the measures introduced by many former owners in tsarist times, such as fines to increase profits and indiscriminate dismissals.

This punitive spirit in dealing with the workers may have sprung from the State's anxiety about the proletariat's political allegiance. There is no doubt that many workers were Mensheviks; but placed as they were, in dire economic need, they would have responded better to more humane treatment than tribunals, fines and trials.[32] And the crucial mistake in the party's reasoning was that the State could not afford to lose what qualified industrial labour it had, yet the steps it was taking led directly to this loss. No amount of militarization of labour in later years would compensate the government for creating ill-will among the workers, where it might with very little effort, have laid down a basis for peaceful co-operation.

56

It was in this way that two socialist experiments were squashed by the Bolshevik government. We can have little good to say for the Poor Peasants' Committees; while possibly less wanton than the crowds which had danced round the guillotine, they were just as harmful to the cause of the people. This is not to deny that some organization for poor peasants at that period would have been extremely useful. The poor peasant, suffering from hunger, ignorance and exploitation, needed some body which would look after his interests and show how to alleviate his lot. The Bolshevik solution of arming him and setting him against his more prosperous brothers was extremely short-sighted, and exacerbated the rural situation for many years to come.

Workers' management of factories is another matter. As we know, this idea was not a short-term revolutionary measure in the way the Poor Peasants' Committees were. It had grown slowly from the nineteenth-century ideas of co-operatives and socialism, and had a lot to recommend it. The very fact that many years later the experiment (though in a much weakened form) is being tried out in countries of both the Western and Eastern blocs adds credibility to its usefulness. Very little doubt remains that the dual fear of a Menshevik revival and of an organized proletariat led Lenin to oppose the continuation of this form of socialism, though we must allow that his fears about productivity may have been justified in some instances. But his decision undermined the essential trust which might have grown up between the government and the working classes and contributed in a great measure to the many ills from which Soviet industry suffers even today.

NOTES

1. Lenin at the eighth party congress, op. cit., p. 20. Also at the sixth congress of the soviets.
2. Prokopovich, op. cit., vol. 1, p. 150.
3. Ibid., pp. 154–5.
4. Ibid., p. 151.
5. Carr, *The Bolshevik Revolution*, op. cit., vol. 2, p. 158; Prokopovich, op. cit., vol. 1, p. 155.
6. Carr, *The Bolshevik Revolution*, op. cit., vol. 2, p. 159.
7. KPSS v. Resolutsiyakh i Resheniyakh, part 1, pp. 424–5.
8. S. Zagorsky, 'Sotsialno-ekonomicheskaya reaktsiya v sovetskoi Rossii' in *Sovremennye Zapiski*, No. 1, 1920.
9. *Izvestiya*, 10 June 1920.
10. *Derevenskaya Kommuna*, No. 98, 1920.

11. For a full discussion on the merits and demerits of communal land tenure which developed in the period 1923–27, see chapter 7.

12. In support of this, one need only quote from a work by S. K. Chayanov et al., *Experimental Farming of the People's Commissariat for Agriculture of the RSFSR*, in which it is said that 'The first of these periods [1917 to 1923] was chiefly concerned with the preservation of the experimental system from destruction. . . .' (p. 7). Though the author has in mind, in the first place, establishments for actual experimentation, he also refers to model farms, soviet farms and collective farms.

13. Louis Fischer, *The Life of Lenin*, p. 472.

14. Ibid., p. 467.

15. Carr, *The Bolshevik Revolution*, op. cit., vol. 2, pp. 281–2.

16. Zakony rabochego i krestyanskogo pravitelstva, decree No. 148, signed by Lenin on 28 March 1921. One pud = 36 lb.

17. Carr, *The Bolshevik Revolution*, op. cit., vol. 2, pp. 283–4.

18. Zakony rabochego . . ., decree No. 426, 22 May 1922, issued by VTsIK.

19. Zakony rabochego . . ., decree No. 68, Zemelnyi Kodeks, 15 November 1922.

20. Florinsky, vol. 2, op cit., p. 1220.

21. Florinsky, vol. 2, op cit., p. 1102.

22. Land Code, section V, paragraph 86.

23. On estimated figures, see chapter 2. The above figures are quoted from E. H. Carr, *The Bolshevik Revolution*, op. cit., vol. 2, p. 194. Carr gives the 1913 figures as 2,600,000 workers.

24. Lenin, *Sochineniya*, vol. 27, 'Doklad ob ocherednykh zadachakh sovetskoi vlasti', 29 April 1918.

25. Lenin, *Sochineniya*, vol. 21, p. 160.

26. A. Ya. Gorman, 'O sotsialisticheskom preobrazovanii promyshlennosti' in *Voprosy Istorii*, No. 2, February 1957.

27. The author has met several people who claimed that they were still (in the period 1940–50) managing factories they had formerly owned; this seems to have been quite a normal occurrence.

28. Carr, *The Bolshevik Revolution*, op. cit., vol. 2, p. 195. It is notable that at that time official hire of hands was still allowed only in exceptional circumstances.

29. Tomsky, eighth congress, op. cit., p. 84.

30. K. I. Bobkov, 'Iz istorii organizatsii upravleniya promyshlennostyu v pervye gody sovetskoi vlasti, 1917–20' in *Voprosy Istorii*, No. 4, April 1957.

31. TsGAOR, quoted ibid.

32. Bobkov, op. cit.

33. Doklad kontrolnoi komissii Bogorodsko-Glukhovskoi manufactury . . . s 1 marta po 1 avgusta 1918 g., in: *Rabochii klass Sovetskoi Rossii v pervyi god diktatury proletariata*, No. 120.

34. This was in keeping with the resolution of the first All-Russian Congress of Trade Unions, in January 1918. See Carr, *The Bolshevik Revolution*, op. cit., vol. 2, p. 107.

35. It is certain that the workers themselves were fully aware of the injustice with which they were being treated. Their grievances were taken up by the party faction, which came to be known as the 'workers' opposition'. This faction commanded a great deal of support for a time; for instance, M. Fainsod states that 'Although the workers' opposition was able to mobilize but eighteen votes (at the tenth congress) . . . the vote was far from reflecting the real strength of the workers' opposition among the party rank and file' (*How Russia is Ruled*, op. cit., pp. 143–4). Had Professor Fainsod added 'the rank and file of the proletariat' he would have been even more correct.

4 'We have to work untiringly to organize the soviets'

While the Bolshevik government was so unsuccessful in establishing viable relations with the two working classes in the country, it had little more success in its efforts to create an efficient administrative network. The issue of 'government by the soviets', which had become a major propaganda point at an early stage of Soviet power, had very intangible results in practice. Unfortunately, though the soviets had little real power, their functions have been taken seriously by most scholars—more so by Western historians, perhaps, than by Soviet ones, who have had more contact with the realities of Soviet administration.

There have been many attempts to classify the network of soviets: to break them down into classes as regional, district, etc., and to establish their functions, their composition and so on. This has resulted in rigid studies which presuppose that because soviet A in α performs certain functions therefore soviet B in β, which corresponds to it in size, is also doing these things.[1] Close reading of Soviet sources on the work of the local soviets, however, gives an impression of variability, fluidity and lack of precisely defined functions. To avoid making any far-fetched comparisons, it is best to be realistic and do what the Soviet writers have nearly always done: divide the soviets into local soviets (i.e. all the soviets in the countryside; in the 1920's they were at the rural—not necessarily village—level, *volost* level, and *uezd* level upwards) and into city soviets. The two types of soviet are completely different institutions. Since the city soviets were

59

little more than enlarged city councils, only the organization and functions of the country soviets will be considered here.

Naturally enough, the early years of Soviet rule are difficult to reconstruct. There are some statistics, but they must be quoted very cautiously, as their compilers often had to rely on limited, uncertain data which were impossible to check. In 1924 the National Commissariat of Internal Affairs in Moscow compiled statistics for ten guberniyas for the years 1919, 1920, 1921 and 1922.[2] According to these the number of rural soviets (that is, the lowest unit) was 17,557 in 1922, and their membership totalled 61,751.[3] It is not specified whether this number comprised only paid officials or whether it included elected members as well. The number of rural soviets for the whole territory of RSFSR is given as approximately 120,000, with over 484,000 members. The election data are more interesting, for they prove the narrow range of participation in the elections to the soviets. In the ten guberniyas surveyed, an average of 22·3 per cent voters took part in the elections. For individual guberniyas these figures varied from 9·5 to 51 per cent. This small number of electors is explained by the fact that very few women voted; the percentage of women is given as 14. As a result, the soviets were composed almost entirely of men—99 per cent in fact. In rural soviets, peasants were firmly in the saddle; 94·3 per cent of members were peasants. Education was not one of the strong points of the members of rural soviets: the number of members with higher education was minute— 0·06 per cent, and 1·7 per cent had had secondary education. 86·6 per cent had had primary education, and there were 11·6 per cent of illiterates. Illiteracy is more noticeable in non-Russian provinces; for instance, the Altay region and Cherkess *oblast* show 28–30 per cent of illiterates in the soviets.[4] On the whole, the electors tended to elect deputies better educated than themselves; for instance, in some regions there were 25·7 per cent illiterate electors, but only 14·3 per cent of elected deputies were illiterate. If literacy was not very high, neither was party membership. The average number of party members is given as 6·1 per cent, with one stipulation: in non-Russian guberniyas the percentage of Communists in the soviets ranges from 11–25 per cent, but in Russian guberniyas from 0·3–1·8 per cent.[5] This would appear to have been caused by the inclusion of Russian Communists specially sent from the centre to keep an eye on the population of non-Russian origins, rather than by the population's interest in Communism.[6]

60

While the rural soviets were thus almost completely in the hands of non-Communist peasants, the situation changed slightly in higher offices. The *volost* soviets, the next higher grade, had a rather different composition. The number of women rose slightly, from one per cent in rural soviets to 1·2 per cent in *volost* soviets. Party membership was almost doubled: on average there were 11·7 per cent of Communists in these soviets. The data are fuller for the executive committees of the *volost* soviets, that is, the small professional core of each soviet which is the chief executive arm. Here the social composition is of most interest: there were 82·2 per cent peasants, 7·9 per cent people of working class origin and 9·9 per cent officials. The educational picture shows a change as well. There were 4·3 per cent people with higher and secondary education, 94·4 per cent with elementary education, and only 1·3 per cent of illiterates.[7]

If the lower and homelier administrative bodies were relatively non-professional and non-Communist, the higher up the ladder the more radical the change became. The executive committees of the *uezd* soviets show a remarkable change in composition. 5·2 per cent of their members had higher education, 18·3 per cent secondary education and 76·5 per cent primary education.[8] Their social breakdown shows that there were 44·1 per cent officials, 31·5 per cent workers and 24·4 per cent peasants. (The growth in the numbers of workers is explained by the fact that the *uezd* soviets comprised provincial town soviets as well as rural soviets.) The high percentage of officials can be explained only by higher professionalization of these more important offices. Party membership in the executive committees stood very high in 1922—81·2 per cent members and candidates of the party. But of all the party members, 76 per cent had joined the party between the years 1917 and 1919, that is, after the Bolsheviks came to power. More interesting is the fact that by 1922 42 per cent of the executive committee members had already been serving for longer than three years, which took them back to before 1919.[8] This seems to confirm the suspicion that these were the old civil servants, or Zemstvo employees, who carried on the main business of administration as they had done in earlier years.

To sum up the impression given by these data, there seems to be no doubt that the lower soviets were completely in the hands of unprofessional and often uneducated peasants, with a consequent loss of efficiency in their work. The higher the office, the more professional officials were found, for naturally it was impossible to carry out more important administrative business with illiterate or semi-literate people. The party membership figures are fascinating, for if the high percentage is taken into account, many former civil servants who had stayed on in their offices must have become Communists, possibly to keep their jobs rather than from conviction.

The figures quoted above have established that by 1922 there was a network (even if some of it was only on paper) of district and rural organizations which were capable of carrying out administration in the country. We know, by reading complaints at the congresses and the resolutions passed by the party, that the organization worked badly most of the time. But to get a clearer view of the problems involved it is always best to rely on first-hand reports, and these are not easy to come by. Sometimes, however, one comes across a painstaking and honest report, written by a local soviet official, which explains the difficulties of local administration and hence the failures of the central government. One of the reports published in 1925 traced the history of provincial and rural administration, through all the vicissitudes of civil war, banditry and changes from the centre, in Tambov guberniya.[9] Tambov was a town situated south-east of Moscow, about half-way to Saratov, so it was a typical provincial Russian town. The guberniya of Tambov was mostly agricultural. In many ways, what had happened in Tambov must have been duplicated in many other parts of provincial Russia.

The author divides the development of the administration into several periods. The first, March–December 1918, is typical only in so far as it shows that no organized institutions could work at that time. The soviet apparatus of the guberniya was not organized till quite late; only in February 1918 did the collegium of the National Commissariat of Internal Affairs in Tambov accept a motion to organize soviets of workers' and soldiers' deputies. The collegium of this particular commissariat was not an isolated phenomenon; it would appear that the guberniya had a complete government working on a provincial level and, even more interestingly, issued instructions to localities (at *uezd* level) to organize a similar network, with commissariats of administration, finance, economics, agriculture, labour, communications, posts and telegraphs, education, justice, health and administration of socialized property. The change-over to the new administration was made by the simple expedient of parcelling out the former guberniya Zemstvo offices among the corresponding commissariats. This happened on 17 March 1918 in Tambov itself, somewhat later at a local level. The whole procedure was devised and carried out by local initiative, since in most instances there had been no instructions from the centre. The guberniya administration then sent guberniya soviet members and agitators to liquidate the *volost* Zemstvo offices and to organize *volost* soviets. Local soviets were not in fact established until July 1918. According to the author of the report, every rural soviet had a national commissariat to correspond with the Tambov commissariats, including a commissariat for the struggle with counter-revolution.

If the initial organization was successful (and in most cases it could not have meant more than the re-naming of the tsarist offices), further measures were not. The Tambov Commissariat for Internal Affairs had sent out organizational instructions, but nothing else, to the localities. There were no directives about elections, and there were no instructions as to who was to be deprived of electoral rights. There-fore no one was disfranchised and in many cases the electors put in charge people who were not eligible for office under Soviet laws. The organizers sent out from Tambov had had no time to investigate the new soviets sufficiently to exclude the rich peasants and anti-Soviet elements who got into them. When the local soviets began to function, they began spontaneously to send the minutes of their meetings to the guberniya soviet; as there had been no instructions on this score, one must assume that this was also a continuation of the tsarist practice. It was only by the end of July that the guberniya authorities issued a circular about minutes. There seems to have been little point in sending the minutes, however, for they did not arrive in Tambov until two or three months after a meeting, and any action arising out of them was overdue. In five months the centre vetoed 455 decisions, most of which dealt with religious matters. One *volost* soviet decided to keep ikons hung up in soviet offices; another petitioned for religious education to be retained in schools; still another, obviously sectarian, wanted to build a meeting house for prayers. One entrusted the office of the registrar of births and deaths to the local parish priest (an office which he had performed up to the revolution); another put the parish priest on the pay-roll in this capacity. It often happened that the local soviets levied their own taxes, exhorting contributions from 'bourgeois' elements, who, oddly enough, were often ordinary working people; there were also soviets which were in fact the old rural administrative offices under a new name, i.e. with new stamps and seals.

In July 1918, almost immediately after the soviets were established, it was decided to liquidate all the commissariats, with the exception of guberniya commissariats of supply and war. In rural soviets, these commissariats became departments, usually seven in number, and an office with a secretary and some officials was introduced. All *volost* and rural soviets had executive committees of seven people, and praesidia of three people (the chairman, his deputy and the secretary). About August 1918, Tambov received the new republican constitution, after which organization became more orderly.

The real test of the new administration came when the civil war started, and 'sacrifices were required from volost and rural soviets'.[10] As soon as they were asked to confiscate surplus food supplies, the soviets proved to be slow and unsuited to revolutionary activity; and this happened just at the time when they were liable to be annihilated themselves. The self-seeking and counter-revolutionary element showed its hand in the soviets at this critical time, says the author. In the meantime the food crisis had become so bad that the second guberniya congress of the soviets gave the following directives on 27 May 1918: barriers to be set up on stations and at guberniya boundaries to fight the kulaks and 'sackmen'; food to be confiscated from the population, allowing only 25 lb per person to be left; confiscation of property from kulaks selling grain to speculators, and other similar measures. Rationing was established, with 25 lb of flour per month per person, 5 lb of wheat or millet per month per person, and 5 lb of grain per month per horse, allowing up to two horses for each family. However, the rural soviets were so weak that they proved incapable of carrying out these measures. The situation was eased, according to the author, by the spontaneous formation of the Committees of Poor Peasants. The decree calling them to life allowed them only a narrow range of activities: collection of grain and other necessities of life from kulaks, and distribution of these among all the population. But in fact the committees gradually took all power away from the rural soviets, and from October 1918 onwards carried out proletarian dictatorship in the villages. As a result, the peasants began to revolt, and liquidated both the rural soviets and the Committees of Poor Peasants (see chapter 3).

The situation was not improved by the frequent call-up of workers delegated to work in the local soviets. When the national commissar Podbelsky was sent from Moscow to strengthen the work of the soviets, he sent this report on 26 July 1919, after touring the guberniya:

Strictly speaking, there is no soviet government in the majority of the uezdy. At present the soviets exist in most places only on paper; in reality, representatives of kulaks and speculators, or self-interested people, or cowards, who carry out the work without any definite direction, work under the name of soviets.[11]

The soviet workers were described as indifferent, barbarous, formalist. When the White forces (Mamontov's cavalry) occupied Tambov, a temporary halt was put to soviet activity. When this territory was regained by the Bolsheviks, a new activity began to occupy the Soviet authorities. Stricter measures for requisitioning and fighting the kulaks were taken. But this brought a lot of trouble, for representatives of outside institutions would come to *volost* soviets and demand various services from them. In case of refusal, they often arrested soviet officials; as a result, people began to avoid being elected for office, and soviet offices worked in fear. The guberniya office was forced to issue a decree forbidding the arrest of soviet officials without previous notification to higher organs, and this restored the soviets' authority somewhat.

In the autumn of 1920, the guberniya was again troubled by disorders; this time Antonov forces were advancing. Once again the soviets proved unable to control this phenomenon. Therefore when the disturbances were finally liquidated, towards the end of 1921, a reorganization of the soviets was initiated. This consisted mainly in replacing the soviet workers with people who had by now returned from the front and in tightening up centralization. However, these measures were put into action at the beginning of the New Economic Policy, which within a short time hit soviet work very hard. Only members of the *volost* executive committees were left on the State budget; all the others and the technical staff had to be financed out of local funds. As a result of this and the introduction of payments for postal and telegraphic services, the workers of the *volost* executive committees began to leave. To counteract this, the guberniya executive committee levied an extraordinary tax on the population, which improved the situation slightly. As a step towards NEP reorganization, the soviet staff was cut by 44 per cent, without any loss of efficiency. By 1923 the work of the soviets seemed to have settled down to more regular ways.

No one could call this account rosy; no one reading it could say that the soviets worked with any degree of efficiency, if they worked at all. And yet a fairly recent publication dealing with the rural

65

soviets asserts that they were active, strong and healthy as early as 1918.[12] Oddly enough, the author chose Tambov guberniya to prove his assertions. Commenting on the re-elections to the local soviets in the winter of 1918–19, the author says that, according to guberniya reports, re-elections to the soviets gave the following delegates in Spasskii *uezd*: 25 per cent Communists, 25 per cent non-party members and 50 per cent sympathizers (with the party). The elections were attended by crowds of citizens. The soviets were filled with poor and medium peasants. The kulak elements, despite their attempts, were unable to take part in the elections.[13] Another *uezd* of Tambov guberniya sent a similar report. All this reads very strangely after the early Soviet publication; a glance at the sources the author used explains it, though: he was relying on an article published in *Sovetskoe Gosudarstvo* in 1934, when the information about the early campaigns had already been edited.[12]

It may be argued that these events were typical of the early period of Soviet rule and that in later years there was an appreciable difference in the peasants' attitude to the soviets. This is not borne out by the scanty information which is available. In 1925 a party instructor in another guberniya had the following comments to make about the electoral behaviour of the peasants:

In the last months of 1925 there was discontent among some of the poor peasants against the Soviet government and the party, for reasons of alleged over-taxation with agricultural tax, and because of lack of attention to peasant complaints on this question. This discontent was exploited by the prosperous and kulak population in the countryside. From the time that work among poor peasants was begun and all possible questions were explained, this partial discontent has been liquidated. At present the poor peasants are well disposed to the party and the Soviet government. Among the medium peasants there were also small hidden discontents, because of problems of taxation and slow land redistribution. The prosperous part of the peasants used the medium peasants at the time of re-elections to the soviets and to the co-operatives, and at times they stood as a united front. Part of the medium peasants sided with the poor peasants.

At present, in connection with proper distribution of the agricultural tax, work is being carried out among the poor peasants, and it is noticeable that the medium peasants are moving over to the poor peasants' side. The prosperous peasants in the villages show a lively activity at elections to the soviets and the co-operatives and attempt to get elected into managements. This top 3 per cent of prosperous kulak element still has a certain amount of influence in the volost. . . . There are no open protests against the party or Soviet government. There is no information about the attitude of the teachers. The majority of the teachers are descended from clergy or

66

from the middle classes, but there are some who come from the peasant class and are loyal to the party and the Soviet government. The clergy still have some influence and there are some monks left. All of them agitate slightly against the Soviet order.

The re-election campaign for the soviets passed reasonably well. There is evidence of leadership from party organizations and volost executive committees. 123 members of rural soviets were elected; of these two were party members, five were Komsomols and 115 were not party members. The composition of rural soviets was replaced by 40 per cent of new members. The volost executive committee comprises seven members and two candidates. Of these, five are party members and two are non-party men.

The rural soviets work very badly. No reports are prepared about the execution of directives and plans. Out of seven rural soviets two work reasonably well, the rest badly. No attention is given to agricultural work, there is no peasant participation, meetings are held irregularly; there is no [party] leadership at general gatherings of peasants. At the meetings, the questions are passed mechanically. The commissions (three of them are attached to each rural soviet) hardly work at all. The revision commissions also work badly.[14]

This confidential report by an observer sent to the *volost* to survey all facets of the political situation sums up all the ills of the Soviet administration. We see that the peasants were easily turned against the government when they felt the effects of the economic squeeze; there is confirmation of the fact that the poor peasants were unfairly taxed, and that because of that they were ready to side with the richer peasants. There is also evidence of apathy on the part of official organizations. It would appear that all their efforts were directed at collecting taxes, and beyond this they left the peasants alone. As usual, the more efficient—that is, the more prosperous— peasants wielded great influence over all the rest of the population. The so-called 'rural intelligentsia', aware of its vulnerability, did not take part in any controversies, but the party instructor had no illusions about their real feelings. Neither did the personnel in soviet offices improve—as formerly, the clerks did not prepare reports, the meetings were not held at appointed intervals, and the special commissions existed only on paper. This situation persisted throughout the 1920's, when the alliance with peasants was in force. Later on, when it had been broken by collectivization, the position grew even worse, but for many years, in the state of near-war with the peasantry, the authorities had no time to worry about it. The revival of anxiety about the work of the rural soviets did not occur till the beginning of the Khrushchev period.

The failure of rural administration to function efficiently in the provinces sprang from many factors. Some of them have been shown in this chapter; many others were deeply grounded. They included the administrative inefficiency which had obtained under the tsarist regime, habitual 'sitting' on decisions, and similar vices—all of which made Lenin say that the Russians were incapable administrators. This of course was nonsense; given the right conditions and training, anybody with a modicum of intelligence can become a good administrator. Administrative training in Russia had always been weak; under Soviet conditions it had become non-existent. Even literacy seems to have been at a premium. Another vice from which the administration had always suffered was arbitrariness; again, Soviet conditions tended to reinforce this, though there were some efforts to devise better ways of dealing with administrative decisions. Bribe taking by civil servants had been a traditional practice. In tsarist times it sprang from bare necessity, for civil service salaries were usually below subsistence level. Under the conditions described above, it would have taken an outstandingly courageous and honest man not to use his office to obtain some additional benefits.

These were the general reasons why local administration was getting worse instead of better. But there were also some specific reasons. The failure of the Bolsheviks to gain the peasants' trust has often been cited as one of them. It is true that a system of administration, such as had originally been devised in the rural soviets, presupposed a great deal of co-operation from the participants. It is also true that the peasants had little trust in the Soviet government, and their participation was extremely weak. But there is little evidence to suggest that the peasants would have trusted any other government, even if it had pursued a more conciliatory policy. For that matter, they had never trusted the tsarist governments. The peasants were both suspicious of governments and not politically minded. They had received their land from the Bolsheviks but they had no sympathy at all with the Bolshevik ideology. And until later on there was no compulsion for them to become Communists. The party was rather glad to keep the peasants out in those early days. According to recent statistics, in 1917 there had been 9·2 per cent of peasants in the party; in 1921, 32·7 per cent. But in the purge which followed, 170,000 members were excluded, and of these 44·8 per cent were peasants.[15]

It is more than probable that had the system of rural soviets proved at all viable and efficient there would have been more support for it. The lack of interest in the soviets was partly caused by their utter and complete inefficiency, but the main reason was the growth of internal peasant organizations as a result of the legislation passed in 1922. This will be discussed later; here it is only intended to show how the government attempted to endow the rural soviets with at least a part of the authority they were originally meant to have. The lack of interest in an elective body is best shown by the percentage of votes cast. We have already seen that this percentage was extremely low in 1922. In 1923 the figures improved somewhat. Members of the trade unions who voted constituted 39 per cent of those entitled to vote; the percentage of voting peasants was 30 per cent. In 1925 the percentage of trade union members rose to 52·2 and that of peasants to 45. After this the full weight of the party organization was thrown in to increase the number of voters. The percentages began to rise slightly, but not dramatically; 51 per cent of all voters entitled to vote voted in 1926, 50 per cent in 1927 and 64 per cent in 1929. This shows that the tightening up of party policy had some influence on the voters in this period.[16]

By 1926, as the 'Face to the countryside' campaign developed, articles began to appear in the Soviet press which revealed that the search for a new solution had already begun:

The re-election campaign in the country this year [1925] passed in somewhat different conditions to those in former years. The rapid growth of all parts of the national economy, great progress of agriculture and the party's measures to create better conditions for productive initiative on the part of the peasants—all these have reinforced the growth of economic and political activity among all classes in the country.[17]

Nevertheless, there was still room for improvement. The co-operatives remained weak and did not fulfil their functions. There was little evidence of stratification, and capitalist elements played a large part in the life of the village, asserted this author. This last complaint was well founded. Reports found in the Smolensk archives for a period very near to the one mentioned above show how small was the participation of poor peasants in the co-operative movement (a complaint which persisted right up to collectivization). The first report states that experience of the past year has shown that:

There was insufficient co-ordination of the dates of the [election] campaign, as a result of which in some instances there was no preparatory work in the localities, and the attendance at meetings was very low.

69

Preparatory meetings of poor peasants were not always held. Not enough attention was paid by party organizations to arranging these meetings in good time. Because of this, a considerable number of labourers and poor peasants remained outside the ranks of members of the co-operatives, and there was no party leadership to ensure organized appearance of poor peasants at the meetings.

No attention was paid to local conditions: the dates of the meetings coincided with [peasants'] departure for forest work, and also with former local holidays.

Sometimes there were instances of insufficient attention to the independence of the elections, and candidates were appointed; in other places, on the contrary, there was a complete absence of party leadership.

The activity of members of the Komsomol was weak, and the percentage of their participation in the management of the co-operatives diminished.

Trade unions and political education organizations took almost no part in the campaign.

The percentage of women taking part in the campaign was insignificant and their numbers in the organs of management had decreased.

To combat this bad state of affairs, the following measures are proposed for future campaigns:

> ... To discuss and widely explain all the most important problems of the work of co-operatives; to suggest as candidates more experienced and tried comrades for active work in management and control organs of the co-operatives. To turn special attention to increasing the activity of poor peasant women, wives of Red Army men and authoritative Komsomols.
>
> The raion committees are to organize pre-election meetings of poor peasants, and to prepare them particularly carefully in these localities where the influence of kulaks on the work of co-operatives is noticeable. To safeguard organized speeches by poor peasants as well as by medium peasants at these meetings, under the leadership of party organizations.
>
> To co-ordinate with the raion committees the question of co-operating the poor peasants, using for this purpose pre-election meetings of poor peasants. To carry out the work in such a way as to safeguard the joining of co-operatives by labourers and poor peasants.[18]

However hard party organizations may have tried to introduce agricultural co-operation among the poor peasants (though there is evidence in the Smolensk archives that these attempts were merely sporadic, and unsupported by a broad plan), their efforts broke down because of factors over which they had no control. The hard fact was that to become a shareholder of a co-operative, a peasant had to have some capital. In the majority of cases, the poor peasants had none. In some instances (as will be seen in documents quoted later) soviet organizations made attempts to loan money to the peasants. They never succeeded, because the soviets were chronically hard up themselves. As a rule, the poor peasants were excluded from co-operatives, they were shouted down at meetings, and they were not organized.

A report of a co-operative in the Smolensk guberniya, though not exhaustive, gives some inkling of the position:

There is no list of poor peasants who entered co-operatives in Gzhatsk network—data of their numbers are missing. . . . Gzhatsk is linked with Viaz'ma only on paper. Instructions to the network are bad: they [the union agents] go there, bury themselves in data, and then they come back. This [bad state of affairs] has to be taken into account. . . . Poor peasants receive less credit; the kulak top [verkhushka] get more credit.

To remedy this situation, the commission considering the work of the union approved the following resolutions:

Having listened to the report of the work of the fraction of G K . . . on 24 September 1927 . . . we note:

1 That the work of co-operating peasant households is carried out badly, particularly as regards the kolkhozes and communes in the uezd.
2 That the union has paid little attention to strengthening agricultural machinery societies.
3 That there is no leadership . . . (insufficient instructions, lack of communications).
4 That poor peasants are not joining the co-operatives fast enough, that there is no clear policy about allowing them to join on easier conditions . . . [or help] in repaying loans.

6 That it is noticeable that debtors who are better off are allowed larger credits . . . .[19]

It is difficult to see that these weak and inadequate measures could improve the situation very much with regard to the poor peasants. They were simply resolutions, passed to prove that the authorities were aware of the difficulties facing the poor peasants who were unable to join co-operatives. The author of the article quoted earlier had few illusions about the peaceful solution of the dilemma. He had this to say on the kulak influence in the villages:

Since the soviets have begun to take a share in the village life, the kulaks have increased their efforts to subordinate them, and bring them within the sphere of their influence. Though party organizations have shown more strength in these elections [1926?] than in previous years, yet in some cases the directive not to apply pressure or administrative measures [on the electorate] were interpreted as an order to stop party interference in the

F

71

election campaign. The class struggle of the present time had to be equated with the fight to gain the medium peasants for socialism. The main feature of this fight must be the party's stress on the alliance of medium peasants with the poor peasants. Left alone, the medium peasant naturally gravitated towards the richer peasant. Without the party's persuasion, victory in the last elections would have gone to the kulaks. As it was, the kulaks won some victories, for the poor peasants still had the mentality of dependants and no faith in their own strength.[20]

But it was difficult to expect much improvement among the lower organs, continued the author, when even the highest organs gave a bad example. It was well known that article 69 of the Soviet constitution disfranchised seven categories of people; they could neither vote, nor stand for nominations. However, article 18 of the electoral instruction allowed several of these categories (peasants using hired labour, people owning mills, smithies and other agricultural enterprises, people receiving income from government or co-operative shares, merchants, and members of families of people disfranchised under article 69) to vote, while article 19 permitted members of the parish councils (apparently including parish priests) and other religious functionaries (including those of other faiths—that is, not Orthodox) to be electors. On 9 June 1925 Stalin asserted that this instruction merely meant a broadening of democracy, not a change in the character of government:

Lenin spoke in 1918 of the necessity of 'extending the Soviet constitution over the whole population, as the opposition of the exploiters weakens'. ... From that time to Lenin's death, five years passed. However, Lenin did not mention this possibility even once again. Why? Because the time for such extension had not yet come. But there is no doubt that it will come some day. ... That is why we, foreseeing a further extension of democracy in the future, consider it necessary for the time being to limit concessions to those envisaged by the fourteenth party conference and the third congress of the soviets.[21]

Translated from Stalinist ambiguity, this meant that the party felt the time had come to extend the franchise. The reasons for this must have been manifold; they will be discussed in the next chapter.

The article on elections in the countryside continued by enumerating how many cases had occurred in which voting rights were extended even to those people excluded by articles 18 and 19. A regional executive committee in Tula guberniya petitioned the electoral commission to enfranchise 51 citizens (in all, 112 people were disfranchised); this number included 29 ex-police officials and

72

one priest. Tyumen *raion* excluded only 0·4 per cent of the whole population from voting rights. The central committee in Kuban stated that those voting illegally were kulaks, merchants, White Guard elements. The correspondent of *Pravda* wrote:

In Chernikhov Stanitsa the right to vote was extended to rich owners of tobacco plantations. . . . The same happened in Pshekhskaya Stanitsa. And in Khanskaya Stanitsa. Who are these 'artisans' with voting rights? Every one sows some 10 to 18 dessiatinas with tobacco and hires from 30 to 120 seasonal workers. 'But how to exclude them when all of them belong to the union?' say the local party workers. What is the effect of such policy on the whole population, and particularly on the poor peasants? Obviously, the poor peasants are frightened; they don't even dare to vote in the districts where the rich tobacco planters live. That is understandable; of all places, it is particularly in Maikop region that the poor peasants depend on the kulak; they are tied down by credit, advance payments, loans, all of which make them very careful not to offend the kulaks. It must be clearly understood that permission to rent land, to hire labour and other measures were all introduced to raise the level of agricultural productivity, and were not meant as political concessions. . . . A few words must be added about the rural intelligentsia, particularly the teachers and the agronomists. The percentage of intelligentsia elected for the soviets has risen sharply. And while nobody denies that these cultural workers are in the main party sympathizers, it must be remembered that while they live in a society which is not very sympathetic to our aims . . . they are bound to interpret the party slogans differently to what is advisable.[22]

This article is interesting, because it was printed late in 1926, when the policy of 'Face to the countryside' was still in full swing. It quoted Stalin's speech, and followed it with information which was clearly meant to compromise him. And apart from the fascinating insight into regional affairs it provides, it also demonstrates that this course was leading the party back to the toleration of limited capitalism inside the country. The richer elements were exercising an undue influence on the poorer electors, and were illegally taking part in the elections themselves. The electoral instruction mentioned above was issued by the Central Committee, obviously with Stalin's approval. Therefore, the local party organizations which were including the more prosperous elements in their voting lists were acting according to instructions from above. In fact, we know from one instance in the Smolensk guberniya how and why such apparent anomalies happened. But even apart from the special circumstances, the poor peasants were at a great disadvantage in normal dealings with the authorities. One party instructor complained in his report[23]

73

that at the time of the survey there were two communes and five *kolkhozes* in the *uezd*:

All the kolkhozes are undergoing a financial crisis at present. . . . It must be noted that the educational work in the kolkhozes is extremely poor, and the life of women is hardly distinguishable from the life of other peasant women.

Traditional practices have not been eliminated, for instance:

'Novospasskaya Artel' is a family commune, which has not grown in the last eight years. Till the time of my joining, the secretary of the party cell did not mention the possibility of accepting medium peasants. The commune 'Nikolskii Krest'yanin' admitted the kulak Paukov, whose grain had been confiscated by the GPU. 'Overishchenskaya Artel' borrows money from Nepmen in Elninsk, and leaves a former land-owner in his flat, while members of the kolkhozes need accommodation.

Though party organizations have begun to pay more attention to the problems of the *kolkhozes,* the leadership of separate artels and practical help were insufficient.

The instructor was equally pessimistic on the question of rural soviets. Giving the figures for rural soviets as follows (all figures per cent):

	Poor peasants	Medium peasants	Prosperous peasants	Others
Composition of rural soviets in 1925–26 (assessed by questionnaire)	29·1	66	1·09	4·1
Composition of rural soviets in 1926–27 (assessed by tax)	50	43·1	1·1	4·48
(Assessed by questionnaire)	37	56·1	–	–

he stated:

If one accepts the soviet activ according to the questionnaire assessment, then the result is that the soviets in Elninskaya volost are full of medium peasants; in addition, this picture is made clearer if one looks at the chairmen of rural soviets, who constitute 76·1 per cent, and even at the presidia of volost executive committees, in which, out of eighteen members, eleven are medium peasants.

The same instructor described the work of the soviets in this way:

There is no doubt that the work of rural soviets as executors of directives from higher organs has improved; it is certain also that rural soviets hold
74

meetings at appointed periods; but together with this, it is necessary to state that as yet the rural soviets are generally badly organized. . . . Commissions of rural soviets work badly and in some soviets they do not work at all. They mostly work on matters of [political] agitation, and because of this the education of peasant activs goes very slowly. Because of this . . . there is no organized influence by poor peasants on everyday work.[24]

Little comment need be added to this realistic assessment of the situation by a man who was both a peasant and a Communist. Unlike the theorists in the capital, he realized that while the social and family structure of the village remained untouched, and while there was no hope of massive financial help from the State to create a new social structure, the system of rural soviets, co-operatives and artels would remain an empty word. The rural crisis was not the result of any measures the government undertook; rather it was the result of the measures the government failed to undertake.

We have seen in this chapter how the different strands of government policy were imposed on the countryside, and on the soviets in the first place. The soviets did not work satisfactorily, and were unable to implement their directives. The second strand consisted in the stratification of the peasants. This was to be effected in many ways, but the main one pertained to electoral rights: the rich peasants were to be disqualified from voting. This could not be done for various reasons, some of which have been enumerated. Some of the more bizarre ones also occurred, and documentary evidence will be provided to show that in one region no one could be disqualified because the authorities had failed to compile any electoral lists whatsoever. Closely allied with the rural soviets and the stratified peasants were to have been the co-operatives. Though their standing in the Bolshevik scheme of things had never been clearly elaborated (even in Lenin's famous essay), they were to provide a means of linking the soviets, the party and the peasants together. In fact, they proved to be vehicles for the continued survival of the more prosperous peasants— a fact which could be neither hidden nor counteracted. All the imposed elements of government had come to grief with the introduction of the Land Code at the end of 1922; and the reason for this lay not only in their inefficiency, but also in the code's re-establishment of the commune.[25] It was the commune which carried out administration in the countryside. But the commune was only one of many types of agricultural system to be found in the European part of the Soviet Union. We have already noted that one of the tendencies in

75

agriculture since 1905 was the break-up of the commune and the growth of individual peasant farming. These individual farms took many forms, but most of them presented problems of an administrative, economic and social nature. Before turning to the analysis of communal agriculture and administration, we must first survey what was happening to the individual farmers in the period 1923-27.

NOTES

1. The works on the system are so numerous that it would be impossible to quote them here. However, some early Western studies deserve a mention: W. R. Batsell, *Soviet Rule in Russia*, a work of classification; Karl Borders, *Village Life under the Soviets*, an account by an eye-witness; S. and B. Webb, *Soviet Communism—A New Civilization*, a naïve but acute account of the soviet system. One ∣post-war work is worth mentioning for it carries its institutional analysis further than most: Julian Towster, *Political Power in the USSR, 1917-47*.

2. *Sovety, S'ezdy Sovetov i Ispolkomy*, NKVD, 1924.

3. Ibid., pp. 5-6.

4. This may simply take into account lack of reading ability in Russian; in Moslem provinces many people knew how to read in the indigenous language.

5. *Sovety, S'ezdy Sovetov i Ispolkomy*, op. cit., p. 12.

6. This is only a hypothesis, but seems quite in keeping with the Soviet nationalities policy. If it is true, then it would appear that the government trusted the Russian peasants to remain loyal.

7. *Sovety, S'ezdy Sovetov i Ispolkomy*, op. cit., pp. 17-20.

8. Ibid., p. 29.

9. Znamensky, 'Iz istorii razvitiya sovetskogo apparata v Tambovskoi Gubernii in *Sovetskoe Stroitelstvo*, sbornik I, pp. 261-73.

10. Ibid., p. 264.

11. Znamensky, op. cit., p. 266.

12. B. Morozov, *Sozdanie i Ukreplenie Sovetskogo Gosudarstvennogo Apparata*, p. 187.

13. Ibid., p. 186.

14. Smolensk archives, reel No. 3, Smolensk 1926, WKP 25, 'Conditions and work of the cell of VKP (b) in Selishchenskaya volost from October 1925 to 1 August 1926'; report signed by responsible instructor of Smolensk guberniya committee, Borodkin.

15. M. Vasser, 'Voprosy vnutripartiinoi raboty pri perekhode k Nepu' in *Partiinaya Zhizn'*, No. 15, 1957, pp. 48-57. See also M. Fainsod, *How Russia is Ruled*, op. cit., p. 250. Fainsod gives the percentage of peasants in the party as 7·6 in 1917 and 28·2 in 1921.

16. 'Iz istorii partiinogo stroitelstva' in *Partiinaya Zhizn'*, No. 20, 1957, pp. 80-96.

17. I. Bogovoi, 'Perevybory sovetov v derevne i rasshirenie demokratii' in *Bolshevik*, Nos. 9-10, 1926, pp. 38-44.

18. Smolensk archives, reel No. 4, Smolensk, 1927, WKP 30, appendix to protocol No. 4 of the meeting of the Bureau of Velikolutskii Okruzhkom of VKP (b), held on 20 October 1927: 'Resolution about the report on the re-election campaign of the rural and urban network of consumers' co-operatives'.

19. Smolensk archives, reel No. 4, Smolensk, 1926, WKP 28, 'Report of the Gzhatsk Credit Rural Union [*Kredselsovet*]', 15 October 1927.

20. I. Bogovoi, op. cit., p. 39.

21. Stalin, *Sochineniya*, vol. 7, 'Rech' v Sverdlovskom Universitete', p. 185. For a fuller commentary on this speech and its importance, see J. F. Karcz, 'Thoughts on the Grain Problem', *Soviet Studies*, No. 4, April 1967.

22. Bogovoi, op. cit., pp. 42–4. It must be added that once again the party theorists did not understand rural problems. The growing of tobacco can only be done successfully with the help of a large number of work-hands at the crucial harvest time. Thus every small tobacco planter must have this large pool of labour at his disposal—it is not a proof of wealth, but a simple necessity.

23. Smolensk archives, reel No. 5, Smolensk, 1928, WKP 33, 'Report of the instructor of Gubkom VKP (b) Sinitsyn about the position and work of Elnya organization of VKP (b) on 1 April 1928'.

24. Ibid. Note also the instructor's cautious classification of peasants according to their wealth which is given in the quoted table of soviet composition. It will be seen that he uses a dual kind of assessment, one according to tax assessment, the other according to questionnaire. Though it is not clear what he means by 'questionnaire', it is almost certain to have been filled in by the householders themselves; and seems to have been a more correct assessment, for the instructor accepts it, rather than the assessment by tax. In this matter of classification, very little work has yet been done. One must be grateful to Dr M. Lewin, who in his book devotes two chapters to the problem of stratification, analysing the meaning of poor, medium and rich peasants, as well as the breakdown of these into sub-classes; this work is certain to bring our understanding of the problem much closer. See M. Lewin, *La Paysannerie et le pouvoir soviétique*, 1928–30, chapters 2 and 3, 'Le problème de la différentiation de la paysannerie'.

25. On the term 'commune' and other terms relevant to the new legislation, see the Glossary.

5 'All measures must be taken to improve the position of the peasant household'

The debate on various kinds of agriculture, which had persisted for some fifty years before the Bolshevik revolution, was based mainly on the social and economic values of the commune versus individual farming. To be sure, it had acquired a degree of political meaning after the Stolypin reforms, which were expressly designed to create a 'strong peasant' as a bulwark against the revolutionary forces of the cities. Nevertheless, it was only with the advent of the Bolsheviks that the political problems took on the sharp form of political conflict, with which all questions of private wealth were treated by the new government.

There were good reasons for this aggravation, however. While in the old commune there used to be both rich and poor peasants, the differences were often masked by the common use of labour and pasture land, and by the periodic redistributions of land. It was difficult to become very rich while remaining in the commune. The individual farmer could become rich in theory, but in practice he was held back by a variety of cogent factors as varied as the amount of land held, the amount of productive land, the ratio of arable land to pasture, the degree of consolidation of land, and its fertility. Apart from these factors, there were others equally important: the number of persons in a family, the number of work-hands among them, the number of cattle held by the household, and the number and quality of agricultural implements. All these were subject to the most important factor of all: the division of farms—an evil of possibly greater portent than the redistribution of land by the communes.

The assessment of peasant wealth had always been of economic importance. Bolshevik ideology made it a political issue as well. But it soon transpired that there were no clear-cut guide-lines in this matter, and that the social needs of the peasants, as well as their economic needs, were more instrumental in shaping the wealth structure of the countryside, and the consequent stratification, than the party ideology. In addition, the countryside (as we have already noted) had undergone significant changes during the war, in that the richer farms grew still richer, while the poorer ones often disappeared. Or, as an early post-revolutionary writer preferred to put it:

Class interests during the war clashed more sharply, and if, earlier on, a large farm received benefits from a smaller farm in the form of cheap labour, then at the time of the war it (the large farm) used all the conditions for its own benefit, and the small peasant farm was left to its fate.[1]

The assessment was not made any easier by the lack of pre-war and war-time data. In some guberniyas (e.g. T'verskaya and Tul'skaya), Zemstvo censuses had been taken; in others it was possible to take into account only a few reliable figures. The only possible way of surveying the position was to take the existing data and break the districts down into 'productive' and 'non-productive', as well as into those affected by the war and those not affected by it. When this was done, the general state of population and agriculture in the regions surveyed produced interesting results (see Table 1).[2] Population had increased in all the productive regions and decreased in non-productive guberniyas. Non-productive guberniyas which were affected by the war showed a greater decrease in population than those which were not affected. The number of cattle fell heavily in areas seriously affected by the war. The area under cultivation was reduced everywhere, but the reduction was greater in the regions affected by the war. However, although the general area under cultivation had grown noticeably smaller, certain crops were increased under war-time conditions. For instance, the area under rye increased in 1919, and in the productive area potatoes were grown in larger quantities than in 1917. It follows, therefore, that the increase supplied the immediate needs of the population, for other crops were grown in the same proportions as before.

79

Table 1

Effect of the war on population and agriculture

Groups of guberniyas	Population			Work horses	Cows	Dessiatinas under crops
	Men	Women	Both sexes			
(a) Productive guberniyas*						
Affected by the war	+1·9	+5·4	+3·7	−13·7	−8·0	−19·8
Lightly affected by the war	+1·0	+3·7	+2·4	−4·8	+2·6	−11·2
Not affected by the war	+1·1	+3·1	+2·1	−2·9	+6·5	−12·2
(b) Non-productive guberniyas†						
Lightly affected by the war	−2·7	−0·5	−1·6	−13·6	−0·3	−35·7
Not affected by the war	−2·4	−0·4	−1·4	−0·5	+5·3	−22·1

All figures per cent. + = more, − = less in 1919 compared with 1917.

Extracts from table given by Khryashcheva

* Productive guberniyas affected by the war:
  Perm', Ekaterinburg, Samara, Orenburg, Astrakhan.
Productive guberniyas slightly affected by the war:
  Tula, Ryazan, Tambov, Saratov, Simbirsk, Kazan' and V'yatka.
Productive guberniyas not affected by the war:
  Marxshtadt, Penza, Smolensk, Nizhegorod.
† Non-productive guberniyas slightly affected by the war:
  Petersburg, Vitebsk, Olonets.
Non-productive guberniyas not affected by the war:
  Yaroslavl, Novgorod, Cherepovets, Tver', S. Dvinskaya, Vologda, Moscow, Kaluga, Kostrom, Ivanovo-Voznesensk, Vladimir.

And although every war means destruction, the civil war brought in its wake great damage, influencing the main elements of agriculture: cattle and the area under cultivation. But this direct effect of the war does not have a deep character, other circumstances being equal; the loss in numbers can be made good in a few years[3]

opined the author. This opinion was to be proved wrong in the following years of the Soviet government, but the author was right in one respect. She insisted that the main damage to agriculture lay not in material losses suffered during the war and the revolution, but in the system of division of peasant farms:

The divisions have a dual effect on peasant agriculture. The positive side of the effect of division lies in the multiplication of farms which are able to make economic changes; the negative side . . . is the increase in the number of landless households which, as a result of this process, are pushed out of the countryside. If [one farm] divides into two farms, this

80

THE MAKING OF THE SOVIET STATE APPARATUS

gives as a result 15 per cent of landless households; if it divides into three farms, this gives 17 per cent [of landless households]; those dividing into four or more give 19 per cent of landless households. But after all this, as a result of division, there is a greater number of individual farms in the countryside, so that their growth is increasing thanks to the divisions.[4]

There were some, though not many, data in existence to prove the extent of division. These pertained to the guberniya of Tula, where a census of households was taken in 1899–1900 in two *uezdy*, and where there was an agricultural census in all the guberniyas in the years 1910–12. These censuses could be compared with a later period, and the results shown in Table 2 were obtained. It can be seen from

Table 2

The division of farms, 1889–1917

Uezd	Year of census	No. of years	Dividing farms (%)
Thirteen *volosti* of Epifanskii *uezd*	1899–1911	11	22·3
All of Epifanskii *uezd*	1899–1911	11	22·6
Seven *volosti* of Tulskii *uezd*	1900–12	11	24·7
Thirteen *volosti* of Epifanskii *uezd*	1911–17	6	8·5
Seven *volosti* of Tulskii *uezd*	1912–17	5	6·2
Three *volosti* of various *uezdy* of Tulskaya guberniya	1911–17	6	6·8
Five *volosti* of various *uezdy* of Tulskaya guberniya	1912–17	5	6·2

Source: A. Khryashcheva *Krestyanstvo v voine i revolyutsii* page 11.

these figures that the intensity of divisions dropped noticeably during the war period. This was seen even more clearly in a table for eight *volosti* of Tulskaya guberniya, where the percentage of dividing farms was 20·6 per cent in 1912, 34·9 per cent in 1913, 21·6 per cent in 1914, 16·0 per cent in 1915, 3·7 per cent in 1916 and none in 1917.[5] The effect of the war, which took away from the countryside a large number of work-hands, showed clearly in the reduction of the divisions of the farms. However:

The creation of new individual farms by way of division during the war decreased not only because the number of divisions decreased, but also as a result of . . . some households being strongly pushed out of the country-side. . . . In this case, consequently, we have to do with a dual influence of war on the peasantry: on one side, the process of creating new farms by way of division fell, and on the other, the process of migration of poor peasants from the village increased.[6]

81

To sum up, it can be said that the war weakened the process of division of farms, increased migration from the countryside, increased the rate of liquidation of poorer farms, and finally, in some cases, increased the return to farming of families which could afford it.[7] The author's general conclusions (on the strength of the scant material that exists) are that:

1 The birth rate fell sharply.
2 The average size of the family became much smaller.
3 Production fell.
4 Women's share in production increased.
5 Agriculture changed, and the crops that were grown were those which could be sold or exchanged easily.
6 There was a sharp increase in the stratification of peasant households, and the number of households without arable land or cattle increased.
7 The migratory processes increased, and many peasant households left the countryside, while other, absentee, peasants returned to the villages.[8]

As will be seen in this and subsequent chapters, the statistical survey carried out and assessed by Khryashcheva at the inception of the New Economic Policy was remarkably accurate in almost every respect, save one: the prediction that the Russian peasant would be able to make good the losses in working horses, cattle and cultivated area in a short time. However, the author was right about the evils of migration from the countryside, the danger of further subdivision of farms, and the trend towards growing crops that gave a quick financial return, while neglecting those which were necessary to the economy in the long term.

A year later, the Central Statistical Board published a full survey of the economic stratification of peasants, using the existing figures for 1917 and 1919.[9] This extremely interesting publication was prepared by the same author, and contains an introduction to the material in it. It is important for us because it contains the first conclusions about land redistribution arrived at by a noted expert. In 1922 Khryashcheva was not as optimistic about the position as she had been in 1921. She notes:

. . . here we have to deal with changes as a result of war and revolution which were so deep that they influenced the very structure of analogical farms . . .

82

In general, the smaller farms now had a larger area under cultivation, but slightly larger farms had less land under the plough. More important,

The number of persons per one cow has also become slightly higher in landless households, and farms under one dessiatina; but all the other groups have more persons per cow in 1920 than before the war.

The extreme traditionalism of small peasant farmers was one of the factors which hampered progress:

The small peasant household, which does not change, cannot make any progress. It will either have to change or, as in the old times, submit to the stronger one and disappear. We know that under former conditions, emigration, dying out, and liquidation deprived the countryside of a mass of small farms, proletarian and semi-proletarian. But emigration from the countryside was earlier determined by the industrial market, which was able to absorb a considerable part of rural over-population. In 1920 these conditions did not exist, and the small farm had to solve its problem . . . without leaving the framework of agriculture.[10]

This acute and far-sighted observation was to be borne out by the facts in the following six, or even seven, years. The agricultural position, despite the additional area under cultivation, became very grave.

Research carried out by modern Soviet historians confirms these early findings. Recent Soviet studies point to the fact that the redistribution of land created many more problems than it solved. According to one contemporary authority, however, it was not the divisions of farms but lack of agricultural machinery and of draught animals which created the biggest crisis:[11]

In the Ryazan-Tula region the peasants had 51·8 per cent more soil and 19·8 per cent fewer horses in 1923 (in comparison with pre-revolutionary years). . . . On the middle and lower Volga the peasants had an acreage of 49·3 per cent more land . . . but they lost 48·4 per cent of cattle compared with 1916.[12]

The same authority states that mechanization of farming seemed impossible at this stage. By 1926 there was only 1·7 per cent mechanical means of haulage, not counting motor cars. The planners in the Gosplan said in 1923 that there was not a high enough ratio of horse-power to implements in the countryside; there was too much man-power. There were, however, other ways of creating working cattle: cows could be used to work in the fields; horses could be worked from an earlier age, oxen could also be used; all animals could be given bigger loads to haul and bigger areas to work. Bigger plots of land would allow work with fewer working cattle. But there is no need to produce agricultural machinery as yet, stated the Gosplan theoretician, there is enough manpower in Russia, and the area under cultivation is not so big.[13]

Thanks to the hard-working Russian peasants, and to the milder political climate, the area under cultivation returned to its pre-war level by 1926, though the number of horses was at that time only 81·6 per cent of the 1916 figure.

The lack of working cattle was made up by its more thorough exploitation, by increasing the loads for a working unit, and also by the use for agricultural work of non-working cattle (cows, heifers and others).

Apparently the working norm per head of cattle was 160–180 per cent compared to the pre-revolutionary norm.[14] After 1925 the cattle situation improved, or conversely it was found impossible to sow any more land without more working cattle. In 1926 the number of horses grew by 7·8 per cent, while the cultivated area grew by 5·7 per cent. In 1927 the number of horses grew by 8·1 per cent and the cultivated area by only 1·9 per cent; in 1928 the corresponding figures were 6·2 and 0·5 per cent. The distribution of horsepower among the peasant households shows that there was very little change after the initial revolutionary redistribution (see Table 3).

Table 3

Distribution of horsepower among peasant households (per cent)

(a) *European Russia only*, 1917

Households without horses	Households with one horse	Households with two horses	Households with three horses	Households with four or more horses
28·7	47·6	17·6	4·0	2·1

(b) *RSFSR*, 1919–27

Year	Households without horses	Households with one or two horses	Households with three or more horses
1919	25·1	*	*
1922	37·1	59·9	3·0
1924	31·0	*	*
1926	30·4	64·0	5·9
1927	28·3	*	*

Source: Danilov, op. cit., pp. 52–4.

* Data missing.

Table 3 proves that the years of Soviet rule made little difference to either the poorest or the medium peasant as far as the ownership of working cattle went. And although the statistics are incomplete, it does not appear that the number of rich peasants grew very dramatically, if it grew at all. The author attempts to prove by these figures that rich peasants exploited the poor ones by hiring out work horses at exorbitant prices; but all the evidence proves is that horses were a rare commodity, that the demand for them was great, and that they would have been expensive under any other form of hire.

If the peasant economy was closely tied to the number of working cattle, it was to an even greater extent dependent on farm machinery. This does not mean the more sophisticated implements, but simply primary tools, like ploughs and harrows. In 1910 there were 11,659,400 ploughing implements on the territory of the present RSFSR, of which 1,575,700 were wooden ploughs, 3,189,100 were iron ploughs, and the rest were *sokhas* or *kosulyas*.[15] Of other machines, there were 180,500 seeders, 529,900 reapers, 322,700 horse or steam threshers and 168,600 hay mowers. By 1920 the number of all these implements is said to have fallen by half.[16] The supply of agricultural machines during NEP was extremely poor, for in 1927 45·2 per cent of peasant households in the middle Volga district were without any agricultural machines, and almost the same picture is shown in other districts, with the exception of the western and north-western districts.[17] The report of the Moscow city soviet for 1924 said, 'the plough is forcing out the *sokha* gradually but slowly.' [18]

The distribution of machinery was another source of annoyance to the left wing: in 1927 poor households comprised 26·1 per cent of all households but owned 4·9 per cent of all machinery. The medium peasants owned 79 per cent of all machinery, but the 3·2 per cent of richer households owned 30·8 per cent of the more complicated machines.[19]

Data quoted from Kursk *oblast* archives speak of a survey of two households, one poor and one rich, in Kursk *oblast* from 1913 to 1923. The poor family lived in the village of Chuykovo, in Ivanin *volost*. The household consisted of ten people up to 1917, when one more child was born. In the period 1913–17 the head of the family, I. G. Chuikov, had one horse and one cow, and about three dessiatinas of land from the commune. The average yield over these years was about ninety puds of grain. In 1918, as a result of redistribution, Chuikov received ten dessiatinas of land and had an annual yield of

85

220 to 270 puds of grain. He also owned two work horses and a foal, three cows, three ploughs, one harrow and one *sokha*. Almost all the food produced was eaten by the family, and Chuikov was classed as a medium peasant.

The rich family lived on the homestead of 'Chernaya Gryaz' (*sic*), in Novo-Derevenskaya *volost*. The head of the family, V. D. Mukhin, owned or rented 48 dessiatinas of land in 1913. He had nine horses, three milch cows and four heifers. As a result of land redistribution he was compelled to enter the commune after 1917, and received (for seven people in the family) nine and a half dessiatinas of land, which decreased to eight and a half when the family diminished. By 1923 he had only two work horses, two cows, one heifer and one calf. But his machinery was not taken away, and he still owned eight ploughs, three harrows, a cultivator, a winnower, a threshing machine, a seeder, a *kosulya* and a roller (*katok*). In 1920 he had also opened a millet mill.[20]

Granted that these examples might have been chosen by a writer well known for his interest in agricultural matters, since they illustrated the phenomenon described by some Bolsheviks as exploitation of poor peasants by the kulaks; but other sources demonstrate that they were typical. They do not suggest exploitation (though no doubt it existed in places), but they do illustrate the fallacy that land alone was enough to make the peasants rich. They also show that a man with capital had a better chance of earning a living than one without capital. Here again, the Bolsheviks were slaves to their own ideology. They ranted at private capital but ignored the fact that capital was needed to bring the poor peasant up to the rich peasant's standard, and to revive agriculture. State capital loaned to the peasants—even State-supplied machinery—would soon have stopped one sector of the peasantry lagging behind another. But the government could not, or would not, provide capital for the development of agriculture. It has been said that it did not 'plough back' the surplus it received from agriculture into the countryside. Certainly the government expended as little money as it possibly could on the peasants, as will be shown later.

Here is what a serious student of Soviet agriculture has to say on this matter:

The Soviet leaders were not empirical economists. Their theoretical commitments led them to distort economic realities and to overlook or misunderstand the effects of their own measures. An example of outright distortion—and one very widely repeated in Western works—is the claim that the peasants hoarded a grain surplus. Grain production had not regained its pre-war levels even in 1925–27 and 'there was not the slightest reason to expect marketings of farm products to reach pre-war magnitudes'. The production of grain—the mainstay of the diet—was still below the pre-war level, while the population had grown, and the problem was not hoarding but low production.

Some of this has already been noted by the eminent economist, N. Jasny, of whom the author says:

Many of the criticisms of the Soviet economic rationalization are taken from Jasny and Lawton. It is indeed surprising how the more significant conclusions of both of these scholars concerning Soviet economic life in the 1920's have been ignored, even by specialists in Soviet economic development.[21]

The author then states that the Bolsheviks blamed low production (when it was discussed) on the inefficiency of small-scale peasant farming—an assumption which, he says, was contradicted by West European experience. But this is the main point; the Soviet government was not dealing with the literate German farmer, or the highly civilized French wine grower; it was dealing with Russian peasants and Russian agriculture. And in Russia:

. . . Soviet peasant agriculture was backward. Land tenure rights were vague, and with the persistence of communal tenure and the strip system over most of Great Russia the individual holder had no security of tenure. Efficient farming was frustrated by the constant division of households and multiplication of ever smaller holdings. Nearly half of the households lacked draft animals; technique was generally at an exceedingly low level, and poverty was more the rule than the exception.[22]

In view of this obvious contradiction, we must insist that despite the setbacks suffered by agriculture through the policy of War Communism (and they were both serious and wounding in their future consequences), it was *not* the Bolsheviks who had caused the low productivity in agriculture. They merely increased it by their cessation of credits and low production of machinery. It was the in-built, almost in-born, problem of backwardness among the peasantry. Before the revolution this problem was partly solved by the large number of progressive land-owners, who used modern methods to get higher productivity, and by the co-operatives. These had stopped farming after the revolution, and the pre-revolutionary experts who were retained as 'specialists' were too small in number to be effective.

The clash between ideology and economic necessity came to a head in the mid-1920's about the time the 'Face to the countryside' policy was proclaimed. The real difficulties of this policy, as well as the problems of improving agriculture without it, are well illustrated by reports of meetings held in rural areas at this period. A conference held in Smolensk guberniya at the end of May 1925 noted that the party's tasks in the countryside were as follows:[23]

In connection with the temporary stabilization of capitalist states, the first task of the party in the countryside is the improvement of agriculture.

We must now deny the principle of refusing to allow kulak and medium peasant farms to increase and develop; we must destroy all obstacles stopping their development. Our ultimate problem . . . shows the necessity of introducing a definite course for the development of agriculture. The development of agriculture will be possible only through kulak and medium peasant households. If, because of earlier measures giving help to poor peasants only, we obtained as a result stagnation in the development of agriculture, then we must now take a course to support the medium peasant, and while exploiting the kulak households we must simultaneously give help to the poor peasants.

Clearly, the conference found it impossible to remain within correct ideological policy and at the same time give the new course its complete support. Yet, since these people were closely connected with the countryside, they had a clear grasp of the practical needs of the peasants. The theses of the conference stipulated the following points:

On the question of RKP (b) and Soviet government policy in developing agriculture:

Point I. Work in the countryside has become the centre of party attention since the thirteenth party congress a year and a half ago. But very little has been accomplished as yet.

1 There are no goods in the shops—even articles of essential importance are missing.
2 There appear to be more and more unemployed, who lead a pitiful existence and who cannot find work in towns (all the jobs are taken there) or in the countryside (no one needs any hired hands).
3 The majority of farm land is not redistributed. Some farms, even some villages, have too little land and they are very poor.
4 Local organization is bad. There is no mass peasant participation in the soviets.

Point II. To improve agriculture it is necessary to lower the agricultural tax even more.

Point III. Land redistribution is the burning question of the day. The third all-union congress decided:

1 To accomplish land redistribution within the next ten years.
2 That the government should cover the cost of land redistribution for poor peasants.
3 That peasants should be allowed more credit for land redistribution.
4 That in guberniyas with less land, the government should turn nationalized land over to private farmers.
5 That in raions with little land, State farm land should be distributed to the peasants. In our own district it is expected that 6,300 dessiatinas will be given from State funds to private peasants.

Point IV. There are not enough consumer goods, and farm machinery is particularly scarce.

Point V. Artisans and craftsmen are unable to produce goods for the market. They must be helped in order to:

1 Produce more goods for the peasants.
2 Find some employment for the unemployed.

Point VI. The unemployment situation is getting worse. To improve it, the peasants must be allowed to become more prosperous, which will enable them to hire more work-hands. War Communism must go. One cannot close one's eyes to the fact that the top layer of peasants will become better off.

Point VII. Nevertheless, this policy is necessary for the State.

Point VIII. This policy is dangerous, but the kulaks will be controlled by banking credits and the growth of co-operatives.

Point IX. Wide masses must be drawn into participation in social activities and elections.

Point X. The cultural level of the peasants is very low. When they abuse the Soviet government, it is because of their ignorance of its nature. In order to improve this state of affairs, the level of literacy in the countryside must be raised.[23]

The report points out the difficulties of carrying out a pro-peasant policy in Smolensk guberniya under the existing economic conditions. Other documents illustrate the fact that the discontent among the rural population was also the result of bad administration, though some of them attempt to minimize the dangers by showing a degree of ideological agreement. The plenum of the Roslavl *uezd* committee of the party, held on 13 August 1925,[24] decided to:

Include in the plan of land redistribution for the summer of the present year 18,960 dessiatinas of land. The corresponding work is being carried out in the present year. Land organs are carrying out important work in

89

connection with analysing disputed land questions; the number of those settled since December 1924 was 302. Unsettled questions number 330. *... It is observed that poor peasants are dissatisfied because of heavy fees for land redistribution.*

As regards the choice of forms of agriculture, it is noticeable that lately there was a *great inclination* on the part of the peasants towards *separate settlement agriculture* [italics in text].

The uezd has 60,654 farming households; of these 53 per cent are poor peasants, 45 per cent are medium peasants and 3 per cent are prosperous kulaks.[25]

This was obviously a particularly poor *uezd*, with poor peasants predominating; their discontent over land redistribution and its heavy cost would have to be taken seriously. Perhaps because of this, the plenum hastily assured the higher authorities that political attitudes were satisfactory:

The attitude of peasants in all branches of industry is satisfactory. There is slight discontent among the workers and officials on the railways, who receive low rates of pay, in connection with higher prices for agricultural products. . . . The attitude of peasants on political questions is steady. There is, however, some discontent with lower organs of government, and with some members of the local government, because of their incorrect behaviour to the population. . . . As regards religion, there is a very comforting picture in the uezd, which can be summed up by saying that religion is beginning to die out gradually. Many facts from village life testify to this. For instance, the citizens of Seslavl, in Seshchinskaya Volost, decided to close the church and use it as a school; clergymen, seeing that peasants are refusing to support them, are trying to get a land allotment and take up agriculture and other occupations. On the other hand, sectarianism is beginning to develop.[24]

An appendix to the same protocol[26] makes the ills of rural government even more explicit:

It was decided to:

1 Accept that the activity of the volost committee is weak.
2 Note that there are squabbles and groupings among the members of the volost party organizations. Suggest to the volost committee that these be got rid of at all costs.
3 Note the insufficient adoption by the volost organization of party policy for the countryside, owing to which the ordering of people about, rudeness and other habits are noticeable. Suggest to the volost committee that it should seriously study and carry out the resolutions of the fourteenth party conference and directives of the uezd committee of RKP on these questions.
4 Ask the volost committee to pay attention to the necessity of observing

revolutionary legality. The noticeable ordering about of the population on the part of Soviet apparatus and other organizations must be stopped and good relations with the population must be established.

5 Suggest that the volost committee begins preparatory work for the re-election campaign to the soviets, and takes care not to be thrown into a panic by this work.

6 Immoral acts which can be observed in the volost organization must stop.

7 Increase the work of finding non-party peasant activ, which should be grouped around the soviets and other volost organizations. *This activ is not to be given an organized form* [italics in text]. The best part of revolutionary-minded activ is to be drawn into the party.

8 Strengthen the leadership of the Komsomol, particularly in order to stop tactless actions by separate members of the Komsomol.

9 Strengthen the leadership work of co-operative organs.

Such were the attitudes of the party organs after the fourteenth party conference. It is clear that some attempts were made to limit the authoritarian and often brutal behaviour of those in charge of rural administration. However, the real test of the rural Communists' discipline did not come till after the fourteenth party congress, which reinforced the decisions of the conference. The ensuing turmoil can be seen in the following selection of extracts.

During the discussion of the resolutions of the fourteenth congress, in Semenovskaya *volost*, one of the party members expressed himself thus:

This is State capitalism. In this question they [the party congress] are trying to demonstrate that there is no difference from the past; that in the past the workers were exploited, and that they are being exploited now; that in the past there were masters and workers, and nowadays there are workers and executives.[27]

Another party member said:

The essence of the peasant policy is particularly striking, because the decisions of the fourteenth party conference are solely a compromise with the kulaks, while the poor peasants are ignored; there is no real help for the poor peasant, and from this it follows that the poor peasant is hostile to the party.

Members of the Komsomol were particularly bitter in their opinions:

. . . our factories could not exist if they did not demand surplus work from the workers. By this very fact, whatever is said about the exploitation of the workers, one must make an analogy with the past. . . . workers are hired by factories through connections. . . . our 'red directors' are tsars, gods and masters in industry. . . . by developing productive forces in the

91

countryside, we are transforming our economy into a capitalist one. . . . the decisions [of the congress] about poor peasants are very good, but there is no actual help for the peasants; in essence there are only concessions to the medium peasants and the prosperous stratum of the countryside.[27]

This sample of Communists' views about the policy of 'Face to the countryside' shows the essential danger of the course for the government. The government was vulnerable on every count—it risked alienating the loyalty of the lower echelons of the party without gaining much in peasant loyalty, or at least in the loyalty of the poor peasants. This will be seen in the following extracts.

When the Shumyach *volost* organization discussed the fourteenth party congress, it was reported that:

[as regards] the mood of the peasants: the medium peasants were full of goodwill about the resolutions of the congress; the poor peasants were rather sympathetic towards the opposition, particularly the slogan about equality. This [slogan] they understood as referring not to political equality but to material equality; but when the organization worked with the groups of poor peasants, and the decision of the October plenum of the TsK was explained to them, the poor peasants' attitude towards the opposition began to change.[28]

It was easy to convince the poor peasants, who after all had no support anywhere, but more enlightened elements were more difficult:

The kulaks' attitude is almost unknown. It is true that often there were kulaks who stated that the opposition also tried to get equality for the richer peasants in the party line and in particular to allow them electoral representation. But other kulaks showed little faith in the opposition's statements. . . . One Social Revolutionary said to the lecturer, 'Please tell us honestly: the Bolsheviks are good people for the cities, but they cannot find a good policy for the countryside. Should we not organize a union of peasants?' . . . A great many such questions were asked by anti-Soviet elements.[28]

When the guberniya organization drew up a list of questions about peasant and industrial policy after the fourteenth party congress, it added up to a massive indictment of the highest party organs on the part of rank-and-file Communists. The following are some of the points made in the guberniya:[29]

Your views about peasant masses have been expressed. But there are strata of peasants who, when their economic condition is improved, will turn away from the party:

92

said one questioner. Another noted:

What does the congress say about raising the prosperity of the poor peasants? After all, the poor peasant depends economically on the kulak.

Still another questioned the validity of elections to the soviets:

In the guberniya elections, four prosperous peasants were elected; but how many labourers, real labourers?

And on the kulaks:

How are we to retain the [loyalty of the] medium peasant? When the position of the medium peasant is improved—and this is now happening—then the medium peasant turns to the kulak side. He becomes a kulak himself. . . . What to do with these kulaks who appear to sympathize with the Soviet government? They confuse the poor peasants, and it is difficult to say whether they are in fact on our side, or not. . . . Is long-term renting of land a transition to capitalism? . . . How are we to achieve a union of the medium peasant with the poor peasant, with the proletariat, since the medium peasants are very numerous?[29]

In summing up, the party secretary noted:

As is seen from the above, the problem of peasants agitates the party organizations very much. The problems which came to the fore were these. How is the task of increasing the productive forces of the countryside to be connected with directing them towards socialism? Will this development not lead to capitalism? And how are the poor peasants to be supplied with practical help? The party organization stated correctly that the opposition did not do anything practical to fight the kulaks, and that the attitude to the opposition's peasant policy is negative.[29]

But while the rank and file of the party could be disciplined, the higher officials were rather more truculent about the policy. One of them, Gusev, said in a guberniya committee meeting:

. . . we have buying and selling, which can only be called capitalist. . . . In connection with our co-operation, I have doubts whether it can be called socialist—it would be a mistake to call it socialist.[30]

And another official said that:

. . . part of the peasantry is under-taxed; the poor peasants cannot receive loans; the peasants with money are getting richer. There was and is *a danger that the poor peasants will turn away from us* [italics in text].[29]

The course which began tentatively in 1921, and took a sharper form in 1923, finally arrived at its fullest expression in 1925—the policy of 'Face to the countryside'. We have seen in this chapter that

93

the policy was fraught with danger in every way. From the Communist point of view, it was not ideologically sound, and in its economic aspects, it required far more investment than the government was prepared to undertake. It will be noticed that even in this brief outline of the agricultural problem, we have been able to isolate the following problems: the difficulties of the imposed administration, the problem of a hostile population, the problems created by the redistribution of land, and the difficulties caused by the general pauperization of the countryside. There is no doubt that all these added to the quandary of the government, uncertain what action to take in relation to its peasant population or to agriculture in general. For the Bolshevik government was neither omnipotent nor omniscient (though, like many governments before and since, it often pretended it was); in questions of agriculture it had to rely on the advice of experts. It so happened that the experts themselves, independent of their political complexion, were not agreed on the policies best suited to the needs of the countryside. A short survey of what the experts considered to be the merits and demerits of individual and communal agriculture[31] will perhaps illustrate the government's dilemma best of all, for these two systems were so closely allied to the administrative machinery that it is impossible to think of one without simultaneously considering the other.

Before considering the problems of rural administration, however, we should take another look at a matter which was closely allied to it—the state of the industrial workers. We have seen in this chapter that the problem of rural pauperization was closely connected with the lack of industrial occupations for those peasants who were forced to leave the land. We have also outlined very briefly the difficulties the government encountered in its short period of pro-peasant policy. These were not so much an index of the peasants' discontent over the agricultural policy as an expression of their despair because, in the absence of agricultural work, they were unable to do what they traditionally used to do: leave the land in order to seek industrial employment. We shall try to explain why this was so in the following chapter.

NOTES

1. A. Khryashcheva, *Krestyanstvo v voine i revolyutsii*, p. 3.
2. Ibid., pp. 5–6.

3. Ibid., p. 9.
4. Ibid., p. 10.
5. Ibid., p. 12.
6. Ibid., p. 13.
7. Ibid., p. 18.
8. Ibid., pp. 31–2.
9. 'Ekonomicheskoe Rassloenie Krestyanstva v 1917 i 1919 g.', *Trudy Tsentralnogo Statisticheskogo Upravleniya.*
10. Ibid., pp. 19–20.
11. While fully agreeing with Danilov on the need for more cattle and farming machinery in the period 1923–27, we should also like to stress that Khryashcheva's approach, which had a strong sociological content (rather unusual in a statistician), was of great importance. My conclusions are that the three phenomena: division of farms, lack of machinery and lack of cattle, played an equal role in the pauperization of the countryside during this period.
12. V. P. Danilov, *Sozdanie materialno-tekhnicheskikh predposylok kollektivizatsii selskogo khozyaistva v SSSR*, pp. 28–9.
13. P. Popov, 'Vosstanovlenie selskogo khozyaistva v golodayushchikh raionakh' in *Planovoe Khozyaistvo*, Nos. 3–4, March–April 1923.
14. V. P. Danilov, op. cit., p. 30, quoting Otchet Nar. Kom. Zemledeliya RSFSR za 1924–25 god.
15. An authority on farming implements has this to say about the *sokha*: 'The Russian *sokha* has many variations which allow us to trace its evolution; if one adds to it Ukrainian and Belo-russian forms of ploughing implements, the variations will be even bigger. . . . in one guberniya only . . . one could count up to thirty kinds of *sokha*, and all of them had their local names. . . . All East Slav ploughing implements, *sokhas* and other implements belong to the type which has no runners (and is unstable). . . . Both single-tooth and double-tooth implements can be sub-divided . . . into two categories: symmetrical and asymmetrical ploughs and *sokhas*. With the former, one can plough back and forth from one end of the field . . .; the latter only [plough] in one direction, therefore they are used to plough around the field. . . . In the central region of Russia . . . a feather *sokha* was widely used: its ploughshares were widened like a triangle, these were turned towards the field, to the left and to the right of the middle axis. These widened ploughshares were the beginning of the mould-board. Besides this, this *sokha* always had . . . a small spade, attached to the ploughshare. . . . This *sokha* was more suitable for the light forest soils of the central forest and forest and steppe zone.' S. E. Tokarev, *Etnografia Narodov SSSR*, pp. 38–40. A *kosulya* is a local variation of the *sokha*. This variety of tillage implements makes it very difficult to assess the actual need for modern farm machinery. It is possible that in some cases (on narrow strips) these were as efficient as the more modern iron plough, though a *sokha* always turned up less soil than a plough.
16. V. P. Danilov, op. cit., pp. 31–2.
17. Ibid., p. 59.
18. M. I. Rogov, 'Deyatel'nost' Moskovskogo Soveta za 1924 god i blizhaishie zadachi na 1925 god' in *Sovetskoe Stroitelstvo*, sbornik I.
19. V. P. Danilov, op. cit., pp. 60–1.
20. E. A. Lutsky, 'O sushchnosti uravnitelnogo zemlepolzovaniya v Sovetskoi Rossii' in *Voprosy Istorii*, No. 9, 1956.
21. H. J. Ellison, 'The Decision to Collectivize Agriculture' in *The American Slavic and East European Review*, February 1961, p. 195.
22. Ibid., p. 195.
23. Smolensk archives, reel No. 3, Smolensk, 1925, WKP 23: 'Protocol No. 1

OLGA A. NARKIEWICZ

of the uezd conference of the managers of rural libraries in the uezd of
Yartsevo on 29 May 1925', issued by Agitpropotdel Ukoma RKP (b).

24. Smolensk archives, reel No. 3, Smolensk, 1925, WKP 22: 'Protocol
No. 8 of the plenum of ¡Roslavl uezd committee of RKP (b) jointly with the
secretaries of volost' committees of RKP (b) on 13 August 1925.'

25. There is a mistake of 1 per cent in these data; the total comes to 101 per
cent, not to 100 per cent. It is not known whether this is a typing mistake, or an
error in the addition.

26. Protocol No. 8, op. cit., 'Report of Khislavishskaya Volost' Committee of
RKP (b) about its activity.'

27. Smolensk archives, reel No. 4, Smolensk, 1926, WKP 29: 'Information
bulletin of the secretary of the Semenovskaya volost' committee of VKP (b)
about the studying of the resolutions of the fourteenth party congress'; undated;
entered by the Smolensk guberniya committee on 12 April 1926.

28. Smolensk archives, reel No. 4, Smolensk, 1926, WKP 29: 'Report
about the study of the fourteenth party congress by the Shumyach volost'
organization', 14 April 1926.

29. Smolensk archives, reel No. 4, Smolensk, 1926, WKP 29: 'Additional
information to the report about the work of the guberniya committee for the
fifteenth guberniya party conference' (summary of the study of the resolutions of
the fourteenth party congress), 9 June 1926.

30. At a later meeting Gusev was made to retract these remarks, and he then
said that he supported the resolutions of the fourteenth party congress.

31. By a 'communal' system of agriculture we mean, like the authors of the
1920's, solely the traditional Russian commune, re-created by the Land Code;
the question of creating completely new communal units like the *kolkhozes* on a
national scale (though they admitted their usefulness on an experimental scale)
does not seem to have entered the authors' calculations.

6 'Russia's biggest troubles are hunger and unemployment'

There are many excellent studies, both Soviet and Western, on various aspects of the 1920's. In the main, however, they deal either with the chief political issues of the time or with specialized topics. A fairly recent historiography, for instance, lists some twenty works published between 1919 and 1927 on 'socialist Saturdays' and 'socialist emulation' but, the author says, 'Despite this, there are still few scientific works which study the process of the development of socialist emulation . . . *in the general framework of the country*' (my italics).[1]

We know a lot about the political struggles of the time, and there are certain data on the economic position. But the overall pattern is hazy. The industrial position definitely began to improve in 1923, after the financial crisis:

The resolution of the scissors crisis in the winter of 1923–24 opened the way for a fresh advance of industry all along the line, thus defeating the gloomy prognostications of the opposition and illustrating once more the validity of the underlying principle of NEP that the revival of industry, like everything else in the Soviet economy, depended on a revival of agricultural production.[2]

Though the industrial position had improved, it did not raise the people's standards of living much. Party resolutions acknowledged the fact that unemployment was growing.[3] The reasons for the decline in prosperity were manifold, but one of the most important was the increase of population. In 1913 the population in the

97

territory of the Soviet Union had been 139 million; in 1926 it was 147 million. This growth was a process foreseen by Malthus and Ricardo rather than by Marx. Ricardo had said that:

If the country is to have increasing capital and product, profits must be good. But then as product expands the population will increase. The food requirements of the population will press on the available land supply. . . .[4]

This principle applied in the Soviet Union during the 1920's with a precision that would have pleased its formulator. The pressure of population on the land was increasing and, as has been pointed out in previous chapters, the land was yielding less food than in the pre-revolutionary period. Industry had recovered slightly, but the recovery was partial, regional and sporadic.

In the major industries which came under the control of Vesenkha, an average of only 36 per cent of pre-war production had been reached; and this average represented a wide variation in achievement. The metal industry, which accounted for the major part of the output of capital goods, registered only 28·7 per cent, and the textile industry, the largest consumer goods industry, 35 per cent. According to another calculation made at this time, heavy industry, which in 1913 accounted for 22·6 per cent of all industrial production, produced only 17·7 per cent in 1922–23 and 17·4 per cent in 1923–24.[5]

In later years the position improved. One economist tells us that:

In 1926–27 big industry had on the whole regained its 1913 pre-war level, but the degree of recovery varied from one industry to another. Whilst coal-mining had reached 107 per cent of its 1913 production and the oil industry 109 per cent, the production of iron ore was only 52 per cent, that of pig iron 70 per cent, and that of rolled iron 76 per cent of the respective figures for 1913.[6]

These figures are confirmed by another economist who assessed the industrial situation in 1928,[7] but it is notable that both these economists used sources which had been published after 1928, and in one case a source published in 1936. In addition, it is now well known that the calculation based on 1913 output has become increasingly doubtful.

Even if industrial production rose slightly, consumption of manufactured products was almost uniformly lower. The average consumption of an inhabitant per annum was expressed in the following figures:[8]

98

	1913	1926–27
Cotton fabrics (metres)	20·6	16·7
Leather and boots	0·33	0·34
Sugar (lb of 410 grammes)	19·3	15·0
Salt ,,	28·5	31·1
Paraffin ,,	14·9	14·6

The consumption of foodstuffs by an average member of a working class family is given later in this chapter. Figures for peasant food consumption are more difficult to find, but documents quoted later in this book provide certain data on peasant diets.[9] All these data are quoted as an average, and presumably are based on a cross-section of general consumption. However, there were some people, and an increasing number as the years of NEP progressed,who had a far smaller share in this modest enough consumption. These were the growing ranks of the unemployed, both peasants and workers.

Unfortunately it is impossible to assess the full extent of unemployment in Russia in the 1920's. In the early years it would have been both wasteful and useless to keep track of unemployment figures; skilled men were needed for constructive tasks, and very little could be done for those who were unemployed. 1921, 1922 and 1923 are all full of grim tales of human misery and stoppages of production. But 1924, the year of the apparent revival of industry, brought no relief. The numbers of the unemployed grew, and the government merely masked the problem by refusing to register the unemployed:

The reform of labour exchanges which began in August 1924 and was accompanied by a mass reduction in the registration of the unemployed, and cessation of registration for some categories of the unemployed, unfortunately deprives us of the possibility of obtaining figures reflecting the real state of the labour market for almost a year.[10]

stated a contemporary author. But some estimates were made of the extent of unemployment. If the unemployment is expressed as 100 per cent in January 1923, it was 165·8 per cent in July of that year; 193·5 per cent in January 1924; 209·7 per cent in July 1924; 171·6 per cent in July 1925 (that is, a year after the reduction of registration) and 156·5 per cent in August of that year. The conclusion he reached was that unemployment was officially on the decrease, but we are warned:

This seems to be true even if one takes into account the fact that the latest figures of unemployed are somewhat smaller as a result of restrictions placed on registration by some labour exchanges.[10]

99

Later in this chapter an attempt will be made to analyse the policy of the labour exchanges, and to estimate the numbers of unemployed who were not registered. At the moment we must survey what categories of people were registered as unemployed. In January 1923 the industrial group constituted 22 per cent, white-collar workers[11] 46·6 per cent and labourers 20·0 per cent. In July 1925 the industrial group amounted to 28·8 per cent, the white-collar workers to 23·3 per cent and labourers to 36·1 per cent.[10] Of all those registered as unemployed, the group of trained industrial workers constituted from a fifth to almost a third of the total—a considerable number in a country short of skilled workers. The figure for white-collar workers had fallen by half in two years, probably because they simply ceased to be registered, not because they became employed.[12] The figures for labourers—that is, mainly unskilled peasants arriving in towns to seek work—are completely unreliable, for the majority of them did not register.

The numbers of the unemployed swamped the labour exchanges, and would have made them completely ineffectual if they had not already been so. A contemporary correspondent complained that the registration was very incomplete. In the first place, the unemployed lost faith in the exchanges, and preferred to look for work themselves. In the second place, the exchanges operated a policy of limited registration. This was envisaged in the reform, but the method of carrying it out differed from place to place:

In some places non-union members are not registered (Leningrad, Arkhangelsk); in others, those who have not worked before (Novgorod); in other places, those who have connections with agriculture (Votskaya Oblast). Many exchanges do not register 'less valuable' professions, they themselves defining the meaning of this term. . . . In Saratov at one time there existed an extremely curious institution—'candidates for "unemployed" ', a reserve list kept by the labour exchange; the candidates' transfer on to the 'unemployed' list depended on the need to fill the ranks of the unemployed registered at the exchange. . . .[13]

In Voronezh in the first quarter of 1925, 40 per cent of those wanting to register were refused registration. The problem created by the arrival of peasants in towns to look for work was very grave. In Moscow in the first quarter of 1925, peasants constituted 32 per cent of the registered unemployed. The same percentage was recorded in Leningrad. But it is certain that the majority of peasants arriving from the country did not register at the labour exchanges. This
100

could be inferred from the fact that in a short period of time 20,000 people found work in Leningrad, while at the same time only 600 people registered at the labour exchanges.[13] There were one million registered unemployed in the Soviet Union in 1925. Even if the ratio of those finding work outside the labour exchanges to those registered was above the average in this case, it still shows that the problem was at least ten times bigger than was officially allowed.

The social picture that one visualizes on looking at the unemployment figures for 1925 is a mixed one. First of all, the breakdown is along the lines of skilled and unskilled labour, which is rather interesting, for despite the restrictions a lot of unskilled (that is, peasant) labour was registered. Second, the sexes show an almost equal proportion in some localities. Third, and more disturbing, the number of adolescents looking for work for the first time was relatively large. The available data collected by the Department of Social Insurance at the Commissariat of Labour refer to the Ukraine in the autumn of 1925; thus they are by no means complete, nor even typical (the Ukraine has no conceivable counterpart in the Soviet republics). However, they do provide certain pointers to the situation in the country at large. In the autumn of 1925 there were 180,000 people registered as unemployed in the Ukraine. 141,000 of this number were registered at the twenty biggest exchanges. This in itself points to a great concentration of the unemployed in the larger centres. 42,700 people were registered in the industrial regions (not enumerated). 63,000 (38 per cent) of the total number were registered in Kiev and Odessa. The social problems of the period are well illustrated by the fact that women constituted 40 per cent of the registered unemployed. The number of adolescents looking for work for the first time and registered as unemployed was very large: the percentage oscillated from 14 to 29 per cent of all unemployed.[14] The difficulties of employing women and young people will be discussed later, but even skilled industrial workers had great difficulty in obtaining employment.

Despite the great number of industrial workers who were registered, it was often impossible to employ them even when industrial work was available. In Kharkov only 50 per cent of the demand for skilled workers could be met in August 1925; in Lugansk, only 32 per cent. This was because the skills the industries required were often of a different sort. In Kharkov, no skilled lathe operators, pattern makers, milling machine operators or instrument-makers could be

101

found among the metallurgical workers who were unemployed. However, industrial workers at least stood some chance of getting work in 1925. In the Ukraine, the starting up of factories in May–August 1925 provided work for 50,000 unemployed. The agricultural labourers provided the greatest problem. In the Ukraine at that time (the harvest period) there were 50,000 unemployed farm labourers registered. What their numbers were likely to be with the onset of winter it was difficult to estimate, but the increase was bound to be very considerable, said the correspondent.

If the figures for the Ukraine—always a proverbially rich agricultural country, whose natural resources also made a larger range of industries possible (though they were to a great extent ruined by the civil war)—were pretty bad, those for Leningrad, a large industrial centre, show the enormous extent of unemployment among the industrial workers. The number of registered unemployed in the middle of 1925 was 60,000. This was an improvement on the beginning of the year, when the number must have been much greater, because in the six months January–July some 75,000 people had already been directed to work. Besides those registered as unemployed, it was estimated that the number of unregistered unemployed was in the region of 90,000 to 100,000 people. In 1925 the problem in Leningrad was still that of directing the old industrial workers to new jobs; 73 per cent of those directed were members of the trade unions.[14] But the composition of the unemployed was changing rapidly. One correspondent estimated that while in 1926 some 400,000 people would find work in newly opened factories, they would be replaced every year by some 300,000 to 400,000 people arriving from the countryside to find work in the towns.[15] Other estimates went even further. It was admitted that though one million people were registered as unemployed, this figure did not even begin to show the full extent of unemployment. The restrictions on registration had 'reduced' the numbers, but even those who were registered may not be properly accounted for because the labour exchanges kept only rudimentary statistics. The number of those who were unemployed but not registered was impossible to arrive at.[16]

The problem of unemployment in the 1920's grew to unmanageable proportions because of rural over-population. Unfortunately, it was as impossible then as it is difficult at present to make an exact estimate of what the Russian demographers often called 'surplus population'.

Though complete statistics for the period are missing, some Soviet writers have made an attempt, on the basis of limited surveys, to estimate the excess of rural population in the 'twenties. One of them used the survey of the State Colonization Institute, which gave limited information on unused labour in the countryside.[17] According to this survey, the excess in only four regions of the Soviet Union in 1923 already exceeded the unused labour force in 1897 (see Table 4). The author, while cautiously stating that the whole nature

Table 4

**Percentage of unused labour
basis: five hectares for one worker**

Raion	1897	1923
Severo–Zapadnii	49·9	45·1
Zapadnii	42·1	49·4
Tsentralno–Promyshlennii	34·9	54·1
Tsentralno–Zemledelcheskii	27·6	47·1

of over-population was not yet sufficiently understood to make very rigid estimates possible, nevertheless assumed on the basis of these percentages that over-population for these regions of Russia alone was about twenty million people.[18]

This survey was carried out in 1923, when the population was smaller, but industrial employment was very difficult to find and the article based on it was not published until 1929. Nevertheless, the author took the view, based on recent work of the Commissariats of Agriculture and Labour in connection with the resettlement of peasants, that the situation was getting worse and not better. He also took into account the apparent absurdity of the data:

There are no exact figures of over-population, and they would be impossible to obtain. It must be accepted that 'surplus' population is not a constant phenomenon. Its dimensions can change significantly, depending on a whole series of reasons incumbent in both agriculture and . . . industry. . . .

An uninitiated person may find the reports of our labour exchanges, such as 'During the past period unemployment rose as a result of opening such-and-such factory or works', quite preposterous. The secret of it is that the countryside, or its surplus, reacts briskly to any openings which allow it a possibility of obtaining work in town.[17]

The author, who was closely connected with the problem, saw no easy solution. The government advised colonization, but the conference of workers connected with colonization insisted that this could be only one of the means of dealing with surplus labour and 'hidden unemployment' in the countryside: 'Colonization can serve only to ease somewhat the sharpest manifestations of over-population.'[19]

Part of the complexity of the problem was that it was often uneven distribution of labour that was to blame for unemployment. There were industrial workers in localities where there was no demand for them, yet suitable work was available in other places. The difficulty lay in moving those concerned to places where employment could be found—a task which centred not on social problems, but on mere matters of bricks and mortar. And at that time housing was perhaps the biggest of all headaches in the Soviet Union. It was hard enough to keep pace with repairing decayed housing; new building had to be relegated to the bottom of the list.

Where plans for resettlement were made, it was on an inadequate scale. The management of the Ivanovo-Voznesensk Textile Trust decided to start up seventeen textile mills in 1925–26. Some forty thousand workers were required. Recruiting officers sent out to the provinces reported that this labour force could be found if the workers were provided with accommodation. But the settlement the Trust was then building for the workers would accommodate only some six thousand families—about a quarter of the required labour force.[14] Many similar cases can be found in industrial newspapers.

The men who managed to get factory jobs were extremely fortunate in comparison with those who remained out of work. The programme of social insurance, and other measures to help the unemployed, were so small that their impact on the mass of the unemployed was insignificant. We can take a look at one case study. Tambov, a guberniya town in south-eastern Russia, had a severe unemployment problem in 1925. In September unemployment was growing among the non-productive groups, and there were no prospects of employing these people in industry without retraining them. Tambov was trying to cope, but more public works would have to be instituted, and it was absolutely necessary to increase the number of those receiving unemployment benefit. The difficulty lay in obtaining funds to do this. In August 1924 the Tambov labour exchange had 22,171 people registered on its books; 8,466 remained on the register in September 1924, after a re-registration had been carried out. Despite the new regulations, the number of those registered steadily grew again, and

104

the percentage of peasants arriving from the country reached 27 per cent of the total registered by August 1925. Those who were registered as unemployed were entitled to a benefit. The current rate in Tambov was from six roubles to eight roubles fifty kopeks for an unspecified period of time. Little as this seems, there was enough money to pay the benefit to only 20 per cent of the registered unemployed in January 1925, to 21 per cent in February, 24 per cent in March, 26 per cent in April, and 21 per cent in May and June of 1925. A special fund, apparently established from collections from private persons, allowed the labour exchanges to make extra grants of three roubles each to 162 additional people.

These benefits did not exhaust the amount of help given to the unemployed. Tambov had received a total of 56,954 roubles from guberniya and central funds to carry out a programme of public works. In the main, these funds were used to tidy the town up: pavements were repaired, the river wall strengthened, squares and avenues were cleaned. About 375 people were employed on this work every day, and their wage was eighteen to twenty-five roubles a month.[20] In the first six months of 1925, 1,008 people were sent on these public works. In order to ease the situation of the unemployed it was agreed with trade union organizations to employ the same people for a month only, and then to take on others who had not yet worked. Another effort for the unemployed was the organization of collectives. They were to produce simple goods, like brooms or bast sandals. Unfortunately, by the time the number of these collectives had risen to 106 and their members numbered 1,475 they were either liquidated or transferred to State supervision.[21]

Lest it be thought that the situation in Tambov was exceptional, there is ample evidence that elsewhere it was no better. Very often it was even worse. Odessa, a big and formerly rich port, had a huge programme of public works which employed over 28,000 people in 1924–25. The work was divided up over sixty points, and included such enterprises as strengthening the quay, clearing out the canals to fight malaria, and similar projects. Twenty per cent of the workers were women and 10 per cent adolescents, for whom the work seems to have been of an unduly strenuous character even by Russian standards. This showed in the low productivity of labour, which exasperated the authorities:

The attitude of the unemployed to their duties is not always responsible. The majority of them look upon public works as public charities. It is

105

OLGA A. NARKIEWICZ

impossible to keep them under supervision, for the area concerned is too large.

In consequence, the results of the work were very small. But here the correspondent relents, and suddenly becomes human:

On the other hand, the pay could not provide a great stimulus to higher productivity. While the average industrial worker earned 2 roubles 44 kopeks a day . . . the unemployed received 82·3 kopeks to 93·5 kopeks a day.[22]

It is clear from these official data that the unemployment position was acute in the critical year of 1925. In 1926, at least in one region of the Soviet Union, it was still bad, as a report from party archives tells us. This report[23] was compiled on the basis of figures supplied by the three labour exchanges administered from Smolensk. It states at the outset that organizational measures which had been undertaken in 1925 did not decrease unemployment, but they made the task of the labour exchanges easier and pointed the way to new methods of work. These measures consisted solely in enforcing changes in the registration rules, which had been discussed earlier. The report stated that on 1 January 1927 there were 16,315 trade union members and 5,532 non-trade union members registered as unemployed. As a result of changes in the registration rules there were 16,950 trade union members registered as unemployed on 1 January 1928, and only 3,173 non-trade union members.

The figures of those registered at labour exchanges for the last three years are given as follows:[24]

I January 1926	8,917
1 January 1927	11,227
1 January 1928	11,162

The newly established labour exchange at Yartsevo had 1,674 people registered on 1 January 1928,

but this figure does not fully reflect the unemployment at Yartsevo, for only those who had managed to register since the exchange opened on 10 November 1927 are accounted for.

On the basis of the figures quoted, the report goes on, there was a picture of decreasing unemployment, particularly among non-union members.

One must not, however, draw the conclusion from that that unemployment in the guberniya has decreased. The decrease in the number of unemployed non-union members has come about as a result of re-registration

106

of the unemployed, which was carried out in April–June 1927. At that time a means test was carried out which also led to many unemployed being taken off the lists of the exchanges.

The report then follows with yet another set of figures for the unemployed. On 1 January 1927 there were 5,695 trade union members registered, and 7,989 on 1 January 1928. The total number of members of trade unions registered in 1926 was 10,033; of those registered in 1927, 15,989—an increase of 59·3 per cent.

There was quite a large number of directions to work. In 1926, 4,348 trade unionists were directed, out of the total number of those registered who were found work. In 1927 work was found for 11,456 trade unionists and 10,323 non-union members. Unfortunately, after 1 January 1927 the number of unemployed increased greatly, owing to the reduction in staff everywhere in connection with the new budgetary year.[25]

Perhaps it is hardly surprising that when contemporary Soviet statistics were in such disorder, the Soviet writers of the present era are unable to make an exact assessment of the actual numbers of unemployed. It would be better, however, if they admitted the difficulties frankly instead of attempting to prove the impossible.

A highly enthusiastic contemporary writer on the subject has to admit, albeit somewhat reluctantly, that by 1927 the unemployment situation seemed worse than ever. This writer ascribes the whole problem to rural over-population, and draws up statistics to show that the peasant element finding work in industry played an important role at this time. Unfortunately, the author's figures, never highly accurate, seem at this point to be in even worse order. This is probably due less to carelessness than to the fact that her work relies on sources published after 1930. Thus we are given the figure of 920,000 registered unemployed in 1925, rising to 1,041,000 in 1927, the first figure being clearly lower than that given by authors writing in 1925. We must therefore accept the statement that industrial workers constituted only 16·5 per cent of those unemployed in 1927, and that some 40 per cent of those employed in industry in the years 1926–27 were arrivals from the peasantry—a figure which even the author says is only approximate. The figure of 400,000 adolescents reaching working age in towns alone every year seems rather large compared with the 100,000 mentioned earlier in this chapter, but since it was taken from the central archives it may be right. Further, the figure of 7 million superfluous people in the countryside is

107

taken from Kuibyshev's interview in 1927, and must clearly be suspect.[26]

But figures apart, it is the author's logic that is suspect. According to her, there were some two and a half million industrial workers in 1927. The population was 147 million in 1926. Therefore the workers constituted barely a sixtieth part of the whole population. To say, under such circumstances, that 'in the USSR, in contrast to capitalist countries, the unemployment was not "industrial" ' seems to be shirking the issue. This might be overlooked if the author could have stated that the industrial proletariat was doing really well. But even with the help of Stalin's figures, the best she can say is that the consumption of rye bread grew less and that of wheaten bread greater; the basic foodstuffs quoted[27] as consumed by a worker's family make one wonder what the unemployed ate. In 1927 an adult member of a worker's family consumed monthly 8·25 kg of rye bread, 19·67 kg of wheaten bread, 1·82 kg of sugar and sweets, 0·32 kg of butter, 5·03 kg of meat; although meat consumption rose by half a kilogram over 1927, this still seems little enough to rejoice about.

We have seen in this chapter how the Soviet Union had to contend with the problems bequeathed by the policy of War Communism, as well as those which arose out of the relative lack of restrictions on labour and small producers during the NEP period. Most of these troubles were not new, they were simply accentuated by several years of war and disorders. Their basic content was not uncommon for under-developed countries in general. They consisted of rural over-population (or lack of a rational organization of labour in the countryside); insufficiently developed industries, which were unable to absorb the surplus labour; bad distribution, geographically and educationally, of trained labour; a poor transport system and completely insufficient urban housing. All these ills, together with a rising birth rate, resulted in a rapid growth of unemployment which may have been unprecedented in the country.

These circumstances created a huge social and economic problem at a time when the government was already under serious stress because of internal party conflict. The influx of unemployed peasants into the cities added to the difficulties of food supply, housing problems and employment opportunities. Thus, in addition to the already existing problems of a peasant class which was difficult to control, and a proletariat which was badly off and therefore dissatisfied, a new dilemma arose in the shape of the hungry masses of

108

unemployed swamping the industrial and semi-industrial centres in search of food, work and accommodation. Some measures were tried half-heartedly, as we have seen. There is no doubt that colonization on a large scale was seriously considered. There were precedents for it from tsarist times, and naturally the large uninhabited areas of Siberia had always been uppermost in every government's mind. It was unfortunate that under the conditions existing in the 1920's, it was impossible to plan a voluntary and orderly process of colonization, and that it was not until the notorious measures of the 1930's that some Siberian areas were populated after a fashion.

If colonization was impossible because it was an expensive and complex process, further migration to the towns had to be prevented. In some districts this was attempted as a voluntary measure, but with little success, as the following report[28] shows:

According to data for 1924–25 and 1925–26, peasant migration is increasing. In 1924–25, out of 1,783,804 inhabitants of the volosti in the guberniya, 41,502 people migrated to look for work in towns (this constituted 2·3 per cent of the population). In 1925–26, out of 1,558,260 inhabitants, 42,869 people migrated, that is, there was a 0·5 per cent increase in migration.

In order to regulate and study the migration of peasant population to industry, a network of labour correspondents and information points was organized in the guberniya, particularly in places where the migrants were concentrated in the greatest numbers. These correspondents had as their basic function the restraining of the influx of peasant migrants into towns in search of work, and the regulation of this migration. They were not fully able to fulfil this task. When the information points were unable to give the peasants a satisfactory answer about the possibility of obtaining work [in towns], the peasants moved to the towns independently to look for work. On 1 October of the current year [presumably 1927] the information points were liquidated.

It is obvious that the local authorities were unable to cope with this additional problem of peasant migration, and in this instance preferred to allow the movement to continue, possibly even in the hope that the surplus population would leave the guberniya and ease the position locally. It was a problem which the central government had to tackle on a national level; it did it in some measure with the promulgation of carefully worded decrees. It is not known whether these decrees were ever actually put into practice.

Some decrees were promulgated in order to prevent peasant migration. One, entitled 'About the duties of raion and volost central committees and rural soviets in co-operating with the organs of the National Commissariat of Labour of RSFSR in their efforts to stop the unorganized migration of peasants in search of work',[29] though ambiguously worded, shows that even if no physical force was to be used to stop migration (and probably this would have been impossible in view of the large numbers involved), all means of persuasion and threats were to be freely employed. These laws seem to have been largely unenforceable. Simultaneously, the problem was mounting every day, and turning from a social issue into a political one.

A parallel can be drawn here with the recent lesson of Commonwealth migration into Great Britain. The immigrants, who in the first instance presented a social and economic problem, soon turned into a political problem which both the major parties had to tackle if they wanted the support of the electorate. In Soviet Russia, the political issue took a different turn; nevertheless it loomed large in the eyes of the government. While the Soviet government had never claimed to be government by consent, it could rightly be classed as a government for lack of organized dissent. In the years of NEP, the lack of dissent was generated not by terror[30] but by a certain measure of agreement between the ruling class and the people. Thus the peasants were left with a degree of independence, in return for increased agricultural output. The workers, at that stage a less important but nevertheless vital part of the population, were slowly recovering their standard of living: their wages had risen slightly, more housing was available than there had been after the civil war; the food supply was becoming easier. Provided this slight improvement continued, it may be accepted that the employed part of the proletariat would have become reconciled to the government's policies in not too distant a future.

This temporary equilibrium could not survive for long the disruption caused by mass immigration from the countryside. The people arriving in the towns were no less culturally alien to the urban population than the West Indian immigrants in Britain and they were far less welcome, for the public services were overstretched in any case. Unless the government could supply work and accommodation in the towns on a far larger scale than had ever been contemplated, it could expect one of two possible outcomes: either the poor peasants would become desperate if they were forbidden to leave the countryside and would form the hard core of a peasant insurrection;[31] or the influx of peasants would disrupt the food supply, put an unbearable strain on existing employment and accommodation, and disorders in the cities would follow a period of famine or larger unemployment.

110

There is no doubt that the government was at least partly aware of these dangers. But convulsed as it was by the internal struggle for power, and powerless to plan ahead as a result, it resorted to a policy of masterly inactivity which in 1927 culminated in a mild industrialization programme. Hoping to avoid trouble in the countryside and to keep the urban population quiet at the same time, it finally had to face disorders in the cities when the 1928 famine struck, and a full-scale civil war with the peasants when it attempted to pacify the urban population with bigger food supplies.

This chapter has attempted to illustrate in some small measure the realities of the position in Russia in the early and middle 1920's. It is by no means an exhaustive survey; there are sufficient data for this period to reconstruct the events year by year and district by district. While it would be of great interest to do this in a separate work, the present sketch merely outlines the background to the remorselessly advancing crisis which erupted in late 1920's. I have also tried to show the close connection between agricultural crises and industrial developments, and to demonstrate that this was not simply a matter of the supply of foodstuffs to the cities but a much more momentous problem of population movement, unemployment, rural impoverishment and lack of a consistent policy on the part of government agencies. We have seen how the peasants who had been forced off the land fared in the cities and provincial towns. It is now necessary to look at those peasants who had been able (or obliged) to stay in the countryside.

NOTES

1. A. L. Oprishchenko, 'Voprosy Sotsialisticheskogo Sorevnovaniya Rabochego Klassa SSSR v Sovetskoi Istoriografii' in *Nekotorye Problemy Istorii Sovetskogo Obshchestva*, pp. 147–51.
2. E. H. Carr, *Socialism in One Country*, vol. I, p. 329.
3. 'KPSS v Rezolyutsiakh . . .', op. cit., Part 2, 'Fifteenth conference of VKP (b)', October–November 1926, pp. 323–4.
4. J. K. Galbraith, *The Affluent Society*, p. 22.
5. E. H. Carr, *Socialism in One Country*, op. cit., vol. I, pp. 331–2.
6. A. Baykov, *The Development of the Soviet Economic System*, op. cit., p. 121.
7. Ch. Bettelheim, *L'Économie Soviétique*, p. 21.
8. Ibid., p. 22. Units not stated for leather and boots.
9. See particularly the Smolensk documents in chapter 10, though these refer to crisis conditions.
10. Nikolsky, 'Bezrabotitsa i ee perspektivy' in *Voprosy Truda*, No. 10, 1925.
11. This group is described loosely as 'intelligentsia', but it cannot mean professional people and teachers alone; it is bound to include clerks and lowergrade civil service personnel as well.

12 Though this is not certain, for the bureaucratic machinery was still expanding.

13. E. Mokhov, 'Organizatsionnoe sostoyanie i deyatelnost birzh truda', in *Voprosy Truda*, No. 10, 1925.

14. 'Khronika Truda i Sotsialnogo Strakhovania po SSSR', *Voprosy Truda*, No. 10, 1925.

15. A. Bakhutov, 'K 8-oi godovshchine Oktyabr'skoi Revolutsii' in *Voprosy Truda*, No. 11, 1925.

16. Ya. Gindin, 'Nash Khozyaistvennyi pod'em i novye zadachi regulirovania rynka truda' in *Voprosy Truda*, No. 11, 1925.

17. Z. Mokhov, 'Pereselenchestvo, izbytki truda i bezrabotitsa' in *Voprosy Truda*, No. 6, 1929.

18. This article may have an historical value. The title page carries a note from the editors of the periodical, saying that they disagreed with the author's incorrect comparison of capitalist population policy with socialist population policy. Despite the disagreement, the article was printed in full in the middle of 1929. It would be interesting to find out whether any 'incorrect' views were allowed publication at a later date.

19. Conference theses, quoted ibid.

20. For comparison, the average pay of a timber feller was 75 kopeks to 1 rouble 5 kopeks a day, provided he worked twelve to sixteen hours a day; figures given in *Voprosy Truda*, No. 10, 1925, p. 167.

21. V. Shavlov, 'Rynok Truda v Tambovskoi Gubernii' in *Voprosy Truda*, No. 10, 1925.

22. I. Shumsky, 'Itogi Obshchestvennykh Rabot v Odesse' in *Voprosy Truda*, No. 11, 1925.

23. Smolensk archives, reel No. 5, Smolensk, 1928, WKP 33: appendix to point 2 of protocol No. 17 of the meeting of the Bureau of guberniya committee, on 16 February 1928, 'The state of unemployment of Smolensk guberniya on 1 January 1928'.

24. It will be noticed that these figures, and those quoted later, are completely at variance with the figures quoted at the outset of the report. This may be due less to the bad state of statistics than to the fact that some labour exchanges may not have been included in some sets of figures, or that the figures fluctuated monthly and the compiler did not see fit to include this fluctuation; or it may be because the unemployed were broken down into different categories, and the statistics only show certain categories. In any case, it illustrates the difficulty of dealing with the figures for this period, and the caution with which any figures must be treated.

25. Appendix to point 2 of protocol No. 17, op. cit.

26. L. S. Rogachevskaya, *Iz Istorii Rabochego Klassa SSSR v Pervye Gody Industrializatsii, 1926–1927*, pp. 55–7.

27. Ibid., p. 60.

28. Smolensk archives, reel No. 5, Smolensk, 1928, WKP 33: 'The state of unemployment in the Smolensk guberniya on 1 January 1928. Regulation of (peasant) migration.'

29. 'Ob obyazannostyakh raionnykh i volostnykh tsentralnykh komitetov i selskikh sovetov okazyvat' sodeistvye organam Nar. Kom. Truda RSFSR v ikh predpriyatyakh po preduprezhdeniu neorganizovannogo otkhoda krestyan na zarabotki', No. 116, *Sobranie Uzakonenii i Rasporyazhenii RSFSR*, Part I, 14 November 1927; signed by Kalinin, Lezhava, Kisakov.

30. This is, of course, only in comparison with the Stalinist terror, and not with conditions obtaining in countries other than the Soviet Union.

31. Evidence that this happened in one district at least is presented in chapter 10.

7 'Our most difficult task is to nationalize production in fact as well as in theory'

We have seen that the Russian peasant had for a long time played a lively part in managing his own affairs. For obvious reasons, this administration was traditional and had little to do with theoretical administrative practice. It had two things to recommend it, though: it was an inherent part of rural life, and it worked. Rural administration was often carried out by the commune, which, though described by this one word, took many forms and indeed depended in its organization not so much on decrees as on the type of agriculture which was practised in a specific region. These factors combined to make the problem of imposing any new forms of administration on the agricultural population one of the most complex issues of the period. The problem became acute during the last years of NEP, but it had been one of the main bones of contention long before. The two main types of agriculture which the experts had to consider were the commune and individual plot farming. Each had something to recommend it. From an economic viewpoint, the commune represented larger-scale farming and the pooling of labour and machinery resources; individual farming provided a greater incentive to the more enterprising families. More important, however, was the political significance which attached to the two types of farming. While there were many opinions about this, two general viewpoints have already been isolated: (1)—that commune farming was the first step towards a socialized agriculture; (2)—that individual farming was more productive and therefore likely to be of more ultimate

113

benefit to the State. Both these points of view had to take into account the enormous complications arising out of the traditional Russian system of agriculture. This had for a long time depended on such devices as the three-course system, strip farming and communal redistribution of land. As a result, it was well nigh impossible to consider administrative changes without first rationalizing the agricultural system.

The debate had a long history but it received additional impetus after the revolution. There is a classic example of such discussion in a book published by an agricultural expert in 1917.[1] It states that in order to reorganize agriculture and intensify production, the 'ignorant, impoverished masses' must have the friendly help of the State:

This help . . . is concretely expressed in three forms: in the form of agronomic help . . ., in the form of economic help—the organization of credit and co-operation . . . and in the form of land redistribution in its narrow meaning—that is, *in the change of the configuration of the area of each farm, according to new systems of agriculture.*[2]

The commune farmers suffer from four ills, says the author: compulsory crop rotation, over-exploitation of common lands, narrow strips and distant fields. The most important are the narrow strips and distant fields, because they intensify cross-strip farming, which has very dangerous effects. The first and foremost task in this field, he suggests, would be to bring the peasants nearer to their land; resettlement into farmsteads appears to be an ideal solution to this problem. He finds the solution wanting in some respects—for instance, it does not solve the problem of how to use large mechanized machinery on small holdings and how to transport it from farmstead to farmstead. Resettlement, as suggested by other experts, is also difficult in regions where the geographical features (such as water supply, the distribution of pastures and forests) are inconveniently placed. These features vary with particular intensity between the black soil and non-black soil regions. If in the black soil regions the majority of peasants are crowded into small villages, there are sound geographical reasons for it.

There are advocates of the farmstead type of agriculture, continues the author, who say that pasture can be produced artificially, and that forests can be planted. However, this process would take a long time, and in the meanwhile lack of these amenities would bring even more misery on the peasants. In addition, a farmstead peasant

114

needs some capital and more agronomic knowledge than he generally possesses. Neither of these requirements is easily met. But the most important need in farmstead agriculture is water. Stolypin himself had said that farmstead resettlement depended completely on the conditions of water supply; the tiny wells on the new farmsteads would not support the peasants or their cattle. Farmstead agriculture without sufficient irrigation is possible only in dry regions, on a large scale and solely with grain crops, and even this will prove to be only plundering agriculture, for it will erode the soil in a few years or at best a few decades.[3] Even if all these conditions could be satisfied, there still remains one major necessity: a network of roads. This would have to be the first step towards farmstead agriculture.

If the farmstead type of agriculture, properly established, is ideal from a technical point of view, it leaves a lot to be desired from the economic and cultural viewpoints. Farmsteads mean living in isolation for most families:

It is possible . . . that drunkenness is rarer, but in our conditions, the culture of the population also decreases: they stop visiting not only the inns, but also schools and churches.

In particular, their income falls because the isolated peasants are not familiar with current prices and sell their produce to travelling middlemen at lower rates. They are also unable to increase their income by casual labour. In countries with a higher cultural standard—particularly Denmark—the farmsteads are models of farming methods and their co-operative organization is excellent. But under Russian conditions the farmstead has led to a lowering of cultural standards and a decrease in social consciousness, the author concludes.[4]

The attempts to introduce a farmstead type of agriculture were often successful, and this led the advocates of farmsteads to assume that it was the right type of agriculture for the whole of Russia. In fact, these farmsteads have prospered mainly in the Vitebsk, Kovno, Grodno, Mogilev and Volynia regions, as well as in the guberniyas of Pskov, Smolensk and St Petersburg. These regions were far from typical, and the survey of 1907 said in summing up the situation that:

While in many localities of central and southern Russia nature itself seems to object to the creation of farmsteads, here in Pskovskaya guberniya their creation seems to be a logical necessity . . .

In the south-eastern parts of European Russia, particularly in the guberniya of Samara, where farmsteads had existed since the times of Catherine the Great, they were on the whole unsuccessful, and one of the main reasons was lack of water. The most successful of all farmers here, says the author, were the German sectarian colonists, the Mennonites, whose level of culture was far higher than that of the Russian and even other German peasants. When faced with inadequate government-built wells they built their own, and obtained crops which were better than those on private estates, and much better than peasant ones. But the Mennonites' farmsteads were on average three times bigger than those of Crown peasants and eighteen times bigger than those of the former serfs. In addition, they were exempt from military service. Therefore, the author concluded, they were nearer to the American farmers in every respect than to the Russian peasants, and it was hardly surprising that they were able to make a success of farmstead agriculture.

In other German colonies (those which were not so rich) the farmstead peasants who started to divide their holdings were now at the same level as the medium peasants:

The general conclusion of researchers on farmsteads in Samarskaya guberniya is that the form of individual ownership of land alone is unable to create farms which are economically rational under given conditions.[5]

To strengthen these arguments the author referred to Stolypin again, and to his affirmation that land redistribution on its own is only a means to an end: it gives an opportunity for productive work but no more. The Stolypin reforms were directed at strong peasants. It was assumed that they would leave the commune and provide a basis for a rational agriculture:

In fact, ... the results did not justify these hopes. ... those who leave the communes are poor peasants who have no deep roots in the village and who obtained their livelihood by other means than agriculture. [The government] counted on the commune, which was a brake on agricultural progress, making the peasants from more intensively cultivated regions take up individual farming. In fact, the Russian commune is being destroyed in the extensive regions of the south and south-west, where it did not take root because of its short existence. ... Obviously, the destruction of the commune develops social differentiation: semi-proletarian households ... turn into fully proletarian ones, the town ends its links with the countryside, the countryside becomes isolated from the town . . . our industry is not large enough to give work to millions of new workmen. ... On the other hand, those who remain in the commune are unable to use the plots which have been left [by the migrants] because they have no

116

capital, . . . these plots are bought by village kulaks, who count on treble profits from renting the land.[6]

Therefore it seems useless to destroy the collective form of agriculture without putting anything better in its place: 'Farmsteads in Russia, at least at present, are impossible on a large scale.' In place of farmsteads, asserted the expert, the government ought to aim at the creation of group agriculture in settlements. Every group would comprise thirty to forty households, with a land area of 300–400 dessiatinas. With the proper configuration of land, and the houses in the centre, this would facilitate transport, access to schools and other communal facilities, and water supply. Land reclamation and the use of large farm machinery would also become possible without much trouble. Such settlements would make it possible to develop co-operation, particularly labour co-operation, and they were an ideal towards which the more progressive peasants should work.[7]

This work, written just before the revolution and obviously under the influence of the Stolypin reforms, attempted to prove that the farmstead type of agriculture was possible only in certain geographical regions. It stated explicitly that it was undesirable for economic, technical and cultural reasons. The implication was that this type of agriculture was also politically and socially wrong: it led the peasants away from collective work, discouraged co-operation and developed an individualistic spirit, of which the author disapproved.[8]

It is interesting to note that a few years later another authority on agriculture used the same examples to prove that the farmstead system had in fact arrived in Russia and that the tide against the commune had finally turned. This work was published at the very inception of the New Economic Policy, and in view of the author's eminence it must have provided guidance for the advocates of the strong peasant until 1927:

In the agrarian system of peasant Russia up to the beginning of the twentieth century [says the author] there was cross-strip farming almost everywhere. It was characteristic not only of the commune village in the greatest part of Russia, but also in those western guberniyas where the farmstead type of agriculture prevailed. The individual plot type of agriculture had for a long time been prevalent, but only in Poland, Latvia and Estonia, from where it began to pass only recently to the neighbouring guberniyas with a Russian population. At the beginning of the present century, many regions of individual plot agriculture had been noted in the following guberniyas: Suvalkovskaya, Kovenskaya, Volynskaya,

117

Vitebskaya, Grodnenskaya, Smolenskaya, Peterburgskaya, Pskovskaya, Kievskaya.[9]

Thus the author uses the same regions as Oganovsky, but he draws exactly the opposite conclusions:

The total of individual farms in various categories of land in the 47 guberniyas of European Russia (for the years 1907–16, that is, on the 1 of January 1917) can be expressed by the following figures:

Category of land	Number of Farms	Area (dessiatinas)
Endowment	1,317,320	12,777,108
Crown	15,505	223,747
Credit banks'	279,865	3,020,062
Total	1,612,690	16,020,917

If these figures are compared with the number of households of the peasant type registered in the same guberniyas by the census of 1916 (15,026,785)—excluding from these the guberniya of Grodno, which was not included in the 1916 census—which will give 1,579,933 households, then the households set up on the basis of individual plots on 1 January 1917 will comprise 10·5 per cent of all households of the peasant type . . . and it follows that as a result of ten years of pre-revolutionary land redistribution, one-tenth of peasant households passed to individual plot agriculture.[10]

In some guberniyas individual farming comprised more than 10 per cent of households. This applied in the north-western regions and in the south and south-eastern regions, as the following percentages show:

North-western regions	
Petrograd guberniya	28·7
Pskov guberniya	17·6
Kovno guberniya	18·6
Vitebsk guberniya	28·7
Smolensk guberniya	15·9
Mogilev guberniya	14·6
South and south-eastern regions	
Poltava guberniya	12·9
Kharkov guberniya	22·5
Kherson guberniya	22·6
Ekaterinoslav guberniya	30·9
Taurida guberniya	30·6
Donskaya oblast	10·4
Saratov guberniya	16·4
Samara guberniya	19·0
Stavropol guberniya	24·9

Commenting on this, the author added that:

As was to be expected, farmsteads break completely with communal agriculture, and in the majority of cases concentrate their land in separate
plots. However, almost three-quarters of plot farms retain commune
facilities, which comprise the seventh part of their lands.[11]

After the revolution many farmsteads and plot farms were liquidated, particularly in the guberniyas where the commune was still
accepted as the right form of agriculture. In Samarskaya guberniya
it was said that:

Plots and farmsteads are unnecessary from the economic viewpoint, and
because of the great harm and destruction brought about by any kind of
change in the forms of agriculture, particularly if it is joined with the
moving of buildings and all the farmstead. . . . Because of this all farmsteads and plots . . . are returned back to the commune.[12]

Fortunately, in the regions where the farmstead system had been
accepted for a long time, it was in general decided to retain it. Data
from 1918 show that in the northern guberniyas (Vologdskaya,
Kostromskaya, Novgorodskaya, Smolenskaya and others) this
problem was discussed by local congresses—on the whole, positively:

So, for instance, in Novgorodskaya guberniya, farmsteads and plots were
accepted as one of the best forms of agriculture (after communes [kom-
muna] and artels), and moving to farmsteads was considered possible,
after mutual agreement by the inhabitants.[13]

In Vologdskaya, Kostromskaya, Smolenskaya and Brianskaya
guberniyas, passing to the farmstead type of agriculture was considered not only possible but even desirable:

The growing trend towards farmsteads was apparently due to the fact that
peasant agriculture . . . during the revolution found itself in a condition
of constant re-partitions. Logically, therefore, it was inevitable that there
would be a desire to acquire land, to adapt it for correct agricultural use
on the basis of individual farms . . . the example of which peasants had
seen in pre-revolutionary farmsteads and plot farms.

However, this desire for individual farming arose at a time when
agrarian policy was directed towards the collectivization of agriculture. At that time, communes (kommuna) and artels were considered
to be not only ideologically correct but also a practical possibility in
the near future. For this reason, local land organizations attempted
to stem the tide of the movement, and when it happened they
characterized it as 'disorderly' or 'spontaneous'.

OLGA A. NARKIEWICZ

'Local organs often took measures to stop such phenomena.' This happened particularly often in 1920 in the guberniyas of Petrograd and Arkhangelsk, as well as in Kostromskaya guberniya, Smolenskaya guberniya and Vladimirskaya guberniya. But the measures were usually to no avail.

This shows that in some guberniyas in Russia, particularly in the northwest, individual agriculture had become such an accepted form in the eyes of the population that a prohibition was unable to halt the trend towards farmsteads.

An agrarian revolution means in the first place a liquidation of nonworking landlordism, and then the destruction of large peasant farming (which is semi-capitalist and kulak), and general equalization of land among all the peasants. Farmstead and plot farms, in so far as they were the expression and the consequence of the social-economic differentiation of the peasants, had been in a large measure destroyed in the process of the revolution; and they were destroyed mainly in those places where the village divided into classes [*rassloilas'*], where plot farming was not, and had been unable to become, the basis of a progressive transformation of the organizational and productive structure of the economy. Revolution destroyed the plot system in the black soil region first, which is extremely characteristic and significant. If one compares this phenomenon with the analysis of plot farming in the south and south-west, then the conclusion is obvious. Plot agriculture here had not yet found a historical justification, as a result of almost exclusively social-economic transformation of the countryside, as an expression of growing agricultural capitalism; it had not yet consolidated and had no economic basis; it contradicted strongly the living spirit of the equalized-distributive commune, and it was not required by any pressing need to reorganize the agricultural system.[13]

In the north and north-western regions the revolutionary process took a completely different form. Here the destruction concerned only the plot farms, whereas the farmsteads, already traditionally consolidated, were seldom touched. Farmstead agriculture had already become a model of the most progressive and productive type of agriculture:

With the existence of sufficiently favourable natural and historical conditions, this organizational transformation of the economy was the result of the conditions of the market, which required the reorganization. Revolution did not destroy, and could not destroy, this process of economic evolution.

Because of these trends, it would be quite unrealistic to forbid the process of breaking up communes by decree:

Measures taken to forbid healthy economic aspirations did not kill them, . . . and they only began to take the form of fictitious types of collective

120

farms. . . . Because of this, the policy of prohibiting farmsteads and plots under the new conditions of national development . . . does not appear to be expedient in any way; its continuation would be a great historical mistake which would doubtless stop the development of our agriculture, which is so necessary in our country.[14]

It is easy to see that this author completely reverses the arguments while still using the same material for his research as Oganovsky. One inescapable conclusion is that the type of agriculture practised in Russia had an influence not only on the economic system but also on the administrative, and therefore on the political, system. It has always been known that from a political point of view the debate on private agriculture versus collective agriculture was of primary importance. What has not been acknowledged, however, is that the intricate connection between the commune, the transition to individual farming, and the changes that this would involve in the administrative system, had a crucial influence on political thinking.

The commune was not only a way of life and a system of farming; it was also an administrative structure. The farmsteads fractionated the peasant mass; the commune coalesced it. The simplest way of looking at it was that peasants broken down into individual farmsteads would in many ways be easier to influence, but they would require a new and more powerful administration than that afforded by the inefficient rural soviets. On the other hand, the commune, while representing a communal way of living and a basic communal system of agriculture, was instrumental in giving the peasants a feeling of power, which they could not possibly obtain under an individual system of farming. Leaving the commune system intact (though even this was impossible by then, for so many of them had become a dead letter) would be a step towards socialism, if it were possible to ensure that the majority of them were loyal to the government. As we shall demonstrate later, this was unrealistic. To allow the peasants to disperse to individual farming could lead to serious political repercussions among the city supporters of the government, and might create a rich peasant class which would be directly hostile to the party. In addition, the agricultural experts themselves were in conflict about which kind of agriculture was economically more viable. We have seen above how two experts disagreed on the economic questions relating to the two types of farming. It would be as well to look at another writer, this time an emigré, to see what arguments he put forward for complete land redistribution.

121

According to this author, the importance of individual farming lay in the fact that the farmer could make plans freely for his production, without having to consider the commune.[15] In a farmstead all land was contained in one piece, and in this way cross-strip farming, a source of great waste, was avoided.

In communal agriculture the land belongs to all the commune, *and separate members of the commune are only . . . temporary users of allotments.* In such a case a farmer is not free in the use of the area under cultivation; he has to submit to the overall plan for agriculture of the whole commune. Generally this plan consists in this, that from time to time (every nine to twelve years) all the arable land is redistributed among the members of the commune according to the number of people in the family . . . or in some other way. Pasture is divided into three fields. In every field, land is divided into strips according to its quality; each member of the commune receives his share in every strip of every field. He uses his share until the next redistribution, but even this use is carried out within the general framework of the communal plan. Grassland for hay is often distributed every year, depending on the hay crop; sometimes the hay is mown communally and distributed among separate households [italics in text].[16]

Obviously, this type of farming failed to satisfy many of the peasants. Therefore it often happened that the commune was retained as a form, but did not carry out land division. Such a state of affairs was the most pernicious of all, because it led to the extreme proliferation of strips. In the example quoted, all land belonging to the members of the commune was within one boundary but the land of each farmer was in strips. One particular peasant held his land in thirty-three strips, of which nineteen were pasture land.

In general, the harm of cross-strip farming can be summed up thus: it requires communal grazing of cattle on the fields . . . and limits the individual farmers as to the choice of crops for sowing . . . it means a less intensive use of non-arable land which is in communal use . . . it increases the average distance of fields from the dwellings, which does not happen in farmsteads; and the deterioration of agricultural techniques because of the great number of small fields, and the time spent in going from one field to another.[16]

There was even a case in the village of Kurovo, in Moscow guberniya, where each farmer had forty narrow strips of pasture, five strips in each of the eight pasture fields; in this way about 10 per cent of land was lost in boundaries. Clearly, this state of affairs was wasteful and unsatisfactory. Of the three types of agricultural organization,

farmstead (or plot farm), communal-distributive, and individual strip farming, we must point out that, from the point of view of agricultural

122

organization, *only in farmstead agriculture does the farmer receive full freedom of organization*; there is less of it in *individual strip farming* and *hardly any in communal-distributive farming* [italics in text].[17]

Because of this, the author considered that only the farmstead system conferred the following benefits: it allowed the farmer to make his own plans; it wasted less land on boundaries; it wasted less time; it was easier to supervise the work; it was easier to improve land either by irrigation or in some other way; it allowed for easier construction of roads and paths; it eliminated arguments and quarrels with neighbours.[17]

Sufficient arguments have been quoted to show that the problem facing the government in the 1920's, as far as agriculture was concerned, was not simply the choice between two kinds of land ownership. Centuries of traditional communal usage, on which governments successively imposed Emancipation communes, Stolypin reforms, post-revolutionary land distribution, War Communism and finally the commune of NEP, combined to make this problem one of the most intricate that any government had ever had to tackle. And it must be remembered that land ownership and rural administration were only one small aspect of the general peasant question. The system of taxation, agricultural productivity, peasant attitudes to the government and dishonest administrators all loomed large among the factors that shaped general policy for the countryside. It is hardly surprising, therefore, that when some of these questions came under discussion later in the 1920's there was little agreement on the measures to be taken.

Faced with conflicting views from agricultural experts and with accusations of 'feather-bedding' the peasants from the left wing of the party, the government was on the horns of a dilemma. The additional burden of having to work within a set of political desiderata proved yet another cause of hesitation and temporization. Like the proverbial ostrich, the government put its head in the sand, declaring its goodwill towards productive peasants while oppressing them with taxes, and hoped the problem would solve itself in the end. But the position was too grave to be neglected.

Despite the growth of farmstead agriculture, the village commune, which had been disintegrating before the revolution, had on its re-introduction after 1922 become a major force in the countryside. Oddly enough, this problem of strong rural organization has been neglected in the West, though the Soviet writers of the 1920's were acutely aware of it. The resurgence of peasant organizations proved highly alarming to the left wing of the party, while the right wing consoled itself with the thought that a strong peasant meant a contented peasant, and that a contented peasant was unlikely to be revolutionary. There were few clear-cut recommendations on the course to take. The weight of the commune was extremely traditional, and all the writers on agricultural questions (left or right wing) were forced to acknowledge that traditional elements in Russian agriculture were of the utmost importance.

While it was clear that no solutions could be offered, there was little doubt about the functional value of the commune. The commune had a triple purpose, in the view of the one modern scholar who has concerned himself with its functions and structure.[18] In the first place, it was concerned with the distribution of land. Each village was interested in the redistribution of land, and in this respect was isolated from every other village. The second function was the provision of public services: the commune dealt with properties and operations such as buying and selling, as well as providing welfare services for the inhabitants. The third function was administrative.[19] It was with this aspect that the party authorities in the 1920's had to come to grips, but always within the framework of the general discussion of the political function of the commune.

The question of land tenure was, of course, heavily weighted politically. After 1925, with the increased prosperity among richer peasants, it gave rise to sharp discussion. The more moderate elements accused the left wing of considering the question of the communes not from the point of view of developing agriculture, but from the point of view of communizing it. The left wing was indicted with supporting populism in its emptiest form, since the peasants showed no propensity to develop communal forms of agriculture and there were insufficient State means for developing such forms. Like the populists before them, these left wingers thought the commune was the best means of socializing the peasantry. Indeed, one of them had said, in connection with the more moderate theorists, that:

These people make the mistake of thinking that the form of land tenure conditions the communizing of agriculture. But it is not the form of land tenure which creates the system of economy; rather, the system of economy creates the form of land tenure.[20]

The more moderate elements contended that if one took into account
124

the writings of Marx and Lenin, it was necessary to leave the development of socialism in agriculture to historical processes. The traditional commune, far from being a road towards socialism, was an obstacle to progress because of its constant re-partitions, the three-course system and the demarcation system. Even so, the commune could not be abolished immediately; that would be too expensive and demand too much effort. It would be impossible to carry out such a measure, asserted the author. The commune should be liquidated gradually, to give way to individual farming; this in turn would be gradually socialized. But he contended that some party and Narkomzem organs were even now forbidding the consolidated farmstead type of farming, justifying this action with the excuse that it introduced the peasants to large-scale Western-style farming (*fermerstvo*). The author considered this argument ridiculous, for it was the richer peasants who preferred the commune (and it has been proved that they were its mainstay), for in it they could exploit the poor peasants; the more progressive peasants wanted to farm individually.[21] The superiority of the farmstead system of agriculture over the commune type can be shown by quoting some figures.[22] The output of rye under farmstead agriculture was 22 per cent higher than under the commune system; that of oats was 18 per cent higher; that of buckwheat, 70 per cent higher, and that of grasses, 42 per cent higher. Nor was there proof that the farmstead peasants were anti-socialist. On the contrary, they co-operated better than the peasants farming in communes. In Moscow guberniya only 45 per cent of the commune peasants went into co-operatives, while 95 per cent of the farmstead peasants did so.[22]

There have been communes in Russia from times immemorial, but as shown earlier, the 1922 Land Code had created something far stronger than even the post-Emancipation commune with its paternalistic hold over the whole population. The strength of this new commune was noted by the party authorities with alarm. In the winter of 1926–27 the Commissariat of Workers' and Peasants' Inspection for RSFSR (henceforward referred to as RKI) made a survey of land communes and rural soviets in the RSFSR. As a result of this survey, the fifteenth party conference passed a resolution stressing the need to improve relations between the rural soviets and the communes, and to ensure the soviets' leading role in the villages.[23] Left wing comments on this resolution make it plain that it was a case of paying lip-service to ideology while the actual state of affairs in the

125

OLGA A. NARKIEWICZ

countryside was completely neglected. The polemic which developed was interesting less for its political content—after all, there had been a left wing and right wing position on the agricultural question as long as the Soviet state had existed—than because it showed that among a welter of suggestions very few were of a positive nature. On the other hand, every protagonist was absolutely sure that his position was the only right one.

One point of view was that the commune was not disappearing but that the contemporary land commune[24] was identical with the pre-revolutionary village commune. According to this author, Lenin had characterized the commune as 'a society to administer the allotments of land'. Up to the revolution a lot of communes were still in existence; almost 50 per cent of peasants in forty-seven guberniyas of European Russia were in communes at the beginning of 1917. According to Pershin, an authority on peasant communes, of all the land-owning peasants in 1917, 49 per cent were organized in communes; in the greater part of the USSR the commune remained the most widely used kind of land tenure.[25] The RKI investigators came to the conclusion that the general gathering was very similar to the pre-revolutionary commune gathering, and that the land commune was not in any way different from the pre-revolutionary village commune. An investigator of the work of land communes at the end of 1926 stated that in two *volost* districts in Tver' guberniya there was no difference between a general gathering and the land commune gathering. Similarly, a Central Committee investigator who surveyed Penza guberniya in the summer of 1927 found that in most villages the gathering was called by the agent of the land commune.[26] This agent was in fact (if not in name) the agent of the general gathering and not just of the land commune. It was found that the agent was the leading figure in the village, with all the inhabitants supporting him. In Beznosovka and Solovtsevo the agent appeared to be the headman (*starosta*) of the whole region, probably because he had sufficient financial resources for his work.

Zdanovich took to task those who maintained that the Soviet agrarian legislation of 1919–22 artifically tried to create communes under the name of land communes. This was untrue, he asserted, for the communes had existed in the first years after the revolution, just as they existed now. The contemporary land commune was also a society for land tenure. Apart from that function, it settled—like the village commune before it—other economic and cultural questions

126

not directly concerned with land tenure. It must be clearly understood that the pre-revolutionary village commune had survived up to present times under the name of land commune. Those who suggested that this communal form of land tenure and cultivation should be abolished had never *suggested what should be put in its place* (Zdanovich's italics). One of the critics of the communes, Ustinov, attempted to show that the form of land tenure made no difference to the system; he even quoted Engels's letter to Tkachev in 1875, in which Engels had said that if there was a revolution in Russia the commune could be changed to a socialist commune. Ustinov also stated that the government now had sufficient funds to transform Soviet agriculture along socialist lines (as Stalin had reported to the fifteenth congress). Ustinov and his supporters said that using the commune in building socialism meant frustrating Lenin's plan for co-operation. But this was untrue, said Zdanovich: the government had developed the forms of co-operation which suited the peasants—the consumers', credit and agricultural co-operatives. Land tenure co-operatives could not play such an important part as the other co-operatives.

The author of this involved argument therefore suggested that instead of encouragement for land tenure co-operatives, there should be more support for communal land tenure. At the sixteenth Moscow guberniya party conference, it was stated that 91 per cent of land in the guberniya was cultivated communally. Moscow's experience had shown that communal cultivation was better, since it solved the problem of distant fields and narrow strips, and thus produced better results than individual farming. Zdanovich reminded his readers that Molotov had committed himself to non-farmstead agriculture, when he said at the fifteenth party congress that the party must help all forms of land cultivation which would lead to the development of co-operation and mechanization in agriculture, and that the practice of putting land into consolidated farmsteads and holdings must be discouraged or stopped completely, for it led to the growth of peasant elements. The author continued that experience had shown that there were forms of communal agriculture which were productive. These were the new village settlements (*poselki-vyselki*), where land was in communal cultivation and where there were no distant fields, no cross strips, and no strips.[27] According to experts, the new village settlements were also land communes, but they had a more progressive type of land cultivation than the orthodox land commune. Moreover, since they were inhabited by the more enterprising

127

peasants—that is, those who could not farm their land as well as they wished to in the old type of commune—they had a tendency to develop collective forms of agriculture.

Another evil in the countryside was that the land commune and its agent had great power. The main reason for this was the failure of the rural soviets to make their influence felt in the villages. The rural soviets in the villages existed only nominally; they were simply offices carrying out the imposed directions of administrative and judiciary organs. The rural soviets seldom held meetings of their members and it was left to the chairman to fill in the necessary forms.[28] The two-year campaign to enliven the soviets improved matters somewhat. They now met to discuss various questions: some even met twice a month, and the presidia, where they existed, met once a week. In addition, the rural soviets now took their own initiative; they tried to solve not only rural problems of an administrative and organizational nature, but also economic and cultural problems. Many rural soviets attempted to introduce the villagers to collectivized agriculture. In places where these soviets were supported by the poorer and medium peasants they were quite successful. But these were the exceptions. Many soviets did not work at all, or only sufficiently to justify their existence. Where this happened, the most important rural organs were the land commune gatherings and their headmen. Even the working soviets did not touch such matters as the transition to a multi-course rotation, co-operatives, collectivization or the regulation of labour hiring arrangements, and they did not draw in labourers and poorer peasants into their organization.

I have quoted so widely from the writings of contemporary authors on agricultural problems in order to show that informed Soviet opinion was fully aware of the problems of the countryside—both those which had existed since pre-revolutionary days, and those created by the Bolsheviks themselves. But there was a wide gap between being informed and being able to act on the information. As demonstrated earlier, there were few concrete suggestions for resolving the situation. There were political, economic and social obstacles at almost every point, not the least being (as a careful student of Taniuchi's monograph will notice) the fact that whenever the agricultural situation was discussed on a higher level, at central congresses and conferences, it was invariably in the spirit of attempting to impose a partial solution from the outside, rather than in a genuine quest for a radical reorganization. In the meantime the

villagers were left to manage as best they could almost entirely on
their own.

NOTES

1. N. Oganovsky, *Revolyutsiya Naoborot* (*Razrushenie obshchiny*).
2. Ibid., p. 33; my italics. This definition of *zemleustroistvo* is the best I have
encountered, being free from the political meaning which later definitions
ascribe to it.
3. Cf. the 'Virgin Land' scheme in recent years.
4. N. Oganovsky, op. cit., pp. 34–9.
5. Ibid., pp. 46–9.
6. Ibid., pp. 62–4.
7. Ibid., pp. 68–70. Compare these arguments with the almost identical ones
put forward by Rzhanitsyn as late as 1927 (outlined later in this chapter).
8. We see here how the Social Revolutionary views on communal agriculture
coincided with Bolshevik views at the time of mass collectivization. However,
the Social Revolutionary point of view preceded the Bolshevik change of heart
by more than a decade.
9. P. N. Pershin, *Uchastkovoe zemlepolzovanie v Rossii*, p. 5.
10. Ibid., p. 8.
11. Ibid., p. 17.
12. Ibid., pp. 37–8.
13. Ibid., pp. 40–3.
14. Ibid., pp. 43 5.
15 N. Makarov, *Organizatsiya Selskogo Khozyaistva.*
16. Ibid., pp. 64–6.
17. Ibid., pp. 67–8.
18. Yuzuru Taniuchi, *The Village Gathering in Russia in the mid-1920's*. See
particularly pp. 21–2 on the nature of the commune.
19. Ibid., pp. 49–50.
20. M. Ustinov, 'K voprosu o formakh zemlepolzovaniya', *Bolshevik*, Nos.
19–20, 1927, p. 144.
21. This was rather different to the pre-revolutionary position as regards the
desire to leave the commune. But even this is not certain. Florinsky states that
'There is no factual evidence . . . to substantiate the widely accepted view that
the movement for severance from the commune and enclosures drew its main
support from the very rich and the very poor peasants . . .' (Florinsky, op. cit.,
vol. II, p. 1220). We are not certain, therefore, that the pre-revolutionary rich
peasants wanted to leave the commune as a rule; nor are we completely convinced that they wanted to stay in the commune after the revolution. This must
have varied enormously, according to local conditions. See also Taniuchi, op.
cit., p. 10.
22. Ustinov, op. cit., p. 147.
23. The author of this article is somewhat mixed up in his dates. The
fifteenth party conference took place in October–November 1926, and hence
before the results of the RKI inspection were known. Its resolution on agricultural policy is very interesting but has little to say on the subject of the rural
soviets (see: *KPSS v Rezolyutsiyakh i Resheniyakh*, vol. II, pp. 299–331). It was
the fourteenth party conference, held in April 1925, which had a long resolution
about reviving the rural soviets and their position in the countryside (*KPSS . . .*,
op. cit., pp. 133–8). The sixteenth party conference was not held until April

1929. It is therefore not quite clear to which party event the author is referring, though no doubt resolutions to this effect were passed frequently by various official bodies.

24. S. Zdanovich, 'Selskie Sovety i Zemelnye Obshchestva', in *Bolshevik*, No. 1928, 6, pp. 32–53.

25. Professor Pershin in *Selsko-Khozyaistvennaya Entsiklopediya*. Pershin's findings are borne out by N. Oganovsky in *Revolyutsiya Naoborot*, op. cit. Quoting figures for 1915, Oganovsky says that the 'process of destruction of communes in the non-black soil region was correctly evolutionary and directed from the east to the west; in the black soil region, it included more or less equally almost all the *raions* in the Povolzhie, fluctuating within the limits of 41–53 per cent, with the exception of Sredneie Povolzhie, where it was as low as 23 per cent. However, if one is to take into account only those commune members who left the commune of their own accord [the argument is about the law passed in 1910 which made some classes of commune peasants liable to leave the commune], then in the non-black soil regions we will see the same correctness, and in the black soil regions a contrary phenomenon: the largest number of those leaving the communes occurs in underpopulated *raions* of extensive cultivation Novo-rossiya and Nizhnee Povolzhie, and in the *raions* with a higher standard of living —Malorossiiskii and Central Agricultural—the percentage of commune leavers is much lower' (p. 100). Oganovsky wanted to show in this work that the commune was a better instrument of agriculture than allotment farming, and he concludes that '. . . one cannot say that leaving the commune is connected with a desire to improve peasant agriculture, still less that communizing all forms of agricultural work in small farms is the main medium of raising the productivity of labour' (ibid., p. 100).

Taniuchi, quoting R. N. Sharova, *Kollektivizatsiya Selskogo Khozyaistva v TsChO*, says that 'A commentator who directly observed rural Russia and participated in its life in the mid-1920's reported that all agricultural villages were more or less keeping communal relations. . . . Before the overall collectivi-zation in the central black earth oblast . . . 94·5 per cent of land held in common . . . was organized in communes. An investigation of TsSU in 1922 revealed that in the main agrarian regions more than 98–99 per cent of all the peasant land was in communes; even in western and north-western regions it was 65–75 per cent and in guberniyas of the central industrial oblast 80–95 per cent' (Taniuchi, op. cit., p. 23). It is impossible to assess, without further data, which figures are correct, or, indeed, whether both are correct, but Pershin's data applied to pre-revolutionary times, and Taniuchi's to the middle period of NEP, after the Land Code had worked this amazing transformation in the countryside. If the Land Code was responsible for organizing almost half of peasant households into tightly-bound communes, then the government's alarm about the strength of the peasants could have been justified.

26. Zdanovich, op. cit., p. 42. See also Taniuchi, op. cit., p. 27, 'Relations between the Rural Soviet and the Gathering'.

27. According to Zdanovich, this had been proved by A. A. Rzhanitsyn in his book *Vnutriselennoe Zemleustroistvo*, published in 1927. Unfortunately, I have been unable to locate a copy.

28. On the great powers of the commune and its agent, see also Taniuchi, op. cit., pp. 35–9.

8 'The country still suffers from an element of petty bourgeois habits'

The overall result of this vacillation was that there were two types of rural administration in the countryside throughout the 1920's: an ineffectual network of rural soviets, and a strong communal administration (see Appendix I, Fig. 2). The essential difficulty facing government bodies was that the network of the soviets could not be strengthened without pouring large funds into the countryside. Since this was impossible, theoreticians writing on the subject suggested various piecemeal remedies. One idea was that the land communes should be completely abolished. Another suggestion was that the rural soviets should become the administrative organs of the land communes (a point envisaged in the 1922 Land Code). There were also some people who suggested that the land commune should be

changed into a public body, the smallest unit of the Soviet State, while the rights and functions of the commune are blended into the rights and functions of the rural soviet.[1]

According to Zdanovich, none of these suggestions was realistic. The wish to abolish the land commune sprang from the fact that kulaks played an important part in them, to the detriment of progressive (i.e. pro-Communist) peasants. But the faction suggesting this forgot that the economic relations of small peasants could not be regulated by administrative means. Moreover, he argued, the suggestion was utopian, for the rural soviets had not the strength to lead an unorganized mass of peasantry. *Any policy of commune liquidation*

131

would mean the use of force against the medium peasants (Zdanovich's italics), a thing Lenin had always warned against.[2] Nor could force be used to introduce better agricultural methods. The idea that the rural soviets should be abolished and land communes put in their place was clearly anti-proletarian. The only possible way to proceed, as Zdanovich saw it, was to leave the land communes alone and take strong measures to turn the rural soviets into real centres for building socialism in the countryside. This could be done by allowing them some funds at present allocated to higher executive committees, and by transferring to them certain land commune functions. Even this would not be entirely satisfactory, because the transfer of all the communes' functions to the soviets would mean the death of the communes: 'The government should aim *at winning the communes over from the inside*, by organizing the labourers and medium peasants in them to diminish the kulak's influence' (my italics).[3] All the Soviet organizations—the rural soviets, the party and the Komsomol—should work towards this end. Though rich peasants had a great deal of influence in the communes, there were many cases of medium and poor peasants being very active in them. This showed that it was possible to win the land commune over with the help of party organizations.

Zdanovich suggested that the first step towards this end would be to strengthen the rural soviets. This could only be done by allowing them a budget of their own. Of 57,310 rural soviets, only 1,720 (or 3 per cent) had an independent budget in 1926–27.[4] Lack of financial independence exerted a negative influence on bringing the poor and medium peasants into soviet work. It often happened that they were asked to form sections and discuss matters of local importance, but the decisions they took could not be put into practice, as the rural soviet had no funds. The practical peasant said, 'We don't come to you for empty talk' (*Pustozvonit' k vam ne poydem*). And yet the survey carried out by the Central Committee commission showed that there was a sharp difference between the work of budget and non-budget soviets. For instance, the North Caucasus Executive Committee said in its report for 1926–27 that the greater number of local economic and cultural questions in most rural soviet districts were decided by a land commune gathering. The reason was that the rural soviets, unable to carry out such work as the repair of roads, bridges or fire-fighting equipment without funds, turned to the land commune for help. Why had the rural soviets no budget? The author

132

thought that there was a simple explanation: the Commissariat of Finances insisted that rural soviet budgets could be set up only as an experiment. Kuznetsov[5] wrote that 'differentiation of budgets must, for the time being, stop at the volost and regional level'. This point of view found expression in the decree about broadening the powers of local organs promulgated in 1927.[6] Article 146 of this decree stated that as the *volost* and regional budgets became stronger, the practice of giving independent budgets to rural soviets should be widened. In the bigger or richer villages this could be done even in the current year. But this same article set out the following conditions for independent budgets: a strong regional or *volost* budget was necessary; the rural soviet in question should be in a large village or group of villages; there should be sufficient local resources to cover a large proportion of the expenses on offices and measures undertaken to serve the locality. In view of such stringent conditions, the guberniya executive committees were very cautious about allowing independent budgets to rural soviets; some (i.e. Arkhangelsk and Kursk) did not allow any budgets at all. In Ivanovo-Voznessensk *oblast* there were twenty rural soviet budgets in 1925–26, and only sixteen in 1926–27; this despite the fact that experience has shown that where the budgets were tried they were fully successful. In the North Caucasus region, where there had been 259 independent budgets in 1925–26, there were already 787 in 1926–27. Their income grew by almost 50 per cent within the year, but it was balanced by greater expenditure. In both years, there had been no deficit.

While the central organs did not allow the rural soviets any money, the land communes had ample means to cover their own and even part of the soviets' expenses. The RKI inspection showed that, in contrast to the lack of funds in rural soviets, the land communes had their funds replenished not only from peasants' self-taxation but also through profit on the various enterprises they ran. These communal funds sometimes reached quite large proportions, and were used not only for the land commune's own needs but also to cover the needs of the rural soviet, even to the extent of covering the payment of debts contracted by the rural soviet. As an example the budget of the Olgin land commune in North Ossetin *oblast* was quoted from the RKI report[7] (see next page).

There were many more examples of such budgets, but this one showed satisfactorily that while peasant self-taxation covered quite a few of the expenses which (had there been any definite ruling on it)

133

Income for 1925–26 (by self-taxation)	2,679 roubles
Expenses for 1925–26:	
Four months' salary for clerk	100
Salary for the militiaman	65
Salary for the scribe	40
Lighting for the rural soviet	10
Salary for the caretaker (school and soviet)	40
Settling land distribution questions	1,150
Rent for reading room	50
Rent for ambulance room	42
Fee for agronomist	42
Salary for the soviet's treasurer	50
Fee for forest inspection	840
Forest work	250
Total expenses	2,679 roubles

would logically belong to the soviet, it was the expenses connected with the commune's economy that were really large.

The sums mentioned in Olgin are not very big, but in richer and larger communes the situation was similar. In the Ivanovo-Voznessensk region, the village of Pershino in Teikovskii *uezd* had an income in one year of 3,000 roubles from its enterprises, and collected another 2,400 roubles by self-taxation.[8] This was not an isolated case but one of many, stated Zdanovich. All this merely reinforced the necessity for independent budgets for rural soviets. In answer to those who said that there were no sources of income for them, Zdanovich pointed to self-taxation and income from local enterprises; these sources by-passed the rural soviets and went to organizations which were hostile to the government; it was quite common for commune income to go to the local kulaks, or to be spent on drinking at a gathering. If the soviets had under their management mills, hulling mills, smithies and local forests as well as ponds, market places and similar enterprises, they would get sufficient income from them to satisfy local cultural and economic needs now taken care of by the land communes. As a first step, therefore, it would be necessary to deprive the peasants of the local means of production; as it was well known in the countryside that he who controlled mills and commons was well on the way to controlling the peasants, it would be half the battle won. This was not enough, however. Only the rural soviets with their own budget had the status of a corporate body (while all land communes had it by law). This meant that the great

134

majority of rural soviets could not own property, arrange trading transactions or sign a contract; they could not carry on any economic activity, and they could not even use the funds allowed them by *volost'* executive committees for economic purposes. This should be changed immediately, as should the law which did not allow the rural soviet to control the actions of the land commune.

Last but not least in this catalogue of malfunction came the complaint about the lack of distinction in the villages between the general gathering and land commune gathering. This is perhaps not very surprising, for the central organs themselves seem to have had difficulty in differentiating between the organs of the land commune and the rural soviet. A decree on this matter had been published by the All-Russian Executive Committee in 1927; unfortunately it gave no results, and produced only confusion in local offices.[9] The reason was that the rural population had been used from pre-revolutionary times to discuss communal matters in common, and did not know how to divide problems into land commune problems and other problems. In addition, the general gathering attracted only some 15–20 per cent of the local population, while the land commune gathering attracted 60–80 per cent of the population. This was natural, for every peasant was interested in the first place in the commune from which he received land for cultivation. Zdanovich thought that if the communes were treated in the same way as factories in towns the situation would be simpler. The factory was the lowest unit of production and so was the land commune. The only difference consisted in the fact that the workers were members of one class and the commune included poor as well as rich peasants. If the right to vote was taken away from the kulaks, matters would change for the better. This, however, could only be done by more party work, and by way of infiltration, for administrative measures would never succeed in breaking the power of the communes.[10]

The authors of the various remedies quoted above had every right to feel worried about rural administration. According to original sources, it was both ineffectual and corrupt. One report from the provinces describes the work of general gatherings and the conduct of election campaigns in strong terms. No pre-election campaign to the soviets took place because at that time there were two non-party peasant conferences taking place in the *uezd* and it would have been impossible to hold this additional campaign as well. The preparatory campaign was generally weak at the local level.[11]

... there was inadequate preparation for carrying out the re-election campaign up to the time of the arrival of the [election] agents; for instance, lists of people deprived of electoral rights were not drawn up, and no steps whatsoever were taken to draw up lists of electors by name. Directives on these two tasks were given in good time before the arrival of the agents, and as regards the drawing up of lists of those disfranchised, such directives were given several times in the course of the present year, from the very beginning of the year.

In the second place, the notification about the course of the campaign was not on time, and there was a careless and inattentive attitude on the part of volost executive committees and particularly agents, in drawing up reports and sending them out at the set time. In the third place, there was insufficient contact in the work of carrying out re-elections on the part of organizations concerned.

This carelessness and lack of interest by the authorities themselves showed in the election results: in general, says the report, the population was well disposed to the elections. Peasants took an interest and participated actively. However, in some *raions* this did not happen, for instance

in Ponikovkii, Mozhaikovskii and part of Mikhailovskii—Mostovaya volost—and in the raions Glukhovskii, Zemtsovskii and Leninskii. In these raions, because insufficient numbers of electors—34 to 35 per cent—turned up the first time, elections were held a second time. It must be noted that the repeated elections in Ponikovskii, Mozhaikovskii and part of Mikhailovskii rural soviets showed a much lower percentage of attendance—17–20 per cent—which served as a reason for confirming the first election results in these raions.

In other volosti a much higher percentage of the population participated in the elections: 39 per cent to 56 per cent. In some [electoral] districts, electoral participation reached 85 per cent; on average, electoral participation in the uezd was 46·8 per cent. This figure is lower than the actual figure (51 per cent) but since it had already been accepted by the TUK [the electoral commission] it is being left. The increase in voting figures in comparison with last year was 12 per cent. Bad weather, owing to which work in the fields was still going on, played a great part in lowering the attendance. Eleven per cent of women voted this year, as against 5 per cent last year.

The report goes on to say that 1,817 people were elected to the rural soviets, 38 per cent of whom were former soviet members, 8 per cent women, 4 per cent members or candidate members of the party, and 6 per cent Komsomols. Party membership in the rural soviets increased by 50 per cent, and 3 per cent more peasants were elected. The membership of poor peasants in rural soviets decreased by

136

11 per cent, medium peasants increased by 14 per cent and prosperous peasants increased by 1·3 per cent. (The party membership
was rather higher than average for the whole of the RSFSR; the
percentage of more prosperous peasants was not unduly high, for the
report says that Belskii *uezd* was a prosperous one.) Nevertheless,
the work of the rural soviets was poor:

The meetings of the soviets are held irregularly. In place of fortnightly
meetings, only 32 per cent of the meetings were held. These are the percentages for separate volosti:

Belsko-Prigorodnaya	54
Baturinskaya	14
Verkhovie-Malyshkovo	38
Glukhovskaya	23
Zemtsovskaya	87
Leninskaya	50
Mostovskaya	22
Nelidovskaya	39
Selishchenskaya	57
Kholmovskaya	69

The greatest number of meetings was held in the following volosti:
Zemtsovskaya, Kholmovskaya, Selishchenskaya and Belsko-Prigorodnaya;
the smallest number of meetings in the following: Baturinskaya, Mostovskaya and Glukhovskaya.

While the soviet meetings were irregular, the general gatherings
were in an even worse state. They were held very erratically. In the
whole territory of the *uezd* there were 115 general gatherings. This
meant that one gathering was held every nine months. The biggest
number of meetings took place in Zemtsovskaya, Kholmovskaya and
Leninskaya *volost'*; the smallest number in Verkhovie-Malyshkovo,
Mostovskaya and Belsko-Prigorodnaya *volosti*. We are not given the
numbers of attendance of general gatherings, but the report states
that there were soviets in which meetings were held with an attendance lower than that required by law. In such cases steps would be
taken to ensure regular attendance at meetings by the members of
rural soviets.[11]

A year later, in the neighbouring *okrug* of Velikie Luki, the party
bureau noted a number of deficiencies in the work of the rural
soviets and in the leadership of general gatherings.[12] There was
insufficient activity by peasants and agricultural labourers in the rural
soviets. General gatherings were called for the whole of the rural
soviet area but the peasants were not notified in time; many did not

137

turn up for the gathering. General gatherings were called as though they were campaigns—there was no planned convocation. To remedy these shortcomings, the bureau ordered that 'Sections of rural soviets must travel to distant villages and discuss local problems on the spot':

It must be put to the raion committees, the raion executive committees' fractions and the union of agricultural labourers that as many agricultural labourers as possible must be drawn into the work of the sections; it must also be ensured that agricultural labourers and poor peasants should have greater influence at general gatherings of the peasants.

As regards the field of improving the work of general gatherings, it is necessary:

(a) To forbid finally the convocation of general gatherings over the whole territory of the rural soviet; these must be called solely in pre-scribed electoral districts. The peasants must be well informed about the place and time of the gathering, and about the problems which are to be discussed . . .

(b) To secure that the rural soviets inform the peasants at the gatherings fully about the implementation of previous decisions of the gather-ings, and about measures taken for their implementation, in order that the population should not be of the opinion that their wishes are not given any attention. . . . That general gatherings must be utilized in every possible way to inculcate cultural and collective-economy principles in the countryside.[12]

It is not difficult to see from the above fragments that the de-ficiencies of the rural soviets lay not only in bad personnel, nor in the peasants' unwillingness to lose work-days in order to attend meet-ings. They were of a more fundamental nature. The apparatus of meetings, conferences and gatherings held by party organizations, non-party *activs*, co-operative organizations, soviet organizations, trade union organizations, and other institutional bodies, was so widely developed that in the very nature of things it was impossible to run so many activities with any degree of efficiency. In addition, the soviet apparatus (at least in some localities, though the situation must have been duplicated in other districts too) lacked the man-power or the efficiency to prepare such elementary materials as lists of voters. Other practices seem equally dubious. The repeat elections which turned out to have a smaller attendance than the first; the subsequent confirmation of the results of the first elections; the absence of lists of disfranchised persons; the irregular convocation of election meetings—none of these could be eradicated by a simple improvement of the rural soviets' personnel.

138

Nevertheless, this was almost the only remedy which was being offered. The author of the article quoted earlier[10] suggested that to increase the importance of rural soviets the pay of their workers should be raised. The majority of guberniya executive committees, he stated, admitted the poor quality of rural soviet staff, both elective and technical. The Arkhangelsk guberniya executive committee reported:

The permanent staff—chairman and secretary or clerk—in the majority of rural soviets is still weak, the chairman in particular. The majority of the apparatus are inefficient because of the technical illiteracy of the secretaries, and their quick turnover, due to low salaries.

During one year in Penza guberniya, in 807 rural soviets 123 chairmen and 130 secretaries (that is, 14 per cent of the total) left work of their own wish; 58 chairmen and 51 secretaries were dismissed because of dishonesty or for other reasons.

If any more proof was needed that the state of rural administration was unsatisfactory, it was forthcoming in another work published at the same period.[13] This book confirmed all the points made by Zdanovich and reinforced them with many more case studies. On the financial issue, the author stated that the budget for the USSR allocated 16 million roubles to the rural soviets (year not stated), while according to the Commissariat of Finances the combined land commune budgets stood at 80 million roubles. The RKI put this sum even higher, at 100 million roubles.[14] Many communes kept the services going by their contributions, in Voronezh guberniya some land communes paid for the postal services, for education and for the soviet itself. In some villages the land commune ratified the minutes of the rural soviet, which was against the law. In villages where the richer peasants had more influence, things were difficult for the poorer peasants. In one village a forest was divided by the land commune gathering: the richer peasants got one share each, the poor ones a quarter to half a share each:

The chairman of the soviet belongs to the ruling elite. He stated that the poor ones would be satisfied with their share; if given a full share, they would not know what to do with it.[15]

Unless the communes' funds were taken away scandal upon scandal would result, warned the author. Some land communes spent their money on shocking things. The Bezobrazov land commune in Penza guberniya spent its money on an Easter mass, entertaining a visiting commission, and giving somebody a bribe. This was not an isolated case; payments to the clergy for 'rain-making' services were often recorded, and so on.[16]

Events such as those led Molotov to say at the fifteenth party congress that unless collectivization of the villages was implemented, the slogan 'All power to the soviets' would lose its force. But collectivization must be carried out very carefully, warned the author, so that the masses will be carried by the party, instead of turning against it. Two experiments in this direction were already under way: one in the Ukraine, where the decisions of the land commune gathering had to be confirmed by the rural soviet; the other in the German Volga Republic, where all the communes' income was given to the soviets, the commune officials had been abolished, and their functions given to soviet officials. The Ukrainian experience showed that such a partial measure was inadequate, for the soviet depended on the commune, which controlled its finances. In the German Republic the officers of the land commune were still being elected unofficially, and money was being raised outside the budget.

In this matter of early experimentation we have the confirmation of a modern authority. This author recounts the many attempts between 1926 and 1928 to induce the peasants to collectivize: the setting up of grain winnowing stations, which cleaned the poorer peasants' grain free or on credit; credits granted to poor peasants' co-operatives to buy tractors; also an interesting and symptomatic campaign to take tractors away from richer peasants and give them to *kolkhozes*. This last started in the Ukraine and in Siberia as early as April 1928.[17]

All the measures the government undertook, or professed to undertake, were completely inadequate in dealing with the situation. The root cause lay not so much in the hostility of the population to the Soviet administration (as Taniuchi suggests) as in the inefficiency of that administration. It stemmed mainly from the government's failure to pay enough attention to local administration in the years up to 1925, and in its lack of financial aid after 1925. A massive effort at training able local administrators, and a big outlay on financing local offices, would not have produced a democratically governed countryside—but it might have helped to build up an efficient administration. In this way, the tragedy of 1929–30 might have been averted.[18]

The opposition of the Commissariat of Finances to any increase in
140

spending on provincial administration frustrated the improvements. Nevertheless, this was not the only reason for the neglect of local administration. A great deal of blame must be attached to the mystique with which the soviets had been endowed by Lenin as organs of real popular government. The Soviet government believed (because it was convenient to believe so, and because it had been stated by the leader that it must be so) that there was intrinsic virtue in the administration by the soviets, and that, given time and a mysterious element of faith, their administration would begin to work properly. Hence any steps which were taken were designed not to improve the administration directly, but to improve it by improving the citizens. One of these means was drawing more peasants into the party. In a memorandum (classed, for unknown reasons, as secret: far more disturbing news was disseminated at open party meetings) one of the regional party bureaux called for a new assessment of party membership:[19]

Having listened to the report about practical measures on the part of raion committees and cells as regards the drawing into the party of workers, agricultural labourers and peasants from the plough—the Bureau of the Okrug Committee notes the following deficiencies in this work:

(a) Up to now the discussion on the growth of the party organization . . . in order to draw into the party new cadres of active workers, farm labourers and peasants from the plough, has been non-existent in raion committees and particularly in cells. As a rule, the cells approach this question only when they discuss voluntary applications for membership.

(b) The growth of party organizations from the ranks of workers is not developing fast enough in comparison with the former period (in two months—September–October—nineteen people were accepted, and these were in the majority unqualified workers; out of nineteen workers only two were qualified, with a short trade union membership).

(v) In the cells, and also often in raion committees, the members accepted as peasants are often officials or semi-officials, which shows, on one hand, that the cells have not understood the directives of the party in the field of regulating party growth; and on the other, that the cells are unable to define the social standing of the people applying for the membership of the party.

(g) The cells and sometimes the raion committees do not always take financial status into sufficient account; they over-emphasize the pre-revolutionary services and social activities of those who are accepted into the party, and do not always follow the principle of individual selection, which results in a large drop-out at the okrug committee

141

level (70 per cent drop-out among peasants and 96 per cent drop-out among officials).

(*d*) There is not enough information about those who have applied—particularly as regards their financial standing and social activity—which creates difficulties and unnecessary delays in acceptance and in the final formulation to the okrug committee.

Because of the above, the Bureau orders that:

(1) Practical measures be taken to draw into the party workers, agricultural labourers, poor peasants and revolutionary medium peasants.
(2) Their applications to join should be encouraged in group discussions.
(3) Non-party activists should be drawn into cell meetings.
(4) In the two succeeding years the numbers of workers and agricultural labourers in the okrug party organizations should be doubled.
(5) The peasants' trade unions and groups of poor peasants be used to increase the insignificant percentage (1·4 per cent) of agricultural labourers who are at present party members.
(6) That it should be made more difficult to admit white-collar workers and semi-white-collar elements to the party.
(7) That the general level of party activity be raised.

The party's concern to recruit peasants, particularly landless labourers, was the direct consequence of the malfunction of rural administration. We shall cite evidence further on (see chapter 10) that in this particular district it was already too late to improve the relations between the party and the poor peasants. Years of neglect, bad executive work and oppressive taxation had set the poor peasants against the government. But there was still some hope that workers from the factory bench might be induced to become good Communists, instead of admitting officials with only a distant peasant or worker background—in fact, the directive orders that it should be made more difficult to admit white-collar and semi-white-collar workers to the party. The party directives underline the essential unity of these two elements, the peasants and the workers, and with good reason. Not only in Smolensk guberniya, but all over the territory of former European Russia, the NEP measures had created an even more flexible type of worker than had existed before the war. The central party authorities noted this fact in late 1926, when the fifteenth party conference passed a resolution on unemployment. It read:

Notwithstanding a significant increase in industry . . . which led to an increase in the numbers of workers and officials (from 6,035,300 in 1925 to 7,700,600 in 1926 . . .), unemployment not only has not decreased, it even continues to grow. On 1 April 1925 there were 992,900 trade union

142

members unemployed. On 1 April 1926 there were 1,182,500 trade union members unemployed—an increase of 19·1 per cent. For some categories of labour (labourers, servants, badly qualified office workers and so on) unemployment threatens to become chronic in the near future, because of *rural over-population and the unbroken influx of work-hands from the countryside into the towns* [my italics]. This puts before the party . . . the task of deciding the general problem of how to use the labour of the surplus population.

The party . . . must lead the most decisive struggle against favouritism and nepotism in hiring and dismissing workers and officials, and must show support for all measures of . . . Soviet organs directed at fighting unemployment.[20]

This was a succinct statement of the situation obtaining at the end of 1926.

We have already considered in chapter 6 how serious the problem of unemployment was in the cities, and how it threatened to upset the delicate balance with which the government was hoping to retain power. This chapter has attempted to show the ephemeral nature of power in the countryside. It now remains to see by what means the government intended to retain its hold over the proletariat, and how it planned to increase industrial productivity—the second factor absolutely necessary for the new State to survive.

NOTES

1. This suggestion had been made by N. Sukhanov in his article 'Obshchina v sovetskom agrarnom zakonodatelstve', *Osnovnye Nachala Zemleustroistva*, p. 102. See also M. Kubanin, *Obshchina pri Diktature Proletariata*, ibid., pp. 105–24. For a fuller treatment of the legal problem, and proof that this idea would have been completely fruitless, see Taniuchi, op. cit., pp. 46–9.

2. Zdanovich, op. cit., p. 47.

3. Ibid., p. 53.

4. Ibid., p. 49.

5. The author is referring to an article by S. M. Kuznetsov, 'K prorabotke pyatiletnogo perspektivnogo plana', in *Vestnik Finansov*, No. 5, 1927. In this article Kuznetsov warned against over-optimistic planning which envisaged considerable rises in workers' earnings, and stressed the necessity of anti-inflationary measures. He was also against the considerable rise in the State budget which was planned for the following five years. As far as local budgets were concerned, he had this to say: 'Local budgets ought to develop on the basis of decrees which are in existence now' (p. 9). That is, while he was against basic changes, he had no objection to development of the existing local budgets.

6. Sobranie Uzakonenii RSFSR, 1927, No. 79.

7. Zdanovich, op. cit., pp. 50–1. For other figures, see Taniuchi, op. cit., pp. 57–8.

8. Zdanovich, op. cit., p. 51.

9. Zdanovich cites a decree of the VTsIK (op. cit., p. 52). I understand that

he refers to the decree on land communes published on 7 April, 1927, No. 172. This decree conferred on the rural soviets exactly the same rights as those which the land communes already enjoyed. Since this is not exactly a differentiation of functions, it is not to be wondered at that the local offices were confused. Taniuchi mentions 'the law of the village soviets', op. cit., p. 31, and notes its ambiguity.

10. Zdanovich, op. cit., p. 53.

11. Smolensk archives, reel No. 3, Smolensk, 1926, WKP 25: 'Report of the Belskii uezd executive committee for the period 1 October 1925 to 1 August 1926', signed by the chairman of the executive committee, Tsyganov.

12. Smolensk archives, reel No. 4, Smolensk, 1927, WKP 30: 'Protocol No. 15 of the meeting of the Bureau of Velikolutskii Okruzhkom of VKP (b) on 28 December 1927.'

13. M. Rezunov, *Selskie Sovety i Zemelnye Obshchestva*, Moscow, 1928. This book provides an excellent commentary on the preoccupation in party circles with the power of the communes. It relies heavily on the findings of the R K I survey and in addition draws fully on little-known local newspapers and bulletins. The author exhibits a strong anti-peasant bias, which should not prejudice one against his findings, for the factual material presented is of unique interest.

14. Ibid., p. 12.

15. A Sapunov, 'Vzaimootnosheniya skhodov i selsovetov' in *Vlast' Sovetov*, No. 21, 1927, p. 22.

16. Rezunov, op. cit., p. 52.

17. V. P. Danilov, op. cit., p. 315.

18. For the direct influence of inefficient local administration on the crisis of 1929, see chapters 10 and 11.

19. Smolensk archives, reel No. 4, Smolensk, 1927, WKP 30. *Secret.* 'Appendix to protocol No. 11 of the meeting of the Bureau of Velikolutskii Okruzhkom of V K P (b) on 3 December 1927' (resolution about practical measures on drawing workers and peasants into the party).

20. 'KPSS v rezolyutsiakh . . .', op. cit., vol 2, 'Fifteenth conference of V K P (b)', October–November 1926, pp. 323–4.

9 'All power is in the hands of the proletariat now'

Nineteen twenty-seven, the year of Stalin's victory over the Left Opposition, showed increasingly schizophrenic tendencies in the government. Up to then it was generally agreed, in keeping with Lenin's realism, that things would get a great deal worse before they got better. Now, the worse matters got the better they appeared to be in the words of the leaders. In an interview with the foreign press, Kuibyshev asserted that the seven-hour working day, then officially introduced, would not be harmful to the interests of socialist production:

In the USSR [he said] socialism is not a future dream but the real thing, which is being created not only for the future generations but for the present one. Our building [of socialism] must be accompanied by a systematic improvement in the conditions of the working class and the raising of its labour consciousness.[1]

What was the position of those workers who were fortunate enough to find employment in the 1920's? Here the whole situation was influenced by the fact, noted earlier, that there were few industrial jobs but a great demand for them. This made for fluctuations in the number of workers: old workers were dismissed on the slightest pretext and new ones hired without a thought of what would happen should a reduction in the labour force be ordered from above. And the reductions were ordered with monotonous regularity all through the period of NEP. Until 1925 a worker might find employment in the few private factories that were still allowed to exist. But from

145

OLGA A. NARKIEWICZ

1925 onwards the number of private industrial enterprises grew steadily fewer. The main reasons were restrictions on fuel supplies, raw materials and trade designed specifically to reduce the number of private factories. Thus in 1924–25 the percentage of workers employed in private industry was 2·1 per cent, and in 1926–27 it was 1·7 per cent. It is also possible that the percentage was reduced artificially, because State-owned industry was expanding; but the small number of workers taken on by private factories in 1926–27 —just 3,000 people—out of an estimated total of 50,000—shows that this would be just sufficient for replacements.[2]

Conditions in industry as a whole are difficult to establish, because for many years Soviet writers have been forced to quote party resolutions, or statements such as the following:

Socialist industry . . . not only brought hundreds of thousands of new workers into industry, raising their pay every year (the pay has already, on average, become higher than the pre-war level), but also attained success in setting up a series of new production units, which free our economy from dependence on the capitalist countries.[3]

But certain monographs have appeared in recent years, which allow us to study not only the conditions of labour under NEP but also the negative influence on the working class produced by the devious and uncertain policies of the central planners.

One such study surveys the labour situation in the Ukraine.[4] Ukrainian industry had suffered heavily during the civil war, and the labour crisis was particularly acute when conditions returned to normal. It was considered essential to apply Trotsky's militarization of labour scheme, under which some 80,000 workers were forcibly returned to industry. As soon as they returned the introduction of NEP, and the *khozraschet* which came in its wake, made it imperative to close uneconomic factories, and the numbers of the proletariat fell again towards the end of 1922. But the workers who had managed to stay in industry were gradually getting a better deal. In the middle of 1923 their pay had, on average, already reached 76·2 per cent of pre-war levels, and in the sugar and food industries it had even surpassed them.[5] This improvement did not last long. In 1924 a wholesale closing down of factories during the over-production crisis, a reduction of workers, and the reform of labour exchanges took place in quick succession. These developments caused unemployment on a scale never before experienced in the Ukraine. The workers did not give in without a fight: there was bitter opposi-

146

tion to the closing down of factories and the dismissals. To avoid open rioting, a vestige of consultation with the workers was resorted to:

All questions of dismissing or transferring workers were decided only with the knowledge and acceptance of the trade unions. . . . The party cells were watching the correct reduction of the workers' numbers, and allowed no divergence from Soviet labour laws. For example, the party cell of the Kramatorsk metallurgical works was helped in the reduction of workers in 1924 by shop stewards [*tsekhorgi*], trade union organizers, the departmental administration, and cadre workers. All questions . . . were first discussed in a broadened meeting of the bureau of the party cell, and then at a workers' meeting. Altogether 800 workers were dismissed from the factory, mostly peasants who came to town for seasonal work.

The party organization's fear of the consequences of the dismissals can be seen clearly in the velvet-gloved way in which the measure was carried out; and the final sacrifice of 'mostly peasants' shows the orientation of the policy.

In other cases the party cell was strong enough, or indignant enough, to oppose the dismissals ordered from above. In dockyard No. 1 at Odessa the dismissals started in October 1923. In 1924 a reduction in the number of workers was enforced twice:

In connection with this the [party] cell pressed the higher organs urgently to increase the established number of workers, and also to furnish the dockyard with necessary repair materials. At the end of 1924, the cell, whose secretary was comrade Malnikov, was at last successful in having a normal complement of workers approved.

Elsewhere the party cells demanded that factories which were scheduled for closure should be put on a shortened working week instead. The party collective at the mines of Krivoi Rog

in the autumn of 1924 stood up in defence of the workers, whom the management of the mines planned to dismiss for the winter. The bureau of the collective appealed to the okrug party committttee, and with the committee's support obliged the mines' management . . . to retain all the qualified workers.[6]

Party intervention has always been interpreted as injurious to the interests of the economy and as interfering with the powers of the management. It is at least arguable that the party cell, being on the spot and knowing local conditions better than the central planners, had not some right on its side. The human misery such dismissals must have caused, particularly in winter, need not perhaps be dwelt on, although one sometimes feels that the economic slant given to all industrial rationalization is sometimes over-stressed. But even from a strictly economic point of view, shutting mines down for the winter is a particularly expensive and harmful process. In factories, the machinery rusts if not in use. In mines the additional risk of flooding, caving in and similar disasters rises steeply during a long shut-down. These were the things the men in the localities knew about, and to which central managements seem to have been indifferent.

The effect of the shut-downs was not slow in making itself felt. In 1913 there had been 642,300 workers in the Ukraine; by 1926, after nine years of Soviet rule, there were only 607,900—almost 40,000 fewer. None of this decrease could be ascribed to mechanization or labour-saving machinery; on the contrary, the wearing out of machines and the low level of skills required many more workers than had been employed before the revolution. But this was not all. In 1913, 56,200 adolescents worked in industry: 8·8 per cent of the total labour force. In 1926 there were only 27,400 adolescents, or 5·9 per cent of the total. This was not fortuitous. Because of the laws protecting young people, the factories hired them unwillingly and dismissed them at every opportunity. Though a special quota for adolescents had been established by law, it was constantly disregarded. Instead of inducing factory managements to keep to the quota, it was suggested that the laws giving young workers certain privileges (such as no night work and longer holidays in unhealthy occupations) should be abolished, along with special schooling for young people.[7] Thus the only possible way of training new cadres of workers for an expanding industry was not only neglected, it was positively discouraged. Here again, the results could be seen immediately. A survey of young workers in the coal mines of the Kuznetskii basin stated that:

The survey of miners in Leninsk-Kuznetskii in July 1926 showed that the basic group of miners consisted of workers who had come into industry before the revolution and before the introduction of NEP. Young workers who entered the industry in 1923–26 represented barely one-sixth of all the workers. The filling up of gaps in the cadres came from the peasant population and workers from other industries.[8]

Not only was this policy purely regressive in that it neglected to train new cadres of workers, but it also had a frank bias against youth. When another reduction in the ranks of the workers was announced in 1927 (this time called a 'socialist rationalization'), young workers were again the first to be dismissed. Again there was bitter opposition to the reductions among the rank and file of the workers, which expressed itself in rioting (its extent is not specified) and the destruction of new machines. The proletarian youth of Moscow, the Urals, the Ukraine and Georgia 'openly said that the rationalization is being carried out at the expense of young workers'. Describing the disorders, the author says disingenuously that the workers 'did not understand the difference between a capitalist and a socialist rationalization.'[9]

There is nothing new in the fact that the workers were dissatisfied during the earlier stages of NEP. There were widespread disorders in 1925.[10] But the interesting thing about these disorders is that they happened at a much later period and that their background was partially due to mechanization of the industry. Most authorities have always ascribed the workers' dissatisfaction to the high rates of piecework established by the planning authorities and to the low rates of pay. Carr himself says of the 1925 riots that 'The precise causes of the trouble were difficult to discover'. It seems more likely that the real causes were more complex. The sorry conditions of work in the factories no doubt contributed to the general dissatisfaction among the proletariat. But we have already seen that even this was considered preferable to the spectre of unemployment. The workers who had jobs, however badly paid, were in an incomparably better position than those who were unemployed. It would seem clear that just as during the period of workers' control soon after the revolution the main industrial troubles were caused by the peasants employed in industry, so it was during the later years of NEP. This was pointed out earlier when the government's policy towards the proletariat was discussed. It is fully borne out by both contemporary and present-day Soviet writers on the subject of labour.

Industrial unrest was a serious problem for the government. But low productivity was far more serious in its long-term consequences. Many inquiries were held into the nature of both, and the general findings were that the neglected state of machinery, the low level of literacy and poor management accounted for the industry's unsatisfactory output. This is perhaps best illustrated in the rate at which industrial accidents rose during the 1920's. To take but one example, in 1925 the overall rate of accidents in Azerbaidzhan was 58 per 1,000 workers. In Azerbaidzhan's oil industry the rate was 137 per

1,000, and in some cases—for machinery workers, borers and constructors—159–166 per 1,000 workers. The rise of the accident rate and the expected further increase were the subject of a trade union inquiry. The inquiry found that the main reasons for the high accident rate were lack of proper supervision by management, worn-out machines, bad installations and bad organization of work. Other factors aggravated the situation. The workers themselves were to blame for one-third of the accidents. It was agreed that the trade unions must convince them that certain elementary safety precautions must be taken:

> . . . one must somehow influence the consciousness of the workers. . . . They must be made to realize that, for instance, special glasses guard their eyes from splinters, swarf and glare; that guards over transmission belts, saws, etc. (the workers often take them off—'they stop us from working') are not a whim of the machine's designer nor of the technical inspector; that drying damp, dirty clothing in the bedroom, lying down on beds in dirty boots, not airing rooms which are fitted with ventilators, or spitting on the floor, is not only 'uncultured' but also bad for their health.[11]

Elsewhere the situation was not much better. A statistician writing in 1925 had started an inquiry into the rate of accidents over the whole of the USSR; he was obliged to give up, since most of the statistics were missing. However, he did receive statistics from the Moscow guberniya department of labour protection, which stated that while in 1912 the rate of accidents had been 33·3 per 1,000 workers, by 1924 this had risen 2·3 times—an amazingly high rate for one of the most civilized and industrialized areas of the USSR.[12]

It was difficult to expect the peasants, used to sharing their hovels with their cattle in winter, to behave otherwise when the highest authorities showed an amazing lack of understanding of the primary needs of industry. The chemical industry had always been one of the least developed in tsarist Russia. The Soviet government failed to recognize that this industry formed the basis of many modern industrial processes, and neglected it accordingly. Workers in the industry were particularly badly qualified, with the result that whereas in 1913 the percentage of production workers was 54·3 per cent, the rest being concerned with maintenance, in 1923–24 production workers constituted only 44·6 per cent, with a great loss of productivity. There were no qualified fitters, solderers nor boilermen, in place of each of whom several unqualified men had to be employed.[13] The increase in machine fatigue made repair work both frequent and unavoidable. Factories had to train these maintenance workers themselves, owing to the general shortage of mechanics. In two large chemical factories only 36 out of 236 trainees were learning chemical processes; the rest were learning maintenance and repair. A similar situation obtained in every other chemical factory.[14] In 1927 the percentage of qualified workers in the chemical industry was the lowest of all industries, including not only heavy industry but also those processing cotton, flax and hides. The percentage of qualified workers was 25 per cent of the total; among those directly servicing chemical machinery it was even lower—17·2 per cent.[15] The percentage of qualified workers fell still lower in 1927–28. The unqualified workers were mainly peasants arriving straight from the villages, and the rate of illiteracy was high. In 1926 15·7 per cent of all men and 19·5 per cent of all women employed in the chemical industry were illiterate.[16] This state of affairs in a dangerous and complex industry showed in the rate of accidents. While the general rise in the accident rate over the whole of the Soviet Union in 1926–27 was 74 per cent (in itself staggering enough), in the chemical industry it was 103·4 per cent for the same period. Even the officials employed in the central committee of the Chemical Trade Union were obliged to admit that this rise was the result not so much of better accident registration as of a great influx of untrained workers from the countryside.[17]

The official reaction to this state of affairs was interesting. In 1927 the first Congress of Workers in the Chemical Industry took place. The main argument at the congress revolved round the question whether workers needed any special training to work in the industry. The official report reflected the negative views which prevailed in the discussion:

The chemical industry is so diversified in its use of plant . . . and so uncomplicated in the manipulation of this plant that there is no need for special knowledge about the way in which to approach a pressure gauge.

Because of this, the report went on, 'Factory training for the chemical industry proper is, as a rule, unnecessary.' And to make its meaning quite plain, one of the delegates explained:

As far as the preparation of a qualified labour force for the chemical industry is concerned, it is doubtful whether any special skill is necessary, apart from a general level of reasonable development.[18]

It should be mentioned here that this highly dangerous proposition

L

151

was condemned by the delegates from VSNKh and Glavkhim. Nevertheless, resolutions against special training were accepted at the congress and were generally adopted in the industry. The first five-year plan found the chemical industry completely unprepared. In 1929 more than 12,000 out of 28,000 workers had no qualifications. Of the remaining 16,000 only 1,417 had had up to three years' training.[19] No doubt a survey of other industries would reveal that similar policies were carried out elsewhere too.[20]

The general result of government measures during the period of NEP was the institutionalization of a remarkable phenomenon: in place of a small but relatively stable and trained working class there appeared a massive, illiterate, unreliable and fluctuating class of semi-peasant semi-workers. These people, whose appearance on the scene was again the direct consequence of the agricultural policy, must at first have seemed preferable to an established proletariat, both for economic reasons—since they could be paid lower wages and asked to work longer hours—and for political reasons, since they lacked the traditions of class struggle against exploitation. But their appearance coincided with a decisive turn in State policy. In 1927 it was finally decided that industrialization was the only way out of Russia's dilemma. The disaster which followed in the wake of the first five-year plan must be attributed in great measure to this lack of a properly trained work-force. The Soviet government realized the danger of the situation fairly early in the years of NEP, but instead of halting this marked deterioration it allowed the process to go on. The improvement in the workers' qualifications was to be attained not by proper training nor by raising their standard of living—such measures would have been too expensive. Instead it was decided to resort to an extension of the institution of councils, though by that time rural soviets were already thoroughly discredited, and town soviets had become simple executive offices.

One of the forms these measures took was that of meetings of workers' delegates to discuss production problems; hence the whole movement was called 'production meetings'. Where several factories congregated to discuss problems jointly, the meeting received the name of 'production conference'. What it was hoped to achieve through these meetings is not entirely clear, though at a later stage, as will be seen, they were given a specific task. The beginning of the production meetings is shrouded in mystery. The first meeting, said to have been held in 1924, was probably called on the local initiative

152

of a party or trade union organization. In 1925, 17 per cent of industrial workers in Leningrad took part in production meetings. During 1925, 34,000 workers in Moscow and 13,000 workers in Tver attended production conferences. The frequency and size of these meetings can be assessed from the fact that during September 1925 fifty-three such meetings were held in one factory and 1,483 delegates took part in them. There were thirty-one meetings in October, with 847 delegates, and only nine in November, with 419 delegates.[21] Elsewhere the impetus seems to have been smaller; party committees from Baku, the Urals, Leningrad, Sverdlovsk and other places reported that party, trade union and government organs did not pay enough attention to the need for these meetings. The workers were keen enough to attend them, but the managements were resolutely opposed to them almost everywhere. This is understandable in view of the loss of production the meetings caused, coupled with the general nuisance they created. At a Moscow party meeting many managers expressed the view that the production meetings would be 'forced to die out'[22]—another way of saying that their days were numbered. The party organizations which were not directly concerned with production thought otherwise. The party committee of Stalinsk *okrug* wrote in 1926 that:

Such reasoning is extremely harmful and dangerous, since it does not organize the working class and does not call it to active work; on the contrary, it creates indifference and inertia . . .[23]

Not surprisingly, perhaps, the meetings did little to remedy the state of affairs in industry. The fourteenth party congress in December 1925 called for the utmost economy in the use of all resources. In April 1926 the Central Committee of the party and the Central Control Commission sent out an appeal to all party organizations, and to all party members working in industry and other State enterprises, entitled 'The fight of the workers for improving productivity and [introducing] a regime of economy'.[24] This document, bearing the signatures of Stalin and Kuibyshev, listed ten points (giving, incidentally, a better insight into the working of industry than many books on the subject) which had to be considered before any improvement in industry could be expected. The directives established a new and definite role for the production meetings. They were to become responsible for uncovering any abuses by the managements in the regime of economy, and they were to discuss all

153

possible measures for lowering overheads.[25] This very Stalinist approach to the problem gave the production meetings a definite boost.

From 1926 onwards, the production meetings lost their amateur character and became direct instruments for 'activating' the workers towards greater productivity, and for revealing any illegal proceedings. The latter were silent agreements to avoid certain rules, and could be of different types. We have already seen that managements and trade union organizations were often in collusion to keep out some categories of workers. It appears to have been equally common for the party cell to be in collusion with the management, from which it illegally received funds for turning a blind eye to breaches of regulations. The earlier NEP phenomenon, when party cells stood up in defence of the workers against the management, seems to have disappeared completely by 1926—a measure perhaps of the change of personnel in party offices. Special activists were allocated to many factories to organize and supervise the work of the meetings. For a time, as is usual with such measures, the reason for the meetings was forgotten in the process of arranging them; for instance, workers from one factory were often sent on excursions to other factories to find out not how they worked but how they conducted their production meetings. In 1927 two journals wholly devoted to the work of production meetings began to appear. The central committee of the Trades Union Congress found that the trade unions were not taking enough interest in the meetings, and ordered them to take more interest. From about the middle of 1927 a new function was found for the meetings. They were now to start a 'socialist emulation' between the factories.[26] Competitions were organized and prizes awarded to the winners. But the workers remained apathetic; an opinion poll conducted in the leather industry discovered that since their suggestions were never accepted they found the meetings of little interest. Special workers were therefore appointed to see that the managements carried out the suggestions.[27]

This curious institutionalization of the movement did not stop there. In August 1926 the Trades Union Congress issued a regulation that the meetings must be attended by members of industrial commissions, by all interested workers and by administrative and technical personnel. The aim of the meetings was to improve all industrial processes, and the industrial commissions (a rather older institution which were a form of factory committee) were not to be a substitute for the meetings, merely their core. Subsequently, more

154

organizational features were introduced into the meetings: meetings for one workshop or one trade only, questions and answers prepared beforehand by the industrial commissions, printed schedules for several months ahead, inter-factory conferences. This was still insufficient; as a next step, 'concretization' was introduced. Instead of problems of general interest to industry, only narrower problems connected with the factory were discussed. The joy Russians find in talking in general was condemned thus:

It was absolutely necessary that the tasks raised by the Communist party in the first years of industrialization should become the central point in the work of the meetings.[28]

From 1927 onwards the following topics were discussed: introducing maximum economies in factories, the organization of labour, the discipline of labour, rationalization in the use of machines. And, most interesting of all, when the production meetings finally became a whole new bureaucratic organization another topic was introduced: how to fight bureaucratization in all institutions.

Disorganization of production and frightened managements were the first results of the work of the production meetings. The other results seem to have been confined to a great deal of wasted paper, a commodity not over-abundant in the Soviet Union. The meetings had purely consultative powers; they could only make suggestions. In 1926–27, in 683 factories, the meetings approved of 70,000 suggestions. The managements (probably cowed by party authorities) accepted 75–80 per cent of them. Here the statistics break down; it is not known how many suggestions were carried out in practice. Only in Leningrad's metallurgical industry was an attempt made by the metallurgical union to keep track of the suggestions. It was found that out of sixty-seven suggestions for economies in seven factories, forty-six were carried out. According to the figures quoted from central archives, where a suggestion was accepted in full the economy always reached the estimated level.

The disturbing and futile character of this activity was met by apathy on the part of the workers and opposition on the part of trade unions and management. At the fourteenth party congress Tomsky warned that the role of these meetings should not be exaggerated; later, he and

his allies . . . went to the point of saying that the production meetings were set up to distract the workers and the trade unions from their fight to raise their wages.[29]

155

A party survey showed that trade union organizations did not try hard enough to involve the workers in the work of the meetings.[30] Despite direct orders from the party, the technical personnel took no active part in the meetings and even actively prevented the workers from putting their suggestions into practice.[31] Finally, the meetings seem to have degenerated and to have met the same fate as rural soviets. Industrial commissions with a high percentage of Communists in them took over their work, and illegally substituted their own suggestions instead of calling the meetings. A student of the meetings' usefulness has this to say about them:

In our opinion, based on many years' activity in production meetings, they had little practical influence. There was no success in activizing the working masses in this way, and it proved impossible to give the workers the feeling of co-operation in the running of the factories or to make them feel responsible for the results of the factory's work.[32]

But the last word should be left to the workers themselves, and not to the older workers but to the young ones—those who held the future of the nation in their hands. In the spring of 1927 a review was held of the activities of young workers in a Briansk metallurgical factory, Profintern. This was done because the Komsomol organization felt that the young workers were not playing a sufficient part in increasing the productivity of the factory. The review, carried out in an organized way, gave excellent results. Whereas only twenty-eight suggestions had formerly been made per month, during the review young people submitted 467 a month. All these suggestions were commendable:

They all speak of a proprietary interest and love for the factory. The working youth understands the socialist character of the factory, and adopts an interested attitude to it. Not once during the review did anyone as much as hint that 'but you see, we are being exploited here.' The working youth of Profintern showed that it understood its class tasks . . .[33]

But there was a tiny shadow on this uniform picture of class understanding. It would appear that

youths recently arrived from the countryside differed strongly from this group [of proletarian workers] . . . The young people who came from the countryside recently, and who worked in brick-making, foundries and construction work, mainly raised suggestions about the protection of labour (which, on the other hand, is conditioned by the kind of work they perform) and about being allowed to become qualified workers. Doubtless that peculiarity of this group of young people will require special methods of work from all factory organizations.[34]

156

A recently published document shows how much attention was devoted to these time-wasting and cumbersome practices in 1927. It is quoted here almost in full because it contains an exhaustive survey of the mechanism of industrial conferences:[35]

According to the data of the central trade unions and economic organs and the data of the electoral survey [carried out by] the organizational distributive section of TsK, there is development and improvement in the work of the industrial conferences. . . . Up to a very recent period there had been a growth in the number of industrial conferences. In the report of the Moscow committee there are the following data [supplied by] the Moscow guberniya council of the trade unions:

1 From 1 January 1926 to 1 January 1927 the number of industrial conferences grew by 530.
2 By October 1927, 1,779 conferences and commissions were counted in Moscow guberniya, not counting sub-commissions in separate workshops. In Leningrad, in nine productive trade unions, there were 252 conferences up to 1 October 1926 and 260 conferences up to 1 April 1927.

It can be safely concluded that at the present time there are industrial commissions and conferences in all the workshops of basic enterprises, including those where there are no trade union organizations. As regards the general industrial picture, in large factories general industrial conferences are often changed into industrial conferences. . . .

More workers are being drawn into the work of the conferences this year. Moscow: in the metallurgical industry in forty-eight factories the number of participants rose from 3,884 to 5,442—that is, by 40 per cent. . . . Worker participation in the work of the conference is growing in all the regions. While in 1926 the percentage of workers drawn into the work of conferences was about 10 per cent at present in a series of regions and enterprises the percentage is about 15 per cent. In Leningrad 24 per cent of the workers are drawn in; in Tula, in separate enterprises, 20 per cent. Kharkov and Dnepropetrovsk are behind in this; in a series of enterprises the percentage of workers is less than 10 per cent.

Industrial conferences in workshops are becoming the most widespread method of drawing wide masses of workers into productivity work. Industrial conferences and commissions have made great gains as far as the growth of their activ goes. . . .

About half of specialists are active participants in the work of the conferences; they form 10–15 per cent of the composition of the commissions in the activs, which proves that there is an undoubted movement towards drawing administrators and technicians into the work. . . .

The greatest number of promotions during the last year occurred inside factories, and mainly for lower administrative-economic work.

In Tula raion, of 129 metal workers promoted in 1927, 108 were promoted inside their factories, 86 of them, or 70 per cent, to administrative-economic work.

157

In Nizhegorodskii raion, according to the data of the raikom, out of 119 promoted metal workers in 1926–27, 92 were promoted for executive work (director, assistant director, foremen, assistant foremen, norm supervisors, brigadiers and others). In Sormovskii raion 65 workers were promoted, 38 of them for production work.

In Leningrad in the nine months of 1925–26, 554 workmen were promoted to administrative-executive work, and in the first half of 1926–27, 527 workmen . . .

There is a noticeable craving by workmen for raising their qualifications. Courses to raise qualifications organized in some factories are greatly respected by the workmen. . . .

As a result of the development of the work of industrial commissions and conferences, one can observe a better relation of the workers to production. Trade unions note a lowering in the number of absences for unimportant reasons.

Productivity of work has been raised. The work of industrial conferences helped in great measure to lower the expenditure in factories. There have been savings of up to 10,000 roubles in some factories as a result of introducing the suggestions of production conferences. . . .

Some new ways of inducing the workmen to improve the work of the factories have also been found. The one which is most common is the production conference in a trust or enterprise. There were production conferences in Moscow, Leningrad, Vladimir and other places. These conferences included a great number of workers and the activity of the participants was very strong.

In some factories and workshops there were surveys of work in the press (Tver', Leningrad, Ural). Production competitions were carried out not only among young workers but among all workers (competition for the best piece-worker in Sormovskii factory); in Tula' there was an exhibition of 'workers' know-how', and there also a wall-newspaper under the same name is published. In Leningrad sub-commissions have been organized by the general production commission in the Krasnyi Putilovets factory; these are to deal with help for workmen's inventions and with planning and technical matters. In some localities there are conferences of foremen (Moscow, Leningrad). . . .

The improvement in the leadership by party and trade union organs of the production conferences and the life of the enterprises is in the first place noticeable in the increase, by comparison with last year, of production problems discussed in bureaux, general meetings of party cells, factory committees and workshop bureaux. Party organizations are more concerned with the discussion of production problems than trade union organizations. The work of industrial conferences is not discussed thoroughly enough by workers in workshop and delegates' meetings. The reports of production conferences are more often taken up by party meetings and plenums of the factory committees.

These collected excerpts about the work of production conferences which the editors include in a new volume of documents testify better than any other data to the essential futility of the whole idea. We can only guess at how many man-hours were wasted while the workmen were in conference considering how to save a few roubles. The apathy of the workmen is apparent even in this edited collection. No doubt political considerations made it important to continue with them. Later the conferences became an excellent medium for denunciations and accusations—but from a production point of view they were a useless device.

This short survey of Soviet labour policy in the 1920's illustrates the neglect in building up a new labour force which persisted right up to the introduction of the first five-year plan. It is interesting to note that few new workers were being trained, that young men were discouraged from entering industries, and that peasant youths were discriminated against in the competition for skilled jobs. Even more enlightening is the policy of instant dismissals carried out in the name of 'rationalization'. It would appear that when the central authorities were faced with a loss-making concern they remedied the situation in a way very reminiscent of the practice of capitalist owners, and gave no thought to redundancy. The persistence of strikes even as late as 1927, and the disorders among the workers, have not hitherto been suspected, though the bad working conditions and the high rate of accidents have usually been acknowledged.

But the most striking point about the industrial situation is the lack of direction and avoidance of decisions, as shown by all the above phenomena. While (no doubt very necessarily) the workers' education and professional training was neglected in the name of economy, while machines were worked incessantly despite their age, and while there was no time even to clean the windows, countless precious man-hours and resources of transport and industry were used up on 'production conferences'. This waste of scarce resources can be put down to the inexperience in the running of industry which was common in government circles, and to the government's eagerness to activate the new proletarian masses; but in the circumstances it cannot be excused. Badly off as Soviet Russia was at that time, it was presented with a unique opportunity to plan for education, production, transport and other developments on a large scale and for many years ahead. That this opportunity was not even partly perceived is to be seen plainly both in its industrial policy during the 1920's, and in the later failure of the five-year plans. Had Lenin lived to see these developments, he would have called the neglect

159

of basic necessities in favour of pseudo-Marxist trimmings a luxury the State could ill afford.

NOTES

1. V. V. Kuibyshev, 'Otvety na voprosy innostrannykh delegatsii' in *Torgovo-Promyshlennanya Gazeta*, 18 November 1927; quoted by Rogachevskaya, op. cit., p. 62.

2. Percentages given by Rogachevskaya, op. cit., pp. 53–4; private labour force estimated as 2·1 per cent of 2,500,000 industrial workers. The total for 1924–25 was 1,800,000 workers. Private industry therefore employed about 38,000 workers.

3. 'Postanovlenie TsIK SSSR, 20 October 1927' in *Bor'ba KPSS za Sotsialisticheskuyu Industrializatsiyu Strany* . . ., p. 213.

4. V. E. Loburets, 'Vosstanovlenie i konsolidatsia kadrov rabochego klassa Ukrainy v 1921–25' in *Formirovanie i razvitie sovetskogo rabochego klassa, 1917–61*.

5. Figures from Ts GAOR, USSR, quoted ibid., p. 250.

6. Party archives of the Ukrainian SSR, quoted ibid., p. 252.

7. Figures from various sources, quoted ibid., pp. 256–7. On the question of adolescents, discussed in government circles, see Carr, *Socialism in One Country*, op. cit., vol. I, pp. 369–73.

8. 'Chislennost' i sostav promyshlennykh rabochikh kadrov Kuzbassa v 1926–1937 gg.' in *Formirovanie i Razvitie Sovetskogo Rabochego Klassa*, p. 266.

9. Rogachevskaya, op. cit., pp. 75–6.

10. See Carr, *Socialism in One Country*, op. cit., vol. I, p. 393.

11. D. Shneer, 'Profsoyuzy i okhrana truda' in *Voprosy Truda*, No. 11, 1925.

12. A Shvabapovich, 'Tekhnika bezopasnosti v tekstilnoi promysnlennosti' in *Voprosy Truda*, No. 11, 1925.

13. V. S. Lelchuk, 'O nekotorykh sdvigakh v ryadakh rabochikh khimicheskoi promyshlennosti SSSR, 1917–37' in *Formirovanie i razvitie sovetskogo rabochego klassa* . . ., p. 214.

14. 'Kvalifikatsiya rabsily v Osnovnoi khimicheskoi promyshlennosti' in *Osnovnaya Khimicheskaya Promyshlennost*.

15. *Puti Industrializatsii*, 1929, No. 15, Lelchuk, op. cit., p. 219.

16. *Vsesoyuznaya Perepis Naseleniya*, 1926 g.

17. 'Okhrana Truda i Uluchshenie byta' in *Zhurnal Khimicheskoi Promyshlennosti*, Nos. 5–6, March 1928, p. 192.

18. Report of Professor N. N. Vorozhtsov for Glavprofobr RSFSR, *Materialy Pervogo Vseosyuznogo S'ezda po Voprosam Khimicheskoi Promysh ennosti*, 28/III–8/IV, 1927, p. 380. This book is an extremely important document, and provides material of both a social and an industrial nature which is well worth studying. Its importance lies in the fact that the discussions at the congress were conducted by people who were actually running, or working in, the chemical industry, and their very real problems are well presented in the forty or so factual reports by specialists.

19. TsGNKh, quoted in V. S. Lelchuk, op. cit., p. 222.

20. An interesting study of the textile industry by V. A. Kungurtsev, *Tekstilnaya Promyshlennost SSSR*, confirms the neglect of elementary rules of hygiene and labour protection both by managements and by central authorities.

21. Rogachevskaya, op. cit., pp. 84–5.

22. Ibid., p. 86. The history of production meetings is recorded on pp. 82–125 of Rogachevskaya's work.

23. *Sputnik Partiinogo Rabotnika*, No. 1, 1926.

24. Bor'ba Rabochikh za Uluchshenie Proizvodstva i Rezhim Ekonomii, appeal No. 14, in *Pervye Shagi Industrializatsii SSSR, 1926–27 gg.*, pp. 265–70.

25. Ibid., p. 268. Other points noted that it was necessary to 'widely unmask in the press any facts about thriftlessness, laxity or squandering, regardless of the position of persons responsible for these' and, more interestingly perhaps, that 'the party organizations are forbidden to extort any sums, either directly or indirectly, from State organizations; party organizations must keep completely within their budgets; they must be an example of economy . . .' (Ibid., pp. 268–9).

26. 'Socialist emulation', as such, was not of course a new phenomenon. But linking it with production meetings seems to have begun only in 1927.

27. Rogachevskaya, op. cit., pp. 86–100.

28. Ibid., p. 101.

29. Ibid., pp. 113–16.

30. *Izvestiya*, Ts K VKP (b), No. 19, 23 May 1927; 'O postanovke ustnoi i pechatnoi agitatsii . . . i o vovlechenie shirokikh mass v provedenie kampanii po ratsionalizatsii proizvodstva.'

31. Ts PA IML, Rogachevskaya, op. cit., p. 117.

32. V. A. Kungurtsev, op. cit., p. 61.

33. Obzor Otdela Pechati Ts K, VLKSM o Proizvodstvennom Smotre Molodezhy Bryanskogo Zavoda 'Krasnyi Profintern' in *Pervye Shagi Industrializatsii*, op. cit, p. 379.

34. Ibid., p. 381.

35. 'Iz informatsionnogo obzora organizatsionno-raspredelitelnogo otdela Ts K VKP (b) o proizvodstvennykh komissiakh i soveshchaniakh', 21 November 1927, in *Sbornik dokumentov i materialov po istorii SSSR sovetskogo perioda*, pp. 244–6.

10 'We will develop an economic apparatus of a higher type'[1]

Previous chapters have been concerned with the indivisibility of agricultural and industrial matters in the Soviet Union. While we have dealt with this problem at the regional level, there is no doubt that a great deal of difficulty was created by central decisions. The intricate and clumsy network of government, party and cooperative organizations was unable to cope with the emergencies which frequently arose at local level, and the disorders which followed such events had to be quelled by force after an intervention from the capital. The best example of this interconnection is provided by the so-called 'Smolensk scandal'.

The crisis started some time in 1927 and came to a head in 1928. The reason behind it was the fact that the guberniya of Smolensk was an area with a mixed economy, and some districts were traditional producers of flax. For some time past the government had been worried by the low output of technical crops in the country as a whole, and the guberniya was designated as one of the main flax-growing districts. Farmers were encouraged by financial concessions to plant their fields under flax, and the central authorities guaranteed a supply of grain in return.[2] How this policy was carried out in practice and what part the guberniya party organization played in it can best be seen from the following documents.

On 28 December 1927 the guberniya committee of the Smolensk organization met to discuss the grain situation.[3] This had been grave for some months, because the farmers, who had delivered their flax

162

quota, had not been supplied with the grain to which they were entitled. The representative of Khleboprodukt (the grain trading organization) explained the position:

The plan for grain deliveries under-estimated the demand, and because of this the small percentage which has been fulfilled intensifies the state of the market. The irregularity of deliveries in individual months exaggerates this condition. Khleboprodukt has fulfilled its plan of deliveries for December so far: 94 per cent of rye flour and 73 per cent of wheaten flour. In December the plan envisaged a delivery of 90 trucks of rye flour; only 55 trucks were delivered. There should have been 76 trucks of wheaten flour according to the plan, instead of which 66 were delivered. Even so, the fulfilment of the plan is satisfactory, but it is insufficient because the plan under-estimated demand.[4]

So far, this seems like an ordinary case of an inadequate plan for food supplies being under-fulfilled. But further discussion provides more enlightenment; the representative of the co-operatives supplied some of the missing links:

According to the plan, the main bulk of grain deliveries was entrusted to Tsentrosoyuz [the Central Co-operative Union], with which we have made contracts: [this was] for 354 trucks of rye, of which only 72 trucks were delivered. Sixty-four per cent of the plan for rye flour was fulfilled. Despite the fact that down-payments had been made, these contracts were revoked by Tsentrosoyuz. Potrebsoyuzy [the consumers' co-operatives] took down-payments from the population for about 300,000 roubles; these [contracts] cannot be fulfilled. Tsentrosoyuz distributes almost all its grain to Tserabsektsia [the workers' co-operatives]. Khleboprodukt gets grain for distribution in the countryside, but sells it in the towns.[5]

It can be seen from this that the government organization for the distribution of grain made contracts with local organizations for the delivery of grain, took down-payments on account of them and then revoked the contracts. To add insult to injury, it then proceeded to sell the same grain to members of town organizations, presumably at higher prices. The same applied to Khleboprodukt. In some instances the percentage of deliveries was even worse:

Tsentrosoyuz took an order from us for 181 trucks of grain, for which we have paid; we received only 30 trucks, and these were sent to fulfil the September, October and November plans. Not a single truck of grain was sent in December, either in fulfilment of the plan or for free contracts.[6]

The feelings of the peasant population were made plain. One party official said:

The panic is greater than the need for grain, and it is caused by irregular deliveries of grain. The population grinds oats and flaxen seed and uses

163

them as food. . . . Khleboprodukt sells its grain to private traders—when Khleboprodukt has grain, the private bakers have grain as well.[7]

Another elaborated:

The fulfilment of the plan in Sychevskii uezd is 11 per cent, with a few decimals. The situation is tense. When the time of soviet re-elections comes, there could be complications. There are declarations by the peasants of this sort: 'We will come for bread (to you); we will come with red flags.' And one rural soviet announced that it cannot answer for the situation in its area. If we do not provide the grain now, we will not remedy the situation in the future. . . . If we allow free market deliveries at higher prices, then we might be able to overcome the crisis. . . . After we had forbidden Khleboprodukt to take oats out [of the guberniya], this organization announced that it would not let us have any grain, even the quantity which had been promised.[8]

Once the ice had been broken, another member amplified the information:

The grain problem is reflected in the panic among the peasants, who are losing confidence in the Soviet government. The situation is tense. *We are on the eve of hunger demonstrations by the peasants, who will come to the towns* [italics in text]. The peasants are killing cattle for food and grinding oats; oil cake is used not for cattle fodder but as food for people. . . . Speculation in grain is growing. We also need deliveries of potatoes.[9]

Someone else stressed the gravity of the situation, and demanded: 'We must send Pavlyuchenko to Moscow to demand a bigger grain supply for Smolensk guberniya.[10]

It is plain that the highest guberniya party organization was helpless in the face of the inefficiency, double-dealing and possibly dishonesty exhibited by the central trading organizations. It was, in fact, ground between two stones: on the one hand it had to deal with the central authorities, keen to make the best possible profit on their trading operations, and on the other to pacify the local population, incited by hunger to irate demonstrations. Obviously, the local leaders were afraid of an uprising on a large scale (though we cannot judge on the basis of these documents whether this was a balanced view). They were also afraid of the central authorities, and unable to effect any changes without Moscow's consent. The conference passed numerous resolutions, all designed to allay the grain crisis by getting a larger supply of grain and selling it at free market prices. Even for this, however, the agreement of the National Commissariat for Trade was necessary; and the guberniya committee

164

humbly begged the Commissariat 'to hasten its decision on this question'.[11]

Three weeks later, during a further discussion of the situation by the guberniya committee, the local leaders summed it up thus:

We took measures to ensure the procurements in good time, and as far as the procurements [of flax] are concerned, our guberniya is not at the bottom of the list. But our guberniya *is supplied with grain* far less than others [italics in text]. The fulfilment of the plan of contractation in the guberniya is satisfactory. But if one takes into account the actual need, then the plan of grain deliveries is fulfilled by 66·3 per cent. . . . According to the plan, the peasant population is supplied with grain by 57·5 per cent. The supply of manufactured goods to our guberniya is completely insufficient. For instance, our order for cotton fabrics has been satisfied by 75 per cent, for woollen cloth by 29·3 per cent, for leather by 55·3 per cent, for metals by 65·4 per cent, and so on.

In view of this state of affairs, the committee resolved

To turn the attention of the National Commissariat for Trade to the intolerably low level of fulfilment by several central organizations of their obligations in respect of grain for the co-operatives, though they received down-payments in good time and in large sums.[12]

In the meantime Pavlyuchenko had been to Moscow and received a reprimand for allowing the disorders to develop, but was at least able to secure further and more ample deliveries of grain. He still did not get permission from the Commissariat for Trade to buy the grain at free market prices. In February the secretaries of the *uezd* committees discussed further measures:

Up to 25 January, the guberniya will have received one million puds of grain on account of December and January orders. It is hoped, if the National Commissariat for Trade allows, to buy grain at free market prices. . . . The delivery of free market grain is possible in greater quantity than we had thought possible. In connection with the deliveries of grain, we must speed up the deliveries of flax and seed. With this aim in view, those to receive the grain in the first instance, and at conventional prices, will be the flax growers. The rest of the population . . . will receive the grain at somewhat higher prices.[13]

The peasant population, which had received only about half of the already insufficient planned supplies, was to be asked to pay for its grain at free market prices. But this was not the worst of it. The greatest difficulty in which the party officials found themselves was that the flax growers who were to buy grain at controlled prices were already the more prosperous peasants. The officials voiced

165

their objections in many ways. One objected on the grounds that selling grain cheap to flax growers and at higher prices to other peasants would create grain speculation. The flax growers were in any case prosperous peasants, and this operation would benefit them to the detriment of poorer peasants. He was supported by several other secretaries, who argued that a class line had to be followed in the sale of grain. It was useless to supply it at low prices to members of co-operatives, for the poor peasants seldom belonged to co-operatives and 'the poor peasants would starve'.[13] All these objections were met with the ruling that

We receive grain only because we are a flax-growing guberniya, and if we use it otherwise than has been directed [by the centre] we shall receive a corresponding reprimand.[14]

In April of 1928 the guberniya committee began to discuss the Katushka affair (described below). While the industrial purge was being prepared, the agricultural purge was already in full swing, accompanied by the usual action by the GPU. On 3 May, a fortnight before Pavlyuchenko's formal deposition, a meeting of the bureau of the guberniya committee listened to the report on the situation in the countryside.

The third quarter of 1926–27 showed a shortage of grain among the population. At the beginning of the fourth quarter there was practically no wheaten flour and very little rye flour:

The tense condition of the grain market is complicated by rumours about war, to which the countryside (as well as the towns) reacts by maximum demand. . . . With the food supply conditions of the current year (failure of rye, bad harvest of potatoes) and also with the new intensity on the grain market . . . it would be important to ensure correct supply of the guberniya by deliveries of grain right at the beginning of the year.[15]

The apparatus of terror was brought into action:

In February OGPU searched 361 people (millers, traders, kulak merchants) and discovered 68·963 puds of grain. . . . In the countryside speculation in grain is growing, and the price of grain rose to 3 roubles 50 kopecks for a pud . . . and together with this, the political activity of kulaks and prosperous peasants grows, and they attempt to bring medium and poor peasants over to their side. Kulaks demonstrate more often and more openly against the party and the Soviet government. The survey of the GPU says that 'all kulak demonstrations are similar and can be reduced basically to this argument: this is not a government, but a workhouse; as soon as the war breaks out the Soviet government will fall'.[15]

166

Informing, almost classical in its simplicity, was revived:

> Kulaks begin to speak more freely. A kulak from the village of Sozh, . . . Korenkov Egor, while a guest of the chairman of the Sozh Rural Society, Yakovlev, poured himself a glass of vodka, and turning to those present— there were eight people—said, 'Let us drink to the destruction of all Communists; let's drink to the ruin of the soviets,' and when Yakovlev suggested the toast 'Let us drink to the oppressed of all the world,' [Korenkov] did not agree and added, 'Let them kill me, let them put me in prison, but let them know that I am the enemy of the Soviet government.'[16]

More disquieting was the reaction of the poor peasants, who were doubtless angry about the sale of cheap grain to flax growers:

> The files of OGPU record that many medium peasants and even poor peasants are in this respect under the influence of the kulaks. . . . At a meeting in Vskhodskaya volost, Elninskii uezd, medium peasant N announced: 'The government does not help poor peasants; peasants are made to starve, while workers get bread. Give us freedom; we have had enough of the party and the Soviet government.' At the same meeting, poor peasant S expressed his feelings in the following way: 'The Communists will finish themselves off between themselves; they turn about like weathercocks; all the convicts are in the government (an allusion to the revolutionary past of the Bolsheviks); they have a brutish conscience. It is *all the same to them whether it is a poor peasant, a medium peasant or a kulak* [my italics]. They only pretend to care for the poor peasants. . . .'[17]

Nor was the attitude of the party members a matter for congratulation. The guberniya party organization started work on preparing peasants for collectivization in January 1928. We are not told in what this work consisted, but it does not seem to have gone beyond preliminary meetings and directives. The report noted that it was most important for the village Communists to give an example in organizing collective agriculture, instead of asking for private plots for themselves. In general, the Communists were not the first to collectivize, and they did not work actively for collectivization. One *uezd* committee issued a directive in February 1928 which read: '*It is categorically forbidden to the Communists and Komsomols to ask for transfer to farmsteads*' [my italics].[18]

The Smolensk affair came to a head with the dismissal of Pavlyuchenko on 16 May 1928 and a general purge. The purge was justified on the grounds of corruption and drunkenness in the party organization, and inefficiency in a Smolensk factory. Here is the comment of a modern historian:

M

Not only did the Smolensk Party organization remain largely untouched by the ideological struggles of the mid-twenties; it also fell victim to corruption in high places. . . . In the background and providing the organizational preconditions for the scandal was that familiar Soviet institution, the entrenched family circle embracing the leading Party and governmental officials of the guberniya, who did their best to protect each other from exposure of their sins of commission and omission. During the mid-twenties this circle was headed by the gubkom first secretary, D. Beika, of whom it was said that he had a wife in every town in the guberniya. In 1926 Beika was transferred to Moscow, but his successor D. A. Pavlyuchenko, a former worker and Party member since 1918, who had been in charge of Party cadres under Beika, continued Beika's practices. As a result the Smolensk Party organization was riddled with corruption and drunkenness.[19]

The reason for this castigation of the morality of high party officials is revealed by the events at the Katushka factory. Yet the Katushka scandal was matched by the scandal at the Diatlov factory (see Appendix II), and the Soviet press as well as the Smolensk archives abound in examples of this kind. Drunkenness, rudeness and abuse of women workers were common occurrences in Soviet industry.[20] They were not a new phenomenon, but a direct consequence of the influx of peasant labour into industry at periods of rapid industrial development which had already been noted at the end of the nineteenth century. The 'family circle' (in both its literal and figurative meaning) was not very new either. In *Gore ot Uma* the famous dramatist Griboedov, writing at the beginning of the nineteenth century, makes Famusov, the head of an important department, say that all those employed in his office are his own relatives, the only exception being his secretary, Molchalin, whom he employs 'because he is efficient'.

The events which took place at the Katushka factory must have been common at many other plants, but they are particularly well documented. It will be best to start with the resolution of the party bureau:[21]

In the period of the last few years (approximately since 1924) a whole series of offences took place at the Katushka factory. The following offences took place. Some of the foremen, both Communists and non-party men, systematically took bribes from the workers; these took the form of joint drinking parties on pay days. [These foremen] also drank at the factory and compelled the women workers to have sexual relations with them; those who refused to do so were transferred to other work, or even dismissed.

Personal appeals from women workers to the [party] cell and the factory

168

committee were met by a formal, tactless attitude, and produced no result. It was not until the [men] workers themselves started to make representations, and the workers who had joined the party during the October levy took decisive steps, that the situation regarding the offences was cleared up . . .

All the above incidents occurred despite formal democracy [at the factory] and sufficient worker participation in social life; also despite frequent information from the correspondents [rabkory] about the irregular goings-on at the factory. It should be noted that the survey of Katushka carried out by the newspaper Rabochii put did not bring these deficiencies to light. The party cell at the factory grew at an enormous pace, and the raion committee and the cell itself did not take steps to check up sufficiently on those who were admitted to the party. No steps were taken to organize educational work with the workers who had recently joined [the party]. In connection with this, some of the [workers] who had joined [the party] turned out to be connected with the offences.

The analysis of the events in the Katushka factory shows that the basic reasons were as follows: in the first place, the isolation of the party and Komsomol cells from the everyday life and interests of the workers, and the corruption of part of the party cell; in the second, lack of indispensable proletarian democracy and effective defence of the everyday needs of the workers on the part of the factory committee . . . while there was an inattentive attitude on the part of the guberniya trade union office towards the mistakes of the administration. In the third place there was bad selection of specialists and directors, and disgraceful management of industrial life of the factory on the part of the trust . . . the production programme had been changed several times, in connection with which there were five separate reductions in the number of workers during the last year and a half, sometimes comprising more than 20 per cent of the whole labour force of the factory. This situation created abnormal conditions . . . so that fear of being dismissed made the activities of the criminal elements easier, and increased the difficulty of uncovering the offences in good time.

In connection with the above, the guberniya bureau decided to: dissolve the party cell and reprimand the secretary; dissolve the factory committee and organize elections for a new committee, other party functionaries to be expelled from the party and subjected to judiciary proceedings, . . . the director of the factory (a party member since 1924) to be dismissed. Other points: those who had offended in the matter of sexual relations, and those who had lied to the party organs, to be expelled from the party and subjected to judiciary proceedings.[21]

This report was signed by the chairman of the bureau, Pavlyuchenko, and his secretary, Stepantsov. The situation at the factory does not seem to have differed significantly from what obtained in other factories of the period, particularly as regards the isolation of the party cell from the workers' problems and the authorities' indifference to complaints. The staff reduction policy practised by the trust was also widespread and officially approved by the government in the name of the 'regime of economy'. Why then was Katushka singled out for this wholesale purge? It becomes even more puzzling when the report of a survey of the factory is studied. This seems to prove that there had been a great improvement in the factory over the previous two years, though, as usual, management–labour relations were none too good:[22]

1 The deficits in 1926–27 were smaller, compared with 1925–26.
2 Work discipline is better.
3 Productivity per worker is higher.
4 The cost of goods produced is higher, because of the increased cost of raw materials.
5 The constant changes in production plans are bad for the factory.
6 Work among the masses is insufficiently developed.
7 Workers (from the shop floor) are not drawn into the management in sufficient numbers.
8 The factory committee does not function properly and does not react to the workers' needs.
9 The commission for labour protection does not work properly; there are too many workers off sick; too much overtime is demanded.
10 The last trust contract with the labour force lowered the workers' pay illegally, thus causing great disturbances. The party cell was passive, instead of defending the workers' just rights.
11 The party cell is very big. On 1 April 1928 it numbered 200 people out of a total of 511 workers. These numbers are too high for proper party work.
12 There was correct party work, as far as holding the meetings and discussing problems were concerned.
13 General meetings of the cell were regular.
14 Frequent changes in production plans meant constant lay-offs and hiring of new workers, which had a bad effect on the workers' morale.
15 The drinking sessions of foremen with workers and sexual relations with women workers were additional sources of jealousy and quarrels.
16 The bureau of the party cell did not pay enough attention to the above.
17 The fraction of the factory committee did not pay attention to the needs of the workers.

23 The commission requires that the bureau of the Zadneprovskii raion committee of VKP (b) should remedy all these matters. The raion committee of VKP (b), fraction of the Union of Trade Unions and the Union of Woodworkers, are to work out new measures to avoid the above [events] in the future.[22]

When the guberniya committee discussed the situation at the factory among themselves, it was clear from the tone of the discussion that the high party officials were well aware that the Katushka affair was being used by the Central Committee as an excuse for a major purge. One of those present said that

the trust kept the workers in constant fear of dismissals. It also sent bad officials to the factory, a thing about which the party could do nothing. The administrative apparatus was full of Mensheviks and White Guards.[23]

Another bureau member said that the Katushka affair had a special importance, as both the persecutors and the persecuted were party members; 50 per cent of the workers at the factory were party members or Komsomols. There were also those who were not slow to change sides and attack the unlucky chairman. An official called Nikitin said:

The matter of Katushka is analogous to the Shakhty affair; isolation from the masses, suppression [of facts] and so on. It is different from the Shakhty affair only because here there is no economic counter-revolution as such.

Another official said that not everything about Katushka was known yet:

We must draw political conclusions from this matter. . . . In connection with the Katushka affair we must survey other factories in the guberniya as well.

And someone else tried to shift the blame:

At Katushka we have almost a Shakhty affair, except that the active people are Communists. . . . It is mostly the GPU's fault that this matter was neglected, in particular since the secretary of the cell informed them of it . . .

Pavlyuchenko himself summed the position up. He said it was obvious that the party was too slow to act in the affair:

When we talk about the guilty ones, then the guilty ones are, in the first place me, as a member of this cell, and in the second, the guberniya committee. It would have been all right if we had discovered this matter two years ago, but that did not happen. In the past year an instructor from the Central Committee, comrade Baranov, stayed at the factory for two weeks and did not find anything. We must give this matter a political appraisal: we must draw political conclusions . . . from it.[23]

As far as can be discovered from the documents, this was the last meeting chaired by Pavlyuchenko. After the ritual of discovering something which had been known to everybody, including the Central Committee, for several years, and fixing the blame on a victim who had already been chosen for other reasons, explained earlier, the sentence finally came. On 16 May an extraordinary meeting of the bureau was held, at which the temporary chairman, Simonov, announced that Pavlyuchenko had been deposed:[24]

Simonov informs the meeting of the decision by the presidium of the Central Control Commission and the Orgbureau of TsK VKP (b) of the Smolensk organization:

To accept the information on the decision of the Central Committee to remove comrade Pavlyuchenko from his post ... and that other designated comrades are to be removed from the bureau of the guberniya committee.

This announcement caused great consternation among those present, but the discussion was brief, for everyone was afraid to talk at this stage. The purge of the apparatus had already started right at the top. The Katushka affair was by no means exceptional—a very similar situation obtained at the Diatlov factory, where only the manager was deposed, and in many other factories in other guberniyas. Yet in this instance everybody of any consequence in the guberniya apparatus was submitted to interrogation, and many were dismissed. Why were the events at Katushka, a model Communist factory, of such great portent? In the first place, the period is important: as the Shakhty trial had already started, the regime of terror was in its initial stage. In the second place, Pavlyuchenko had to be made the scapegoat for a peasant revolt which had occurred in the guberniya during the winter months. That was why the whole organization had to be purged as well—the apparatus knew too well what had been the initial cause of the revolt. And that was also why Pavlyuchenko was only demoted to industrial work, instead of meeting the same fate as the Shakhty defendants: instead of defending himself against the unjust charges, he had taken the onus of guilt on his own shoulders and saved the central party authorities an unpleasant confrontation:

The resolution of the praesidium of the CCC on the situation in the Smolensk organization, adopted on 9th May, was published in *Pravda* on 18th May 1928. Although denouncing the corruption, drunkenness, and sexual degeneracy in the Smolensk apparatus, its treatment of Pavlyuchenko and the 'leading organs of the guberniya' was relatively mild.[25]

This is what Fainsod said in his short analysis of the Katushka affair, described under the title 'The Smolensk Scandal of 1928'.[26] Unfortunately, Fainsod missed the earlier part of the tragedy which supplied the real reason for the importance accorded to a relatively commonplace factory scandal, as discussed in this chapter.

172

But the main purpose of this chapter is not so much to show what really happened in Smolensk in 1927–28 as to relate the events in the guberniya to the much more momentous movement in 1929–30, known as 'forced collectivization'. We have already seen that in the Smolensk crisis certain elements could be separated: a central decision to raise the output of technical crops, a resultant grain shortage followed by a peasant rebellion, followed in turn by the deposition of the whole party leadership, a purge of the apparatus and a campaign of terror in the countryside. When we analyse these elements, we notice that the central decision was passed on to the central trading and administrative organs, which were ordered to arrange for its execution on the local level. The documents demonstrate clearly how and why implementation failed. The central trading organizations did not adhere to their commitments, but were interested only in fulfilling their targets *vis-à-vis* the central plan; central administrative organizations issued directives to the local organs with no thought about their viability; the local organs were a powerless tool, unable to force action on the central organizations and unable to alleviate the crisis in the region on their own. In the final analysis, the only solution left to the local administrative organs was the application of terror—which they did as a result of panic and fear, rather than from choice. In Smolensk the result of the crisis was a wholesale purge, a famine and violence on a fairly large scale. Where such means were tried out on a national scale, the result was almost certain disaster, as will be seen in the following chapter.

NOTES

1. Parts of this chapter were published in *Soviet Studies*, October 1968.
2. Much remains to be done yet on the state of agriculture in the years 1926 and 1927. Some authorities assert that the grain crisis was caused 'by a succession of bad harvests in 1926 and 1927' (Fainsod, *Smolensk under Soviet Rule*, p. 46). Karcz, whose theory on the 1928 crisis is well worth considering, says that 'Hence, the year 1926–27 is the first in which the tax element was . . . introduced into the system of government grain prices. . . . These measures brought the grain market into a state of serious disequilibrium, which has persisted to this very day. . . . Thus the decision on grain prices for the 1926–27 procurement campaign marks a turning point of the grain problem. It forms a crucial, indeed the initial, link in the chain of events that led to the grain procurement crisis of 1928 . . .' (J. F. Karcz, 'Thoughts on the Grain Problem', op. cit., p. 415). Mr Karcz has a lot to contribute on the shift from the production of grain to the production of higher protein crops; but unfortunately he does not tackle the vital problem of the technical crops. This stress on technical crops contributed in large measure to the grain crisis. We have only oblique proofs of this, as for

instance in the statement that 'Planned supply of grain (in 1928) had to be increased by 1·4 million tons, of which 672,000 were destined for the supply of Central Asia and seed loans alone' (Karcz, op. cit., p. 424); this increased supply of grain to Central Asia was the result of a stress on Central Asian cotton. In the event, little was accomplished, for we are told that 'In January 1928 Uzbekistan received only 39·5 per cent, in February only 66·6 per cent of grain allocated to it from centralized sources' (Karcz, op. cit., p. 422). Compare this delivery rate with that fulfilled in the Smolensk region, which was also a technical crops region, later in this chapter.

3. Smolensk archives, reel No. 5, Smolensk, 1928, WKP 33: 'Protocol No. [illegible] of the meeting of Smolensk guberniya committee of VKP (b), 28 December 1927.'

4. Sinev, for Khleboprodukt, ibid.

5. Trudov, for Koopsovet, ibid.

6. Kolesnikov, for Smolensk *raion soyuz*, ibid. The reader will be struck by the diversity of the organizations dealing with grain procurements and by the price differentiation. Karcz comments 'At one time there were sixteen different agencies (including the State bank) conducting grain procurements alone; by 1926–27 that number was reduced to three' (op. cit., p. 414). The grain prices, as already referred to, provide the basis for a major work. Karcz has made a beginning in his article; we must wait for a further elucidation of this problem from him, or from another economist. I am not qualified to make any statements on the pricing policy of the government and can only repeat, *relata refero*, the opinions of the Smolensk guberniya officials, who were caught in the net of the government's price policy.

7. Shnurov, for Gzhatsk *raion sel'sovet*, ibid.

8. Simochkin, for Sychevskii *uezd* committee, ibid.

9. Makushkin, for Gzhatsk *uezd* committee, ibid.

10. Okhlopkov, ibid.

11. Smolensk archives, reel No. 5, Smolensk, 1928, WKP 33: 'Protocol No. 6 of the meeting of the bureau of Smolensk guberniya committee of VKP (b), 29 December 1927' (about the state of grain market).

12. Smolensk archives, reel No. 5, Smolensk, 1928, WKP 33: 'Protocol of a conference of the guberniya committee of VKP (b) on the procurement of goods, 20 January 1928'.

13. Smolensk archives, reel No. 5, Smolensk, 1928, WKP 33: 'Protocol of the conference of secretaries of uezd committees of VKP (b), 12 February 1928'.

14. Simonov, ibid. The same Simonov presided over the extraordinary meeting at which the bureau of the guberniya committee were told that Pavlyuchenko had been deposed. It is quite possible that he had informed on Pavlyuchenko in the first place, though he does not seem to have benefited in any way by the purge.

15. Smolensk archives, reel No. 5, Smolensk, 1928, WKP 33. *Secret.* 'Appendix No. 1 to protocol No. 28 of the meeting of the bureau of the guberniya committee on 3 May 1928' (report on the results of the economic campaign, 1927–28).

16. Ibid., 'Economic and Political Results of the Grain Crisis.'

17. Appendix 1, op. cit.

18. Ibid., 'Preparations in Party Organizations.'

19. M. Fainsod, *Smolensk under Soviet Rule*, op. cit., pp. 48–9.

20. See O. A. Narkiewicz, 'Surplus Labour and Peasant Migration in the Soviet Union in the 'Twenties', a paper delivered at the conference on *Peasant and Farmer in Europe*, University of Birmingham, March 1966.

21. Smolensk archives, reel No. 5, Smolensk, 1928, WKP 33, protocol No. 27

THE MAKING OF THE SOVIET STATE APPARATUS

of the meeting of the bureau of Smolensk guberniya committee of VKP (b),
30 April 1928: 'Resolution in connection with the situation at the Katushka
factory'.

22. Smolensk archives, reel No. 5, Smolensk, 1928, WKP 33, appendix to
point No. 1 of protocol No. 26 of the meeting of the bureau of the guberniya
committee, 28 April 1928: 'Conclusions after a survey of professional, economic and party work at the Smolensk factory "Katushka" '.

23. Smolensk archives, reel No. 5, Smolensk, 1928, WKP 33: protocol No. 26
of the meeting of the Smolensk guberniya committee of VKP (b) on 28 April
1928.

24. Smolensk archives, reel No. 5, Smolensk, 1928, WKP 33, protocol No. 30:
'Extraordinary meeting of the bureau of the Smolensk guberniya committee of
VKP (b) on 16 May 1928.

25. M. Fainsod, *Smolensk under Soviet Rule*, op. cit., p. 49.

26. Ibid., pp. 48–52.

11 'The transition from capitalism to socialism cannot be made without compulsion'[1]

We must now look at the general agricultural situation between 1927 and 1929. The overall figures showed a rise in agricultural production, but did not take into account two things: the rising population, and the population's desire to make up for the years of famine and privation by eating more. An eminent economist pointed out that the

gross agricultural production reached the pre-war level as early as 1925–26, and exceeded it by 6·0 per cent in 1926–27. This was certainly an excellent showing, considering the great decline in the preceding years and the generally unfavourable situation in agriculture during the recovery period.[2]

The improvement, however, was deceptive:

The population in 1927–28 exceeded that of 1913 by 7·6 per cent. Hence, on a *per capita* basis, pre-war production was not yet fully restored by 1927–28. The importance of the growth in population was fully realized by the Gosplan, which published [a computation on a *per capita* basis showing the reduced amounts of production of certain agricultural products]. These computations are the more significant because, soon after their publication, Soviet officials displayed an obvious inclination to forget that the rural population had increased and consequently needed more food.[3]

None of the three factors which made up the Soviet State—the administration, industry and agriculture—can be said to have been in a healthy state of development by 1927–28. The state of affairs

176

was worsened by disagreements in the top ruling circles, the most important of which was the Central Committee. Though the arguments were often engendered by personal animosity and mutual distrust, their basic cause lay in the realization that the economic situation was getting worse, and that no remedies to improve it would easily be found. The climax of the arguments came in April 1929, at the Central Committee plenum.

Stalin's speech at the April plenum is rightly famous, and some parts of it have been quoted so often as to become commonplace. However, while the speech was ostensibly an attack on the Bukharin–Rykov wing, it is true to say that this attack (though very important) took up less than a fifth of the exposé; the rest of it was almost fully devoted to defending Stalin's theory of industrialization and his interpretation of Lenin, as applied to the contemporary Soviet situation. The slogans of the moment (which Stalin enumerated as self-criticism, the fight with bureaucratization, purge of the apparatus, the organization of new Communist cadres, strengthening of the collective farm movement, attacking the kulaks, lowering the cost of industrial production, improving trade union work and purging the party, in that order of importance) were not accidental, though the party as a whole found them 'stunning and dizzying'. They were part of one unbroken chain of an attack by socialism upon capitalism.

But in order to carry out this [socialist] reconstruction, one must first of all improve and strengthen the cadres of socialist construction, both economic and professional as well as party and co-operative ones . . .[4]

As a second task, Stalin stipulated that the party should remain unified not only on the internal front, but also in relation to the foreign parties. He castigated Bukharin's appeal to the Comintern[5] and accused him of fostering the belief that capitalism was getting stronger, whereas he, Stalin, believed in the rising tide of revolution. (Stalin was quite right: the Great Crash was only a few months off, and Germany was not far from revolution, though not a Communist one.) Stalin believed that the Soviet Union had no chance of settling down to normal relations with other States while factions of the Comintern were leading their own policy of fostering revolution. 'Iron discipline' was necessary, said Stalin. The Comintern had to be brought into line with Soviet policy, and all this was spoiled by Bukharin's manœuvres with foreign Communists.

177

The importance of having a unified foreign policy, he emphasized, was the greater because of the state of internal affairs. In the cryptic fashion which he often used for revealing top secrets to the initiated while at the same time refuting them to the uninitiated, Stalin couched his explanation in the following words:

Was it because capitalist elements are growing faster than the socialist sector of our economy and that because of that they are increasing their resistance to the building of socialism?... But it is untrue that supposedly capitalist elements are growing faster than the socialist sector. If this were true, then socialist construction would already be on the edge of a precipice. ... The resistance [of the capitalist elements] was possible because ... the absolute growth of capitalist elements is happening all the same...[4]

Or, to translate into plain words, although the capitalist elements were not growing, socialist economy was on the verge of collapse. The same trouble occurred in the administration:

It would appear that up to the time of... mass sabotage in the Shakhty region, we had an excellent apparatus, and then... the apparatus became for some reason completely bad. It would appear that up to last year, when grain deliveries were proceeding by the free flow method, our local organizations were good... but from last year, when the kulak opposition took on a particularly sharp form, our organizations suddenly became bad.[6]

Having voiced the fact that the organizations and administrative bodies were so fragile that any additional strain on them could destroy them completely, Stalin then clumsily demolished this hypothesis. But the party was not left in any doubt about the danger:

In what way does Bukharin's theory that capitalism will grow into Communism harm us ...? In this way: that it demoralizes the working class [i.e. the party], that it undermines the preparedness of the revolutionary forces in our country... and that it makes the attack of capitalist elements against the Soviet government easier.[4]

Having delivered these general warnings, Stalin turned to the main attack against the 'Bukharin line'. This did not consist in a condemnation of Bukharin's advocacy of individual farming, because Stalin himself supported individual farming (though he made the classical distinction between the medium peasant and the kulak). Nor had it much to do with industrial expansion, for at that time Stalin's own programme was still in accordance with the earlier estimates. One of his main arguments against Bukharin was the latter's insistence on the restoration of a free market.[7] The New Economic Policy, Stalin

178

argued, had always since its inception meant a certain degree of market freedom. But not a complete freedom:

NEP means the freedom of the market within certain limits, . . . but *safe-guarded by the regulating role of the State on the* [conditions of the]*market.* We have no free play of prices on the market, as is normal in capitalist countries . . . while NEP exists, both sides must be retained: the side directed against a regime of War Communism . . . and the other side, directed against a complete freedom of trade [italics in text].[4]

And after thus apparently giving NEP his blessing, Stalin justified his stress on the regulating role of the State in the case of the Soviet Union by stating plainly that since it was the State which paid the salaries of the apparatus and of the industrial workers, it could not afford to have a free play of prices, with a probable rise in prices as a consequence, as it would then be constrained to raise its bill for wages and salaries, apart from becoming unpopular with the majority of its citizens. 'It is clear that the party cannot follow this perilous road.'[4]

Stalin was firm on the condition of retaining control of the market. He was less certain about agriculture. The party must follow the road shown by Lenin in fulfilling its obligations towards the peasants:

. . . we must insist at all costs on supplying the peasants with agricultural machinery, tractors, fertilizers . . . to reconstruct rural economy on a new technical basis.

Industry was being modernized and developed; the cities were growing, raw materials were becoming even more necessary. But agriculture remained as it always had been: '. . . old tools, archaic methods of cultivation, primitive techniques . . . old, small-peasant forms of individual economy and labour.' It would be necessary to change this slowly, to consolidate small holdings gradually: 'to make a gradual transition from small peasant farms to large-scale collective industry . . .' But there was to be no sudden or forced change:

This obviously does not mean that we should abandon individual medium and poor peasant farms. No, it does not. Individual poor and medium farms have an overwhelming role to play . . . in the very near future. For this reason it is absolutely necessary to support individual poor and medium farming.[4]

But it was impossible to make progress in agricultural techniques without tractors and machinery; the State must supply the peasants with those, and the rest would follow. For this, the development of industry must be quicker: 'Hence the key to the reconstruction of agriculture on a collective basis lies in a rapid pace of industrial development.' It would be impossible to solve the grain difficulties without these two concomitants, and allowing free play of market prices in the meantime would only complicate the situation. That was why it was better, while the ¦grain crisis lasted, to resort to extraordinary measures of grain collection. Bukharin had suggested that '. . . 50 million puds should be imported from abroad; this would cost 100 million roubles in currency. And what if we need [foreign] currency to import machinery for industry?'

While there were people who were terrified of even the mention of collectivization, there were also some who asserted that it was at least two years too late to develop collective forms of agriculture (the argument was addressed to the left wing). This, Stalin stated, was untrue. The party had foreseen the need for collective agriculture even at the time of the October coup (*perevorot*). But it had been impossible to embody the early slogans into reality owing to lack of means.

We must not forget that we represent a *ruling party*, not an *opposition party*. An opposition party can employ slogans . . . which may be realized on coming to power. . . . But the slogans of a [ruling] party are not simple agitational slogans; they have the force of a *practical decision, of law*. They should be carried out immediately [emphasis in text].[4]

Two or three years ago the party had been unable to carry the masses with it: the peasants were too hostile to collectivization.

But now—it is a different matter. Now we have whole strata of peasants, who look at kolkhozes and sovkhozes as a source of help as far as sowing grain, improved cattle, machines and tractors are concerned. Now, given only machines and tractors, the matter of collective farms will move forward with more intensity.[4]

Moreover the State now had the resources to finance the change-over to collective farming, though this would require hundreds of millions of roubles. And the State had a minimum industrial basis for supplying machinery—or 'At least, the very basis is being prepared at a quickened pace.'[4]

None of this was either very new or very revolutionary. As Stalin himself pointed out, the party had foreseen the need to collectivize soon after the October revolution. Collectivization had not been carried out then because the resources were not available. But he did not assert that the resources were there in 1929, merely that the
180

peasants were less hostile to collectivization, and that an industrial and financial basis was being prepared for it. This was April 1929, and forced collectivization was only a few months off. Had Stalin already made his plans in secret? Was he merely deceiving his listeners (the highest dignitaries in the Soviet Union, who would have to carry out the collectivization) by saying that collectivization would be gradual, rational and supported by machinery? The whole tone of the speech belies the supposition. What Stalin supported was the limited extent of collectivization as envisaged by the minimal five-year plan, while the right wing baulked at the very mention of the word. This is not surprising, for that is where the essential difference between Stalin and Bukharin lay.

To understand the nature of their misunderstanding, we must go back to the very beginnings of the State: to the regime of War Communism. At that time the survival of the State depended on the peasants' willingness to co-operate with the new government. Both Bukharin and Stalin had watched the policy of War Communism and seen it end in fiasco—the State had been unable to coerce the peasants into growing food for the government. Both men had seen how Lenin resolved the crisis: first by invoking an alliance with the medium peasants, and then with all the peasants; by restoring the peasants' rights to hire labour, to market freely and to regulate their sowing by a semi-free play of market prices. But the lessons each man drew from this experiment with War Communism were different. Where Bukharin was awed by the strength and resistance of the peasants, Stalin inferred that given a sufficient amount of supervision the experiment, or part of it, could be repeated again, this time more successfully. War Communism had failed, he reasoned, not because the peasant was stronger than the State but because the State was not yet strong enough to discipline the peasant. Provided with a large enough apparatus of coercion, the State could make the peasant sow, grow and harvest the grain, even though most of it would have to be given away to the State at nominal prices. Even so, Stalin was not convinced that his apparatus was strong enough, and it is doubtful whether he would have resorted to extraordinary measures had the circumstances not virtually forced him to.

The 1928 crop had been disappointing, and in the summer of 1929 the food position in the towns was disquieting even to a government used to food emergencies. According to Molotov, the enormous queues for food presented a grave problem in the cities.[8]

Though collectivization was being mentioned as a distant and beneficial solution to the problem, it was clear that quick and decisive measures were needed if the inhabitants of the towns were not to revert to the War Communist custom of disappearing into the countryside in search of food.[9] The danger of this happening was threefold: it would disturb the peasants even more than the extraordinary measures had done up to then; it would send food prices rocketing up; and last—but perhaps most important—it would wreck the industrialization drive by depriving the industries of badly needed skilled workers. In order to avoid all these disasters, Stalin had to introduce extraordinary measures anew, and with a greater intensity than they had been practised before.

Until then there had been three main channels through which the grain was obtained from the peasants: free flow (*samotek*), where the peasant was paid a market price by State agencies; procurements [*Khlebozagotovki*], in which the peasant sold to a nominated government agency at a State-fixed price, and so-called 'contractation'. This last was a process which took as many forms as there were districts, and depended for its execution on the local officials' interpretation. In theory it meant that while the grain was still in the fields an official would inspect the fields and set the grain delivery figure for the whole village. This measure was called an inducement to socialism, for the peasants were assessed by whole communes, and were required to make deliveries not from their own crops but by communes. In reality the measure re-established the hated post-Emancipation 'collective responsibility', but it seemed to the authorities the only possible course, for once the grain had been harvested there were many channels by which the peasants could sell it secretly at higher prices. When they were collectively responsible, it was hoped, the peasants would supervise each other and none would be able to hide or sell grain that was required by the government. The procurements had been tried in a smaller measure earlier on; they were successful when there was a good organization working in the locality and the grain could be collected immediately after the harvest.

As the food crisis grew, however, it was found necessary to intensify all forms of grain collection, but particularly contractation. Since by then the towns were suffering not only from bread shortages but also from vegetable and dairy products shortages, it was decided to extend contractation to them as well. In the future these supplies would come through collectivized industries.

182

In this area [of food supply] we have a big and complicated task before us. It consists in great development of big sovkhozes and kolkhozes in every branch of the rural economy, in maximal development of contractation, in constructing huge stores for perishable produce . . .

said an article in *Pravda* at the end of August 1929.[10] After giving the starving townspeople a tantalizing glimpse of the future, the article continued:

But all this work is only just a beginning. The only significant results have been obtained in the collection of grain products, on which all the efforts were concentrated. In the current year a large proportion of prepared grain, about five million tons, should be obtained by organized means from sovkhozes and kolkhozes and from contractation. . . . The experience in solving the grain problem must be immediately transferred to the field of dairy and meat production, and the production of vegetables.

This increase of contractation (for the production of *kolkhozes* and *sovkhozes* was notoriously low), and its extension to other produce as well, was a signal for a return to the War Communist requisitioning of food from the peasants.

This was not undertaken as a punitive measure: it was devised in order to pacify the starving workers. The tone and emphasis of the article make it clear enough:

The party set . . . *a strong course for produce procurement not in the order of concessions to capitalism, but as a socialist attack*, by way of fighting the kulak, speculator and private owner . . .

Despite many serious difficulties (crop failure in big producing regions, inconvenient geographical distribution of the harvest and so on), supplying the industrial regions went, on the whole, without interruption . . . As in procurements, so *in distribution, the class proletarian policy proved to be the only correct one.* Only thanks to the timely introduction of rationing based on class principles were we able to . . . supply the basic categories of worker consumers. . . . *The problems of food supply for workers and for the toiling masses must be considered as one of the most important fronts of class struggle and socialist reconstruction of the economy.*

We need a radical change [perelom] *here. In order to attain it in reality, it is necessary to activate the community, to organize it with a view to overcoming the food supply problem, in the solution of which it is vitally concerned.* In the coming new budget year we can and should attain a better supply . . . of food. A better harvest, measures just beginning for improving and changing agriculture, give a real possibility of this [italics in text].[10]

Little additional comment is necessary; the article makes the situation perfectly clear. For many reasons (and fear of a revolt could have been one of them) the countryside had to be plundered—not because the peasants were becoming capitalist, but because the towns were starving and becoming restless.

There were thus two main objects of government policy in the autumn of 1929. The first was a short-term one: the procurement of sufficient grain to pacify the towns and guarantee the success of industrialization. The second was a gradual collectivization, based on the developing technological potential of the State. There was no deceit in Stalin's exposé of policy to the April plenum, no hiding of real objectives. Whatever he had to hide, it was not plans for a sudden and complete collectivization—for he had none. Indeed, he knew well that in the existing situation there could be no plans unless and until he had prepared some basis for collectivization. This basis did not consist solely in machinery; given a sufficient amount of currency, machines could be purchased abroad. Nor was it merely a matter of convincing the peasants that collectivization was a beneficial step. This, Stalin knew, could be performed by compulsion in a far shorter time (though he was not yet ready to resort to that type of compulsion). The lack of readiness consisted in something far more important and more difficult to prepare: the administrative incapacity of the State machine to deal with such a drastic reversal of the situation, and the complete lack of trained personnel to carry out the collectivization or guide the new collective farms into the safe harbour of prosperity and productivity. It would be unjust to say that Stalin was not interested in administration. After all it was he, and not Bukharin, who had been in charge of the administration for some eight years; it was he, not Bukharin, who stressed Russia's essential need for trained cadres; finally, it was he who brought about the real revolution in training a sufficient number of skilled men to serve the new Soviet State. Stalin was not an administrator *par excellence*—he lacked both the cultural background and the rigid training which would have made him so—but he had the instincts of a good administrator. He knew what could and what would not work, administratively speaking. Within the rough framework of the Soviet State he made more use of administration with the minimum of resources than perhaps anyone has ever been able to do in any other country.

It must be stressed here that despite the policy of developing terror, which had been growing since 1928 (a policy which was partly designed to frighten the peasants into surrendering their grain, and was partly the result of administrative measures carried

184

out in a clumsy—and therefore frightening—way), Stalin was not on the road to complete collectivization yet, even in the summer of 1929. There were references to collectivization in the press; there was more stress on the necessity for collectivization; but the dominant theme was that of developing industry first. In the summer of 1929 the unbroken working week was introduced in industry; workers were invited to join in socialist emulation; managements were being exposed to the barbs of criticism; party officials were being purged, less for being rightist than for not pushing industrial production sufficiently. Throughout that summer agriculture took a back seat. There was a food crisis, there were ration cards, there were preparations for a grain procurement campaign; but none of these was very important compared with the development of industry. (Though, of course, the main topic in the press was the inhuman attitude of the Chinese government towards Soviet citizens in China.)

There was a certain amount of collectivization, but it was carried out (or at least announced) in such a way as to show that the government was fully aware of the perils and difficulties that awaited it should it attempt a complete collectivization.[11] In September it was reported that 14 per cent of the population in north Caucasus had been collectivized, and 10 per cent in the lower and middle Volga[12] —significantly, the regions where grain collection had met with the greatest difficulties. In addition, four examples of successful collectivization were quoted:[12]

1 Armizonskii *raion* in the Urals, where 74 per cent of arable land had been collectivized, with about seventy-eight households to each *kolkhoz*. The region disposed of a small amount of agricultural machinery but a large number of collectivized cattle, horses and smaller farm implements. Many *kolkhozes* were beginning to plough up virgin land without the aid of tractors.
2 Samoylovskii *raion* on the lower Volga, where 25 per cent of land was collectivized. The collectivization was based on a column of thirty-six tractors which served 1,600 households (*not kolkhozes*) and a column of six tractors serving 200 households.
3 Mineralovodskii *raion* in the north Caucasus, where 40 per cent of the population were collectivized. The western part of the *raion* was populated by Germans, the eastern part by a mixed population of Tartars, Bulgars, Nogaytsy and others. There was a small tractor column of twenty tractors, but many of them were out of order or obsolete.
4 Tiginskii *raion* in Severnaya *oblast*. This was a district of dairy farming. Here collectivization was relatively easy, for it was a highly

185

industrialized and mechanized district with adequate electrical power.

The quoted examples show that complete collectivization was carried out either in distant regions where a quantity of virgin land existed, in districts where the population was not Russian or, finally, in districts where there had been an existing fund of machinery which was being put to communal use. Apart from this detailed description, notices of collectivization with exact details were conspicuous by their absence in *Pravda* till the second half of October 1929, if not later.

Even the most ardent advocates of collectivization could not deny that there was not enough machinery to carry it out on a large scale. Above all, there were not enough men to help with the collectivization where it *was* being carried out. It may be, in Dr Lewin's words, that 'the countryside was mobilized by thousands of agitators and activists of all sorts'.[13] If this was so, then certainly *Pravda* had very little detailed information of such a campaign. It is true that in some districts there was some activity: in Brianskii *okrug* workers' brigades were preparing the peasants for collectivization in the period 15–19 August 1929. This short period of four days was devoted to arranging a communal harvest so that the peasants would recognize the joys of communal work.[14]

The peasants were to be eased into collectivization in other ways as well. On 6 September 1929 the Central Committee passed a resolution to establish an annual day of 'harvest and collectivization', to be held on 14 October every year. This date was set to coincide with the holiday of Christ the Saviour, so as to discourage the peasants from attending church on that day.[15] This day, the Central Committee opined, ought to be conducted as a mass campaign, somewhat in the manner of a production campaign in industry. But there were also articles which testified to the fact that, however much the Central Committee wished it could send thousands of activists into the countryside, it simply had none to spare. Even at the height of collectivization fever, in mid-December, the commission on complete collectivization which was then working took two days to dispose of the problem of where to send the 700 graduates from Communist *Vuzes* and 10,000 *dvadtsatipyatitys'achniki* which were the total human material the government could spare at this crucial moment.[16]

While it was difficult to assemble this relatively unskilled apparatus of coercion at short notice, the matter of trained leaders for the
186

future *kolkhozes* and *sovkhozes* seemed absolutely hopeless. An article in *Pravda* made this clear. The struggle for the socialization of agriculture would require thousands of organizers and leaders, asserted its author. The socialized sector of agriculture was even now badly in need of agronomists, specialists on mechanizing agriculture, organizers, engineers and managers of gigantic production units. The government had doubled the output of grain expected from the *sovkhozes*, and an enormous development of tractor stations was expected during the five-year plan. But the Commissariat of Education had raised its programme of admissions to the agricultural *Vuzes* by only 10 per cent in 1932–33 compared with 1929. On the other hand, it was expected that artistic *Vuzes* would have a 60 per cent rise in admissions in the same period. This was not all. Out of all the students admitted into agricultural *Vuzes* in the RSFSR, only 15·7 per cent graduated. The truly Stalinist solution of making the pass rate higher was offered here, with better teaching methods coming a poor second.

Not a single agricultural *Vuz* had been planned for the RSFSR during the five-year plan, while there were projects for a theatrical *Vuz*, a literary institute and other schools of cultural interest. In 1928–29 650 agronomist-cultivators graduated from all the agricultural *Vuzes* in the RSFSR, a number which was completely inadequate. The number of graduate cattle-breeders was 372. Even these small numbers were lowered in the projects for the year 1932–1933. The position with regard to engineers was even worse: by the end of the five-year plan twenty-nine specialists in tractor construction would have graduated. By 1933 130 agronomists specializing in large agricultural units were expected to graduate (by way of contrast, 302 pianists and 209 singers were envisaged). While Moscow *oblast* alone would need 357 agro-economists under the five-year plan, the output for the whole of the RSFSR was expected to be 360 people. Many more figures were quoted, all attesting that it would be impossible to run full-scale socialized agriculture under the existing cadre limitations.[17]

All these circumstances made it plain that complete collectivization could not be carried out in the near future, and that there could be no question of serious plans for it. In the meantime the grain crisis was growing. This was the direct result of the poor crop (or poor procurements) after the 1928 harvest. There is some confusion about the 1928 crop. Some authorities (Dr Lewin among

OLGA A. NARKIEWICZ

others) state that it had been good, but the peasants were hiding the grain. At the 1929 April plenum Stalin said the poor procurements were the result of a year of severe drought and winter-killing.[4] Jasny, a leading authority on Soviet agriculture, stated clearly that the decline was the result of extensive winter-killing.[18] Whatever the reasons for the poor harvest in 1928, the prospects for 1929 were much better. Molotov reported to the party conference on 14 September 1929 that the harvest was excellent, and that it was proposed to store 100 million puds of grain as a guarantee of economic growth.[8] The only remaining task before the government was to collect this grain, grain procurements being the basis of the economic plan. There, of course, was the rub. Even if sufficient grain were grown, the difficulty consisted in mustering sufficient means and forces to collect it.

The problem facing the government was that the forced pace of industrialization undermined the possibility of agricultural expansion. There was not enough money or manpower in the country to force both; and it was the growth of industry that was to be forced. Therefore agriculture had to be made to give up enough of its produce to guarantee the possibility of industrial development. The attention of the Central Committee turned towards the grain situation from July 1929 onwards. At first, with the promise of a good harvest, things seemed to be going reasonably well. The grain procurements were said to be coming in in August, and it was not till the end of August that Mikoyan sounded the first alarm. It might be as well to stop here for a moment and consider the anti-free trade campaign which, as Dr Lewin pointed out, 'gravely disrupted the normal commercial network.'[13] but which he took to have been just another aspect of the class war. Despite the terror aspect of the wholesale arrests of traders and the shutting down of free markets, this campaign was a practical step designed to obviate the ease with which the peasants could sell their grain at higher prices. This was clearly stated by Mikoyan in August 1929, when he called the free traders 'meshochniki', in pure War Communist tradition, to stress the State's strong resistance to the selling of grain at high prices. Nevertheless, the free traders were only part of the government's problems. It was not the private individuals who were sabotaging the plan for grain procurements, but the ineptitude of government agencies and their internal warfare, which made the targets inaccessible. Mikoyan cited the instance of Soyuzkhleb and EPO

188

(Consumers' Co-operation), which were fighting each other about who had the right to collect the contracted grain.[19] In the same issue of *Pravda*, a correspondent from Armavir filled in the gaps Mikoyan had left in his report. In this district the agricultural co-operative, whose organization was very weak, held the monopoly for collecting contracted grain, while the well organized apparatus of Consumers' Co-operation had to collect what grain it could find by free flow. The managers of EPO refused to collect the free flow and were instead fighting a bitter battle with the agricultural co-operative for contracted grain, even going so far as to refuse to help with storage facilities for the grain already collected.[19] This information, and more reports about the inefficiency of government agencies, do not square up with the picture presented by Dr Lewin, who wrote:

. . . the Party and the specialized services spent that year preparing, with a degree of energy and efficiency rarely to be encountered in other fields, for the procurement campaign, which in fact was to be more successful than ever before because of the unprecedented extent of the resources mobilized for the purpose.[13]

The alarm sounded by Mikoyan on 24 August was but a first sign of trouble. On 15 September *Pravda* reported that the autumn sowing was going very badly because the grain had not been prepared for sowing, and attributed this to the fact that the peasants were frightened to bring it to government cleaning stations, as there had been some rumours that it would be confiscated. The same issue also reported that in some districts only 17 per cent of the procurement plan was being fulfilled. The reason was partly that the peasants, resisting procurements, were taking their grain secretly down the Volga to Stalingrad and Astrakhan, where they could sell it at high prices. But the local authorities must be blamed as well, since they were not speedy enough with grain collections, and had not prepared sufficient storage space, transport or technical facilities—even such basic necessities as weighing machines were lacking in some places.[20] From that day on, *Pravda* was full of tales of disaster. While the headlines spoke of breaking down the kulaks' resistance (and little attempt was made to conceal the fact that this term covered all the peasants who refused to co-operate with the State), the correspondence underneath showed the extent to which the grain procurement plan was breaking down because of lack of organization. On 28 September came the first report of twelve wagons full of wheat rotting in railway sidings. Workers' brigades, formed to help with

189

procurements (another harking back to War Communism) went out into the countryside, only to send back letters of complaint that there were no storage, transport or any other facilities on the spot.[21] Nor could the private growers be blamed any longer, for many *kolkhozes* and *sovkhozes*, alarmed at the extent of grain collections, were hiding their stores. Many *kolkhozes* were being disbanded as a punitive measure.[22] On 5 October *Pravda* announced in large headlines that grain procurements simply had to be fulfilled in October; they were going very badly all over the country, but particularly in Siberia and the Kuban. The *kolkhozes* were the worst offenders in fulfilling their quotas. Everywhere party officials in the localities were up in arms by this time; the party bureau of Zaporozh'ye complained indignantly that the plan 'did not leave a single kilogram of grain for the population'. The secretary of the bureau of the Ts K Ukraine was dismissed from his post for not pursuing the grain procurements energetically enough.[23] That the procurements were in a bad way by this time was shown by the increasingly militant character of the campaign. In the north Caucasus the procurements were called 'fines' (*shtrafy*) and the local administration was applying them to all the peasants, rich and poor, but not alike —they were hitting the poor peasants hardest.[24] The campaign had degenerated into utter chaos, and there was no one to check it.[25] In and around Sverdlovsk hundreds of wagons full of grain (at least 200–250 were arriving every day) were standing, waiting for further orders. All over the country, grain was rotting out in the open because there was nowhere to put it.[26] To counteract the opposition of both the peasants and, in some cases, the local party authorities, the role of the workers' brigades was put on a firmer footing: they were to become 'responsible agents for procuring grain' and were given full powers to proceed in large detachments (presumably it was no longer safe to work in smaller groups) and to clear out district after district of grain.[27] The work of one of those detachments is fully described. Finally, the use of force was given the formal seal of approval:

We must begin to work in a revolutionary way. Only in this way will October become the decisive month for grain procurements;

and for the first time it was admitted that it might be too late to go back to the *status quo*. Too often grain procurements were looked upon as an end in themselves, and not as but one of the measures

190

included in a whole complex of changes—industrialization of the country, collectivization of agriculture and other changes.[28]

On 17 October *Pravda* stated for the first time that the grain procurements were not an end in themselves; on 22 October it carried the first realistic report (as opposed to the rather nebulous earlier ones) of a whole *okrug* which had been collectivized in a few days, and a mention that there were now twenty-five regions of complete collectivization in the country.[29] As late as 10 October there had been a long article indignantly denying that socialization of agriculture was to be quick, or that force would be used; a gradual transformation was to be aimed at.[30] Yet barely a fortnight later it would appear that just such a collectivization was being enforced. What had happened during this short interval? For several weeks there had been constant newspaper reports of grain being set on fire by the peasants, and of grain-collecting officials being attacked. Despite a great degree of frankness in the newspaper reports, it would perhaps be too much to expect the full story from them. That is why it is necessary to resort to the report of a former Communist official, who claims to have been an eye-witness of the disorders:

Isolated peasant outbreaks within the country, in connection with 'extra-ordinary measures' taken to ensure grain collection in the autumn of 1929, were threatening to develop into mass peasant uprisings throughout the country. It was a repetition of the peasant uprisings of 1905, but without the support of the city workers and with the intellectuals silent and the outside world indifferent. Peasants armed with pitchforks hurled themselves at Soviet tanks, which received their first battle honors in the war against the people. Women threw themselves on the bayonets of the Checkists, children wept on the bodies of their dead parents, while tanks, cannon, machine-guns and bayonets collectivized some and liquidated others mercilessly and systematically.[31]

This author states unequivocally that it was the procurements which caused the peasant revolts, not the collectivization. It is a picture which is consistent with the reports in *Pravda*.[32] In the absence of an archival search, this claim cannot be made with complete certainty; but a very strong hypothesis must be put forward that the so-called 'collectivization' was, to start with, merely a series of punitive measures undertaken against the peasants who were opposing the confiscation of all their grain. Even so, disorders on such a large scale might have been avoided had there not been constant proof before the peasants' very eyes that the grain which had been brutally confiscated from them was rotting in open fields, in railway wagons,

191

in churches, schools and even manure stores for lack of storage space. Faced with starvation that same winter while their precious grain was rotting away, it is hardly surprising that the Russian peasants took to rebellion. The punitive measures took the form of ploughing up the boundaries to remind the peasants that, in the last analysis, it was the government which decided their fate. The additional measures of collectivizing livestock and farm buildings may have been of a punitive character, but may also have been undertaken to stop the peasants from killing all the livestock and destroying their buildings in despair. In addition, the city proletariat did not play such a passive role as Avtorkhanov ascribes to it. The proletariat, or part of it, was out in the countryside, actively helping the troops to requisition the grain, in the hope of laying in stocks for the winter in their larders.

It must be assumed that the peasant war started some time in mid-October;[33] it was not until 7 November that, taking advantage of the anniversary of the revolution, Stalin proclaimed complete collectivization. But already, on 1 November, *Pravda* made it clear that a sudden and decisive turn in agricultural policy had been made:

We are developing complete collectivization in whole raiony and okrugi. . . . Tens of tractor columns are furrowing the peasant fields, are wiping out the boundaries.

Workers' brigades were asked to convince the peasants that they had to join the *kolkhozes*.[34] Two days later, an article appeared which called for 'a decisive revision of plans on land consolidation'. The five-year plan, the article stated, would have to be fulfilled in two years. According to this change of plan, large collective farms would have to play a decisive part in the country's economy. There was no time to wait for ideal conditions: the time for consolidation was now.[35] The author might have added 'or never'.

It was against the background of a peasant war, incipient or already flaring, that the November plenum described in detail by Dr Lewin[13] took place. Under the stress of the circumstances, since Molotov plainly said that collectivization had to take place now, the Central Committee decided to set up a commission on collectivization, to 'see that the whole operation . . . was carried out in an orderly manner'.[13] However, the commission was not finally constituted until 8 December 1929, a delay which Dr Lewin finds puzzl-
192

ing. The delay seems perfectly natural, though, when we remember that there must have been a great deal of confusion in the capital and a lack of reports from the districts which were being 'pacified'; and that very few members of the government believed that anything in the nature of a real collectivization could possibly be achieved. Their hesitation is not very surprising, for they had an inkling of the situation and could scarcely be blamed for thinking that a country in which there were not enough weighing machines or clerks to register the grain collected from the peasants was not an ideal ground for a process as complex as collectivization of even half the area under cultivation.

The commission to 'develop complete collectivization' was set up at the beginning of December 1929, under the chairmanship of the commissar for agriculture, Ya. A. Yakovlev.[36] Its members were members and candidate members of the Ts K, secretaries of *kraikomy* and *obkomy*, representatives of central institutions. The first meeting, held on 8 December, set up eight sub-commissions. These were to deal with the speed of collectivization, the type of economy in collectivized regions, organizational problems, the distribution of resources, cadres, the mobilization of peasant property, relations with the kulaks, and other matters. The management of Kolkhoztsentr USSR, with G. N. Kaminsky at its head, was given the problem of deciding the pace of collectivization, with the proviso that it was to be completed in two to three years in grain-producing regions, and to end during the five-year plan in other regions. The sub-commission, consisting of K. Ya. Bauman, I. Ye. Klimenko, T. R. Ryskulov and G. N. Kaminsky, was to work out the problem of relations with the kulaks.[37] To help in its estimates on the speed of collectivization, the commission prepared a summary of the collectivization already achieved by 15 December 1929 (see Figs. 5–8, Appendix IV). The figures were incomplete, but even taking them at their optimum level (that is, the highest percentage in each chart) it will be seen that 29·09 per cent of peasant households were collectivized by then. When taken at an average level (that is, 40 per cent for the 30–50 per cent section, Fig. 6, and so on), then the level of collectivization was 20·75 per cent. Taken at the lowest possible figure (that is, nil for Fig. 8, 15 per cent for Fig. 7, and so on), the level of collectivization for the enumerated districts is 12·4 per cent. In addition, data for twenty-two *okrugi*, five *oblasti*, three '*otdel'nyye raiony*' and two autonomous republics were missing.

OLGA A. NARKIEWICZ

Even the existing data are rather dubious, according to Ivnitsky, who states that:

In the assessment of these data, it must be borne in mind that, first, it is known that the data were not complete, since in a series of okrugi they were missing; second, a certain over-assessment shown in the table must be taken into account. For instance in the Uzbek SSR at the end of 1929 there was not a single raion in which more than 50 per cent of peasant households were in kolkhozes, but table No. 1 [graph] shows one rayon (in the Bukhara okrug) with a level of more than 70 per cent collectivization. There are also other errors. On the whole, however, despite some over-assessments, the table gives a more or less correct picture of kolkhoz construction in the middle of December 1929.[38]

In view of such uncertainty on the part of a leading Soviet authority on the subject, it would be futile to attempt any guesses at the real level of collectivization in mid-December. All one can say is that it was not very high, and certainly nowhere near complete nor almost complete, except in one or two districts.

Two problems exercised the commission's ingenuity most of all: the first was the speed of collectivization; the second, relations with the kulaks. It would appear that Yakovlev warned the commission that undue haste would lead not only to alarming the peasants, but also to the 'substitution of real collectivization by show collectivization—formal collectivization—which we do not want'.[39] No deep double meaning need be read into this opinion. It seems certain that Yakovlev meant exactly what he said—not that the peasants would be terrorized into joining the *kolkhozes* (though he said that as well) but simply that local officials would be forced to show, on paper, levels of collectivization which hard fact did not bear out at all. Another faction (and here Ivnitsky names B. P. Sheboldayev) apparently went all out for the notion that there was a strong desire from below to form *kolkhozes,* and that there was no need to hold it back. Yakovlev was accused of taking the side of those 'who wanted to temporize'.[40] The initial draft of the project was sent to the Politbureau on 22 December; the pace of collectivization was set according to Yakovlev's position. The draft was accompanied, however, by an amendment which T. R. Ryskulov sent direct to Stalin, and later to Ordzhonikidze.[41] This amendment suggested that the pace outlined by the commission was not quick enough, and proposed a maximum pace, with the particular inclusion of districts with technical crops (about which Stalin was beginning to be seriously worried); and, following this, the forcing of the pace
194

in Central Asia, the cotton-bearing territory. The whole project was returned to the commission, which was told to amend it in line with Ryskulov's proposals. We need not dwell here on the question of whether Ryskulov acted on his own initiative or was ordered to table the amendment by Stalin himself, though it is possible that an archival search would provide the answer.

The problem of dealing with the kulaks was the one which had the strongest bearing on the outcome of the struggle. For while it was quite certain that actual, positive collectivization could not be achieved with the limited means at hand, the commission had no doubt that, provided the government was prepared to send out armed forces in strength, the opposing kulaks could be liquidated.[42] The sub-commission, under the chairmanship of K. Ya. Bauman, suggested that in the regions of complete collectivization all kulak means of production should be confiscated and transferred to the *kolkhozes*.

This process of de-kulakization . . . is completely different from de-kulakization under War Communism, when kulak wealth passed to individual peasant households . . .

suggested the commission.[43] But expropriation and condemnation to death were not to go hand in hand. The sub-commission stated clearly that it would be hopeless to try and solve the kulak problem by deporting 'whole masses of kulak population' to distant regions, or similar means (thus admitting that it was not merely a matter of dealing with a few hundred thousand richer peasants, but with large strata of the peasant population). It was therefore suggested that only those kulaks who actively opposed the socialist order or who carried out counter-revolutionary work should be arrested or deported; that kulaks who opposed complete collectivization should be deported or transferred (*pereseleny*)—a subtle difference, but one which could mean the difference between life and death—and, finally, that the majority of the kulak population should be allowed to work in the new *kolkhozes* for three to five years without pay and without franchise, after which those who passed the test would be allowed to become full members of the *kolkhozes*.[44]

This more lenient course was advocated by K. Ya. Bauman, G. N. Kaminsky, T. R. Ryskulov, I. Ye. Klimenko and M. N. Belenkoi. However, other members were in favour of completely excluding the kulaks from *kolkhozes*. Among them was L. M. Vareikis, who, on the strength of his experience in the Central Black Soil

Region, advocated deportation of all the kulaks, transferring them to the very worst districts or, finally, not allowing them even the smallest plot of the worst soil.[45] The decree of the Politbureau took this last point of view and stated that kulaks were not to be accepted into *kolkhozes* anywhere at all, and not just in the districts of complete collectivization. This wording of the decree (which Ivnitsky suggests was inspired by Stalin) made it relatively simple to justify the mass deportations of peasants, which Stalin felt were necessary after the disorders.

Another matter the commission discussed was the question of peasant property and the form which collectivization would take. Here again, most members of the various sub-commissions were in favour of leaving some property in private hands, but Ryskulov expressed the opinion that unless the peasants were made to surrender all their property to the *kolkhozes* they would be tempted to opt out of them at a later date.[46] Ryskulov's viewpoint, as well as the deliberate choice of the artel form of *kolkhoz* because it did not leave the means of production in private hands, were approved by Stalin thus, in Ivnitsky's words: 'witnessing his disregard of the interests of working peasantry . . .'[47] Since Stalin settled most of the outstanding questions in accordance with his own views (and it is quite possible that he believed no other way out remained) and since time was pressing, the commission did not deliberate for long. Less than a month passed from the first meeting in December to the issuing of the decree '*About the pace of collectivization, and measures of government help for kolkhoz construction*' on 5 January 1930.

What happened as far as collectivization proper was concerned in the months from January to March 1930 does not lie within the scope of this work. Under the best climatic conditions, collectivization would have been a difficult matter. In the hard Russian winter, when many districts are cut off for months, the operation appears to have been almost impossible. Adding to these natural factors the breakdown of civilian administration and a virtual civil war, one can only conclude that any action carried out that winter must have been mainly punitive. But, probably thanks to pressure on local officials, Stalin got his figures by March: it was announced that 58·1 per cent of peasant households were collectivized.[48] As soon as the pressure was eased, this figure was reduced to 23·6 per cent in June 1930, thus coming very near to the average of the tentative figures gathered by the collectivization commission in December 1929.
196

Careful piecing together of this new information, together with the older evidence, must lead us to ask whether complete collectivization had been planned by Stalin, if not as early as the fifteenth congress, then at least as late as the April plenum in 1929. The answer must be in the negative. Every piece of evidence suggests strongly that while Stalin (in line with most other Bolshevik leaders) believed that a certain degree of collectivization would be necessary under the five-year plan, in order to ensure a constant supply of food to the industrial centres, he had no intention of carrying out anything so drastic as even a 25 per cent collectivization as late as the beginning of October 1929. He knew very well that, even if he wanted to do so, the means to hand were pitifully inadequate. On the other hand, he believed (erroneously, as it turned out) that he had sufficient means of persuasion and coercion to 'squeeze' every bit of grain out of the peasants in order to guarantee industrial expansion. His miscalculation was due to lack of reliable information about the state of provincial administration. It was the incompetence of the local administration in carrying out the grain procurements, together with the lack of technical resources and transport and storage facilities, which set off the peasant revolts. Once these revolts had occurred, some way had to be found of cloaking them under the overall term of 'counter-revolution'. Little ingenuity was needed to show that the peasants were rebelling against collectivization and not against grain procurements; this was in fact done, thus confusing not only the peasants themselves but also serious students of the situation. Stalin desperately needed this excuse, not so much to protect himself from the population as to protect himself from both the Central Committee and the expelled opposition leaders, who had been predicting just such an outcome for two years.[49]

The commission, on the face of it set up to discuss collectivization, never seriously contemplated that task. Instead it was forced to give the seal of approval to the measures taken to quell the peasants, such as arrests, deportations and confiscation of property—all on a scale undreamed of in War Communist days. Even when the worst was over, in March 1930, Stalin still needed the assurance that the Central Committee was with him, as is witnessed by his statement on 30 April that

the article 'Giddiness from success' was written on Stalin's personal initiative. This, of course, is nonsense. The Central Committee does not exist in order to allow personal initiative by anyone . . .[50]

197

If it is true that Stalin's position was so weak at this time, it might be objected that his enemies would have taken advantage of it to depose him. This must have been more than a passing thought in many a mind. But there was an obstacle—in the face of a peasant rebellion, all the ruling class was in danger. 1928 had already demonstrated plainly that even the former idols could no longer count on the support of the proletariat, which had once followed them gladly. Faced with the choice of Stalin's rule and a peasant revolution, even Trotsky chose Stalin. In addition, Stalin was the best person to subdue a rebellion: rightly, none of the other leaders felt they could be quite so ruthless and methodical as he was. It was the fear of a full-scale peasant revolution (whether real or imagined it is difficult to say without full data, though Avtorkhanov asserts that there were fears that a Pugachev would arise at any moment) which made the commission on collectivization assent to Stalin's drastic measures; it was the same fear that made the Central Committee mute despite the realization that collectivization was a sham and that it was only invoked in order to subdue the rising peasant masses.

When the worst danger was over the war could be relaxed a little in the spring, since it was time to induce the surviving peasants to start work on the land again. But it is immaterial whether Stalin himself or the Central Committee wrote the article on relaxation; what is important is that both parties knew that what had happened during the winter was not a collectivization at all. This would have to be built up far more painfully in the following few years, after the price of the 1929 blunder had been paid in famine and industrial catastrophe.

NOTES

1. Parts of this chapter were published in *Soviet Studies*, July 1966.
2. N. Jasny, *The Socialised Agriculture of the USSR*, p. 202.
3. Ibid., pp. 217–18.
4. Stalin, 'O pravom uklone v VKP (b)' in *Voprosy Leninizma*, sections I and II.
5. A brief account of the struggle with foreign Communist parties will be found in L. Schapiro's *Communist Party of the Soviet Union*, op. cit., pp. 474–80. The German party was particularly affected because of the rise of Nazism.
6. Stalin, op. cit., section III. It is interesting to note that Stalin was using the Shakhty trial in a similar way that Lenin had used the Kronstadt uprising, i.e. to discipline the party and enforce greater unity.
7. On the economic meaning of the disputes at that time, see A. Erlich,

The Soviet Industrialization Debate, 1924–28, op. cit; also N. Jasny; *Soviet Industrialization, 1928–52*, op. cit.

8. *Pravda*, 20 September 1929.

9. It is impossible, on the basis of existing evidence, to prove that the food disorders in the towns were taking on a more serious form and were threatening to develop into a revolution. Nevertheless, the possibility has to be borne in mind.

10. 'Towards a basic solution of problems of food supply', *Pravda*, 28 August 1929.

11. Dr Schlesinger, in his article 'On the Scope of Necessity and Error' in *Soviet Studies*, January 1966, states that the course for industrialization was bound to mean collision with the private grower and entrepreneur. There is no reason to assume, on the basis of his writings, that Stalin thought so till the beginning of November 1929. He required compliant producers but did not identify them with collectivized producers.

12. 'On the Road to Complete Collectivization', *Pravda*, 12 September 1929.

13. M. Lewin, 'The Immediate Background to Collectivization' in *Soviet Studies*, October 1965.

14. *Pravda*, 13 October 1929.

15. *Pravda*, 6 September 1929.

16. N. A. Ivnitsky, 'Istoriya podgotovki postanovlenia Ts K V K P (b) o tempakh kollektivizatsii sclskogo khozyaistva ot 5 yanvaria 1930 g.' in *Istochnikovedenie Istorii Sovetskogo Obshchestva*.

17. 'Struggle for the Cadres,' *Pravda*, 25 August 1929.

18. N. Jasny: *The Socialized Agriculture of the USSR*, op. cit., pp. 220-1.

19. *Pravda*, 24 August 1929.

20. *Pravda*, 15 September 1929.

21. *Pravda*, 29 September 1929.

22. *Pravda*, 3 October 1929.

23. *Pravda*, 5 October 1929.

24. Dr Schlesinger, op. cit., also confirms this state of affairs: 'But in some villages . . . up to 10 per cent of the peasants got an "individual assessment"; in other cases the 3 per cent were made up by inclusion of serednyaki.'

25. *Pravda*, 15 October 1929.

26. *Pravda*, 16 October 1929.

27. *Pravda*, 17 October 1929.

28. Ibid. I am saying 'for the first time' since I have been unable to find an earlier mention linking procurements with collectivization. Dr Lewin places it on 31 October 1929.

29. *Pravda*, 22 October, 1929.

30. K. Tversky, 'Against Trotskyist Relapses', *Pravda*, 10 October 1929.

31. A. Avtorkhanov, *Stalin and the Soviet Communist Party*, p. 159.

32. Peasant disorders during the procurement campaign are fully confirmed by reports from the guberniya of Smolensk (Smolensk archives, W K P 223, Smolensk, 1929). These reports, too numerous to quote here, speak of emissaries being afraid of going out on procurement duties, of commissions being attacked, of shots being fired at Soviet officials, and of bad storage facilities. One letter of complaint is reproduced in Appendix III.

33. This is also consistent with the reports in the Smolensk archives, which place it in the second week of October.

34. *Pravda*, 1 November 1929.

35. V. P'yer, 'For a decisive revision of plans on land consolidation', *Pravda*, 3 November 1929.

36. Ivnitsky, op. cit., p. 266.

o

199

OLGA A. NARKIEWICZ

37. TSGANKh SSSR, f.7486, quoted ibid., pp. 266–7.
38. Ivnitsky, op. cit., p. 269.
39. Ibid., p. 271.
40. TsPA IML, f.17, quoted ibid., p. 272.
41. TsPA IML f. 85, quoted ibid., p. 278.
42. Despite pressure on him, Yakovlev himself was convinced that it would be impossible to collectivize without additional machinery, and remarked that means should be found to make 120,000 tractors available and, if necessary, to buy additional ones abroad, as it would take at least five or six years to construct a technical base in Russia. TsGANKh SSSR, f.7486, IML, f.17, quoted ibid., pp. 276–7.
43. TsGANKh SSSR, f.7486, quoted ibid., p. 272.
44. Ibid., p. 273.
45. Ibid., p. 274.
46. TsPA IML, f.85, quoted by Ivnitsky, op. cit., pp. 280–2.
47. Ivnitsky, op. cit., p. 284.
48. Figures quoted by M. Fainsod, *How Russia is ruled*, op. cit., p. 531. Fainsod himself states that the new collective farms were 'paper' organizations.
49. Avtorkhanov, op. cit., relates in a loose but convincing way the confusion and anti-Stalinist currents in the Central Committee during the winter of 1929–30: see pp. 159–60.
50. Stalin, quoted by Avtorkhanov, op. cit., p. 160. Avtorkhanov asserts that 'Giddiness from success' had not been written of Stalin's free will but was dictated to him by the 'deathly frightened Central Committee', whose members told Stalin to sort out the situation by himself.

12 Conclusion

It will have been noticed that the bulk of this work has dealt with events mainly of a local nature, and that reference to central government has been made only in so far as the local situation required it. There are several reasons for this. It was due partly to my ignorance of the finer points of the political struggle at the top level, and partly to the conviction that this struggle has already been described much better than I could do it in this short essay, by far better scholars. But one of my main reasons has been to underline the fact that though the Soviet government in the 1920's was already highly dictatorial, and contained all the seeds of the horror of the 1930's, it still reacted strongly (though, to be sure, often in a negative way) to the demands of the population. Thus while this work is hardly designed to increase one's faith in politicians, it is yet a work of hope—the hope that with improved social and economic conditions even the most arbitrary governments will be unable to violate the just demands of the people as a whole.

I have shown that such conditions did not exist in the Soviet Union in the 1920's and analysed some of the factors which made for the constant crises and catastrophes of the period. But I should like to make one strong point, even at the risk of being accused of passing moral judgments—a thing which no historian should do. This refers to the ideological bankruptcy of the Bolshevik party after it had attained power. The core of Bolshevik strength before the revolution lay in the fact that they had faith in their ideals, in the withering away

201

of the State, in a world revolution, in human perfectibility—a faith which it may be difficult to understand in the disillusioned years of the late twentieth century, but which stemmed directly from the nineteenth-century thinkers, and which reached at times even such crude manipulators as Stalin himself.

The Bolshevik tragedy was that the party actually came to power and its ideology was put to the test—whereupon it broke up into small pieces almost immediately. The new regime was therefore founded on false premises. Whereas it had started as the movement of the people, it soon found itself to be more autocratic than the tsarist government it had overthrown. It had begun as a protest against the methods used by the old regime, particularly its secret police, summary trials and notorious prisons. But it soon embraced the same methods, and without the limitations imposed on the imperial government by a strong Church, an established law code and the fear of international opinion they soon developed on a scale unheard of before the revolution. Most disappointing of all, to the left wing in particular, was the collapse of War Communism. This naïve belief that a moneyless economy could be introduced into a modern State had the strength of ideological dogma. When it failed, and when partial capitalism was restored under NEP, one of the basic tenets of official policy was removed. Possibly this, together with the ban on discussion within the party, had done more to create totalitarian State capitalism than the terror of the secret police. Thus it was the Bolsheviks' inability to retain power without conceding their ideals which brought about their corruption.

The unpopularity of the Bolshevik government has often been blamed on this corruption. The standard explanation is that the government had no support among the people, that its policies were unpopular, its leaders alien and its means unscrupulous. This explanation contains much that is both true and false. The tsarist government had no support among the people. The peasants did not support anyone, simply because for many centuries they had had no means of expressing their opinions. The newly formed proletariat had been extremely dissatisfied with the imperial government. The only vocal part of the population—the intelligentsia—demonstrated repeatedly its heartfelt desire to overthrow the government. Nor were the tsarist policies popular. The Crimean war, the frustrated Emancipation, the Japanese war, the dissolution of the First Duma and participation in the first world war were all undertaken by successive tsarist governments without consultation with the people, and they all turned into major disasters. As to the leaders, although an aura of mystical importance still clung to the Romanovs the same could hardly be said of their ministers; most of them of foreign origin, hardly any of them in touch with Russian public opinion. Nor was the tsarist government very scrupulous in choosing its means, as the witnesses of Bloody Sunday alone would testify.

On these grounds, then, there was little to choose between the two governments. Nevertheless, the tsarist government had certain advantages over the Bolsheviks. In the first instance, it had acquired a certain security of tenure simply by having held power so long. Second, it had no new and inconvenient theories to try out. Whenever an able minister attempted to introduce new measures, he was almost certain to be asked to tender his resignation. But the Bolsheviks, on coming to power, had two crucial points of their programme to implement: the abolition of private property and the abolition of religion. Among the articulate classes, the Bolsheviks had lost support because of their political ruthlessness and lack of social ethics. The proletariat counted for very little at this particular stage, because of its numerical weakness. It was the peasants' attitude that the new government had to watch most carefully. And the peasants' two bulwarks were their private plot of land and their religion. The peasants helped the Bolshevik revolution along because of the programme for land distribution. At certain periods they were capable of overthrowing the Bolsheviks if the government aroused sufficient wrath against its policies. Throughout the 1920's government policies were geared to implement some of their tenets without antagonizing the peasants too much. However, this is only part of the story.

Little need be said here about the fact that the Bolsheviks had inherited a country which, though potentially rich, had been ruined by a major war, a civil war and a revolution. Nor is it necessary to draw attention to their essential inexperience in government. But it must be stressed that both these factors played a major role in determining the pattern of Bolshevik government from the moment of the October revolution up to the present day. What is even more important, however, is the fact that the revolution and the subsequent government measures tampered with an intricate socio-economic system which had its roots in tradition and which performed definitive functions of both an economic and administrative nature. The reasons for the essential failure of the Bolsheviks (not failure to retain

203

power, of course, for they managed to do that, but failure to introduce satisfactory new policies) were basically that they had disturbed
the existing system without destroying it completely; they failed to
see the connection between the social, administrative and economic
parts of the system; and they were unable to substitute any genuinely
new structure in place of that which they had partially destroyed.

Since Russia during the 1920's was a predominantly agricultural
country, any investigation of Bolshevik failures has to start in the
countryside, among the peasants. I have shown in this book that the
social and administrative system had already been disturbed by the
pre-revolutionary measures of the tsarist governments, with the
result that many of the functions hitherto performed by the landlords
had to be performed by the communes, and on the other hand many
of the functions of the communes became the prerogative of individual peasant farms. The reforms begun by Stolypin led historically to the programme of land redistribution, which was attempted
as soon as the February revolution started and continued, with
Bolshevik approval, after the October revolution. This land redistribution—about which little has been known up to the present,
mainly because it was overshadowed by political upheavals—had
little to recommend it, either politically or economically. It contributed in great measure to the creation of unruly peasant bands, at
first supported by the Soviet government but soon to be disowned
because they created an additional security hazard and were hamper-
ing agricultural production.

The land question was closely connected with the problem of rural
administration. Pre-revolutionary communes played a large part in
the administration, and their powers were enhanced by the Emancipation Act. The Stolypin reforms, while undermining the power of
the commune, created no new administrative organs of equivalent
value. After the Bolshevik revolution the position was highly
anomalous. The new government was committed to the introduction
of new organs of local government which were to blend both the
administrative and the executive functions, and in which all the
members were to be elected by popular franchise and easily recallable.
This form of government by the masses for the masses—which, as we
have seen, Lenin preferred to other forms of administration—was in
fact introduced in the provinces at all levels, starting with the villages.
The difficulties encountered by the new provincial soviets have been
described in some detail. They were of many kinds, but the most
204

important result of their introduction was that they clashed directly with the commune form of administration. The rural soviets encountered problems of staffing, lack of directives and lack of support in the countryside; on the other hand, they had to contend with changing party policy on agricultural questions—for while the debate about the best forms of agriculture went on in the Central Committee, the course favouring administration by the soviets to the detriment of the communes alternated with the course favouring the communes. Meanwhile the commune, supported by certain elements among the party theorists as a road to socialism, began to grow in importance. Its administrative functions began to take on a new complexion and for the first time in its existence since the Middle Ages it began to fulfil a distinct political function. It became the means of expression for the political opinions of the peasants. It also gave the peasants belonging to the commune a new cohesion, which they were not slow to feel. Because of the weakness of the soviets, and the relative strength of their own organization—the commune—the peasants felt stronger in the second half of the NEP period than they had ever done before.

The irony of the situation lay in the fact that the commune was the organ of the richer peasants, who were naturally more articulate and commanded the respect of their fellow peasants. Not only was the commune, therefore, not a road to socialism; it also served to strengthen those elements in the countryside whom the government considered to be least trustworthy. In addition, many peasants were eager to leave the communes. We have seen how the commune hampered the efforts of the more enterprising peasants and how it cushioned the poorer, less hard-working ones. There was also conclusive proof that where the commune had broken down it produced a great number of landless peasants, whose only alternative was to leave the land and seek work in industry.

Though the Soviet government described itself as proletarian, the label was a symbol and not a reality. We have seen that although the Russian workers used to be well organized and concentrated in large centres until the October revolution, this phenomenon had ceased to hold good by the time the Bolsheviks assumed power. Owing to the conscription during the war, call-up during the civil war and the closure of many factories after 1917, as well as acute famine in the cities, the Russian proletariat had been reduced to insignificant numbers. In addition, where genuine attempts were made by the

205

workers themselves to introduce socialist measures in industry, they were summarily stopped by State or party intervention. The contraction of industry, which created unemployment among the proletariat, also hit the countryside. It has been already mentioned that the poorer peasants were forced to leave their villages in search of industrial work. However, industry could not absorb them. This created one of the biggest problems the government had to face during the 1920's. The hungry crowds of peasants streaming into the towns had to face great difficulties in every respect. The former workers, also unemployed, did not welcome their new rivals for industrial work. Nor did the city authorities, unable to deal with the large numbers of newcomers who were overstraining the already inadequate services. Factory managers, in search of cheap labour and often required to cut nationally approved wage rates, were sometimes willing to hire peasant labour, to the detriment of established workers. This created impossible conditions in industry. Frequent changes of plan by central authorities, inefficient management, corrupt trade union and party organizations and an influx of unskilled peasant labour into the factories lowered production, reduced the morale of the labour force and increased the rate of accidents. Though the government attempted to remedy this state of affairs, its measures were completely ineffectual, for they failed to deal with the basic causes of the crisis.

Thus, the period of NEP abounded in difficulties for the Soviet government. It was handicapped by a variety of reasons, some of its own creation, others inherited from the tsarist regime, and yet others it had no control over. It would be correct to say that its main problems were of an economic nature. The standstill in industry and the low productivity of agriculture were a constant brake on any plans for development. The second problem, closely connected with the first, was the cessation of normal relations with wealthy foreign countries, often called by the Soviet leaders an 'encirclement'. Doubtless the loss of foreign credits, on which imperial Russia in a great measure depended, was a great blow to the Bolsheviks. While the government clung to its monopoly of ownership and foreign trading very little could be done in this respect.

The third problem, the one which has been considered in this work, was that of creating harmonious relations between all the elements in the State—the majority of the population, the peasants, the government and the administration—both at local and higher levels. We have seen that this proved impossible because there were too many conflicting interests, because the attempts were piecemeal and hesitant, and because the government failed to grasp the real nature of the dilemma. Though the population was in the main antagonistic to the government, there were grounds for agreement in some respects. The peasants had been granted land by the revolution. Retention of their land tenure, and adequate safeguards for agriculture, might have reconciled them to the government. Nevertheless, I doubt whether this would have been a step in the right direction. Individual farming in Russia tended to become small-plot farming because of land divisions, and thus delayed improved techniques in agriculture. Commune farming had its bad sides, too, and it created an illusion of strength among the peasants, which the government wanted to avoid at all costs. Moreover, both these systems of farming were economically inefficient and created a large pool of surplus labour, which should have been siphoned off into industry.

This is the reason why agricultural and industrial problems were virtually indivisible during the period. The government found it impossible to develop industry without a healthy agriculture, and agriculture could not be improved without a developing industry. As though these problems were not enough, the government found itself facing yet another, this time completely of its own making. The system of local administration, imposed by order, was highly inefficient. In the countryside the peasants bypassed it whenever possible, and it degenerated into a channel for handing down instructions and directives from above. In industry the network of organizations was widely ramified and equally inefficient. The party cells interfered with managements, trusts interfered with the proper running of factories, and nobody knew where the limits of his authority began or ended.

In the long run the party, officially the vanguard of all that was best and progressive in the nation, held itself responsible for the running of the State, both centrally and on the local level. Though this meant certain advantages for the higher party officials, it also carried penalties when their policies miscarried. It was a most unsatisfactory state of affairs, for, apart from official policy-making in the centre, which was carried out by the highest party dignitaries, local party officials had little influence on the running of their districts. They appeared to be all-powerful, and this was true when they set out to carry out certain penal policies. But in the matter of production, agricultural output, the supply of goods, and food supplies, they were perpetually torn between the plans formulated at the centre, agreements concluded by the powerful industrial organizations, and local inefficiency and discontent. In this way the government lost ground constantly through the actions of its own organs, while non-government bodies gained in stature.

It has already been suggested that the problem of the commune was almost insoluble in its complexity, for the commune, where it existed in large numbers, had superseded government-sponsored organizations and had become the agent of a new and organized peasant movement; its social, economic and administrative strength lay in its organic background. We are not here concerned with the question of whether the commune was economically more productive than individual farmsteads (though clearly it was much more productive than State farms and collective farms): as has been demonstrated earlier, that question was interpreted differently by people of different political opinions. There was no direct answer to the problem. Obviously it was a case of individual communes—some were highly productive, others had a low productivity. Their success or lack of it depended on such factors as the regions in which they were situated, the soil they farmed, the quality of their officials and members, and many other circumstances. What is of interest to us here is the political influence of a large number of cohesive and relatively prosperous communes, which performed such diverse functions as planning agricultural production, disposing of produce at the best prices, carrying out day-to-day administration, and in many cases instructing the government offices—the rural soviets—about their tasks, besides paying for their upkeep as well as for that of the local teacher (who was probably the parish priest too), the local militiaman and the land surveyors.

There is little evidence to show that the communes had an external as well as an internal organization, but no doubt the congresses of co-operatives and of various other peasant organizations, held frequently under direct government auspices, provided sufficient ground for informal contacts and for a preliminary measuring of strength of the whole organization. This state of affairs was bound to cause the Soviet government anxiety, irrespective of whether the anxiety was well-founded. Unorganized, individual peasant households were deemed to be dangerous; how much more so were organized, prosperous communes. It was for this reason that 1927 marks the start of acrimonious arguments about the future form of Soviet agriculture. There were alternatives to the power of the commune, but none of them was really satisfactory. The first remedy to be suggested was infiltration of the commune: a slow, laborious and largely unreliable process, for it implied removing solely by persuasion the commune's natural leaders—the more successful peasants —and replacing them by the least successful peasants or by government officials. It also involved taking over the commune's rights of free trading, free bargaining and democratic communal decision making. Even given a long period of time, this process had little chance of success. The second alternative—and this was the one into which the government finally forced itself—was to replace the communes by new, artificially created, collective farms. Little need be said about this development, for it has been studied constantly since 1930. The third alternative was to allow (or force) all communes to break up, and to impose a uniform individual farmstead agriculture on all peasants in all regions. Again, we cannot concern ourselves here with the economic side of this question. We have already seen that it was a multilateral problem which involved such factors as farm division, strip farming, the use of primitive farm machinery and so forth, set against a possible (though doubtful) increase in agricultural production.

It is the political side of the problem which interests us here. Naturally, for ideological reasons, the encouragement of individual farming seemed wrong to the rank and file of the party; nevertheless subtle brains (and most notably Bukharin) saw that there was less danger to the government in an unorganized mass of peasants, each trying to get rich at the expense of the others, than in organized peasant communes. But this was not a sufficient reason for supporting individual farming. The crux of the matter lay in the fact that the break-up of the communes had an extremely important side effect: it led to the pauperization of a large number of peasant households and threw them directly onto the industrial labour market, which was not at that time prepared to absorb them. On the other hand, the commune (and probably the *kolkhoz* up to the present date) helped to cushion the less prosperous peasants and to create marginal employment for them, thus allowing them to stay in the countryside.

The break-up of the communes led directly to an increase in the migration of peasants into the towns and, indirectly, to the transfer of many inherently peasant problems into industrial enterprises. This migration was so harmful, and even dangerous, in the long run that the government felt it had to be stopped at all costs. For this reason the government could not wait much longer; its time was running out. It was not the Politbureau which set the time limits for the change: social and political considerations almost literally forced its hand. I refer here to Karcz's assertion that the government could afford to wait, for agriculture was steadily raising its output:

The inescapable conclusion is that a different policy, based on a clear definition of objectives and their rational implementation, might well have yielded about ninety million tons of usable grain by 1930–31 or a year later. The course of action suggested above does not rest upon a belief in the superiority of small peasant farming, nor is it argued that the existing structure of land holding was in any sense optimal. Nor do we intend to deny the existence of discontinuities that render the process of development difficult. It might also be granted that a policy of raising the productivity of traditional agriculture while embarking on an ambitious development programme was not easily discernible to those who were accustomed to think in terms of dialectic and the class struggle. But the question posed by Dr Lewin is still in order: 'Is there any reason why the time limits which the Politburo chose to set should be accorded the status of immutable historical laws?' It is fully permissible to think that had Soviet grain production followed an even mildly rising trend since 1926 . . . the whole pattern of Soviet industrialization . . . would have been different. Rising productivity and the continuing decline in the agricultural population would have affected the peasant terms of trade in the direction desired by Preobrazhensky and ultimately by Stalin. In principle this was all that was necessary to sustain a larger industrial labour force.[1]

It is odd to note that Karcz, who quoted Adam Smith to support his theory of the indivisibility of agricultural and industrial questions,[2] should have neglected the writings of equally important economists: Malthus and Ricardo. Both regarded population as a dependent variable; according to them, advancing wealth and productivity always bring about an increase in population, and even if the Soviet Union in the 1920's were not sufficient proof of this rule, the events in developing countries in recent years should convince everybody that the principle is sound. This was why the Politbureau felt it had no time, even if (which I do not for a moment concede) it considered itself to be the maker of history rather than the implementer of historical processes.[3] The combination of an increased rural population, organized communes and massive migration of pauperized peasants in search of non-existent industrial jobs, together with other equally valid government problems, gave credence to the fear that things could not continue for long as they were.

210

Ordzhonikidse summed the faults up at the fifteenth congress by saying that the:

apparatus was over-centralized; every trifle had to be referred to the centre; the apparatus had too many parallel bodies, there was a lack of efficiency, a lack of a sense of responsibility in the executive; it was very often impossible to find out who was responsible for what. Paper work ate us up; there was an incredible amount of red tape, and very often party and government directives were distorted.[4]

None of the features described in this book was therefore unknown to the highest bodies in the Soviet government and party. But, while they were well aware of them, they were unable to find remedies. It may be that a total relaxation of controls, both economic and administrative, might have served to improve the position. It may be that the continued inefficiency of the system without the application of a greater measure of terror would finally have brought about another popular revolution. These questions belong to the realm of Kremlinology and need not concern us here. But we have some indications that the Soviet Union's position in the late 1920's was not unique—that there are exact parallels even at the present time, in other countries which were made to embrace the particular brand of State capitalism, combined with a degree of private enterprise, which characterized the Soviet Union in the period of NEP.

Seen in perspective, the Soviet troubles of the late 'twenties appear in a different light. The government had erred in every way. It had not taken the trouble to produce an efficient administrative system; its efforts at education, while better than those of the tsarist regime, were directed at other objectives; its industrialization programme was badly timed and badly introduced; above all, its indecision in agricultural matters harmed the country immeasurably for many years to come. It is doubtless true that all these troubles were the direct consequence of a brutal take-over of the State by a group of inexperienced revolutionaries, but it must be said that the Bolshevik government merely exacerbated conditions which were already inherent in Russia at that period.

Could a different government have achieved better results? It is difficult to say on the basis of limited experience with new socialist governments. None of them seems to have performed very well, even though they were not isolated and bereft of allies, as the Bolshevik government was in the 'twenties. A continuation of the tsarist regime would not have been feasible after the first world war. Try as one

211

OLGA A. NARKIEWICZ

may, it is impossible to imagine that Russia was ready for a truly democratic government at that time. Here, analogies are not lacking. Almost every under-developed country which has tried democracy since the second world war has lapsed into dictatorship. There is little reason to suppose it would not have happened in Russia, particularly in the conditions of economic crisis which would have followed the first world war, whatever government was in power.

But given that the Bolshevik government was as good (or as bad) as could be expected under the circumstances, we must enquire whether it could have improved its methods, and avoided the horrors and excesses of both political purges and economic disasters. It seems certain that this could have been done, and with very little effort. Even political tenets need not have precluded a more peaceful solution of the problems. I think it is true to say that the conflict of personalities had as much influence on the solutions offered to that unfortunate country as any objective situation. Had the government been united, had quarrels been forgotten, had the leaders attempted to understand each other, the policies could have been worked out on a different basis, and they might have been better policies (in any event, they could hardly have been worse). The basic difficulty of the 'twenties, therefore, lay not in the fact that a small clique of Bolsheviks came to power with a desire to try out new policies, but in the fact that this clique, small as it was, could not agree among itself. This is not a condemnation of Stalin alone, though he was one of the chief culprits. Other members of the clique were equally ruthless and intransigent while lacking Stalin's genius for quick decision making. Thus, while it is ridiculous at this stage to look for scapegoats, it would perhaps be useful to point out that any government which comes to power in ways other than through democratic elections, and which therefore cannot be removed by peaceful means, should be careful not only to devise policies that will suit the population but also to be sure to agree within itself. Otherwise it will hardly be able to avoid the fate of the Bolsheviks in the 1930's, and the ruin which it brings to its country will be of far greater consequence than the downfall of the clique itself.

NOTES

1. Karcz, op. cit., p. 429.
2. Ibid., p. 400.
3. In addition, while Professor Karcz constantly and correctly states that the

government pursued an inconsistent policy—e.g. 'While the subject of trends in economic policy cannot be exhausted here, it will be made clear that the government pursued inconsistent policy objectives, that it failed to define its priorities in an unmistakable manner, and that it failed to implement them with the aid of policy tools employed at the time' (p. 413)—he yet suggests, fifteen pages later, that there was no need to panic, for all that was needed was a consistent policy on the part of the government. Professor Karcz cannot have it both ways; both his theory and mine hinge on the inability of the government to pursue a consistent policy, and the subsequent disasters. This government *did* panic, and in the process probably did itself more harm than good; we have no means of knowing what another government would have done in its place.

4. Fifteenth congress of the VKP (b), December 1927, vol. I, p. 447.

Appendix I

The organization of commune and soviet

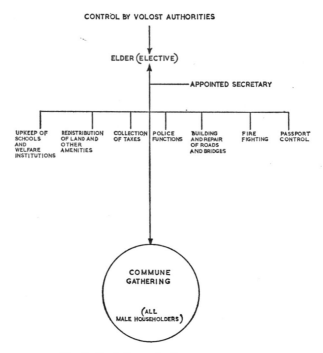

CONTROL BY VOLOST AUTHORITIES

ELDER (ELECTIVE)

APPOINTED SECRETARY

| UPKEEP OF SCHOOLS AND WELFARE INSTITUTIONS | REDISTRIBUTION OF LAND AND OTHER AMENITIES | COLLECTION OF TAXES | POLICE FUNCTIONS | BUILDING AND REPAIR OF ROADS AND BRIDGES | FIRE FIGHTING | PASSPORT CONTROL |

COMMUNE GATHERING

(ALL MALE HOUSEHOLDERS)

Fig. 1. Post-Emancipation commune

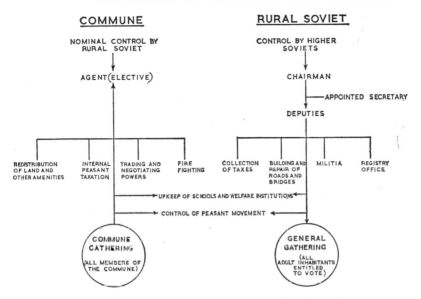

Fig. 2. Commune and rural soviet during the NEP period

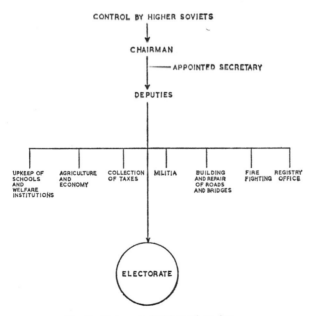

Fig. 3. The post-1930 rural soviet

215

Appendix II

Report of the agent of GKK about the persecution of the *rabkory* in the Diatlov factory

Smolensk archives, reel No. 3, Smolensk, 1926, WKP 22, protocol No. 17 of the meeting of the bureau of Belskii *uezd* committee of VKP (b) on 28–29 September 1926: 'Report of the agent of GKK about the persecution of the *rabkory* in Diatlov factory.'

This document tells of persecution by the management of two 'workers' correspondents' (*rabkory*) who had discovered some irregularities in the running of the factory.

Two 'workers' correspondents', Golosov and Gondelev, were persecuted by the manager of the Diatlov factory, Chibisov, and his assistant, the specialist Kaufman. Chibisov, who was a Communist and a former worker, had been running the factory with the help of the specialist. The working conditions in the factory were very bad, and the workers were badly treated. The two correspondents (who, clearly, were also employed as workers in this factory) had tried to make the irregularities public, and were subjected to persecution by the management. Chibisov had apparently found it difficult to run the factory to start with, but he was now feared by all the workers. At one time things were so bad that the inspector of labour was obliged to intervene because 'there was a violation of the law code about labour'. The outcome of this intervention is not given, but obviously Chibisov did not change, for 'Many workers made complaints against comrade Chibisov for his rude behaviour to them, and they intended to put this problem before the [party] cell, but since they were family men they were frightened that they would be dismissed from the factory as Gondelev [one of the *rabkory*] was dismissed. Chibisov and Kaufman spent their travelling expenses money unlawfully . . . Clerks received ten roubles above their salary. The workers work two shifts [running], that is, sixteen hours, and do not receive their full pay for over-time . . .'

The reported meeting was a full party organization inquest on the situation in the factory, at which the unlucky Chibisov was present, and
216

the judiciary organizations were represented by the assistant procurator, Narkevich. Narkevich confirmed the above-noted facts and said that the national prosecutor was already handling the matter. Additional information should be sent to him to help expedite the case. Narkevich suggested that Chibisov should be left in his post for the time being. Chibisov begged to be released from his position and sent to a shop-floor job. There is no record of the meeting's decision on Chibisov. The only resolutions are that party work at the Diatlov factory should be improved; that the [party] fraction of the trust managing the factory should be asked to dismiss Kaufman; and that a commission should be set up to supervise all the activity in the factory.

Appendix III

Letter of complaint about disorders during the procurement campaign, 1929

копия'

Газетам: 'БЕДНОТА' 'ПРАВДА' 'КРЕСТЬЯНСКАЯ ГАЗЕТА', СТАЛИНУ и' РЫКОВУ.—

Ужаснейшие безобразия творятся в Мещовском районе, Сухинического Округа, Западно й области.

Есть хозяйства ниже средняцких у которых выгребли весь хлеб до зерна хлебо заготовители. А что делается с хлебом, так жутко сказать! В Мещовске хлеб ссыпают прямо под навесы без всяких стен. По хлебу ходят коровы, свиньи и люди грядными ногами. Тяжело и больно смотреть мужику как взятый у него за безценок хлеб совершенно не производительно в грязь затаплтывается и скотами поедается. Отнимают у мужика хлеб говорят для Красной Армии, для рабочих, а вместо этого просто в грязь его топчут. Ужели нет у нас в Республике никого, кто бы мог прекратить эти безобразия? И разве нельзя было записанные в добровольном порядке хлебные излишки забронировать за записавшими их хозяевами, чтобы в нужную минуту предложить подвести к месту назначения. Не подготовили ни места, ни тары словом ничего, а двинули тысячи обозов с хлебом который и ссыпается можно сказать под открытым небом, несмотря на наступившую осень.

Это—вредительство, а не хлебозаготовки. Тысячи пудов гниют. Десятки тысяч рабочих семейств можно было прокормить за счет гниющего совершенно напрасно хлеба.

Где та бережливость и экономия, о которых говорил Ленин? Здесь мы видим только одно издевательство надь хлебом мужиком и мужнцким трудом. Многие крестьяне вывезли букваль— но все, до последнего зерна, и на их те глазах, по их хлебу ходит, скот, топчет хлеб в грязь, а дома совершенно без куска хлеба осталась семья.

Ужели в интересах Революции полнейшее разорение и обнищание крестьянских хозяйств.—

[*Note:* all spelling mistakes are in the original.]

Appendix IV

The rate of collectivization

Figs. 4–8 summarize the extent of collectivization achieved by 15 December 1929. Data missing for the following districts:[1]

Orenburgskiy okrug	Middle Volga
Karachaevskaya avtonomnaya oblast'[2]	
Cherkesskaya avtonomnaya oblast'	North Caucasus
Chechenskaya avtonomnaya oblast'	
Kurskiy okrug	Central black soil region
Staryi Oskol' okrug	(Ts Ch O)
Barabinskiy okrug	
Tarskiy okrug	Sibirskiy Kray
Tulunskiy okrug[3]	
Zlatoustovskiy okrug	Uralskaya oblast'
Kurganskiy okrug	
Rzhevskiy okrug	Zapadnaya oblast'
Moskovskiy okrug	Moskovskaya oblast'
Kineshemskiy okrug	Ivanovskaya oblast'
Votskaya avtonomnaya oblast'	Nizhniy Gorod Kray
Nenetskiy natsional'nyi okrug	Severnyy Kray
Luzhskiy okrug	
Murmanskiy okrug	Leningradskaya oblast'
Novgorodskiy okrug	
Karel'skaya ASSR	

THE MAKING OF THE SOVIET STATE APPARATUS

Adaevskiy okrug
Akmolinskiy okrug ⎫ Kazakhstan
Gur'evskiy okrug
Kara-Kalpakskaya avtonomnaya oblast'

Belaya Tserkov' okrug
Volynskiy okrug
Tulchinskiy okrug[4] ⎬ Ukraine
Chernigovskiy okrug
Moldavskaya ASSR

Kashka-Dar'ya otdelnyy raion
Khoremskiy otdelnyy raion ⎬ Uzbekistan
Kenimekhskiy otdelnyy raion

Notes
1. The above data are quoted by Ivnitsky, op. cit.
2. Karacharovskaya avtonomnaya oblast in text.
3. Gulunskiy okrug in text.
4. Gulchinskiy okrug in text.

In Figs. 4–8 the key to the horizontal axes is as follows:

1 RSFSR:
   (a) Nizhne-Volzhskiy kray.
   (b) Sredne-Volzhskaya oblast.
   (c) Severo-Kavkazskiy kray.
   (d) Tsentralno-Chernozemnaya oblast.
   (e) Sibirskiy kray.
   (f) Uralskaya oblast.
   (g) Zapadnaya oblast.
   (h) Moskovskaya oblast.
   (i) Ivanovskaya oblast.
   (j) Nizhegorodskiy kray.
   (k) Severnyy kray.
   (l) Leningradskaya oblast.
   (m) Kazakhskaya ASSR.
   (n) Dagestanskaya ASSR.
   (o) Krymskaya ASSR.
2 Ukrainian SSR.
3 Belorussian SSR.
4 Uzbek SSR.
5 Turkmen SSR.
6 Armenian SSR.
7 Azerbaydzhan SSR.

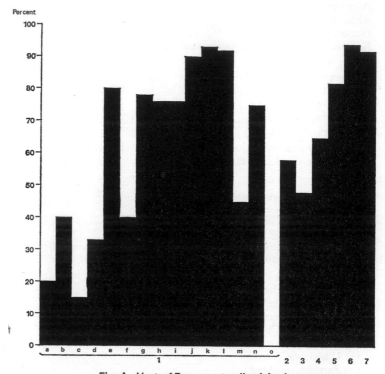

Fig. 4. Up to 15 per cent collectivized

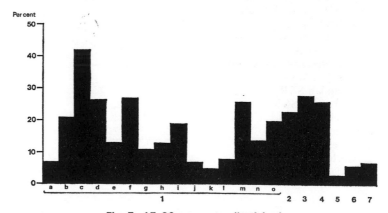

Fig. 5. 15–30 per cent collectivized

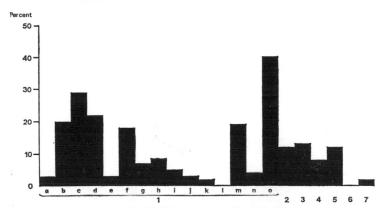

Fig. 6. 30–50 per cent collectivized

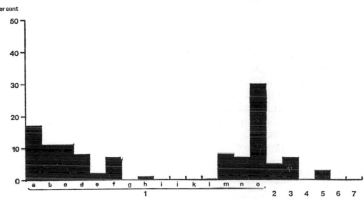

Fig. 7. 50–70 per cent collectivized

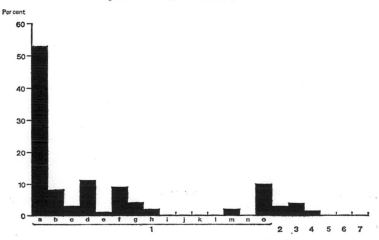

Fig. 8. 70 per cent and over collectivized

223

Q

Glossary

Agitprop   Agitation and Propaganda Section.
Batrak   Agricultural labourer.
Edinyi selsko-khozyaistvennyi nalog   Agricultural tax.
Glavk   Main committee or central board.
Glavkhim   Central Board of the Chemical Industry.
Glavpolitprosvet   Central Department for Political Education.
Glavprofobr   Central Department for Industrial Training.
Gosplan   State Planning Commission.
Guberniya   Region.
Istpart   Commission for the Study of Party History.
Khozraschet   Profit and Loss Accounting.
Khutor   Farmstead.
Kolkhoztsentr   Central Collectivization Board.
Narkomzem   National Commissariat of Agriculture.
NEP   New Economic Policy.
Obshchii skhod   General gathering (of all village inhabitants entitled to vote in soviet elections).
Obshchina   Pre-revolutionary village commune.
Orgraspred   Organization and Distribution Section.
Otrub   Plot of land.
Poselok   Settlement.
Proizvodstvennaya konferentsiya   Production conference.
Proizvodstvennoe soveshchanie   Production conference.
Rabkor   Workers' correspondent.
Raion   District.
Rassloenie   Stratification.
RKI   Workers' and Peasants' Inspectorate.
RKP   Russian Communist Party.
RSFSR   Russian Socialist Federal Soviet Republic.
224

Selkor   Rural correspondent.
Skhod   Pre-revolutionary village gathering.
Sovnarkom   Council of National Commissars.
Soyuzkhleb   Agricultural Co-operatives' Union.
Uchastok   Plot of land.
Upolnomochennyi   Agent of the land commune.
VChK   Extraordinary Commission for the Struggle against Counter-revolution.
Volost   Township.
VSNKh   All-Union Economic Council.
VTsPS   All-Union Trades' Union Council.
Zemelnoe obshchestvo   Land commune (as set up by the 1922 Land Code).
Zemelnyi Skhod   Gathering of the land commune.
Zemleustroistvo   Land redistribution.

Bibliography

1 Sources

Z. A. Astapovich and K. V. Gusev (ed.), *Nekotorye Problemy Istorii Sovetskogo Obshchestva*. Moscow, 1964.

A. Bakhutov, 'K 8-oi Godovshchine Okt'yabrskoi Revolyutii'. *Voprosy Truda*, No. 11, 1925.

K. I. Bobkov, 'Iz Istorii Organizatsii Upravleniya Promyshlennostiyu *v* Pervye Gody Sovetskoi Vlasti (1917–20)'. *Voprosy Istorii*, No. 4, April 1957.

I. Bogovoi, 'Perevybory Sovetov v Derevne i Rasshirenie Demokratii'. *Bolshevik*, Nos. 9–10, 1926.

Bor'ba Rabochikh za Uluchshenie Proizvodstva i Rezhim Ekonomii, appeal No. 14, Pervye Shagi Industrializatsii SSSR, 1926–27 gg. Moscow, 1959.

Brokhaus and Efron, *Entsiklopedicheskii Slovar'*.

S. K. Chayanov *et al.*, *Experimental Farming of the People's Commissariat for Agriculture of the RSFSR*. Moscow, 1929.

'Chislennost' i Sostav Promyshlennykh Rabochikh Kadrov Kuzbassa v 1926–37 gg.', *Formirovanie i Razvitie Sovetskogo Rabochego Klassa (1917–61)*. Moscow, 1964.

D. A. Chugaev (ed.), *Rabochii Klass Sovetskoi Rossii v Pervyi God Diktatury Proletariata*. Moscow, 1964.

R. P. Dadykin (ed.), *Formirovanie i Razvitie Sovetskogo Rabochego Klassa (1917–61)*. Moscow, 1964.

V. P. Danilov, *Sozdanie Materialno-Tekhnicheskikh Predposylok Kollektivizatsii Selskogo Khozyaistva v SSSR*. Moscow, 1957.

—'Sotsialno-Eknomicheskie Otnosheniya v Sovetskoi Derevne Nakanune Kollektivizatsii'. *Istoricheskie Zapiski*, vol. 55, 1956.

Ekonomicheskoe Rassloenie Krest'yanstva v 1917 i 1919 gg.', *Trudy Tsentralnogo Statisticheskogo Upravleniya*. Moscow, 1922.

226

L. S. Gaponenko, 'Rabochii Klass Rossii nakanune Velikogo Oktyabrya'. *Istoricheskie Zapiski*, vol. 73, 1963.
Ya. Gindin, 'Nash Khozyaistvennyi Pod'em i Novye Zadachi Regulirovaniya Rynka Truda'. *Voprosy Truda*, No. 11, 1925.
A. Ya. Gorman, 'O Sotsialisticheskom Preobrazovanii Promyshlennosti'. *Voprosy Istorii*, No. 2, 1957.
E. N. Gorodetsky, *Rozhdenie Sovetskogo Gosudarstva*. Moscow, 1965.
M. P. Iroshnikov, 'O Tekste Leninskogo Dekreta "O Zemle" '. *Issledovaniya po Otechestvennomu Istochnikovedeniyu*. Moscow, 1964.
N. A. Ivnitsky (ed.), *Istochnikovedenie Istorii Sovetskogo Obshchestva*. Moscow, 1964.
N. A. Ivnitsky, 'Istoriya podgotovki postanovleniya Ts K V KP (b) o tempakh kollektivizatsii selskogo khozyaistva ot 5 yanvaria, 1930' in *Istochnikovedenie Istorii Sovetskogo Obshchestva*. Moscow, 1964.
'Iz Istorii Partiinogo Stroitelstva'. *Partiinaya Zhizn*', No. 20, 1957.
'Khronika Truda i Sotsialnogo Strakhovaniya po SSSR'. *Voprosy Truda*, No. 10, 1925.
A. Khryashcheva, 'Krest'yanstvo v Voine i Revolyutsii'. *Tsentralnoe Statisticheskoe Upravlenie*, 1921.
M. P. Kim (ed.), *Istoriya Sovetskogo Krest'yanstva i Kolkhoznogo Stroitelstva v SSSR*. Moscow, 1963.
M. Kubanin, 'Obshchina pri Diktature Proletariata' in *Osnovnye Nachala Zemleustroistva*. Moscow, 1927.
V. A. Kungurtsov, *Tekstilnaya Promyshlennost' SSSR*. Munich, 1957.
S. M. Kuznetsov, 'K Prorabotke Pyatiletnego Perspektivnogo Plana'. *Vestnik Finansov*, No. 5, 1927.
V. S. Lelchuk, 'O Nekotorykh Sdvigakh v Ryadakh Rabochikh Khimicheskoi Promyshlennosti SSSR (1917–37), *Formirovanie i Razvitie Sovetskogo Rabochego Klassa (1917–61)*. Moscow, 1964.
V. I. Lenin, 'Gosudarstvo i Revolyutsiya'. *Sochineniya*, vol. 25, Fourth edition, 1949.
—'Rough outline for the draft of a programme of the Russian Communist party'. Document No. 152, *Trotsky papers*, vol. I. The Hague, 1964.
—'Chto Delat'. *Izbrannye Proizvedeniya*, vol. 1. Moscow, 1960.
—*Sochineniya*, Fourth edition.
M. Lifshits, 'Sistema Oblozheniya Krest'yanstva v 1924–25'. *Vestnik Finansov*, No. 3, March 1924.
V. E. Loburets, 'Vosstanovlenie i Konsolidatsiya Kadrov Rabochego Klassa Ukrainy v 1921–25'. *Formirovanie i Razvitie Sovetskogo Rabochego Klassa (1917–61)*. Moscow, 1964.
E. A. Lutsky, 'Vosproizvedenie Teksta Dekreta "O Zemle" v Sovetskikh Publikatsiyakh', *Problemy Istochnikovedeniya*, vol. XI. Moscow, 1963.
—'O Sushchnosti Uravnitelnogo Zemlepolzovaniya v Sovetskoi Rossii'. *Voprosy Istorii*, No. 9, 1956.
M. Makarov, *Organizatsiya Selskogo Khozyaistva*. Berlin, 1924.
Materialy I-go Vsesoyuznogo S'ezda po Voprosam Khimicheskoi Promyshlennosti. Moscow, 1930.

Z. Mokhov, 'Pereselenchestvo, Izbytki Truda i Bezrabotitsa'. *Voprosy Truda*, No. 6, 1929.

E. Mokhov, 'Organizatsionnoe Sostoyanie i Deyatelnost' Birzh Truda'. *Voprosy Truda*, No. 10, 1925.

B. Morozov, *Sozdanie i Ukreplenie Sovetskogo Gosudarstvennogo Apparata*. Moscow, 1957.

N. Nikolsky, 'Bezrabotitsa i ee Perspektivy'. *Voprosy Truda*, No. 10, 1925.

N. Oganovsky, *Revolyutsiya Naoborot* (Razrushenie Obshchiny). Petrograd, 1917.

A. L. Oprishchenko, 'Voprosy Sotsialisticheskogo Sorevnovaniya Rabochego Klassa SSSR v Sovetskoi Istoriografii', *Nekotorye Problemy Istorii Sovetskogo Obshchestva*. Moscow, 1964.

Osnovnaya Khimicheskaya Promyshlennost', Moscow, 1925.

P. N. Pershin, *Uchastkovoe Zemlepolzovanie v Rossii*. Moscow, 1922.

Yu. A. Polyakov, 'Sotsialno-Eknomicheskie Itogi Agrarnykh Preobrazovanii Oktyabrskoi Revolyutsii (1917–20)'. *Istoriya Sovetskogo Krest' yanstva i Kolkhoznogo Stroitelstva v SSSR*. Moscow, 1963.

P. Popov, 'Vosstanovlenie Sel'skogo Khozyaistva v Golodayushchikh Raionakh'. *Planovoe Khozyaistvo*, Nos. 3–4, March–April 1923.

A. G. Rashin, *Formirovanie Rabochego Klassa Rossii*. Moscow, 1958.

M. Rezunov, *Selskie Sovety i Zemelnye Obshchestva*. Moscow, 1928.

L. S. Rogachevskaya, *Iz Istorii Rabochego Klassa SSSR, v Pervye Gody Industrializatsii, 1926–27*. Moscow, 1959.

M. I. Rogov, 'Deyatelnost' Moskovskogo Soveta za 1924 god i Blizhaishie Zadachi na 1925 god'. *Sovetskoe Stroitelstvo*, sbornik I. Moscow, 1925.

A. Sapunov, 'Vzaimootnosheniya Skhodov i Selsovetov'. *Vlast Sovetov*, No. 21, 1927.

V. Shavlov, 'Rynok Truda v Tambovskoi Gubernii'. *Voprosy Truda*, No. 10, 1925.

I. Shumsky, 'Itogi Obshchestvennykh Rabot v Odesse'. *Voprosy Truda*, No. 11, 1925.

D. Shneer, 'Profsoyuzy i Okhrana Truda'. *Voprosy Truda*, No. 11, 1925.

A. Shvabapovich, 'Tekhnika Bezopasnosti v Tekstylnoi Promyshlennosti'. *Voprosy Truda*, No. 11, 1925.

M. Snegirev, 'Velikaya Okt'yabrskaya Sotsialisticheskaya Revolyutsiya i Raspredelenie Zemel' v 1917–18 godakh'. *Voprosy Istorii*, No. 11, 1947.

Sovetskoe Stroitelstvo, sbornik I. Moscow, 1925.

Sovety, S'ezdy Sovetov i Ispolkomy. Moscow, 1924.

J. V. Stalin, *Voprosy Leninizma*, Eleventh edition. Moscow, 1941.

—'Rech v Sverdlovskom Universitete'. *Sochineniya*, vol. 7.

—*Sochineniya*.

N. Sukhanov, 'Obshchina v Sovetskom Agrarnom Zakonodate lstve'. *Osnovnye Nachala Zemleustroistva*. Moscow, 1927.

S. A. Tokarev, *Etnografiya Narodov SSSR*. Moscow, 1958.

G. V. Tsiperovich, *Sindikaty i Tresty v Rossii i v SSSR*. Leningrad, 1927.

M. Ustinov, 'K Voprosu o Formakh Zemlepolzovaniya'. *Bolshevik*, Nos. 19–20, 1927.

M. Vasser, 'Voprosy Vnutripartiinoi Raboty pri Perekhode k Nepu'. *Partiinaya Zhizn'*, No. 15, 1957.
B. S. Vlasov (ed.), *Bor'ba KPSS za Sotsialisticheskuyu Industrializatsiyu Strany i Podgotovku Sploshnoi Kollektivizatsii Sel'skogo Khozyaistva*. Moscow, 1960.
I. M. Volkov (ed.), *Sbornik Dokumentov i Materialov po istorii SSSR, Sovetskogo Perioda*. Moscow, 1966.
S. Zagorsky, 'Sotsialno-Ekonomicheskaya Reaktsiya v Sovetskoi Rossii'. *Sovremennye Zapiski*, No. 1, 1920.
Znamensky, 'Iz Istorii Razvitiya Sovetskogo Apparata v Tambovskoi Gubernii'. *Sovetskoe Stroitelstvo*, sbornik I. Moscow, 1925.
S. Zdanovich, 'Selskie Sovety i Zemelnye Obshchestva'. *Bolshevik*, No. 6, 1928.
Zhurnal Khimicheskoi Promyshlennosti, Nos. 5–6, 1928.
Z. K. Zvezdin and L. S. Rogachevskaya (ed.), *Pervye Shagi Industrializatsii SSSR*, 1926–27. Moscow, 1959.

2 *Studies*

A. N. Antsiferov *et al.*, *Russian agriculture during the war*. Yale, 1930.
A. Avtorkhanov, *Stalin and the Soviet Communist party*. Munich, 1959.
W. R. Batsell, *Soviet rule in Russia*. New York, 1929.
P. T. Bauer and B. S. Yamey, *The economics of under-developed countries*. Cambridge, 1957.
A. Baykov, *The development of the soviet economic system*. Cambridge, 1946.
Ch. Bettelhelm, *L'Economic soviétique*. Paris, 1950.
K. Borders, *Village life under the soviets*. New York, 1927.
A. Broderson, *The soviet workers: labor and government in soviet society*. New York, 1966.
E. H. Carr, *The Bolshevik revolution*. London, 1954 (2 vols).
—*Socialism in one country*. London, 1958–59 (2 vols).
R. V. Daniels, *The conscience of the revolution*. Harvard, 1960.
Margaret Dewar, *Labour policy in the USSR, 1917–28*. London, 1956.
G. Drage, *Russian affairs*. London, 1904.
H. J. Ellison, 'The decision to collectivize agriculture'. *American Slavic Review*, February 1961.
A. Erlich, *The soviet industrialization debate, 1924–28*. Harvard, 1960.
M. Fainsod, *Smolensk under Soviet rule*. Harvard, 1958.
—*How Russia is ruled*, revised edition. London, 1963.
Louis Fischer, *The life of Lenin*. London, 1965.
M. T. Florinsky, *Russia, a history and interpretation*. New York, 1961 (2 vols).
J. K. Galbraith, *The affluent society*. London 1961.
N. Hampson *A social history of the French revolution*. London, 1965.
E. Holzman (ed.), *Readings on the Soviet economy*. New York, 1962.
G. Ionescu, 'Eastern Europe' in *Populism: its meanings and national characteristics*. London, 1969.

OLGA A. NARKIEWICZ

N. Jasny, *Soviet industrialization, 1928–52*. Chicago, 1961.
—*The socialized agriculture of the USSR*. Stanford, 1949.
J. F. Karcz, 'Thoughts on the grain problem'. *Soviet Studies*, April, 1967.
M. Lewin, *La Paysannerie et le pouvoir soviétique, 1928–30*. Paris, 1966.
—'The immediate background to collectivization'. *Soviet Studies*, October 1965.
P. I. Lyashchenko, *History of the national economy of the USSR*. New York, 1949.
James Mavor, *An economic history of Russia*. London, 1914 (2 vols).
O. A. Narkiewicz, 'Surplus labour and peasant migration in the 'twenties' a paper delivered at the University of Birmingham, April 1966.
T. J. Polner, *Russian local government during the war and the union of Zemstvos*. Yale, 1930.
S. N. Prokopovich, *Narodnoe Khozyaistvo SSSR*. New York, 1952 (2 vols)
G. H. Sabine, *A history of political theory*, Third edition. London, 1963.
L. Schapiro, *The origins of the Communist autocracy*. London, 1955.
—*The Communist party of the Soviet Union*. London, 1963.
M. Shachtman, *The struggle for the new course*. New York, 1943.
R. Schlesinger, 'On the scope of necessity and error'. *Soviet Studies*, January 1966.
S. M. Schwarz, *Labor in the Soviet Union*. New York, 1952.
S. G. Strumilin, *Ocherki ekonomicheskoi istorii Rossii*. Moscow, 1960.
Yuzuru Taniuchi, *The village gathering in Russia in the mid-1920's*. Birmingham, 1968.
J. Towster, *Political power in the USSR, 1917–47*. New York, 1948.
M. I. Tugan-Baranovsky, *Geschichte der russischen Fabrik*. Berlin, 1900.
S. and B. Webb, *Soviet Communism: a new civilization*. London, 1935.
Karl A. Wittfogel, *Oriental despotism*. Yale, 1964.
S. O. Zagorsky, *State control of industry in Russia during the war*. Yale, 1928.

3 *Unpublished documents (in chronological order)*

Smolensk archives, reel No. 2, Smolensk, 1917–18, WKP 1 and WKP 2; various documents relating to land and cattle inventories.
Protocol No. 1 of the Uezd Conference of Managers of Rural Libraries in the Yartsevo Uezd on 29 May 1925; Smolensk archives, reel No. 3, Smolensk, 1925, WKP 23.
Protocol No. 8 of the Plenum of Roslavl Uezd Committee of RKP (b) jointly with the secretaries of Volost Committees of RKP (b) on 13 August 1925; Smolensk archives, reel No. 3, Smolensk, 1925, WKP 22.
Report of the Belskii Uezd Executive Committee for the period 1 October 1925 to 1 August 1926; Smolensk archives, reel No. 3, Smolensk, 1926, WKP 25.
Conditions and Work of VKP (b) Cell in Selishchenskaya Volost from October 1925 to August 1926; Smolensk archives, reel No. 3, Smolensk, 1926, WKP 25.
Protocol No. 17 of the meeting of the Bureau of Belskii Uezd Committee
230

of VKP (b) on 28–29 September 1926: 'Report of the agent of GKK about the persecution of the workers' correspondents in Diatlov factory'; Smolensk archives, reel No. 3, Smolensk, 1926, WKP 22.

Report about the study of the fourteenth party congress by the Shumyach Volost Organization, 14 April 1926; Smolensk archives, reel No. 4, Smolensk, 1926, WKP 29.

Information bulletin of the Secretary of Semenovskaya Volost Committee of VKP (b), c. April 1926; Smolensk archives, reel No. 4, Smolensk, 1926, WKP 29.

Additional information to the report about the work of the Guberniya Committee for the Fifteenth Guberniya Party Conference, 9 June 1926; Smolensk archives, reel No. 4, Smolensk, 1926, WKP 29.

Report of the Gzhatsk Credit Rural Union [Kredselsovet], 15 October 1926; Smolensk archives, reel No. 4, Smolensk, 1926, WKP 28.

Resolution about the report on the re-election campaign of the rural and urban network of Consumers' Co-operatives: appendix to protocol No. 4 of the meeting of the Bureau of Velikolutskii Okruzhkom of VKP (b), held on 20 October 1927; Smolensk archives, reel No. 4, Smolensk, 1927, WKP 30.

Appendix to protocol No. 11 of the meeting of the Bureau of Velikolutskii Okruzhkom of VKP (b) on 3 December 1927; Smolensk archives, reel No. 4, Smolensk, 1927, WKP 30 (secret).

Protocol No. 15 of the meeting of the Bureau of Velikolutskii Okruzhkom of VKP (b) on 28 December 1927; Smolensk archives, reel No. 4, Smolensk, 1927, WKP 30.

Protocol No. [illegible] of the meeting of the Smolensk Guberniya Committee of VKP (b) on 28 December 1927; Smolensk archives, reel No. 5, Smolensk, 1928, WKP 33.

Protocol No. 6 of the meeting of the Bureau of Smolensk Guberniya Committee of VKP (b) on 29 December 1927; Smolensk archives, reel No. 5, Smolensk, 1928, WKP 33.

Protocol of a conference of the Guberniya Committee of VKP (b) on the procurement of goods on 20 January 1928; Smolensk archives, reel No. 5, Smolensk, 1928, WKP 33.

Appendix to point 2 of protocol No. 17 of the meeting of the Bureau of Guberniya Committee on 16 February 1928: 'The state of unemployment in Smolensk guberniya on 1 January 1928', Smolensk archives; reel No. 5, Smolensk, 1928, WKP 33.

'The state of unemployment in the Smolensk guberniya on 1 January 1928: regulation of peasant migration'; Smolensk archives, reel No. 5, Smolensk, 1928, WKP 33.

Protocol of the Conference of Secretaries of Uezd Committees of VKP (b) on 12 February 1928; Smolensk archives, reel No. 5, Smolensk, 1928, WKP 33.

Report of the Gubkom Instructor of VKP (b) Sinitsyn about the condition and work of Elniya organization of VKP (b) on 1 April 1928; Smolensk archives, reel No. 5, Smolensk, 1928, WKP 33.

Protocol No. 26 of the meeting of the Smolensk Guberniya Committee of

VKP (b) on 28 April 1928; Smolensk archives, reel No. 5, Smolensk, 1928, WKP 33.
Appendix to point No. 1 of protocol No. 26 of the meeting of the Bureau of the Guberniya Committee on 28 April 1928: 'Conclusions after a survey of professional, economic and party work at the Smolensk factory "Katushka"'; Smolensk archives, reel No. 5, Smolensk, 1928, WKP 33.
Protocol No. 27 of the meeting of the Bureau of Smolensk Guberniya Committee of VKP (b) on 30 April 1928: 'Resolution in connection with the situation at the factory "Katushka" '; Smolensk archives, reel No. 5, Smolensk, 1928, WKP 33.
Appendix No. 1 to protocol No. 28 of the meeting of the Bureau of the Guberniya Committee on 3 May 1928; Smolensk archives, reel No. 5, Smolensk, 1928, WKP 33 (*secret*).
Protocol No. 30: 'Extraordinary meeting of the Bureau of the Smolensk Guberniya Committee of VKP (b) on 16 May 1928'; Smolensk archives, reel No. 5, Smolensk, 1928, WKP 33.

4 *Published documents*

Eighth congress of the RKP (b), March 1919, *Protokoly*. Moscow 1959.
Ninth congress of the RKP (b), 1920, *Protokoly*. Msocow, 1960.
Tenth congress of the RKP (b), 1921, *Stenograficheskii Otchet*. Moscow, 1963.
Fourteenth congress of the VKP (b), 1925, *Stenograficheskii Otchet*. Moscow, 1926.
Fifteenth Congress of the VKP (b), December 1927, *Stenograficheskii Otchet*. Moscow, 1961.
Decree No. 148, Zakony Rabochego i Krestyanskogo Pravitelstva, 1921.
Decree No. 426, Zakony Rabochego i Krestyanskogo Pravitelstva, 1922.
Decree No. 68, Zemelnyi Kodeks; Zakony Rabochego i Krestyanskogo Pravitelstva, 1922.
Decree on the hiring of work-hands, *Izvestya*, 10 June 1920.
Decree No. 79, Sobranie Uzakonenii RSFSR, 1927.
Decree No. 172, Zakony Rabochego i Krestyanskogo Pravitelstva, 1927.
Decree No. 116 (about the regulation of peasant migration), Sobranie Uzakonenii i Rasporyazhenii RSFSR, 14 November 1927.
Doklad Kontrolnoi Komissii Bogorodsko-Glukhovskoi Manufactury . . . s l marta po l avgusta 1918 g., Rabochii Klass Sovetskoi Rossii v Pervyi God Diktatury Proletariata, Collection of Documents. Moscow, 1964.
Iz Informatsionnogo Obzora Organizatsionno-Raspredelitelnogo Otdela TsK VKP (b) o Proizvodstvennykh Kommissiakh i Soveshchaniakh; Sbornik Dokumentov i Materialov po Istorii SSSR Sovetskogo Perioda. Moscow, 1966.
KPSS v Rezolyutsiyakh i Resheniyakh, part I, Seventh edition, 1954.
Lenin, Doklad ob Ocherednykh Zadachakh Sovetskoi Vlasti, 29 April 1918. *Sochineniya*, vol. 27.
Postanovlenie TsIK SSSR, 20 October 1927: 'Ob Itogakh Khozyaistvennogo Stroitelstva SSSR'; Bor'ba KPSS za Sotsialisticheskuyu Industrializatsiyu Strany. Moscow, 1960.

232

THE MAKING OF THE SOVIET STATE APPARATUS

The Trotsky papers, 1917–22; vol. I., ed. Jan M. Meijer. The Hague, 1964.

5 *Newspapers, journals and periodicals consulted*

American Slavic and East European Review, Bolshevik (Kommunist), *Derevenskaya Kommuna, Doklady i Soobshcheniya Instituta Istrii, Ekonomicheskaya Zhizn', Istoricheskie Zapiski, Izvestiya, Izvestiya TsK-VKP* (b), *Partiinaya Zhizn', Planowoe Khozyaistvo, Pravda, Puti Industrializatsii, Soviet Studies, Sovremennye Zapiski, Sputnik Partiinogo Rabotnika, Vestnik Promyslovoi Kooperatsii, Vestnik Finansov, Vlast Sovetov, Voprosy Istorii, Voprosy Truda, Zhurnal Khimicheskoi Promyshlennosti.*

Index

234

237